To Virgie A. Ramey, Effie Baker, and Marvel R. Scarberry, three real-life victims of the Buffalo Creek disaster of February 26, 1972.

Chosen at random, as they were by the water.

Julia Keller was b̲ ▓▓▓▓▓▓▓▓▓▓▓▓▓▓▓▓▓▓▓▓ a.
Previously the ▓▓▓▓▓▓▓▓▓▓▓▓▓▓▓▓▓▓ e has
also ▓▓▓▓▓▓▓▓▓▓▓▓▓▓▓▓▓▓▓▓▓▓ ton, the
University of Notre Dame and the University of Chicago, and
won the Pulitzer Prize for feature writing in 2005. Her previous
novels, *A Killing in the Hills, Bitter River* and *Summer of the
Dead*, were highly acclaimed and are also available from Headline.

By Julia Keller and available from Headline

A Killing in the Hills
Bitter River
Summer of the Dead
Last Ragged Breath

Digital Short Stories

The Devil's Stepdaughter
A Haunting of the Bones
Ghost Roll
Evening Street

Julia
Keller

Last Ragged Breath

The paper in this book is made from wood grown in sustainable forests.

<!-- faded reversed text -->

HEADLINE PUBLISHING GROUP
An Hachette UK Company
Carmelite House
50 Victoria Embankment
London EC4Y 0DZ

headline

First published in Great Britain in 2015 by
HEADLINE PUBLISHING GROUP

First published in Great Britain in paperback in 2016 by
HEADLINE PUBLISHING GROUP

1

Cataloguing in Publication Data is available from the British Library

ISBN 978 1 4722 1564 2

Typeset in Sabon LT Std by Palimpsest Book Production Limited,
Falkirk, Stirlingshire

Printed and bound in Great Britain by Clays Ltd, St Ives plc

MIX
Paper from
responsible sources
FSC® C104740
www.fsc.org

Headline's   recyclable
products   nd other
controlled   pected to
confo   igin.

There is always one moment in childhood when the door opens and lets the future in.

Graham Greene,
The Power and the Glory

In the end, stories are what's left of us, we are no more than the few tales that persist.

Salman Rushdie,
The Moor's Last Sigh

Part One

1

Goldie was a six-year-old shepherd-retriever mix with a thick yellow coat that had inspired her name, a riotous tail, and chocolate-brown eyes that suggested profound depths of mysterious wisdom. At present that wisdom had coalesced into a conviction that something smelled mighty good – that is, powerful and unusual – somewhere along the slanting bank of Old Man's Creek. Wet black nose plowing a shallow trench across the rugged terrain, body balanced expertly to accommodate the steep grade, Goldie rammed forward along the upper brow of the creek bank, sniffing and quivering. The smell, as it intensified, became even more intoxicating. It was like a string pulling her along, winding itself tight on a bobbin at the other end. Everything else dropped out of Goldie's thoughts.

From behind her came the distant syllables of someone calling her name: 'Goldie! Here, girl! *Go-o-oldeee!* Come on!'

She didn't hear it. Rather, she heard it, but the hearing part and the subsequent ignoring part constituted a single supple action that had nothing to do with volition, nothing to do with stubbornness or calculation. Goldie wasn't being disobedient. Goldie was being a dog.

'*Go-o-o-ldee!* Come on!'

She didn't even lift her head. She knew her name, and she had a definite affection for the man yelling it, but those two facts counted for nothing now. She was All Nose. Her nose was her destiny.

'Goldie, you ornery girl, you. Taking off like that. Leadin' me a merry chase. Never seen the like.' The yell had subsided into a running grumble. Andy Stegner was getting closer, following the trail of mashed-down dirt and still-trembling branches that testified to Goldie's hasty journey past them.

He was, at the moment, sorely regretting the fact that he'd stopped to pick her up that morning. Goldie was turning out to be Trouble-with-a-capital-T. His neighbor, Royce Dillard, had seven dogs, including Goldie. That was down from the fifteen he'd had a year ago, which sounded like the aftermath of a massacre but was actually due to the fact that eight of the dogs were dreadfully sick when Royce first took them in, and it was only through Royce's kindly labors that they'd lasted as long as they did, and were granted, one by one, a serene, dignified death. Stegner couldn't keep a dog – his wife was allergic to the fur, her only fault as far as he was concerned – but he liked to have company when he checked his raccoon traps. Royce never minded lending one out for a morning's patrol.

Today, though, Goldie was climbing Andy's last nerve. The instant they ventured near the creek bank she'd taken off as if she had firecrackers tied to her tail. She seemed determined to ignore him. It wasn't like Goldie to act this way; she was a good dog. Something had gotten hold of her and wouldn't let her go, just as surely as Andy's traps captured skinny gray-black raccoons from October to February, the official trapping season allowed by state law.

Goldie plunged forward, whipping back and forth between the leafless trees. She crossed the dirt and the rocks and the low scrubby bushes and the scat and the sloughed-off hunks of bark and the burrs and the seed pods and the dead insects and the dented green Mountain Dew cans. All emitted excellent smells, smells that under normal circumstances would have caused her to pause and savor – but the smell drawing her forward asserted its dominance. It separated itself from the others. It was the King of Smells. It ratcheted up in deliciousness a few notches more, even after it seemed that it couldn't get any more wonderful.

Goldie was getting close.

'I *mean* it, you rascal! You get back here! Goldie, come on!'

He was wasting his breath. The dog had it in sight now, mired down there in the creek itself, a broad hump of brown. It was snagged between a rock and a batch of cattails that, wind-whipped and top-heavy, arched low over the greenish-silvery water like skeletal fingers reaching into a fingerbowl. Goldie's hearty bark startled two turkey vultures, newly returned from their winter journey south, in mid-feast. They rose quickly and corkscrewed away, broad wingspans catching the circular updraft of air currents. They would be back. They had infinite patience.

Goldie slid deliriously down the bank – not even trying anymore to maintain her balance, enjoying the free fall of four scrambling paws and a glorious sense of anticipation – and collided with the hump. The smell exploded in her nostrils. She uttered a brief yip of joy.

She was up to her belly in the frigid water, water that had recently made its late-winter pilgrimage down from the mountain to creeks like this one, and she was thrashing and nipping at the hump, trying to unravel the core source of its splendid stink. She didn't mind the cold one bit. She pulled at a section of the brown mass. There was a quick sound of ripping cloth as something came away in her teeth – but it tasted bland, and she spat it out, flapping her tongue to rid herself of the unimportant. A few brown threads dangled from her left incisor as she returned to the mysterious mound. She moved to the other side of it, parting the water with her wide golden chest, prodding the object repeatedly with her muzzle.

'There you are, you ornery dog, you!'

Andy looked down at her from the top of the bank, hands at his sides, breathing hard. The left sleeve of his denim jacket was torn and his ball cap had been knocked askew. Low-hanging branches had done the damage. A few years ago he might've been able to keep up with her when she broke loose that way, running a good half mile like a furry streak of lightning. But he was sixty-one years old now. And creaky as hell. Arthritis pinched at his joints as if somebody – a mean somebody – had taken a pair of pliers to them.

'Whadda you got there, Goldie?'

He descended the bank carefully, gingerly, heel-hard, keeping his body sideways so that he wouldn't go head-long if he stumbled, grabbing at the thin branches of spindly trees and then releasing them again after he'd descended further. Goldie had gone for the water at another angle, but he went this way because there seemed to be a bit of a path here already, two faint parallel lanes of pushed-down plants, a running indentation. Then a branch snapped back and whacked him in the face – *Dang*, he exclaimed – and he broke it off and kept going.

Down below, Goldie splashed around like a young pup. Her tail was going in wild, incessant circles. She was obsessed with whatever it was that slumped by the creek, half-in and half-out, nudging it with her nose, then backing off and barking. Her barks rang sharply in the frigid air of the mountain valley.

'What's got into you, girl?' Andy muttered as he neared the spot where the dog pranced and bounced and shimmied. Her glee was giving way to agitation. The strong smell was still pleasurable but also perplexing, and Goldie seemed eager for him to help her solve it.

Moving closer, he saw that the hump was covered by a big brown coat. He picked up a wrist-thick black branch at water's edge. Used it to poke at the object. A few more pokes would be required to dislodge the thing. He pushed at the far end and something broke off, swaying briefly until it spun onto its other side, like a bobbing beach ball. He leaned toward the broken-off piece, holding the stick in both hands now so that he could hook it. He drew it closer to the bank.

Goldie instantly backed off, setting up a hysterical barking. Andy felt his stomach drop. Rational thought fled from his mind. Vomit rose in his throat.

It was a human head. Andy was staring at the place where the face ought to be. He knew a face belonged there because of the gray ear-shaped objects on either side of the central cavity and because of the presence of matted hair at one end. At the other end was the ragged fringe of what Andy now realized was a severed neck. The soft chasm in the center – where you would expect to see eyes and nose and mouth – was scooped out, replaced by a wormy mess.

Goldie, sensing his shock, not sure what she ought to do about it, went from barking to a kind of eerie, sirenlike crooning, an ancient song of lament that was as mindlessly instinctive to her as was her earlier devotion to the voluptuous smell of death.

2

The Highway Haven truck stop occupied six and a half acres of asphalt at Exit 127 along the major route linking Acker's Gap, West Virginia, with points east and west. It was divided into two distinct halves, with six rows of pumps – two pumps per row – on either side. One side was marked TRUCKS ONLY. The other was designated ALL OTHER VEHICLES. On the trucks-only side, the lanes between the pumps were wider, allowing the drivers of the eighteen-wheelers to maneuver with relative ease as they lined up their famished vehicles for lengthy refills. The heavy odor of diesel fuel was like a truth you couldn't turn away from.

Belfa Elkins parked her Explorer in front of the glass-walled building, a combination snack bar, coffee shop, convenience store, video-game arcade, lavatory, and, for truckers, shower facility. The building divided the truckers' side from the other side. She had made the drive here from Acker's Gap in a surprisingly quick fifteen minutes, but knew better than to chalk it up to skill or even luck: There was always a lull between 5 and 6 A.M. on this stretch of interstate, and the clock on her dash told her it was just before 6. Later this morning the place would be packed, crammed with buglike compacts and massive RVs and only slightly less massive SUVs that had turned off the highway and swung hungrily toward the pumps, along with all the big rigs driven by the professionals, the men and the very few women who could handle an eighty-foot length of steel and chrome and momentum – a vehicle that weighed forty tons even before its load was factored in – with apparent ease. After fuel, the next most-desired items for travelers were bathrooms and food, and so most of the drivers of the regular vehicles, after they'd finished their business at the pumps, nosed their cars into parking spots in front of the store. If it were any later in the day, there would've been no open slots left; Bell would have been forced to use the spillover lot in the back.

She was an attractive woman with a slender build, medium-length wavy brown hair, and a quiet intensity in her gray eyes. Those eyes seemed to take in everything all at once, filing most of it away for later; there was nothing cursory or slack about her gaze, nothing casual. She was closer to forty-four years old than she was to forty-three, but she looked younger than that, owing in part to an edgy restlessness, a sort of spirited impatience, in her manner. She wore jeans, a taupe barn coat with a dark brown collar, and a blue cable-knit sweater. The thin strap of a black leather purse made a diagonal slash across the front of that sweater.

Just before she opened the double doors with the giant red *H* painted on each side of the glass, she glanced to her left. The last parking place on that side was occupied by a white Chrysler LeBaron. Nick's car. She felt a slight but definite pang. In years past, when she arrived at a crime scene and looked around for his vehicle, her eyes would search automatically for a black

Chevy Blazer with an official Raythune County seal on both sides. This wasn't a crime scene, but she'd automatically had the old expectation. Since November, however, when Nick had handed over the Blazer keys to his successor, he had been driving his own car. He had decided not to stand for reelection. His deputy, Pam Harrison, had won easily.

She gave the car a quick going-over with her glance, same as she'd done the three previous times she'd come out here to see him. The Chrysler didn't suit him. Nothing suited him but the Blazer.

On the curb in front of his vehicle was a pert warning delivered in red stenciled letters: RESERVED N. F. He had his own spot. Unreasonably, that also bothered her; it gave his new job an aura of permanence, of finality. This wasn't some temporary gig – which she already knew, of course, but seeing it spelled out that way forced a firmer kind of knowing.

Nick Fogelsong worked here now, as head of security for the Highway Haven chain. He wasn't coming back to the courthouse.

She and Fogelsong had worked together for six years. She was the prosecutor; he was the sheriff. They had been friends since Bell was ten years old – he was one of the few people she allowed to call her by her given name, Belfa – but it was as colleagues, as professionals, that they had truly bonded. They had solved difficult cases. They had faced death together, more than once. They had sparred and argued. They had gone long days without speaking after especially intense quarrels over tactics or priorities or ethical issues – and then resealed their friendship over long chats while chain-drinking cups of black coffee at JP's, a diner in Acker's Gap.

They'd run the justice system as best they could in this beautiful, beleaguered patch of West Virginia.

All of that was over now. In the fall, after his testimony at a trial that concluded one of their most challenging cases – the middle-of-the-night murders of two defenseless citizens, and other revelations that had shocked a town whose residents thought they were well beyond that kind of dark astonishment – Nick Fogelsong announced he was giving up the sheriff's post. He didn't notify Bell before he did it. He was afraid, he told her later, that she'd talk him out of it. *And I would have, too,* she'd snapped back at him. *You bet your ass I would've done just that.* She was still upset when she said it, still mourning the loss of him as her comrade.

She'd had an inkling he was losing his enthusiasm, losing his keen edge, losing his relish for the job – but who didn't, from time to time? Who didn't occasionally falter, wondering if it was all worth it? This was a place that would challenge anybody's optimism. It featured, after all, a steady cascade of falling-down shacks and crumbling roads and slow slides into alcoholism and drug addiction, along with red spikes of random violence. To believe in the future around here required a unique kind of fire. You needed your anger, an anger that initially had to be directed at the long line of public officials who, throughout the last century, had sold out the state and its uniquely bounteous natural resources to unscrupulous corporations. An anger that was creative instead of destructive. A vigorous, motivating anger. A righteous anger. Without it, you ran the risk of sinking down into the same sticky pit that had swallowed up the very people you were trying to help.

Fogelsong, though, had given up. That's how Bell saw

it, anyway: He knew as well as she did how much was at stake around here, how much they were needed, and he'd put a *Gone Fishin'* sign on the front door of his life. He'd shed his sheriff's badge and his hope that things could ever change, and he'd walked away.

'Excuse me, ma'am.'

Bell stepped aside, realizing that she was blocking the narrow sidewalk and thus impeding access to the store. Moving past her, a heavy man in a green plaid wool coat pulled at the ragged bill of his Peterbilt cap. 'Ma'am,' he repeated.

She followed him in. Rolling off his shoulders was the odor of nonstop tobacco use and truck-cab staleness, a sour, adhesive smell that seemed to be a distillation of everything she was feeling about the day that lay before her.

The store had few customers at this hour on a Saturday, but still felt crowded on account of all that it stocked: stairstepped wire racks of candy, mini doughnuts, gum, cookies, mints, nuts and sunflower seeds; bright rows of crackling bags of chips and pretzels and popcorn and two-liter plastic bottles of soft drinks; barrels filled with discounted DVDs of John Wayne movies and complete seasons of *The Andy Griffith Show*; waist-high freezers featuring ice-cream bars and Popsicles. On account of the snapped-in tubes of fluorescent lighting that hummed overhead there was a bright, sunrise feel to the place, an atmosphere bound to eventually surrender its taut freshness over the long course of the day but that had yet to begin that unraveling.

Nick was over at the self-serve coffee section, topping off his chipped gray mug. Bell knew that mug. She'd

seen it on the desk in his courthouse office every day
– including Saturdays and Sundays, because neither she
nor Fogelsong were inclined to take weekends off – for
the past half-dozen years, which meant that she'd started
her morning with that mug as part of her visual landscape at least two thousand times, give or take.

It didn't belong here in the Highway Haven, any more
than Nick did.

Alerted by the two-note chime that cheerfully did its
job each time the glass doors popped open, he looked
up and saw her. He waved and tilted his head. She got
it, and nodded. He wanted her to meet him in his office
at the back of the store. She lifted an imaginary cup to
her lips; now it was his turn to nod. She'd be there as
soon as she'd fortified herself with some coffee.

His office was located down a linoleum-floored
corridor, past the squat red YOUR WEIGHT AND FORTUNE
FOR A PENNY machine and the knockoff brand-name
cologne dispenser and the locker room and the waiting
area for the shower facilities. At peak times, this hall
was packed with truckers waiting for their assigned
numbers to be called over the public address system;
the summons meant it was their turn for a shower.

'Good to see you, Belfa,' Nick said.

'Likewise.'

He edged his way behind the black metal desk, turning
sideways to do so. He had a large square head topped
by sprinkles of short-cut gray hair and a linebacker's
body – wide shoulders, big hands, but with a certain
nimbleness, an essential balance, in his movements. As
he sat down, he placed his mug on the blotter so that
he could grip both arms of his chair and lean back.
Both sides of his suit coat fell open, revealing a snowy

expanse of snug-fitting white shirt. Bell noticed the beginnings of a belly on him. Maybe, she thought with a sour little grimace, he ought to spend a penny now and again to keep tabs on that.

The observation was mean and small and unworthy of her, but Bell couldn't help herself; she was mad at him and she needed to get it on the record, even just in the privacy of her own ruminations. She knew the truth of the old West Virginia aphorism: *Hit dogs howl.* If you felt like someone had done you wrong, you reacted. You had to. Didn't you?

The office was small but neatly organized. It had been a mess when Fogelsong first took over: file cabinets askew; monitors linked to the ancient security cameras stacked up every which way, their cords twisted and dangling; dirty cinder-block walls dotted with taped-up notes that constituted a never-ending to-do list. Nick's wife, Mary Sue, had helped him restore order here over a couple of weekends. The man who'd held the job previously was a retired West Virginia state trooper named Walter Albright; at the company's insistence, he had agreed to give it up after seventeen years. Nick couldn't figure out how Albright had gotten anything done – hell, he told Bell, he didn't know how the man had been able to think straight – amid the frantic, impossible jumble that had seemed to churn around one's ankles back then, bubbling up like storm water from a backed-up sewer drain in a deluge.

'Cold as all get-out this morning,' Bell said. She took the only other seat in the room, a black metal folding chair facing the desk.

'Thought it might be warmer by now,' he said, by way of agreeing with her. 'Never sure if spring's really coming.

Every year about this time, I start to worry. What if it just stays like this? What if somebody somewhere decided that we don't deserve that pretty spring weather and we get stuck year-round with the cold and the sleet?'

'Know what you mean.' Bell pulled off her jacket and twisted around so that she could hook it over the chair's rounded back. Seeing Nick Fogelsong in a suit and tie was something she had to get over in stages; she couldn't assimilate it all at once. His suit was light gray, with a narrow black tie. Even with a couple of extra pounds, he looked good. Dapper, even. Professional. She couldn't deny it.

But it still wasn't right for him. He ought to be in a sheriff's uniform, in the ugly brown polyester pants and shirt, topped off with the broad-brimmed hat and the thin band of gold braid encircling the sweat-darkened crown. There was a part of her that wanted to tell him so right now, to bust through the crust of all the politeness and the nice greetings and the talk of weather – weather! – and to lean forward and say, *For Christ's sake, Nick, stop this nonsense and get back to the courthouse.*

To be sure, most people thought Nick Fogelsong's move a wise one. He was getting older, and this was a sweet deal. Highway Haven's president had read about his success in a number of cases and made him a generous offer: Fogelsong would oversee security procedures and personnel screening at the company's eight locations in southern West Virginia and eastern Kentucky, and he'd still be able to keep his home in Acker's Gap. The tiny office was only in use when he was visiting this location. His real office – a spacious one, Bell had heard, with a secretary and a wet bar and pictures on the wall, all frills that Sheriff Nick Fogelsong would've disdained – was at the chain's headquarters in Charleston.

Nick pointed toward her Styrofoam cup. It sported a pattern of interlocking red *H*s around the white circumference. 'Coffee suit you?'

'It's fine.'

'Good. How's Carla?'

'Confusing the hell out of me, but otherwise – she's great.' Bell's eighteen-year-old daughter lived in Alexandria, Virginia with Bell's ex-husband, Sam. Carla had graduated from high school the spring before, but decided – just for the time being, she'd said, just for now, adding *Really, Mom, I promise* – to put off college. Carla had explained that she didn't know what career she wanted to pursue, and then further explained that it was totally pointless to spend a boatload of money on tuition until she'd made up her mind.

'Kids're required to drive you crazy at regular intervals,' Nick said. 'There's actually a law on the books to that effect.'

They were quiet for a run of seconds. The catch-up question had been necessary; not only had Bell generally avoided the place since Nick started his new job, but their paths didn't cross elsewhere, either. She didn't buy her gas here. The Lester station was closer to Acker's Gap. Bell didn't like the crowds that normally thronged the Highway Haven. And there was the other thing, too. There was the fact that driving out this way meant getting just a small, tantalizing taste of what she'd had before on a regular basis, and maybe had taken for granted: Nick Fogelsong's company and counsel. Sometimes it was better, she thought, to move on. Try to forget.

When she'd called him the night before and requested

a meeting today on official business, he said, 'Sure, come on by.' She had started to make a counter-proposal – maybe he could head into town and save her a seat at JP's? – but realized, just in time, that that would be even worse: Sitting across the table from him at the place they'd met almost daily would be borderline unbearable. She preferred to drive out to the interstate and see him here. In new surroundings. In a place where she didn't have to bump into memories every other second.

'So what can I do for you?' he said.

'Had a briefing from the state police. Wanted to make sure you were aware of what's going on.' She'd found a paper clip on his desktop and proceeded to take it apart while she talked, twisting and bending it. 'Major new distributor of oxy. Need to be on the lookout.' Oxy meant oxycodone, one of the prescription drugs that had drastically increased the crime rate in the area.

Only Nick Fogelsong had ever seemed to understand, in the same visceral way that Bell did, just how prescription drug abuse had gotten a deadly purchase on the region. Recreational drugs, by contrast, were easy to deal with. Pot, cocaine, even methamphetamines – those were familiar blights, the users easy to spot, the dealers bottom-feeding louts whom deputies could scoop up like excrement in a public park. But prescription drugs were different. They were legally supplied, in many cases, by physicians, physicians who either didn't know – or didn't care – that the pills were ferociously addictive. After only a few weeks, people who had sought relief for a torqued back or an infected tooth found themselves dependent on the pills, with no way to pay for them – except criminal activity. And by that time, they'd moved on from doctors to dealers.

These were people who never before in their lives would have contemplated an illegal act – but who, when confronted with a clawing, ravening need for the golden ooze of contentment that slid through your gut when you swallowed a pain pill, would do anything to feel that settle-you-down sensation, just one more time. And then one more time after that. *Just once more. Swear.* They weren't looking for a way to get high. They were looking for a way to feel okay again.

'Shit,' Fogelsong said, putting as much frustration into a single syllable as it could hold. He and Bell hated the drugs, but they hated, too, the circumstances that sent people hurtling toward them.

By what right could you tell a family from back in the hollows that things would ever get better? That if they worked hard and got an education and avoided traps like alcohol and drugs, they'd be able to find a good job and know a different kind of life? It wasn't true. The mines were dead. The pay at the shiny fast-food places along the interstate was laughably low, not even close to being enough to live on, much less raise a family on. The real enemy was an invisible one, a force that trapped people even more definitively than the mountains did. It was an attitude, a default setting of defeat. You could always leave; but if you stayed, you faced long odds and, more than likely, a short life.

'So that's all we know so far,' Bell said. She twisted the paper clip back and forth until it was no longer a paper clip, but a short straight piece of steel. She didn't have to tell him what he already knew: Truck stops were notoriously common distribution points for the pills – and for the heroin that was, perversely, cheaper than pills and thus had begun an entirely new spiral of addiction in these hills, an auxiliary misery. 'The state police are being extra attentive,' she added. 'Notifying local law enforcement, prosecutors, school authorities – everyone who understands the drug trade and has a stake in stopping it.'

He fingered his tie gingerly, as if he'd just discovered it was there. 'Not a good time for the bad publicity,' he said. 'What with the new resort coming, I mean.'

A Virginia-based firm that called itself Mountain Magic had recently purchased a twelve-hundred-acre parcel stretching across portions of Raythune, Collier, and Steppe counties. The plan was to build a resort to rival The Greenbrier, the historic and palatial facility in White Sulphur Springs that had hosted kings, queens, senators, presidents, and CEOs. Because no matter what else was going on with the people of West Virginia – poverty, addiction, despair – the landscape was a thing apart, a separate and unassailable fact. In the spring to come, like all the springs before it, the mountains would rise into a seamless blue sky, the massed interlocking trees on the sides of those mountains would make a solid block of spectacularly vivid green that drifted its way into your dreams, and the brown rivers would move so fast that their supple surfaces resembled the sleek back of a muscular animal in a stretch run.

'Oh, come on.' Bell's response to his point was sharp and dismissive. 'Won't matter a damn. The billionaires who're putting up money for that thing don't care about local crime stats. They hire their own armies. Once the resort's up and running, the place'll be crawling with private security.' Too late, she remembered that Nick was now private security himself; her remark could be construed as a dig.

Well, hell. He was a big boy. He could take it.

'Might cut down on their bookings, though,' he said. There was no indication he'd felt insulted. 'The negative press, I mean.'

Bell shook her head. 'No way. That resort won't be connected at all with what's going on locally. The guests'll come and go and never set foot beyond the tennis court or the golf course or the sauna or whatever the hell else they build.'

'You don't sound too happy about it.'

She shrugged. 'If it means new jobs – good-paying ones – I'll be over the moon. But there's been no word yet about how many local people they intend to hire. If they're going to use our land, the least they can do is put our people to work.' She was getting wound up, despite herself. 'This state's been exploited long enough, don't you think? We've suffered for years from absentee landlords and all of their promises. Maybe it's time we just told them to go away and leave us alone. Go use up somebody else's natural resources. These are our mountains. Ought to be our decision about what happens to them.'

Nick created a crooked arch with both sets of fingertips. He waited a few seconds to let some of her anger burn off, and then he said, 'It's progress, Bell. Progress and change.'

'And you think I'm against all that.' She was irritated. What did he take her for – some barefoot granny back in Briney Hollow who still reminisced about the superiority of horse-pulled wagons and outdoor privies?

'No,' he said. 'I just think you're anticipating the extra aggravation that strangers always bring – even strangers who're investing money in the region. Can't say you're wrong about that. I've met the company's marketing guy. Name's Ed Hackel. Not exactly the shy, retiring type, that's for sure. Slicker'n goose grease. After he shakes your hand, you feel like you oughta check for your watch and your wallet. But then again – that kind of job, you've got to be a hustler.' He let the arch collapse and put his palms flat on the desktop. Scooted his chair in closer. 'Heard any timetable yet for breaking ground?'

'They've run into a snag.' She watched as the news altered his posture, causing him to sit up straighter. 'That marketing guy you mentioned – Hackel – has been calling the county commissioners about twice an hour all month long and raising nine kinds of hell. There's a thin strip of land on the southern border of the acreage that the company's already purchased. They've got to have it. Provides their best access to the interstate.'

Fogelsong nodded. This was old news. 'Belongs to Royce Dillard. They're giving him a pile of money for it.'

'Yeah. Trouble is, he changed his mind. Doesn't want to sell.'

'Lord,' he said. 'That's Royce for you.' Dillard was a recluse, a man who lived in rural Raythune County in a cabin he'd built with his own hands, amidst a silence broken only by the barks and howls of a retinue of old dogs – mutts and castoffs, mostly, dogs whose homelessness had destined them, before Dillard's intervention, for legally sanctioned elimination by an animal control officer. Dillard was only seen in Acker's Gap every few months or so, when he walked into town pulling an old wagon and bought his supplies. He stopped as well at the post office, where he'd sweep the accumulated mail out of his post office box into a plastic grocery sack.

'It's not like they're asking him to give up his home,'

Nick mused. 'His cabin's on a little sliver of land over by Old Man's Creek. They've got their eye on a bigger chunk he bought back in the eighties. With the settlement money given to Buffalo Creek survivors. Way I hear it, he's always planned to open some kind of animal sanctuary on the spot. Dogs, I believe, are about the only living creatures Royce has any use for. The parcel's just been sitting there, though, all these years.'

'Company's got to have it. No land – no resort.'

Nick nodded. 'Predictable, I guess, that he's making a fuss. Royce is an odd bird. But he's got his reasons for being a bit peculiar. Had more than his share of tragedy, that's for damned sure.' He thought about it. 'When he was five, six, seven years old, there'd be a TV crew here every February twenty-sixth, on the anniversary of the flood. Wanting to do an update. Wanting to know how much he remembered about that day. Then it tapered off. Folks forgot.' Nick rubbed his chin. 'Don't imagine Royce ever forgets. Not for a day, maybe not even for an hour.'

Bell stood up. Time to go. She could have handled this errand by phone, and right now, very much wished she'd done so. What did she hope to gain by seeing Nick in person? Their relationship had changed too much, too fast.

Restless, not sure if she ought to shake his hand – they'd never followed social rituals like that before, but things were different now – she fingered the uncoiled paper clip and then used one of the sharp edges to scratch at a spot on the back of her other hand. 'I'm sure the whole mess will somehow find its way into a courtroom,' she said. 'And at the end of the day, the only people who profit will be the lawyers.'

'Funny way for a lawyer to talk.' He was ribbing her, just like in the old days. 'Takes one to know one, huh?'

'I guess.' She wasn't in the mood. 'Getting back to the business at hand – keep an eye out, will you? Hate to see another pill mill get a foothold around here. If you see anything suspicious, give Sheriff Harrison a ring.'

'That's what I'm here for.' Nick stood up as well, indicating with a sweep of his big hand the monitors stacked neatly along the wall and their shifting stream of gray-and-white images, recording what went on at the cash registers and in the corridor leading to the showers. Another set of monitors displayed the scenes from the area around the pumps and from the perimeter of the store. 'Had to update everything. Top to bottom. Damn near every piece of surveillance equipment we have. I can't quite figure what Walter Albright was thinking – letting it deteriorate the way he did. Half of the security cameras weren't in working order. Management told me to spend whatever it took to bring us into the twenty-first century. All I needed to hear. By the way,' he said, shifting his tone as he shifted his topic, 'I mentioned to Mary Sue that you were coming by. She made me promise to ask you over for dinner tonight. Nothing fancy – probably venison chili – but it's been way too long. I know it's short notice and all, but—'

'Can't. Tell her thanks, though.'

'Okay. Another time.' He waited. Usually Bell would explain a turn-down. But she didn't, so he had to pry. 'Better offer?'

'As a matter of fact, I have a date.'

'Well. Well, now.' His face broke open into a smile. 'Do I know the lucky fella?'

'No.'

Once again, he waited for more details. Her expression informed him that none would be forthcoming. The silence lengthened, thickened. Many things occurred to her within that silence, and Bell noted them, one by one: Nick was now on the outside of her life, looking in, and even though she'd acknowledged that leaving the sheriff's job was his decision, that he had to do what was best for himself and for Mary Sue, she still wasn't reconciled to the change. She missed him. She knew he missed her, too. But if she acted as if they were still close – if she talked with him about her life, the way she'd always done before – then she would be letting him off the hook too easily. He had abandoned her, dammit. He had to face the consequences of that.

Finally, Nick said, 'Guess both of us had better start our day's work.'

She put the straightened-out paper clip in her pocket and lifted her jacket from the back of the folding chair. Once it was on, she picked up her purse and her coffee cup.

'Hey,' Nick said. She paused at the threshold. 'We offer free refills on the coffee,' he said lightly. 'Make sure you take advantage. For the drive home.'

Bell didn't know what she'd wanted him to say right then, but it sure as hell wasn't about coffee. She was hit by a fusillade of unsolicited memories: cases they'd worked; long afternoons they'd spent together, going over evidence or interviewing witnesses; meals they'd shared while they laughed and swapped stories and demonstrated the kind of support for each other that didn't require words. Just a steady accumulation of days in each other's company.

'One more thing,' he said.

Here it comes, she thought. Now he'd say something heartfelt, something about how he, too, remembered their daily interactions back in Acker's Gap, and missed the camaraderie of a shared purpose. Missed, even, the impossible hours and the constant frustrations.

'No charge for the paper clip,' he said.

She gave him a brief wave to acknowledge the levity.

The front part of the store, when she rounded the corner and returned to it, was a different place now, with all three cash registers going full tilt, with lines of customers snaking around the racks and bins, waiting to pay for gas and gum and coffee and lottery tickets and peanuts and candy bars and sunglasses and cigarettes. Bell moved in a haze, preoccupied by her memories of previous mornings with Nick Fogelsong, work mornings, mornings when they'd felt the weight of the world but never really minded it because each had the other one right there, ready to take up the slack when one of them grew weary. The past was a tricky bastard. It called and called to you – and when you turned around and tried to grasp it, it disappeared.

Reaching the double glass doors, she took a quick look back at the busy store. She was mildly surprised to see the fat man – the one who'd walked in just ahead of her, the one in the green plaid coat and the cap with the oval Peterbilt logo – still on the premises. Must be stocking up. He stood at the start of the soft drink aisle, shoulders hunched, hands in his pockets, apparently torn by an existential dilemma regarding two-liter plastic jugs of Dr Pepper: diet or regular? The only visible motion came from his jaw, as it grappled with a bountiful plug of snuff, and his eyes, which roved restlessly.

3

'I didn't kill him, but I sure as hell don't mind the fact that he's dead.'

Royce Dillard put a stiff nod at the end of the sentence, as if that settled the matter, once and for all. His palms were flat on the tabletop. His spine was pressed against the back of the chair and his feet were spread wide; his legs kept up a steady vibration, causing his boot heels to tick against the concrete floor. His gray-blond hair wasn't long but still appeared flighty and disorganized, as if it never felt the press of a comb. There was a look of apprehension in his black eyes. Those eyes were ringed with dark, the natural tattoo of the chronic insomniac. He was one of those people who blinked so rarely that you'd swear someone was making him pay per blink, and he'd been keeping careful count since the day he was born so that he wouldn't be overcharged.

'We got that.' Sheriff Harrison stood behind him. She was motionless at this point, but seconds before she'd been making a series of slow, deliberate loops around the gray metal table and chair that hosted Dillard in the interrogation room, pausing at irregular intervals: in front of him, behind him, beside him, then in front of him again. She didn't like interview subjects to get too comfortable. From the look of Dillard, there was no chance of that.

It was just after seven on Saturday night. Bell would be showing up at the courthouse soon; Harrison had reached her on her cell. The sheriff sensed that she was interrupting something – she'd been able to hear, in the background, the purr of soft music, the drift and murmur of voices, the courtly clink of cutlery, indicating a restaurant, and not the sort that got by with plastic utensils and paper plates – but Bell didn't seem to mind and promised she'd be there in half an hour. That was twenty minutes ago.

'Good.' Dillard barely opened his thin-lipped mouth to speak. A quantity of suppressed energy appeared to be buzzing and fluttering inside him, power held back only by an effort of will. He was a medium-sized man, but his jangling nervousness made him appear bigger, more volatile, a potential threat. 'Just so we're clear.'

'Oh, we're clear all right,' Harrison snapped. She was in motion again, ambling behind him and then around toward the front of the table. Her arms were crossed. She was a petite, visibly fit woman with short brown hair and a pink birthmark that splashed across one side of her face, lapping down onto her neck. The big hat cast a shadow over her face, and people meeting her for the first time sometimes mistook the birthmark for part of that shadow. When they realized their mistake – the shadow stayed, even when she removed her hat – they were embarrassed, even though no words had been spoken to indicate the error. Pam Harrison was used to it by now, used to people's reactions to the left side of her face. She'd been dealing with it ever since she was old enough to understand how profoundly a superficial anomaly could change one's destiny.

'So why am I still here?' Dillard said.

'Because you lied to us. Twice.' Harrison stopped her march, then started up again an instant later. She traveled behind him, then around the side of the table, then to the front of it, then down the other side. 'Deputies come to your door this afternoon and say a body's been found on your property. You don't ask where. You don't ask who.'

'That ain't a lie. That's just a lack of curiosity.'

The sheriff halted her pacing. She was directly in front of him now, timing the pause and the position to coincide with this particular point in her questioning. He turned his head to one side. He didn't want to look at her. He didn't want to look at anybody.

'The lie came after that, Dillard,' she said. 'As you well know. By then, we had a preliminary ID on the victim. Deputy Mathers asked you if you'd ever heard of a man named Edward Hackel. You said no.'

'I forgot. Forgot I knew him.'

'You didn't forget.'

'Well, then – I was confused.'

'You weren't confused. You knew him well, didn't you? And when I asked you just now when you'd seen him last, you said you don't remember.'

'I don't.'

'You sure as hell *do* remember. You took a swing at him the day before yesterday. In public.'

'Well, if I did, he deserved it.'

'We have witnesses, Dillard. Several of them.' Harrison started her rounds all over again. She was behind him now. He didn't turn in his chair. He didn't watch her, as most people did when she circled the table. He kept his head angled toward the floor, just as he'd been doing since he first arrived here, brought in by Deputy Charlie Mathers.

'In fact,' she went on, 'you'd had many angry confrontations with the victim. He wanted your land. And you didn't want to sell. Isn't that right?'

Dillard snorted. His headshake was vigorous and prolonged. Yet a flicker of tension showed up along his jawline, causing it to flex and settle. It was not the sort of detail Harrison was apt to miss.

'My business,' he said. 'Not yours.' But his voice had shed some of its confidence.

'A lot of people heard you repeatedly threatening him with physical harm.'

He pondered that. 'Okay,' he said. 'Fine. So I knew the man. And, yeah. I'd called him an SOB, a time or two. Said I was gonna knock him flat on his ass. Still didn't have nothing to do with him ending up that way.'

'Convince me.'

'Use your head,' he said, his voice rising until it was just short of a shout. 'If it was me what done it, then why'd I leave him right out in the open like that? If you think I'd murder that rat bastard and not try to hide the body, then you figure me for the biggest fool that ever was.'

Harrison took another break from her pacing, pausing once again in front of the small table. The brim of the sheriff's hat extended so far over her small face that the nature of her expression was unavailable to onlookers. She liked it that way. Not being able to read another person's eyes was unsettling. It rattled a lot of suspects, even more than her questions did.

This was the first major case she'd handled on her own, and she was determined to wind it up quickly.

Efficiently. Gather the evidence, make an arrest, assist the prosecutor in getting ready for trial. Harrison liked Nick Fogelsong, and admired the hell out of him, but sometimes she'd found his methods a little too . . . *slow.* Yes. That was the word. A little too slow. Ponderous, even. He spent a lot of time – too much time, maybe – thinking about things. Contemplating. Must be those books he was always reading, Harrison had told herself. They could turn you into a chin-stroker. A philosopher – a word her daddy always deliberately mispronounced as '*fool*-losopher.' She preferred action. She knew that a female sheriff was not exactly the norm in these parts, and she figured that the faster she moved, the swifter and more forthright her decision making, the sooner her constituents would realize that a young woman could do this job every bit as well as a middle-aged man – maybe better – and that they'd been right to elect her. Nick Fogelsong's endorsement had made her a lock the first time around; next time, she wouldn't need him.

'You're smart,' she said. 'Wily enough to do just that – to kill a man and then leave the body right out in the open, in a creek on your very own land, assuming it would throw off suspicion.' Harrison hooked her hands on the front table edge and leaned forward. He leaned back, his eyes on her hands, not her face. 'Trouble is, Dillard, nobody on God's green earth wanted Edward Hackel dead more than you did.'

'Not true.' He stuck out his chin. 'There's a line of folks a mile long who hated that bastard. Just like me. I ain't the only one who'd be rootin' for the buzzards.'

'You're not helping yourself with that observation. You ought to know that.'

The sheriff had read him his rights, and knew that

Deputy Mathers had done so, too. But Dillard said he wanted to talk. He rejected – repeatedly – the offer of a court-supplied attorney. She halfway wished he'd told her to go to hell and then clammed up, refusing to talk, daring her to charge him with the murder. She wished, fleetingly, that he'd had a tight-knit, pugnacious family to protect him, to speak up for him, a complicated network of angry uncles and prickly aunts and outraged cousins who would've shown up at the courthouse when word got round that he'd been brought in for questioning, a bristling picket line of blood relations who would've demanded that she show her evidence or let him go. But Royce Dillard didn't have any family. Not that such a thing was unusual anymore: By the time they reached forty, fifty years old, a lot of people around here didn't have much family left. Sometimes it was on account of the slow regular way of the world – heart attack, stroke, diabetes, the cancer – but sometimes it happened another way. A quick way, with violence involved. That was how it had happened for Dillard.

Once again, though, that didn't mark him out as special. So many people in this region had violence living in their history, like a snake waiting under a pile of rocks: You knew it was there, but you tried to forget about it, and if you had an errand that took you past those rocks, you walked a wide circle around them.

The only people who seemed to give a damn about Royce Dillard were the old couple from the farm next to his, Andy and Brenda Stegner. It was Andy who'd found the body in the first place; he'd used his cell to call 911, and then had the judgment and good grace to move away a few yards, so that his puked-up breakfast of biscuits and gravy wouldn't contaminate the crime scene. Shortly thereafter, the state police forensic unit had arrived and started its work. When it came to the science component of an investigation, counties as small as Raythune didn't have the resources to run their own show.

'Last chance, Dillard,' the sheriff declared. Maybe she couldn't do the chemical analysis part, but she sure as hell could handle the psychology part. She'd watched Fogelsong do this for years, with dozens of suspects in dozens of cases. She was ready. And she knew a guilty man when she saw one.

'Last chance to tell the truth here,' she went on, swapping out her hard-ass tone for an affable, bargaining one. 'You help me – and I help you. Okay? So maybe Hackel shows up at your cabin. Starts pushing you around again. Trying to get you to sell your land. Won't let up. Hasn't let up for weeks. This time, maybe he threatens you. Maybe you fear for your life. Is that how it happened? You're scared. Maybe you're trying to defend yourself. Maybe you grab a heavy object and you take a big swing at him. Maybe you connect. You're a strong man, Dillard. Anybody can see that, just by looking at you. And so maybe you accidentally kill him. And then maybe you panic. So you drag his body down to Old Man's Creek and you hope that nobody finds him till the spring thaw – and by then he'd be unrecognizable even to his own mother, after the woods have had their way with him. Is that it, Dillard? Is that how it went down?'

The man stared at the cinder-block wall across from his chair. The jiggling motion in his legs had picked up speed. 'Like I told you,' he said, 'I didn't kill him. But I won't lie – I ain't at all sorry he's dead.'

4

Sheriff Harrison left the interrogation room. Deputy Mathers, waiting outside, took her place – not to question Royce Dillard, but just to keep an eye on him. Harrison would do all the questioning herself. She'd be back.

Her office was in the courthouse annex that had been added in the 1960s, when it seemed as if Raythune County, boosted by new jobs in busy coal mines, might continue to grow. It hadn't. The mines died, and the population shrank back. Whole corridors of the original courthouse were swept by shadows now, the offices used strictly for storage.

'Okay, Sheriff,' Andy Stegner said. He spoke the moment Harrison stepped across the office threshold. 'What'd he say? He didn't have nothing to do with this, right? Like we told you.'

Harrison ignored the old man and woman who'd been waiting for her, until she'd first pulled out the chair from under her desk and placed herself in it. She kept her hat on. It was cold in here, for one thing, and for another, she didn't like the air of informality that sometimes ensued when she took it off. This was serious business. Nobody should think otherwise.

34

'Andy, Brenda – please take a seat,' the sheriff said. They obeyed instantly, glad to have an order they could follow. 'It's been a long day for everybody,' Harrison added. 'Let's all calm down.' She sounded affable, friendly, but she needed them to understand that she was in charge. There should be no doubt about that, even though Andy Stegner had known her since she was in grade school. *Okay,* Harrison corrected herself. *Longer than that.* Andy and her father were regulars at the VFW Hall.

'How's he holding up?' Brenda said.

Husband and wife wore thick winter coats, the convex, heavily insulated kind that caused even slender people to look like hand grenades, and they were not slender people. Their boots made it impossible for them to take a delicate step. Brenda was twenty years younger than Andy, but in the way these things sometimes went, she now looked almost as old as he did. She had been a great beauty when she was younger, and you could occasionally get hints of that, faint echoes: The elegant bone structure of her face was still evident beneath the yellowed, hangdog skin, and when her drab shoulder-length hair moved back and forth, it showed a ghost of its soft curl and its radiance, even though the velvety honey-blond shade had been stripped down now to a bland whitish gray.

'I'm just asking him some questions,' Harrison said. 'That's all. The body was found on his property. I think you can understand why—'

'He's pretty fragile,' Andy said. He didn't seem to realize he'd interrupted her. His big, wind-burnished hands were clasped between his knees. 'When I found that body in the creek, I never thought – I mean, it never occurred to me that you'd think Royce would've— It's just not possible that—' The face he showed Sheriff Harrison was bleak, beseeching. 'Royce Dillard is a good man. He's got his peculiarities. Nobody knows that better than us. We're his closest neighbors and we don't hardly see him more than twice, three times a year. I go by and I pick up Goldie from the barn and Royce don't even come out to say hello. It's like he can't, somehow. Wants to, but he can't.'

'He'd die in prison,' Brenda said. There was passion in her voice. 'You know that.'

'Whoa there,' the sheriff said. 'Nobody's talking about prison yet, okay? Nobody. Let's get that straight, first off. But I've got to question him.' She wished Deputy Mathers hadn't stopped at the Stegner house on his way back into town. Seeing Dillard's face in the back of the Blazer, they'd insisted on following the county vehicle to the courthouse in their Tahoe. They'd waited here, standing in her cold office in the lonely annex, while she spoke to Dillard. And then when she returned, they'd fallen upon her like avenging angels in wool and polyester.

'Gentle as a lamb,' Brenda said. She'd perched herself on the edge of her chair, leaning forward, one hand coiled in her lap and the other hand thrust out to rest flat on the sheriff's desktop, as if she wanted to keep a physical tie with Pam Harrison, even one mediated through solid oak. To plead her case. 'That's what I'd say about Royce. What anybody would say, who really knows him. You ask. You just ask 'em. The man's not got a mean bone in his body.'

Harrison nodded. 'Understood. But let me repeat, Brenda – and this is for you, too, Andy – I'm not arresting him. Okay? I'm just talking to him. We've got a homicide on our hands. Anybody with any connection to the victim – no matter what that connection might've been – will be spoken to. Same as you folks were spoken to. It's how it's done.' She used a knuckle to nudge up the brim of her hat, so that she could make eye contact with Andy. 'We appreciate your calling us right away, like you did. And not touching anything.'

Andy shook his head, as if he wanted to shake off the compliment, too. 'Who the hell would touch a dead body?'

'You'd be surprised.' Harrison reached for a pen. Then she lifted the yellow legal pad next to it and turned it around, so that it was facing in Andy's direction. The page was covered in a small barbed-wire scribble. 'I think we have everything we need from you for the time being. But you have to sign your statement, Andy. About finding the body.'

'Okay,' he said. He bent over the page, grimacing. Reliving the experience as he skimmed what he'd written. Brenda watched her husband's hand as he signed his name. His hand was so large that it made the pen look like a toy. Once he was finished, his hand continued to hold the pen; he didn't want to let it go just yet. Brenda's hand stayed on the sheriff's desktop. It was as if they were trying to stop time for as long as they could, to hold off acknowledgment of the grievous reality of the day's events.

'Dogs,' Brenda suddenly said.

Harrison looked at her.

'Royce's dogs,' Brenda went on. 'If you keep him here much longer, who's gonna look after his dogs?' She shook her head. 'We can't do it. I'm allergic. Can't be within a hundred feet of those mutts of his. I start swelling up something terrible. That's why Andy has to borrow Goldie. Can't have dogs of our own.'

'How many's he got?'

'Seven,' Andy said. 'Counting Goldie.'

The sheriff frowned. 'They'll be okay overnight?'

'Yeah, but not much beyond that,' Andy replied. 'Somebody'll have to go by in the morning and see to 'em. They're living creatures.'

That irritated the sheriff. Having known her since she was a baby, Andy Stegner apparently forgot that she'd progressed well past that point intellectually. 'Understood,' Harrison said stiffly.

'How long you gonna keep him here?' Brenda asked.

Harrison had answered enough of their questions. She didn't have to explain herself to them. Or to anyone. She was calling the shots, dammit. They ought to remember that. She could hold Royce Dillard without charging him for at least forty-eight hours.

'I don't know,' she said. 'Depends on what the evidence shows.' *And what the prosecutor says,* Harrison added to herself, but didn't want to say out loud, because she didn't like the sound of it – true as it was.

5

Bell lied. There was no way she could make it to the courthouse in thirty minutes. The distance between Acker's Gap and the Italian restaurant in Dalton Forge where she'd been picking at a decidedly mediocre plate of spaghetti – the sauce was heavily sugared, the pasta a close cousin to crusty shoestrings – required nearly an hour's drive. But she didn't want Sheriff Harrison to call one of the assistant prosecutors in her stead. Both Rhonda Lovejoy and Hickey Leonard had been putting in loads of overtime lately, extra duty for which – the county budget being what it was – she couldn't compensate them. It was her turn, she thought, to have a Saturday night shot all to hell by a work obligation.

Her date had seemed to understand. David Gage was a professor of environmental sciences at West Virginia University. He was in town for a three-month study based in Raythune and Collier counties, gathering information he intended to use in a book about formerly robust coal-mining communities and what decades of renegade coal dust had done to the air quality. Virginia Prentice, a classmate of Bell's at Georgetown Law School who now taught at WVU College of Law, had set up the date, pushing Bell to agree by sprinkling her e-mails with dares and double-dares.

Reluctantly, Bell had finally said yes. One date wouldn't kill her, would it? Even if Gage turned out to be a fool and a bore, it would be a change of scenery. Take her mind off things. She suggested they take separate cars to Luigi's; that was as much for his protection as hers. Maybe he'd be the one who needed a quick getaway. Bell knew she was an acquired taste. So, as it turned out, was Luigi's.

Dating after forty was a risky business. It was like shopping at the Goodwill store over in Blythesburg: Everything on offer was used, picked over, random. It had been discarded by somebody else. *Just like me,* Bell thought ruefully. Sure, you could find some hidden gems, but you had to be especially careful. And definitely selective.

To her surprise, she enjoyed Gage's company. He was forty-eight years old, recently divorced; the split, he said, had been a long time coming. Lesley, too, taught at WVU. They had two daughters, one in college, the other a senior in high school. Bell liked the way Gage talked about his children, with pride and humor and a deep understanding of their individual personalities and ambitions. He didn't just say 'my kids' in that homogenous, glazed-over way that some people discussed their offspring, as if all children were the same, moving at the same pace through the same inevitable stages of development, inevitably causing the same frustrations and heartaches for their parents. Susan, he said, was majoring in biology at Pitt, while Meagan was obsessed with the cello and hoped to go to a university with a top-flight music program.

Gage had close-cropped white hair, a long jawline, watchful brown eyes that lived behind a pair of round gold spectacles, and lean, expressive hands that were in constant motion as he talked, which Bell attributed to his having been a professor for so many years. She liked the way he dressed: olive khakis he hadn't bothered to iron – she didn't trust men who ironed their trousers, probably because her ex-husband had always insisted that everything be ironed, including his pajamas – and a wheat-colored corduroy shirt. Bell's admiration, however, stopped well short of desiring anything more from him than interesting conversation. She didn't like to acknowledge it – especially not to herself – but she was still carrying a torch for a man she'd dated two years ago. In a way, that gave her the freedom to have a good time with David Gage; she knew this couldn't really lead anywhere. Not while she still felt a small but persistent flutter in her stomach at the thought of Clay Meckling, formerly of Acker's Gap, now a grad student at MIT. She and Clay still exchanged the occasional e-mail and letter, still traded phone calls on birthdays and holidays. Bell liked to tell people that her romantic relationship with Clay was over, that the notorious phrase 'just friends' was absolutely applicable. But that wasn't really true, and she knew it.

'I wonder how you stand the thought of it,' Gage had asked Bell as they pushed their entrées around on their plates.

'Of what?'

'Of all the coal mines around here. Knowing what coal has done to the environment of West Virginia – and to the health of the miners, too. Not to mention the entire planet. I mean, the science is irrefutable.'

'That may be,' Bell said, 'but the coal industry has provided a decent living for these people for a lot of years. Is it easy work? Clean work? Safe work? Hell, no. But it's work. Honest work. I don't see any manufacturing plants sprouting up in these valleys anytime soon – do you? Plants that'll replace all the jobs lost if you and your friends in Washington shut down the last of the coal mines? So you might want to think twice before you demonize coal and coal mining. It's not just coal you're coming out against – it's people's livelihoods.'

'We're developing some promising new fuel sources. Renewable ones. Sustainable ones.'

Bell gave him a level look. 'Right. But in the meantime, what happens to the people here? People who depend on coal mining to earn a paycheck? Not many of them left, I'll grant you, but don't they matter?'

'So you're pro-coal.' He said it with incredulity.

'I'm not pro-coal. I'm pro-work. Show me another way for the people of Raythune County to feed their families, and I'll be all over it.'

'Speaking of feeding,' he said, 'I'm thinking about dessert. How about you?'

She grinned and shook her head. She liked this man, liked the way they could disagree vehemently about an issue and yet keep the conversation amiable, liked the way he defused the tension with a breezy comeback. Bell had opinions, and she expected other people to have them, too; if their opinions happened to coincide with hers, fine, but if they didn't – well, that ought to be fine, too.

And the truth was, she would have agreed with Gage if they'd had this talk six years ago, before she moved back to Acker's Gap. Yes, she knew the science. She knew that the burning of coal was doing terrible things to the earth's atmosphere, just as the underground mining of it had done terrible things to the respiratory systems of miners. But if the land was your concern, then strip-mining was even worse. And once she'd come back here to live, she saw another truth: Coal meant jobs. As underground mining dwindled, so, too, had the fortunes of the people in this region.

Bell made a private pact with herself: Next time she and Gage got together – if there was a next time – she'd offer to take him to a coal mine she knew about, one that was all but shut down. Only a few men worked there now, and not regularly. She would show him that there was only one thing more depressing than a mine filled with miners: a nearly silent one. And a community filled with men and women who had no jobs.

Before she'd had a chance to choose between the crème brûlée and the cheesecake, her cell had gone off. A glance had informed her that the caller was Sheriff Harrison. The social part of her evening, Bell knew, had just come to an abrupt halt. The nature of her job as a prosecutor in a small rural county meant that she was eternally tethered to her phone, always on call. There was really no such thing as a night off.

She put the cell to her ear, listened, spoke briefly, then hit End and placed the cell next to her plate. The sleek black rectangle looked out of place on the ivory lace-trimmed tablecloth amid the elegant white china and heavy cutlery, like something strange and futuristic that had fallen out of the sky and invaded an old-fashioned garden party.

'Listen, David, I need to run,' Bell said. 'Really sorry. I've had fun, though.'

'No worries. Ginnie warned me.'

'About what?'

He pointed to her cell. 'About that.'

6

Driving back to Acker's Gap along a road that cut a curving line between two night-shrouded mountains, Bell let herself be brought up to date on the day's events. Sheriff Harrison would be busy in the interrogation room, so she'd called Deputy Charlie Mathers, putting him on speakerphone so she could focus on the white line. His big friendly baritone filled her vehicle.

'The 911 operator took the call about noon or thereabouts,' he said. 'It was a guy named Andy Stegner. Bought a little farm after he retired from the railroad. Out near Sawyer Fork. Said he'd come across a body down in Old Man's Creek. Sheriff sent me and Jake Oakes out there to take a look. We ditched the Blazer and hiked about a mile or so to get to the spot. Mud liked to ruin my boots.' Oakes was the new deputy hired to replace Pam Harrison when she ascended to the sheriff's position. Bell knew very little about him yet, other than the fact that Oakes hailed from somewhere in Georgia and had worked briefly for the Beckley Police Department before applying for the open spot in Raythune County. He was young and muscular and good-looking, a trio of attributes that immediately distinguished him from Charlie Mathers. Oakes had shiny black hair, a dashingly crooked grin, and a tendency to wink at any woman to whom he was speaking, a habit Bell intended to quash the moment she had time to sit down and discuss it with him. He had a certain flourish in his step when he patrolled the streets of Acker's Gap in his brown uniform and big black boots, as if he were simultaneously walking and admiring himself from afar.

'Took one look,' Mathers went on, 'and called for the coroner and the state forensics team. It was a body, all right. The buzzards had started to have their way with the face. Always go for the soft parts first, have you noticed?'

Bell felt her supper stir in her gut. 'Go on,' she said.

'Well, turns out the property belongs to Royce Dillard. Found him in his cabin. Claimed he didn't know the deceased. Corrected himself later.'

'I'll need the tape of the 911 call. And your notes from the initial conversation with Dillard at his residence.'

'Already on your desk.'

'Go on.'

'Okay, well, the state folks made the ID through fingerprints. That Mountain Magic company has a policy of fingerprinting all of their employees when they do background checks, so the prints were easy to match up.'

'Preliminary ruling on cause of death?'

'Blood loss from trauma to the base of the skull. Even with the head being such a mess, Buster found evidence of the nature of the assault.' Buster Crutchfield was the Raythune County coroner. 'Something hard and sharp, applied repeatedly.'

'Time of death?'

'Nothing's set in stone, but unofficially, about a day and a half ago. No more'n that. Sometime late Thursday afternoon. Maybe early evening. State crime lab boys're doing their own autopsy. Might be able to narrow it down better.'

'How about the victim's car?'

'Still parked at the Hampton up on the interstate. That's where he was staying. It's a nice one – a BMW X5 – leased for him by the company. He must've gotten a ride with somebody out to where he was killed. Either that,' Mathers added with a chuckle, 'or he had himself a magic carpet.'

She ignored that. 'Notification of next of kin?'

'State police is handling that. His family's in Falls Church, Virginia. Hackel went home on the weekends to see 'em. His wife's supposed to be on her way here right now. Hope she's bringing a friend to spell her with the driving. It's a five-, maybe six-hour trip – and not an easy one.' He paused. Bell could tell that he was holding the phone away from his face. She heard a belch, and then he was back. 'Sheriff had us pick up Dillard. Being as how he lied initially, and being as how he had a history with this Hackel guy – and not exactly a cuddly one, you know? – she's still talking to him.'

'Okay,' Bell said. According to the sheriff's call that she'd taken at the restaurant, Dillard denied any involvement in the murder, despite the fact that he had no plausible alibi, no one to vouch for his whereabouts for the past two days, and a big reason to want Hackel to go away.

The Explorer's headlights splashed a bucketful of light on a green exit sign with white lettering: ACKER'S GAP. Even after she made the turn, Bell would have a good half an hour of driving before reaching the town, the county seat of Raythune County. No safe way to shave any time off that journey. The county road was considerably less hospitable than the smooth and well-lighted interstate she was leaving behind.

'Any word from Hackel's employer?' she asked.

'CEO of Mountain Magic was already here in town this weekend, going over some blueprints. She's on her way to the courthouse.'

Bell tried to think of another question, even though she knew she'd be seeing Mathers soon. For some reason, she didn't want to hang up; it was as if, as long as she kept the line open, she could put off the moment when the murder drowned out everything else and took over their lives, when the investigation and subsequent trial became a massive intractable fact that spread to every corner of their world. Once she parked her Explorer in front of the great gray courthouse that loomed over the old town like a three-story foretaste of Judgment Day, it was all over. She'd be caught. She would have to see this case through to its conclusion. And that road, too, had to be traveled with caution; that road, too, had things waiting around corners that could not be anticipated, vexing things, maybe even perilous things.

She had a crazy compulsion to just keep right on driving, to glide past the exit and go plunging into the darkness of whatever came next, as long as it wasn't a homicide investigation. At the moment the impulse hit her, she had the clearest understanding yet of why Nick Fogelsong had done what he did last fall, turning his back on his job and, by extension, on her. The weariness she felt was not physical but emotional, even spiritual, as she prepared to embark upon this new case. Duty was a stubborn kudzu vine that looped around her ankle and held her fast. It would never let her go.

Damn you, Nick Fogelsong, Bell fumed. *You think I don't feel exactly the same way that you do? I'd like to quit, too. But there's nobody else to do this. Nobody.* She knew what she'd see on both sides of the road once she left the interstate: a series of dark, hunched shapes. By daylight, the shapes would reveal themselves to be rotted-roofed shacks and scruffy barns and broken-down trailers and scuffed-up cars. Places where nothing green would ever grow.

To hell with you, Nick Fogelsong. You think I can't do it without you? Watch me. You just watch me.

She shook her head. She made the turn.

'Mrs Elkins?'

Mathers, unnerved by her silence, sounded anxious, tentative. He added, 'Still on the line, ma'am?'

'Yeah. Almost there.'

7

Nick Fogelsong had once had a friend named Bert Cousins with whom he occasionally shared a beer or three. Nick wasn't much of a drinker, but Bert was, and thus if you wanted to spend time with Bert, you were better off matching him drink for drink, instead of listening to him take potshots at your manhood all evening long. Bert had made a small fortune as a concrete contractor over in Swinton Falls, and he'd been a reliable contributor to Nick's campaigns during all those successful runs for sheriff, and so Nick owed him. They would get together two or three times a year, have dinner, laugh too loud, drink too much, then call their wives to pick them up. Nick's clanging headache the next day was, he thought, generally worth it. And as it happened, it wasn't a dilemma with which he had long to reckon; Bert Cousins, two years younger than he was, had died in November from colon cancer, a gaunt and stony-eyed ghost of himself.

Nick always remembered one of their earliest conversations. Each man was embarking on his fourth – or was it fifth? – Budweiser at Sloppy Sam's, a bar in Swinton Falls, when Bert leaned over the table in the booth, its wood all liquid-shiny with a slick yellow varnish, and poked a finger in Nick's face. 'Happens to you, too, right?' Nick didn't know what his friend was talking about, and told him so. Bert grinned and shook his head and said, 'Oh, come on. I mean, getting tired of the same thing at home, night after night.' Turned out that Bert Cousins was determined to reveal that he was having an affair. His wife, Gloria, just didn't excite him anymore, at least not in the way that a woman named Liz Something-or-Other, a waitress he'd met over in Chester, could do. Nick didn't catch Liz's last name and didn't ask Bert to repeat it. He didn't care what her name was. And he didn't want to hear Bert's confession, because he knew that it was less about confessing than about wanting to have Nick confirm that he, too, had thought about it, that he, too, had either cheated on Mary Sue or was seriously considering it.

One thing Nick had learned from all those years of being a sheriff was this: People wanted solidarity in their sins. They wanted the comfort of company when they misbehaved. That's why they confessed so often, right on the spot, in those needy, wheedling tones that used to drive him crazy: *You know what I mean, right? Under the circumstances, you would've done the same thing, right? Right, Sheriff?* It was almost as if, Nick thought, people believed the shame and the guilt might be lessened that way, split up and parceled out and spread around, so that no one person bore the total weight of the remorse.

When he told Bert no – no, he'd never cheated on Mary Sue, and no, he didn't desire to do so – Bert hooted his disbelief and his disdain, but Nick didn't care. It was the truth. Nick Fogelsong had first seen Mary Sue at a church picnic more than a quarter century ago. The moment was a dividing line in his life; there was a definite Before and an absolute After. As he tried to explain to Bert, it wasn't that he was some goody two-shoes, or was trying on halos for size; he just had no interest in any other woman, in that way. Mary Sue was funny and smart and beautiful, and there was a life force in her – that was the only description that worked, 'life force,' even though Nick had never previously used the phrase and was surprised when it popped out of his mouth – that seemed to deepen all the colors of the world.

It was still true, all these years later. Despite everything.

Nick sat across the dining room table from her and finished the final bite of his chili. Saturdays were typically his longest days at the Highway Haven, and this one was longer than usual; a few hours after Bell left, a trucker had miscalculated the distance when he was backing up to the pump and had sideswiped it. He hadn't knocked it over – that would've necessitated urgent requests to a dozen different fire-rescue units and the evacuation of half the county, not to mention the filing of about ten thousand forms with the EPA – but he'd bumped it, and that meant a temporary shutoff and a lot of complications. It wasn't a crisis, but it was a major pain in the ass.

And the day had started off with another kind of aggravation: Bell's visit. Clearly, she was still sore at him for giving up the sheriff's job, for deciding not to run for reelection and taking the position at the Highway Haven. Nowadays she was stiff and formal with him, faintly condescending, and too polite, like a damned stranger. What was the statute of limitations for being pissed off at somebody? *Whatever it is,* Nick thought, *Belfa will stretch it out longer. No doubt about that.*

He didn't see her often these days, but when he did, the atmosphere wasn't easy and comfortable. Not like it had been for all those years.

He had arrived home half an hour ago, kicked off his hard black shoes, pulled off his tie, and sat down to dinner. The sight of Mary Sue across the table – her hair, her face, her eyes – had put him in mind of that night with Bert Cousins, and Bert's question, and Nick's quick uncomplicated answer: *No.*

'One more bite,' he said amiably, 'and I swear I'll pop wide open.'

'Well, we don't want that. Think of the mess it'll make.'

He grinned and dropped his spoon into the empty bowl. That produced a pair of nervous plinks as the spoon hit first the ceramic bottom and then the side. He wiped his mouth on a white paper napkin. He crumpled the napkin into a tidy wad and left it next to his bread plate.

The dining room was big, too big, really, for just two people. The whole house was like that: It was a rambling, shingle-sided place that had once belonged to a mine foreman and his family. Four children and an elderly aunt, in addition to the foreman and his wife, had once lived here comfortably. Then the foreman was transferred to a mining operation out in Wyoming – the new West Virginia, Nick had heard it called, although he doubted that the people of Wyoming would embrace the label willingly – and Nick had purchased it. Back then, a decade or so into his marriage, he was still sure that he and Mary Sue would have a family. Not four kids – Lord! – but maybe two. At least one.

Nowadays, the large house got on his nerves sometimes. The rooms had high ceilings and wide windows, and there was a broad backyard that went on and on until finally it ran underneath a jagged shelf of mountain called Smithson's Rock. The day after he and Mary Sue moved in, a proud and happy Nick Fogelsong had taken an exploratory stroll around the property, like a squire with his walking stick and his spaniel, and when he came to that shadowy space beneath Smithson's Rock, he bent over and took a few scooting steps forward. His toe bumped a soft edge. It was a pile of comic books. Nick plucked one off the top. There was a handwritten note taped there:

To the new kid who moves in here. I'm Corey. I'm eight years old and we are going to Wyoming. These are my comic books. I'm leaving them for you, okay? This is a great place for a fort. PS I hope you are a boy.

There wouldn't be any children here, boy or girl. If Nick hadn't known that on the day he and Mary Sue moved in, he surely knew it now.

'If you get hungry again later, there's plenty left,' Mary Sue said.

She had stopped eating after a few bites, her dinner finished, but she continued to sit with him, her chin in her hand, her elbow propped on the table next to her glass of sweet tea. She had once been lovely, but the mental illness with which she had long contended had left its mark, like a line high on the sand where the tide had reached before sliding back again. Her gray face was too long. She was too thin. Too solemn. It was the joy of Nick Fogelsong's life now when he could make her laugh.

'I gotta say, though – man, oh, man, that's good chili,' he said. 'Best yet.'

'Well, I made enough for Bell, too. Wish she'd been able to join us.'

'Said she had a date tonight.' He used the same skeptical inflection he had routinely used for reporting a suspect's exceptionally lame alibi.

'No reason why not. She's allowed to have a social life, isn't she?'

'Not what I meant.'

'Oh.' Mary Sue nodded. 'You mean – what about Clay?'

Nick shifted his feet under the table. 'Not even sure they're in close touch anymore.'

'They are. I hear from Clay myself from time to time. He calls here, looking for you. Never likes to trouble you at work. We end up talking for quite a while. He loves her. I'm sure of it.'

'He told you that?'

'Oh, heavens, no. I'm extrapolating from the things he says. His observations. Being away has given him a new way of looking at the world.'

'I thought the old way was working just fine,' Nick muttered. 'Never understood why he's got to go all that way – Boston, Massachusetts, for crying out loud – just to read a bunch of books.'

'It's called graduate school.'

'I know what it's called.' Nick was a great reader himself, a man who felt half-dressed unless he had a book in his hand. It wasn't the books he had a problem with. 'I just don't think that's where he belongs. Makes no sense to me.'

Mary Sue smiled. Her smile was edged with irony.

'Oh. I see. So Belfa's supposed to give you the benefit of the doubt and accept your decision to leave the sheriff's office – but you won't extend the same favor to Clay about his decision to go to MIT?'

Nick grunted. She was right, dammit. And now he'd have to pretend to be perturbed about that. But he wasn't. Not really. He enjoyed it when she challenged him, calling him out on his hypocrisy, after which they'd laugh. This was how it had been between them all the time, until she got sick. These glimmers from the past, these stray moments of casual happiness, kept him going. They enabled him to get through the hard times, times when her disease seemed to stand in every doorway and block out all the light.

'Anyway,' he said, 'Bell can date anybody she pleases. Not my lookout anymore. She doesn't talk to me. Not about personal matters.'

'That's a shame.'

'I guess.' He shrugged. 'Her loss.'

'Nick, there's nothing wrong with admitting that you miss somebody.'

'I didn't say I missed her. It's just damned awkward, that's all. I still have to deal with her. Security matters at the stores, you know? But if she can't get past the fact that I'm not sheriff anymore – well, too bad.'

'Give it time.'

'Got no choice.'

'Speaking of security – did you ask her about Albright? You've been concerned about that, I know.'

'Nope. Never had the chance. She was in a hurry.' He scratched an ear. 'Maybe I'm worrying about nothing. Not everybody keeps good records. I can get a little sloppy myself. And Walter's an old man. Probably just got tired. All those years with the state police and then a security job. Law enforcement's no picnic. Takes a toll.' Walter Albright's incident reports for the months before his firing were spotty, irregular, with few specifics. It was almost as if he thought he could make the negatives go away by ignoring them. Nick heard that he'd built himself a palace of a house with some money his wife had inherited and settled down into a comfortable retirement. Should've done it sooner.

Mary Sue picked up her bowl. She started to rise, intending to clear the table. Nick waved her back down in her seat.

'We'll clean up in a bit,' he said. He was restless tonight, just as he'd often been after dinner back when he was sheriff and they waited for the next lightning-strike of bad news.

His simple request to delay the cleanup had thrown her, knocking her off her rhythm, but she didn't want him to know that. And so she shrugged – *whatever* – and put her bowl back in the precise spot where it had been. She would try. She always tried.

But she was rattled now. Her plan for the next few minutes had been to collect the plates and bowls and silverware and stack them all in the dishwasher, then to check the contents of the refrigerator and the cupboards and make the penciled list for Lymon's Market. Sunday was food-shopping day. Mary Sue planned her time minute by minute; it was the price she paid for being able to function, for keeping her mood pitched to a livable level.

'Guess I thought Belfa would understand why I had to make the change,' he said. 'You remember how it used to be. I mean, did we ever make it through a whole danged meal – not to mention a week's vacation – without being interrupted by a phone call? Or a dozen phone calls? Always another crisis.' Nick didn't like making speeches but he made one now anyway, revving himself up, because he needed to make sure she understood: *It wasn't you.* He never wanted Mary Sue to think she was the reason he'd given up the sheriff's job. Yes, her illness was part of it – he'd taken a leave of absence the year before, they'd gone to Chicago to see a specialist there, she'd tried a new anti-psychotic medication – but only a part. The biggest reason? He was tired to the bone. And sick of other people's problems. That was it. Really.

'You remember,' he said. 'Know you do. If it wasn't a traffic accident, it'd be a drowning. Or a drug overdose. Or a fistfight. A fire. Or somebody's car getting stolen. Or their cat. Or their lawnmower. Or just somebody bellyaching about something. I got so goddamned *sick* of it, Mary Sue, all the time, year after year. I know you know that, but sometimes I don't think anybody can really know just how deep it ran in me. I was getting to be a cranky old fart. All I saw was people at their very worst. I was starting to—'

Abruptly, he stopped talking. She had come around to his side of the table. Instead of getting up, he wrapped his arms around her waist and turned his face into her apron. She stroked the back of his head. He could smell her hands, and the pungent scent of the onions she'd chopped to put in the chili, and he knew that his head was greasy with sweat, after his long workday. But it didn't matter. She was trying to soothe him, console him, just as he had often consoled her, and those other things – smells and sweat, the body's small persistent betrayals – were irrelevant. Over the years they'd gone back and forth like this, healer and wounded, changing roles as the need arose. If, in the final reckoning, her problems had been more profound than his, if her mental instability had kept their lives churned up while his issues were ordinary, a matter of a bad day every now and again, then so be it.

'You did a good job for this town for so many, many years,' she said, her voice soft, with a gentle ripple moving through it, like a sheet hung out to dry in a mild spring breeze. 'You gave it everything you had. All of your time and your energy and your passion. You were a hell of a sheriff. But it's all over with now.'

She meant to be kind, so he couldn't tell her what he was really thinking: *That's exactly what I'm afraid of.*

Later, dinner dishes loaded and dishwasher under way, the furry thrum of its work sounding like another kind of digestion, they retreated to the big living room. Nick sat in his recliner with a book open on his lap – *An Army at Dawn* by Rick Atkinson – and Mary Sue occupied a small corner of the couch, her long legs tucked up under her, watching a TV show with the sound turned low. The phone rang. They looked at each other. It felt at once like one of those Saturday nights before he'd changed jobs, when they would barely be settled into their chairs when the phone exploded over and over again like a series of benign bombs, leaving the evening in shreds and tatters. Those nights, Nick had rarely bothered to take off his boots after he got home for dinner. He knew he'd just have to put them back on again, along with his hat and his coat and his holster.

'Hey, Nickie, my man.'

Nick recognized the voice of Vince Dobbs, grandson of Bundy Barnes, a Raythune County commissioner. Vince ran a car wash a mile or so outside the city limits. He and Nick had gone to Acker's Gap High School together. That was about the only thing they had in common.

'Just wanna make sure you heard,' Vince went on. He spoke rapidly, so rapidly that Nick had once compared his cadence to a squirrel's frisky scamper. 'Gonna be all over town by morning. 'Member the guy who was running the show around here for the resort? Big man? Lotsa hair? Kinda loud? Real asshole?'

'Ed Hackel.'

'That's the one. Well, they found him dead this morning and it weren't no natural causes. And guess who got dragged in for questioning? Okay, you'll never guess, so I'm gonna tell you. Royce Dillard.'

Nick scratched his cheek. The twinge he'd just felt had nothing to do with any special kinship with Hackel or Dillard; it was the fact that, until a few months ago, no one had had to call and tell him the news. He knew the news. He knew it ahead of everybody else – including a nosy fool like Vince Dobbs.

'Huh.' He didn't want to give Vince the satisfaction of his interest.

'Yeah. Guy's head was all bashed in, way I hear it. Big ole mess.'

Gossip was a commodity, a fungible, tradable article of commerce. It was currency. And always before, Nick had controlled the asset side of things; he was the one who decided to whom to dole it out, and when, and how much. Now he was on the outside. Now he was no different from Vince Dobbs. Or Rhonda Lovejoy, come to that, one of Bell's assistant prosecutors, another renowned purveyor of local information – except that Rhonda, given her position, would already know a hell of a lot more than he did.

Two homicides had occurred since Nick had left the sheriff's office in November, but they were routine, unexciting: First, a domestic violence case in December, for which the crazy-jealous SOB was now serving a life sentence at the Mount Olive Correctional Complex. And then there was a shooting death on New Year's Eve at a tattoo parlor along Route 6; the perpetrator had thoughtfully shot himself after shooting his girl-friend, saving the county the trouble and expense of a trial. At the news of those tragedies, Nick had felt only relief. He wasn't responsible anymore. Let Pam Harrison handle them.

This, though, was the first case that was unusual, compelling. Nick instantly felt a familiar zip of adren-aline, and a slight fizz across the top of his brain, as if someone had doused it with ginger ale and then wiped it dry again, all within seconds. He said good-bye to Vince Dobbs and heard the man on the other end of the line hang up, but Nick still held the phone, aware of a faint tremor in his hand. There arose within him the old fire. He felt a poke in the back, prodding him. That force had a voice, and the voice was his own, and it said, *What the hell happened to Ed Hackel?*, and after that he automatically began to assess, recollect, calculate, speculate. He couldn't stop himself. He took the known facts and he spread them out like the greasy parts of an engine, the tiny levers and gears and washers and springs and bolts, and then he started to put the thing back together again, reverse-engineering it, trying to figure out how the pieces all worked together, how the crime had been committed, and why.

The resort was the biggest new project around here in a long, long time. Tens of millions of dollars were on the line, and Hackel had been right at the center of it. And Royce Dillard – he was an unusual character, you bet, strange as all get-out, but capable of murder? Or maybe it was an accident. Tempers flare, angry words are hurled back and forth, Dillard grabs a weapon – a sledgehammer, maybe, or a post hole digger – and, blinded by hurt and fury, he takes a wild swing, and . . .

'Nick?'

He looked over at his wife. But he didn't see her.

8

The Raythune County Courthouse at night was a different place from what it was during the day. In daylight, it was a haggard, benign-looking building where forms were filled out, licenses applied for, parking tickets either paid or argued over, and copies of birth certificates issued, a place at which people also tended to congregate even when they didn't have specific business there, just because they might run into somebody they liked talking to. At night, though, it was a cold, forbidding Gothic pile that exhaled the sour breath of its buried secrets: a multitude of criminal trials and the systematic passing of judgment on overlapping waves of human souls. The ground-floor windows at the rear – where the booking office of the jail was located – were illuminated all night long, as if the courthouse itself suffered from bad dreams and needed a nightlight.

'Sheriff's waiting for you in her office,' Mathers said.

Bell had gone to the side entrance, the one that led directly to the interrogation rooms, in case Harrison was still in there with Royce Dillard. Deputy Mathers met her. He was a large, dark-haired man with a gut that tormented the bottom two buttons on his brown uniform shirt. He was a reassuring presence in the courthouse.

He'd been doing this job a good long while and even if all hell was breaking loose, chances were that Charlie Mathers had been through worse and was happy to tell you about it; he could make you feel as if the present crisis maybe wasn't so bad by comparison.

'You just missed the guy who found the body,' Mathers added. 'He and his wife finally went home. Wanted to make sure we didn't go all CIA on Royce Dillard, I guess. Victim's boss just got here. The head of Mountain Magic.' He waggled his eyebrows suggestively. 'She's a piece of work, lemme tell you.'

The halls were dim and empty at this hour on a Saturday. The office doors were shut and locked, with no lights behind the frosted glass fronts, no rise and fall of voices – except for the sheriff's office, where the thick door was propped open, its strong orange light spilling out into the corridor like treats from an upended candy jar.

'Bell. Hey,' Harrison said, the moment Bell arrived there.

The sheriff was seated at her desk. By now, she'd taken her hat off. There was someone else present, too, but Bell kept her attention on Harrison for the first instant after entering, as she adjusted to the reality of seeing someone other than Nick Fogelsong behind that desk, the same way her eyes might adjust to the level of light before she could see clearly.

Truth was, Pam Harrison looked as if she'd been destined to occupy this spot from the day she was born, or shortly thereafter. Inscribed on a small gold-plated bar that held down the flap of her left breast pocket was her name and her title. Her forehead was creased by a horizontal red band, the mark where the hat's inside brim had pinched throughout a long day and what was shaping up to be an even longer night.

The first few times Bell had come here after Nick's defection, she was struck by the oddity of it all, by the sense of this office as a drastically altered place – but these days, the shock passed away in less than a second. There was too much work to do to indulge that kind of pointless nostalgia. Bell might chafe at the sight of Nick in civilian clothes, driving his own car and not a county vehicle – but here in the courthouse, she'd accepted the new reality. Pam Harrison now ran the sheriff's department. Her stoic demeanor was a perfect fit with the battered black desk, a desk that, over the years, had endured kicks and body-slams from outraged defendants, innumerable spills from overfilled coffee mugs, and quarter-moon gouges across the top from having Nick Fogelsong's big black boots piled restlessly on it during countless conferences with his deputies.

Right now a very angry woman stood in front of that desk. She exuded a livid hostility. She had wavy brown hair with expensive-looking blond highlights, a black suit, a red scarf draped expertly around her neck, and complicated earrings that shivered and bobbed each time she leaned forward and pointed a finger at Sheriff Harrison. Bell had never formally met the woman, but recognized her from her appearances at county commission meetings. She was Carolyn Runyon, founder and CEO of Mountain Magic. She had a solid-gold CV: Yale undergrad, University of Chicago MBA, ten years as CFO of an international hotel chain, three years as a deputy to the US Secretary of Commerce. *She's got more connections than a junction box*, was how Rhonda Lovejoy put it back in September, when she and Bell were having a cup of coffee after the commission meeting at which Runyon had introduced herself and pitched the resort project.

This was a different woman from the one who had charmed and flirted with county officials that night. She didn't acknowledge Bell. Instead she continued hectoring the sheriff, her voice haughty and cold.

'—and I *demand* to have Ed's body removed *immediately* to a reputable medical facility for an independent autopsy. *This minute*, do you hear? These primitive facilities are absolutely and totally *unacceptable*.' She shivered in disgust, as if she'd spotted a bowl of squirming leeches or a long row of patent-medicine bottles with fading labels. 'It's my understanding that you currently have an individual in custody for this unspeakably brutal and vicious crime. I want your *personal* guarantee, Sheriff, that this man will remain under lock and key until the trial. We simply *will not* tolerate any mistakes or delays. Frankly, it's a question of peace of mind for the rest of my employees as they go about their business here in Raythune County.'

Harrison ignored the insults. She gestured toward Bell. 'Ms Runyon, I'd like you to meet our prosecuting attorney, Belfa Elkins. Bell, this is Carolyn Runyon. She just returned from the coroner's office, where she formally identified the body of the homicide victim. It's Edward Hackel. Vice president and marketing director of Ms Runyon's firm.'

Bell looked closer at Runyon and felt a strange, unwanted flash of recognition: *Another life, another time – could be me.* This woman, whose obvious contempt for Raythune County in general and Sheriff Harrison in particular was as sharp as her heels, was what she, Bell, might have become if she had stayed in the Washington, DC, area and practiced law there, using her Georgetown law degree the way it was intended to be used: to make a lot of money for somebody else, which in turn would make a lot of money for her. She'd be wearing a black suit, sleek as a seal's pelt, just like the one Carolyn Runyon was wearing. And she'd be having her hair trimmed at someplace a bit more expensive than Betty's Kut 'n' Kurl out on Route 6. She and Runyon were approximately the same age, Bell surmised, and there was an eerie, funhouse-mirror aspect to looking at this twisted – that is to say, better-dressed and beautifully coiffed – version of herself.

'So – *do* I have your assurance, Sheriff?' Runyon said. She had yet to acknowledge Bell's presence. Her next sentence sported a canny edge. 'I really hate to bring this up, but my firm has a great many friends in Charleston. Perhaps I should call the governor and ask him to personally monitor the murder investigation here in Raythune County. I'm sure he'd be more than happy to oblige, given what this resort is going to mean to your state's economy.'

Sheriff Harrison looked at Runyon for a few seconds before she spoke.

'You know what, ma'am?' the sheriff said. Polite, but barely. 'This isn't the first time we've undertaken a homicide investigation. We know what we're doing. But if you're determined to hang around the courthouse this evening, making suggestions about how we might do our jobs, we'll take full advantage of your presence. I'll get Deputy Mathers over here right away. He's handling the initial interviews. We've got some questions for you, too, ma'am. Starting with – where were you Thursday and Friday? Last time anyone saw Edward Hackel alive was Thursday afternoon.'

Runyon's face contorted in an expression of outrage. 'I don't believe this. *I'm* a suspect?'

'Everyone's a suspect.' Harrison stood up. When she did, Runyon reflexively backed up a step, as if she weren't quite certain what the sheriff's next move might be. Harrison was a small woman, but a thoroughly imposing presence. Bell wasn't sure how she pulled it off – it might have been the boots or the uniform or the rigid facial expression, which kept you guessing about her mood. Might have been a lot of things. But whatever it was, it worked.

Harrison reached for the big brown hat on the desktop and settled it on her head. She wasn't happy with how the fit felt, and so she lifted it and settled it again. Better.

'I'll let you think about your answer,' the sheriff said, 'while Bell and I go get Deputy Mathers.'

If Runyon were a cartoon, Bell thought, smoke would be jetting out of each ear like the steam whistle on a locomotive.

'What about the governor?' Runyon snapped.

'What about him?'

'Maybe I'll just give him a call.'

'Be my guest.' The sheriff gestured toward the phone on the desktop. 'Dial nine for an outside line.'

9

On the infrequent occasions when Bell got together with friends from law school back in the DC area, they always begged her for details about her professional life. Most of them were either academics, like Ginnie Prentice up at WVU School of Law, or corporate attorneys, and they had no firsthand knowledge of the grubbier, seamier side of things – of the guts of the law, as Bell called it, and they would nod at the description, enjoying the tough, raw sound of the phrase, even though, to them, it was an abstraction. They'd never dealt with drunk or stoned defendants who threatened to dig out their eyeballs with a rusty spoon and then pee in the empty sockets, or with the relatives of convicted felons who left shoeboxes filled with dog shit in Bell's home mailbox. *Really? Dog shit?* her friends would say, shaking their heads, half-amused, half-appalled. *Yeah,* Bell would reply. *Dog shit. Although come to think of it, I suppose it might've been human shit or horse manure – I mean, I didn't get it officially tested. Hard to say. The shit part – that's all I'm really certain of.*

The get-togethers with her classmates would happen in some fancy bar in Georgetown or Adams Morgan, during one of Bell's trips to see Carla. Amid the clink of glasses and the sudden uprushes of laughter from nearby tables, against a background of pop songs banging endlessly out of the sound system, Bell would tell her stories to these people, people she had known very well for a brief, intense period in her life – Ginnie, Ron, Pam, Kim, Trevor, Steve, Paula, and Jeremy – but who now listened to her description of a prosecutor's job in a small, poor rural county as if she were telling them about an expedition to Mars: Everything was exotic and unfamiliar. People with degrees such as theirs didn't become prosecutors. *And prosecutors aren't cops,* Kim would say, challenging Bell. This moment generally came after Kim had finished her third lime margarita and had fluffed up her tawny mane of hair for the fifth or sixth time, hoping to catch the eye of Trevor, whom she'd had a crush on throughout law school and continued to pine for, even though he was now married and had three children.

I don't get it, Kim would continue. She'd never liked Bell, and liked her even less now that Bell held the group's attention, including, gallingly, Trevor's. *You talk about running around and interviewing suspects,* Kim said, *but that's not your job. The cops're supposed to do that. And then they're supposed to bring you the suspects and the evidence and then you take it to trial. What the hell?*

Bell would smile a small, knowing smile. *Yeah,* she'd reply. *That's how it's supposed to work, all right. In theory.* In reality, she explained, the county was poor, the caseload was out of control, and the sheriff's office was short-handed, and thus she ended up participating in the gathering of facts and the interviewing of witnesses and the culling of suspects. She could, she supposed, say something like, *That's not my job,* but she would only be making more work for herself in the long run. Moreover, those people – the sheriff, the deputies, the coroner – were her friends. *Better friends,* she was tempted to say to her classmates, *than any of you.* Which was not a slam against the witty, well-dressed, highly successful people gathered around the table in this very nice bar, ordering another round of expensive drinks. It was, rather, an indication of how far away from all of them that Bell had traveled – in terms of physical distance, yes, but in other ways, too. More important ways.

'She's right in here,' Deputy Mathers said.

At the sound of his voice, Bell's mind snapped back to the present. Mathers stepped to one side. He'd walked with Bell and Sheriff Harrison to the lobby of the courthouse. Mathers had taken the lead, flipping on row after row of lights in successive corridors as they passed through them. The lights had all been turned off on Friday afternoon and, minus this incident, would've stayed that way until early Monday morning. In the sudden swoop of illumination, the ancient building with its water-stained plaster walls and well-scuffed floors reminded Bell of an old man abruptly awakened from a deep sleep. She could've sworn she heard a groan or two.

'Thanks, Charlie,' the sheriff said. She leaned toward him, giving her deputy a brief set of murmured instructions regarding Carolyn Runyon. He nodded and headed back to her office. Except for the lobby area, he turned off the lights again behind him.

The sheriff took advantage of their last second of

privacy. 'You don't have to do this,' she said to Bell. 'It's not your lookout. Not yet, anyway. You can head home.'

'I know.'

'Hated to call you away from your dinner.'

'Wasn't much of a dinner.'

Harrison nodded. They advanced into the lobby waiting area, where two lines of green vinyl armchairs faced each other across a wooden square. The sole occupant hadn't noticed them yet. She was staring at the floor. She was about the same age as Carolyn Runyon, Bell guessed.

'Mrs Hackel,' Harrison said.

The woman flinched, raised her head. Her body looked as if it had been drawn in to make a smaller target, the hands locked together in her lap, the tiny feet crossed at the ankles and tucked under the chair. She had a pink, heart-shaped face that just missed being pretty. Her brown curly hair featured a few streaks of a lighter shade, and was pulled back and corralled by a red scrunchie. Her eyes were dry, her cheeks unmarked by tears, but there was a strained and anxious look to her, a sense that she was readying herself for the next blow.

'Yes?'

'Sorry for your loss, Mrs Hackel,' Harrison said. 'I'm Pam Harrison. Raythune County Sheriff. And this is Belfa Elkins – our prosecuting attorney.'

'Thank you.' She blinked at them, as if uncertain about what was expected of her. 'I got a call and drove right over. I came to the front door and I just – I pounded and pounded. It was dark and – and I thought there might be nobody here, nobody to talk to me, to tell me what happened. Then the deputy came and he told me to wait here. I didn't know – I wasn't sure—' She shook her head. Her eyes made a quick assessment of her surroundings. The courthouse corridors were long and dark, looking as if they led to places nobody wanted to go. 'Ed – is he—?'

'The body's at the coroner's office,' Bell said. 'It's standard procedure. We'll release it just as soon as we possibly can.'

'Oh.' Her gaze strayed back to the floor.

Bell leaned over and touched her shoulder. Diana Hackel flinched again. 'Can I get you something?' Bell asked her. 'A glass of water? Coffee? Maybe a soft drink?'

'Oh, no. No. No, thank you.' She trembled. 'I heard that they found him – outdoors, right? Is that right? And that he'd been – he'd been dead for a while.'

'We'll have a complete report for you soon,' Bell said. 'We're still investigating.'

'Okay. Okay, then.' She took a deep breath. 'But somebody did this to him, right? I mean, he didn't have a heart attack. Which is what I thought must've happened. When they first told me. Because he doesn't take care of himself. He really doesn't. I tell him so all the time. I say, "Eddie, listen, you've got to cut down on the burgers and fries. And the drinking. And you need to quit smoking." He just grins at me. Then he says – I mean, then he *said*—' An arrow of shock struck her as she remembered what had happened. 'Oh, my God. Oh, my God.'

Harrison let the woman weep softly for a bit, and then she spoke.

'I was kind of surprised, Mrs Hackel, to hear that you'd gotten here so soon. It must be – what? A four-hour drive? How did you manage to—'

'I wasn't home,' Diana said quickly. She sniffed, rubbed at her nose. 'Wasn't in Falls Church. I was in Charleston. At a hotel. I'm getting ready to start my own business. Had some appointments there. The state police reached me on my cell.' She blinked a few more times. 'I was supposed to drive over and have dinner with Ed tonight. He's been spending so much time around here lately that he knows all the restaurants. He's been telling me about this place over in Swanville that has—' Once again, recollection smote her. She gave a small cry and shuddered.

'Your husband worked for Mountain Magic,' Bell said.

'That's right.' By this time Diana had located a Kleenex in her coat pocket and used it to dab at her eyes and her nose. Then she looked up, fixing Bell with a hard stare. 'His job is the reason he's dead.' Steel in her voice.

'How so?'

'He's been here for months now. Scouting locations. Taking investors on tours. Checking on logistics for the construction phase. That kind of stuff.' Diana batted a small hand in the air. Disgust had overtaken her. 'If it hadn't been for this damned resort – this stupid fucking hotel out in the middle of fucking nowhere—' She stopped herself. Still holding the tissue, she rearranged her folded hands on her lap. Bits of Kleenex peeped out between a couple of knuckles.

'Look,' she said, starting again, 'I'm sorry I said that. I don't mean to be insulting. I know this is your home. I'm just upset, okay? I mean, if it hadn't been for this job, Ed would've been back in Falls Church. With me and the kids. But, no. He just never quits. It's always been push, push, push. I swear, he'd build the place with his own two hands, if he could work it out. He's a go-getter. And they need that. Mountain Magic needs everything he's got. Eddie's the spark plug and they're using him up. All the delays. All the problems – my God, the problems.' She gave Bell and Harrison a sharp look, as if assessing their ability to understand the complex intricacies of corporate politics. 'They're way behind schedule, did you know that? And they were supposed to be breaking ground by now. Millions of dollars are at stake. *Millions*. The investors are getting pretty skittish. So the management team – you want to talk frantic? They're frantic, all right. And they've been coming down hard on Eddie. They're on his back, day and night. They're—'

Diana broke off her sentence to laugh, a laugh veined with hysteria. The sound startled Bell and Harrison; it was not only sudden but also incongruous, here in a cavernous deserted courthouse that still seemed slightly stupefied by the presence of people at this unlikely hour on a weekend.

And then the grief returned, flooding Diana's face again, distorting her features. 'Oh, my God,' she said. 'I can't believe I'm talking this way. He's dead. Dead. *Dead*.' Pronouncing the word multiple times undid her even more. She slumped over in her seat, face in her hands. When she looked up again, her eyes were red and wet.

'Are you sure we can't get you anything?' Harrison said.

Diana shook her head.

'Can we drive you to a motel? Or somewhere else?'

She took a few deep breaths. 'I'm fine. Really. I've made my own arrangements.' Now she frowned. She'd just remembered something. 'Don't I have to identify the body? I mean, isn't there, like, some kind of official procedure for that?'

'It's been done,' Harrison said.

'What? By who?'

'Your husband's boss. Carolyn Runyon. She was in town for some meetings and when we reached her, she was able to go over to the coroner's office and—'

'That bitch. That *bitch*.' Diana had jumped to her feet, eyes wild and darting. 'How *dare* she. I can't believe it.' She was choking out the words, practically spitting them. 'How *dare* she do that after—' She whirled toward the sheriff. Her hands were bunched into two tiny fists, and she shook them in Harrison's face. 'You had *no right* to let that bitch anywhere near my husband's body. No *fucking right*. Do you hear me?'

10

Just after 8 A.M. on Sunday, as Bell was emerging from the sole hour of sleep she'd managed to extract from the long fraught night, her cell rang. She kept it on her bedside table, within easy reach. She fought through a tangled-up quilt – and some tangled-up dreams – to get to it.

'New developments,' Sheriff Harrison said. She didn't bother with preliminaries; there was no 'Hello,' no 'Good morning' or 'How are you?' Just an earnest, straight-ahead voice. A voice with a one-track mind. It was as if no time at all had passed, as if Bell was still at the courthouse, right beside her. As if Bell hadn't finally gone home, exhaustion having gotten the upper hand, letting Harrison and Mathers deal with Diana Hackel's grief and anger.

'Deputy Oakes got back about twenty minutes ago,' the sheriff continued. 'Been working all night.' Bell's last official act before leaving the courthouse had been to prepare the request for a search warrant. Once Judge Tolliver signed it, the sheriff had planned to send Jake Oakes out to scour Royce Dillard's cabin and grounds. The county owned a set of freestanding halogen lights that could turn night into day. Speed was imperative;

even with Royce Dillard under their watchful eye, she didn't want to take a chance on anyone messing with potential evidence.

'Hit pay dirt,' Harrison said. 'Found a bloody shovel in Dillard's barn. State crime lab already took it for analysis, to see if it's Hackel's blood. The state crew's just about finished, too. They've been collecting soil samples. And that's not all.'

Bell waited. She had an odd feeling in the pit of her stomach, a queasiness she couldn't entirely blame on the lingering effects of the lousy pasta at Luigi's. Some cases were easier to solve than others, but this one – well, this one was shaping up to be *too* easy. If Royce Dillard had killed a man, wouldn't he have taken a little more trouble to hide the murder weapon? She didn't know much about Dillard, but presumably he wasn't a fool.

Yet the sheriff sounded as if they were already in the home stretch. 'We got a call from Rusty Blevins,' Harrison was saying, 'about an hour after you left the courthouse. Word spreads pretty quick in this town, you know?'

'Yeah,' Bell said dryly. 'I noticed.' Rusty Blevins was a retired bricklayer who spent his days shuffling through the streets of Acker's Gap, nosing into other people's business, adding newly acquired information, bit by bit, to the stories he spread, the same way he'd built up course after course of brick during his working days.

'Well,' the sheriff said, 'turns out he's one more person who saw Dillard threaten Edward Hackel. And it's not just hearsay. Rusty took out his cell phone camera and filmed one of their arguments. Took place Thursday afternoon. Right in front of Lymon's Market.'

'You saw the video?'

'I did. Mighty wobbly, but it's watchable. Starts out with Dillard yelling at Hackel. Something like, "You say that one more time, you sonofabitch, and I'll kill you. Swear I will." Then Dillard grabs him and pushes him. Now, Hackel was a big man, so it doesn't faze him. He comes right back at Dillard. Then Dillard picks up something – some kind of stick or rod or something, it's hard to tell on the video – and takes a big swing. Barely misses him. That's on top of the other witnesses, who saw them going at it earlier that day in front of the post office. Sounds like Hackel was maybe following him around on his errands, goading him. Dillard had finally had enough.'

By now Bell was sitting up on the side of her bed.

'You say Dillard doesn't have an alibi?' she asked.

'No, ma'am. Lives alone, so nobody saw him from Thursday – when he left Acker's Gap – to Saturday afternoon, when we picked him up at his cabin for questioning. I'll wait for the forensic analysis of the evidence, of course, but I believe we have to seriously consider booking him.'

She seemed to expect a comment from Bell, and so Bell said, 'Consider it, yes.'

They were both quiet for a few seconds. It was a moment of immense significance – not just for the man whose fate was now entwined with the criminal justice system, like a shoelace caught in the gears of a mammoth machine, but also for the human beings who administered that system: the sheriff and the deputies who would collect more evidence and interview additional witnesses, and the prosecuting attorney who would take the information and shape it into a timeline, a narrative, a story that would help persuade a jury to find him guilty of murder.

Bell never took the process lightly. One life was already gone – the victim's – and now they were putting another life in play as well.

Did they have the right person?

They would do their best to find out. That's all she knew. And if the evidence supported it, they would charge Royce Dillard with the killing of Edward Hackel and they would do everything in their power to prove his guilt.

Sheriff Harrison was talking again. 'Got one little problem.'

'What's that?'

'Royce's dogs. Passel of them out there. Strays he's taken in to raise. If we end up charging him today, and he doesn't make bail, he could sit in a jail cell for weeks. Maybe months. Who's going to take care of—'

'Call the shelter.' Bell had other things to worry about.

'Hate to do that. I really do. I'd handle it myself if I could, but I can't leave the courthouse today. Those neighbors aren't in the running, either. The wife has allergies.' The sheriff paused. 'Because if nobody adopts them from the shelter, then . . .' She let the sentence die a natural death – as if to remind Bell that the dogs wouldn't be so fortunate.

The silence stretched out. Finally Harrison said, 'Royce Dillard may or may not be guilty of murder, but those dogs of his haven't done a darned thing to anybody. Seems a shame for them to suffer.'

'Oh, hell.' Bell stood up. Sunshine was pushing seriously into her room by now, straining its way through the many-paned window and leaving printed squares of light on the front of the dresser. 'How many dogs?'

'Seven. All shapes and sizes.'

'Seven! Christ, Pam, what am I supposed to—'

'It won't be just you,' Harrison said quickly, interrupting her. 'Rhonda Lovejoy volunteered to help round 'em up. Her family's known Royce Dillard for years, much as anybody *can* know the man. She's already started lobbying me – says there's no way a gentle soul like Dillard could've killed anybody. I told her that what I need right now isn't opinions – it's temporary homes for seven dogs.'

Harrison had heard nothing from Bell and so she barreled on, hoping that the lack of a *Hell, no!* was a positive sign. 'The forensic team has already gotten what they need from the scene, so it's okay to go on out there. Dillard keeps the bigger dogs in the barn. Smaller dogs are in the house. They're all as nice as can be. Oakes didn't have any problem at all when he was searching the place – except for the risk of being licked to death, he said. State crew said the same thing. Front door's unlocked. I talked to Dillard a few minutes ago and he was mighty grateful. Only thing he really cares about is those dogs.' The sheriff spoke hastily, to drive home the idea that Bell had already agreed. 'You're doing the right thing. You know that.'

Bell groaned. 'Isn't that what we say to suspects when we want them to confess?' She didn't expect an answer. She didn't get one. 'All right, fine,' she said. Resigned to it now. 'Any last words of wisdom before I head out there?'

'Better take a roll of paper towels. The old bulldog, I hear, has a major drool issue.'

11

The road wore its battered, end-of-winter face. The two-lane stretch that ran from Acker's Gap into rural Raythune County looked like a boxer who'd refused to stand down despite being seriously overmatched, and so had wobbled under the blows in hopes the referee might finally halt the thing out of pity. Repeated assaults by the ice had left deep slash marks. The constant weight of snow had caused substantial portions to heave and buckle and shred. Time and again Bell had to swerve into the other lane, when her own lane suddenly fell away into a collapsing bowl of road kibble. From the passenger seat, Rhonda Lovejoy resisted the impulse to yell, 'Look out!' every quarter mile or so. Above them, the low-hanging ochre sky had a strained, painful look, as if it were holding off a migraine. The sun had retreated behind a bank of haze. Snow-topped mountains brooded in the distance, nursing their own wounds.

'Another four miles or so and we're there,' Rhonda said, employing her most cheerful and optimistic voice. She sensed that Bell was wavering. The morning had started out bright and cold but now was just cold, and the chill seemed to press itself against the windows of the vehicle, demanding to be let in.

'Okay,' Bell said. It was true: She'd considered scrapping the mission at least a dozen times since they'd left her house, and another dozen times once they turned off Route 6 and onto this chunked and rutted road. She'd definitely been tempted to call Sheriff Harrison and say, *Come on. I'm the prosecuting attorney, not the friggin' dogcatcher. SEVEN dogs? What the—?*

Rhonda had arrived at Bell's house on Shelton Avenue twenty minutes after Bell hung up with the sheriff. She was armed with three dog crates and a red box of Milk-Bone biscuits. Somehow, by virtue of passionate pushing and rhythmic grunting and the sporadic application of curse words, Rhonda had managed to wedge the three large crates in the back of Bell's Explorer, after which she stepped back and grinned, winded but proud. Rhonda was a heavy woman with generous hips and a regal bosom, and this morning she was dressed in a manner totally out of sync with the weather conditions. For a week now, daytime temperatures had fluctuated between the freezing mark and a notch or two below, and she was decked out in canvas sandals, a diaphanous powder blue skirt with a gauzy pink T-shirt, and a black velour vest. No coat, no hat, no gloves, no boots. *No sense, either,* Bell wanted to say, but restrained herself. Still, though, if Royce Dillard's dogs got away from them and went tearing across the winter-clawed countryside, Rhonda would be quite a sight going after them in that getup.

'Three dog crates,' Bell had said, eyeing the contraptions jammed up inside the rear windshield, 'and seven dogs.' She stood on the sidewalk next to her assistant, arms crossed, car keys digging into her fist. She was in a bad mood, the bad mood that generally descended after she'd granted a favor under duress and then felt the opening pangs of severe regret. 'I'm no math whiz, Rhonda, but I can tell you that—'

'Not a problem,' Rhonda said, cutting her off. 'I stopped by the jail this morning and talked to Royce about his dogs, so I'd know who's who. The crates'll hold the bigger ones – Goldie, Ned, and Utley – and Connie and Elvis can ride in the backseat. They're real well behaved.'

'Which still leaves two more.'

'I can hold PeeWee and Bruno on my lap up front. They're Shih Tzus. Well – Shih Tzu mixes, anyhow. Maybe Pekinese. Maybe something else. Hard to say. They're pretty small – that's all I know. Anyway, I've already lined up temporary homes for just about everybody. We can deliver 'em on our way back into town. Like toys from Santa.'

'Christmas is over.'

'Treats from the Easter bunny, then,' Rhonda countered with a game grin. 'Coming a little early this year.'

Off they went, the cages jangling and rattling in the back of the Explorer despite the snug fit. The commotion would've given Bell a headache, if she hadn't already had one. As the Explorer headed toward Royce Dillard's property, the height and density of the woods increased. They were in the least inhabited part of Raythune County now, on land that was generally left to do whatever it wanted, and what it wanted was to host trees and other varieties of vegetation that twined and looped until they created a nearly impenetrable living filigree. There was a wildness here, a wildness that started at the edges of the road and grew heavier and more menacing as it progressed toward the mountains, like a mild preoccupation that grows into a dark obsession.

The bleakness of rural Raythune County sometimes got to Bell, working its fingers deep into her mood. This was the territory of her childhood – not this specific road or batch of woods, but land so like it that the longitude and latitude didn't much matter. This was territory she felt as much as saw. It kindled in her a certain melancholy, reminding her of an abusive father, of a dirty trailer in which she and her older sister Shirley had struggled daily for their very lives, and finally, of the night when Shirley murdered their father and burned down the trailer. Bell was ten years old at the time. Sometimes she could swear she still smelled it: not the odor of a trailer turning to ash, but of the past itself changing shape, becoming heat and smoke. She had escaped, yes. So had Shirley. But for both, escape cost them dearly.

Six years ago, Bell had come back to Raythune County. No one forced her to. Quite the contrary: Everyone in her life at the time called it the worst idea in the world. The phrase 'career suicide' appeared in more than one startled, admonishing e-mail from her Georgetown friends. She'd shaken her head. Told them – in her thoughts, at least – to mind their own damned business. And did it anyway. Once back here, she had decided to run for prosecutor, a job that often entailed trips back into the very landscape over which her memories rose like the charred arch of a ruined cathedral.

Landscape like this. Tangled woods, a disintegrating road, a sense of isolation and despair that drifted in and out of the reaching branches and trailing vines and rotting stumps like an insinuating whisper. The whisper of a story told over and over again, until even the rocks and trees seemed to have it memorized.

'Turn here,' Rhonda said. First words she'd spoken in at least ten minutes. She, too, had settled into silence as they made their way beneath the gray-black valance of the day.

Bell braked. There was nobody behind them – they'd not seen another car since leaving the county road – so she didn't bother with a turn signal. 'Where?'

Rhonda pointed.

Twisting in her seat, squinting out the side window, Bell finally caught sight of a thin dribble of what might once have been a path through the tightly furled woods. She wasn't sure the Explorer would make it ten feet before sinking or being swallowed up.

'I'm supposed to go there?' Bell said.

'Yep.'

'It's not a road.'

'Best we're going to get.'

'Lord help us.' Bell swung the wheel.

'No chance of that, boss. He's not been spotted around these parts for a while.'

Rhonda was trying to be funny. Or maybe not. There was evidence all around that she was right: This place had an aura of abandonment, of having been forgotten by all but the agents of decay.

Eight minutes later they emerged into a small dirt clearing. The interval had been filled with Bell's excruciatingly slow and careful driving, necessary to avoid the drop-offs on either side of the road that would've landed them in bogs with indeterminate bottoms.

In front of them loomed the crumbling mess of Royce

Dillard's home. A few of the dogs inside the cabin barked, but the barks sounded tentative, not menacing. One uttered a long, mournful howl. The howl broke off abruptly, as if the animal had suddenly remembered the pointlessness of everything.

In spite of the cold, Bell lowered her window. Rhonda did the same with hers. The silence now was profound. Later in the spring, these woods would be alive with the thrash and crackle of small animals dashing through the underbrush, with the tattered music of birdsong. But not yet.

Once, standing in the middle of an abandoned Raythune County farm on a late-winter day just like this one, Bell had been startled by a dramatic flapping sound as a cauldron of turkey vultures – that was the collective noun, a cauldron, which she knew because she'd looked it up when she got back to her office – passed overhead in a solemn gray wave. The sound was like the sexy rustle of silk or the preliminary shifting of a heavy velvet theater curtain just before the show commences. It was a rare sound, because turkey vultures didn't often flap their wings. They did more gliding than flapping.

You were supposed to be repulsed by the birds, Bell knew; they zeroed in on roadkill and tore out the entrails and eagerly inserted their scrawny heads in the ripped-open cavities of dead animals, burrowing and chewing, burrowing and chewing. She'd been to grisly crime scenes that featured less blood and gore. But somehow, she was never put off by turkey vultures. They were nature's cleanup crew. They were just doing their job. If they were interrupted, they took to the air, and there they were majestic. Wings spread, superbly balanced, they were in their element, rising higher and higher on spirals of air, poised between the red carnage on the ground and the blue promise of the sky. The flap of those wings was a sound you never forgot. It was a sound that told a story. An ancient one, filled with hunger and beauty.

But this was still too early in the season. Bell had seen a few of the birds in the past week or so, but not a cauldron. Here in Royce Dillard's front yard, there was no sound of wings. Only a peculiar kind of silence. A silence that seemed to be waiting right along with them for the next thing to happen.

'Wow,' Rhonda said, still discombobulated from the jolting trip. She straightened her skirt with one hand. With the other, she checked her hair, refastening a barrette that had vibrated loose on account of the violent bounces of Bell's vehicle. 'No wonder Royce Dillard walks everywhere.'

'Not sure that would be much better. I'd rather lose a tire or two than break a leg. Some of those sinkholes are pretty deep.' Bell turned up the collar of her jacket, hoping to protect her neck from the wind. 'I always think I've seen the roughest parts of the county – but then I come to a place like this.'

She turned back to the cabin. Ragged, dilapidated, it seemed well on its way to being consumed by the gray tangle of woods on three sides. Panes of glass in the front windows were badly cracked or missing altogether and replaced by flaps of cardboard. The muddy front yard was crammed with the kind of clutter that would make a hoarder feel right at home. There were multiple piles of garbage bags bulging with whatever Dillard had stuffed them with. Many were leaking fluids of various colors: green, yellow, brown. There were two rusted-out riding lawnmowers tipped over on their sides, uncovering greasy round puddles that had repeatedly frozen and thawed. There were wooden sawhorses and loose rolls of fencing and old shovels and rakes. There were at least a half-dozen open-topped barrels, brimming with the rain that had overflowed and leaked down the blackened sides, leaving long, drippy trails. A scummy green film of algae, taut as a drum, stretched across the tops of the barrels. Behind and to the left of the cabin was a small, humped, sullen-looking barn; the warped gray boards seemed to breathe a toxic exhaustion.

'So what's his deal?' Bell said.

'What do you mean?'

'Dillard. He's got some money, right?'

'Not a lot. There was some kind of insurance settlement when he was a kid. But he hasn't worked in a long time. Can't, the way I hear it. He's tried, but he gets too nervous around other people.' Rhonda had an intricate knowledge of the backstories of an impressive number of Raythune County residents. Bell depended upon that knowledge, and tapped it often. 'He doesn't spend much,' Rhonda added. 'Keeps his head above water – let's put it that way. And he has enough to take care of his dogs. Barely.'

'So he's not destitute.' Bell's voice was hard. 'Then why the hell does he live like this? Like he's some kind of animal himself.'

'Seems to me that people in this world can live howsoever they please.' Rhonda's reaction surprised Bell; clearly Bell had touched a nerve. 'They don't need you or me or anybody else passing judgment on their choices.'

'Come on,' Bell said. 'I didn't mean—'

'You – you of all people – ought to understand. Royce

Dillard lives out here because he's poor. And because he can't deal with all the bullshit of civilization, okay? He just can't. I mean, given what he saw as a little kid—' Rhonda looked down and brushed something off her skirt. An invisible something. She was buying time. Afraid of getting too upset.

'Listen,' Rhonda said, starting again. 'I don't believe Royce killed that man, but nobody asked for my opinion. If he's charged, a trial's gonna do the deciding. When it comes to condemning him, though, just because this place won't be showing up in *Architectural Digest* anytime soon, well—' She stopped. 'Dammit, Bell,' Rhonda said, her tone softer now. 'I really thought that after what you've been through – I thought for sure that if anybody judged Royce Dillard, it sure as hell wouldn't be you.'

Bell opened the Explorer door. Rhonda had a point. And the sooner they got to work, the better. 'Let's go.'

The outside was a junk heap, but the inside of the cabin was clean and uncluttered. The furniture in the one-room structure was simple but serviceable: square wooden table with one chair, rocker, couch, camp bed. Four small dogs made a lumpy mound on the left side of the couch; unperturbed by the arrival of strangers, they watched, but did not bark. They barely stirred. The room smelled of cold, with a touch of cut wood and wet fur.

The log walls were bare of decoration. The oak floor was scratched and stained, but had been recently swept. In one corner was an old gas stove. It was flanked by a makeshift six-plank shelf stocked with canned goods: Hormel chili, baked beans, Chef Boyardee ravioli, green beans. A jar of Jif. A box of saltine crackers. Propped on the highest shelf was a huge slumping sack of Purina Dog Chow, well out of reach of inquiring canine snouts, with a big metal scoop right beside it.

Bell took a few seconds to look around before they dealt with the dogs. This wasn't the first time she had been in a stranger's home without the owner present to explain, to guide, to buffer, or even to hide things at the last minute; she had accompanied the deputies many times as they undertook warranted searches of places from which people had fled or been forcibly removed. It was always a peculiar experience, like catching a glimpse of someone when he doesn't know he's being watched. She'd heard the basics of Royce Dillard's story – everyone in the area had, his unusual early life being as familiar as the chorus of a favorite hymn – but no more than that. People knew what had happened to him at age two; of the long aftermath, they knew very little.

Who is *this man?* Bell wondered, standing in the middle of his home on this cold Sunday morning. More to the point: Was he capable of murder? And if he was, what could have provoked it?

'Better get these pooches outside right quick,' Rhonda said.

One of the dogs sneezed. The others looked at him. Apparently they'd slept right there, snuggled together in the folds of the old couch. They hadn't made a mess. They had persevered through the long dark hours, hours broken up only by the arrival of search teams with too much on their minds to pay attention to pets.

Rhonda led them outside for their communal peeing. It was, she reported to Bell when they returned, copious and prolonged. The look of relief in the dogs' eyes was unmistakable.

'So who's who?' Bell asked, watching the animals warily. They watched her warily right back.

Rhonda was busy rounding up leashes, bowls, blankets, chew toys. She paused to point to each dog and tick off a name: 'There's Connie and Elvis – Elvis, you're a troublemaker, aren't you? – and over there is Bruno. PeeWee's the one with the missing ear. Royce says his ear was that way when he got here.'

'Fine.' Bell was restless. She wanted to get back to town.

They headed for the gray barn. Rhonda was in charge of the dogs, so it was Bell's job to wrench open the rickety wooden sliding door, a task requiring two hands. She grimaced at the shriek it made. The windowless space was frustratingly dim, even with the door wide open, and the floor was padded with a thick layer of dirty straw. The walls were lined with junk: three old washing machines; a cracked leather saddle; two bicycles, one minus its handlebars and the other lacking tires; more scum-topped barrels; a hodgepodge of construction equipment and yard implements. Deputy Oakes had roped off the area where he'd found the bloody shovel.

'Hey, there. Good boy,' Rhonda said. Slowly, she moved toward a shadowy corner, from which a pair of eyes watched her. 'This must be Utley,' she said. She reached forward and scratched at the tangled thatch of gray and white hair behind the dog's ears; her other hand held the leashes of the four dogs from the house, who waited amiably, pawing at the straw, sniffing it.

Bell looked around. Two other dogs waited along the back wall, regarding her with what seemed to be curiosity, not ill will. She wasn't good with dogs. She figured they could probably tell.

'Here you go,' she said to the closest one. The words came out flat and listless.

'Oh, come on,' Rhonda said. 'You can do better'n that, boss. Know you can.'

Still Bell held back. She'd never owned a pet. Her life was too busy, too complicated. Carla had begged for a puppy when she was eight years old, and again when she was nine and ten, but Bell was adamant: No dog. And there was something else: The longer she was a prosecutor, the less Bell trusted animals. Two years ago she'd won a case against the owner of three fighting dogs; the dogs had broken loose from their thick chains and killed a toddler. The year before that, she'd prosecuted a domestic violence case in which a husband had forced his German shepherd to attack his estranged wife, ripping off a large portion of her face. Multiple plastic surgeries later, the victim still wouldn't go out in daylight without a veil. The horrific incidents seemed to validate Bell's instinct to keep all dogs at a distance.

Truth was, she felt the same way about people sometimes.

'These are sweet dogs,' Rhonda said. 'They wouldn't hurt anybody. There's no such thing as a bad dog – only humans who don't treat 'em right. Come on, now. Just walk right up and say hello. Put a little oomph in it. Got to get 'em motivated.'

The cold in the barn had begun to penetrate the fabric of Bell's jacket. She couldn't imagine how chilled Rhonda was, in her flimsy clothes.

Oh, hell, Bell thought, stepping forward. *Here goes.* 'Hey, dog. Good girl,' she said. A bit louder this time, with more enthusiasm. The animal closest to her emerged from the dark corner. She was a kind-eyed, broad-chested animal, with a thick coat the color of buttered toast. Her tail made wide looping circles, sweeping the floor with each downward revolution. The tops of her rounded ears were hiked up in anticipation of something new. She whined softly.

'That's Goldie,' Rhonda said. 'While you put a leash on her, I'll handle Utley and that other one over there. The bulldog. Name's Ned. He's about a hundred years old, give or take. Won't be any trouble – except for the drool factor. We were warned, remember?'

A few minutes later they trooped out of the barn, a motley parade made up of two women, seven dogs, and a crisscrossing confusion of leashes. Rhonda was handling six dogs; Bell, one. Rhonda looked far more comfortable.

'Okay. So I'm keeping Bruno, which means we're done. Everybody's taken care of,' Rhonda said. She smacked the dashboard of Bell's Explorer with satisfaction, which was her way of high-fiving herself. Then she folded up the piece of notebook paper, the one on which she'd been keeping track, penciling lines between dogs' names and the names of friends and relatives. Rhonda had called them all first, naturally, to warn of their approach, but hadn't given too much advance notice. Didn't want to provide time for second thoughts.

She slipped the paper back into her purse. She tickled Bruno's scruffy gray head, which was pushed into the crook of her arm. 'We're going to get along fine, you precious little thing,' she said. 'You're a sweetie, aren't you?'

They had just pulled out of Hickey Leonard's driveway on the south side of Acker's Gap. Hickey and his wife had agreed to provide a temporary home for Elvis. Bell had seen little of Hickey around the courthouse of late; he was working on a major drug case and spent most of his time on depositions in other counties.

Prior to the stop at Hickey's, Bell and Rhonda had made dog drops at Ken and Michelle Burch's house; Roger Cantrell's trailer; Sharon Morgan's apartment; and Curtis and Annie Wehrle's farm, where they deposited, respectively, Utley, PeeWee, Connie, and Ned.

Bell turned the Explorer back toward the county road. At each home, she had remained in the car while Rhonda went inside, toting one of Royce Dillard's dogs under her arm or leading it by a leash. A few minutes later she would come back out again, giving Bell a thumbs-up sign. Then they'd head to the next location.

'Hold on,' Bell suddenly said. She kept driving, but gave Rhonda a sideways glare.

'What's wrong?'

'You miscounted. There's an extra back there.'

Rhonda turned around. In the rear of the Explorer the round golden hump of a large dog, asleep in a crate, rose and fell with deep, untroubled breathing.

'Oh,' Rhonda said.

The fake surprise was utterly unconvincing, Bell thought, as her irritation increased.

'"Oh"?'

'Well,' Rhonda said, sounding flustered, 'I suppose I thought that maybe, if the need arose, you might—'

'No.'

'We can work real hard on finding another home for her, Bell, but for the time being, it sure seems to me that you might consider opening up your heart to a sweet—'

'No.'

'She's housebroken, boss.'

'Don't care.'

'Well, if you look at it right, this is your duty. She ought to be a protected witness. After all, she's the one who found the body. And she surely won't be any trouble or—'

'No. No. No.'

Rhonda looked down at the small dog in her lap. She used an index finger to make a series of soft squiggly paths through the fur on his back, a gesture that clearly pleased Bruno. 'Looks like you're gonna have yourself a roommate, buddy.'

'Oh, for Christ's sake.' Bell shook her head. 'You live in a studio apartment above a pizza place, Rhonda. You don't have enough room for *one* dog, much less two. That mutt back there is bigger than your kitchen.'

'We'll manage.'

They rode in silence for another mile. Bell turned onto Shelton Avenue. She sighed a prolonged, exasperated sigh.

'Okay, fine,' Bell said. 'I'll keep the dog. But just for a few days, okay? After that, we'll have to figure out something else. It's just temporary.'

12

'A dog. Really.'

Carla's voice on the phone combined skepticism and amusement. Bell always called her daughter on Sunday nights – she called her other times, too, but this was a standing date – and on this particular Sunday night, Bell conveyed a piece of news that clearly surprised the young woman. And delighted her, too.

'Yes, but it's just for a day or so,' Bell quickly added. 'Until we can find another place.'

'Geez, Mom. That big old house seems perfect to me. And there's a fenced backyard. Plenty of running room for— What's her name again?'

'Goldie.'

'Right. Goldie. Well, Goldie is one lucky pooch, tell you that.'

Bell took a sip of the Rolling Rock she'd opened just before making the call. Her bare feet were tucked up under her; that was her preferred position when she settled into this beloved old easy chair. The chair had been one of the very first items she had insisted that the movers carry into this house six years ago – ahead of the washer and dryer, or the beds, or the couch, or the boxes that she had packed in a daze back in the condo on Capitol Hill, still reeling from the collapse of her marriage and her decision to return to her hometown.

The chair was torn, dilapidated, printed with stains of mysterious origins – *And let's* keep *them mysterious,* Bell had muttered to herself, when she'd first spotted it in a Goodwill store in central West Virginia when she was nineteen years old – and dozens of holes worn right through the fabric to the meager bit of stuffing beneath. It dominated her living room. The rest of the furniture, fairly new, seemed to be sinking slowly down to the level of the chair, instead of the other way around. Bell didn't mind. This chair had seen her through the milestones, good and bad, of her adult life: marriage, motherhood, divorce, relocation, election to prosecuting attorney, and one passionate love affair, the kind upon which she still couldn't quite close the door, even though Clay Meckling now lived four states and many mountains away.

The chair had been here for her on the painful day two and a half years ago when Carla decided to go live with her father, Bell's ex-husband, Sam, and finish high school there. And on the morning last year when Bell's sister Shirley showed up. Shirley, paroled from prison, had lived with Bell for a few months before moving in with her boyfriend, a musician named Bobo Bolland. Things had settled down now for Shirley; she was holding her own in the world.

Bell had been sitting in this very chair six months ago – with her feet tucked under her, same as now – when she received the call from Sammy Burdette, a county commissioner, telling her that Nick Fogelsong had just announced he wasn't running for reelection. *Can't be,* she'd said, stunned and blindsided. *Bet me,* had been

Burdette's saucy reply. His chuckle of superiority had very nearly put her over the edge.

'Mom? You there?'

'Sorry, sweetie. I'm here. Just distracted. How's the job? You're working out in Bethesda, right? I hope the commute's not too bad.'

'You're changing the subject. I want to hear about Goldie.'

Goldie. Jesus, yes. She had a pet now. Another living creature here in the house.

Bell stood up. She'd left the dog in the kitchen, eating the chow that Bell had slung into a plastic mixing bowl. She had picked up a small bag of dog food at Lymon's that afternoon. She didn't go so far as to buy an actual dog dish, being as how Goldie's days around here were numbered. A mixing bowl would do. She could sterilize it with bleach after Goldie had moved on.

She didn't know much about dogs, but she knew enough to realize you weren't supposed to leave a strange animal unattended in your kitchen just a few hours after you'd brought it home. 'I'm checking on her right now,' Bell said hastily into the phone as she hurried through the hall toward the kitchen. She was envisioning chewed-up chairs, an upended table, and multiple piles of excrement dotting the linoleum like exhibits at an avant-garde art gallery. Bell realized the irrationality of her apprehension – surely she would've heard the commotion of clattering furniture? – but still had persuaded herself that the amiable Goldie might suddenly turn into a demon of destructiveness.

She rounded the corner. Goldie was lying on her side in the middle of the floor, her slightly rounder belly rising and falling contentedly. The bowl was empty. Spotting

Bell, Goldie lifted her big head. Her tail thumped on the floor. Chairs, table, linoleum – everything was fine.

'Good girl,' Bell said. It was the only thing she could think of to say.

Carla laughed. 'Unless that was directed at me, it sounds like you two are getting along great. So what's she like? Text me a picture, okay? I'd love to see her.'

'Sure.' Bell pulled out one of the dinette chairs and sat down. To her surprise, Goldie hoisted herself up and trotted over to sit alongside her, pushing a soft yellow head into Bell's lap. The tail softly brushed the floor. 'But remember, sweetie – I'm not keeping her very long,' Bell said. 'She's just here for a little while, until Rhonda can find her another home. And anyway, she belongs to Royce Dillard.'

'But he's in big trouble. Right?'

'We're not going to talk about that.' When Carla had decided to move back in with Sam, Bell made a pact with her: They would avoid discussion of Bell's cases. Carla already knew too much about the dark side of life, from the days when she resided here in Acker's Gap, daughter of a prosecutor; Bell wanted her to have a chance to forget all that. Carla lived in a different place now. A place that wasn't shadowed as massively and relentlessly by tragedy as it was by mountains.

'Too late, Mom. Kayleigh Crocker already told me all about it. We've been texting a lot. She says Dillard's gonna hang for murdering some guy who worked for the resort.'

Bell was instantly annoyed. She knew Carla kept up with a few of her old friends from Acker's Gap High School, but did that have to include Kayleigh Crocker?

Kayleigh was Rusty Blevins's granddaughter, which meant she was privy to every scrap and rag of gossip that the old man pilfered and scavenged on his daily rounds.

'Okay,' Bell said. Testiness turned her voice into a blunt instrument. 'To begin with, no one's going to "hang" for anything. West Virginia doesn't have the death penalty anymore.'

'Geez, Mom. It's just a figure of speech. Kayleigh just meant that—'

'She ought to keep her mouth shut,' Bell declared, interrupting her. 'And that goes for that meddling grandfather of hers, too. They've got no right to be talking about Royce Dillard or anybody else brought in for questioning. Or about the Hackel murder in general. It's none of their business.'

Silence.

When Carla spoke again, her tone was respectful but determined. 'None of their business, Mom? They live there. It's their town, too. I think it *is* their business. Definitely. And just for the record, I *asked* Kayleigh about it, okay? I saw a thing on the local news here about that guy – the one who was murdered. He's from Falls Church, so they covered it. I heard them say "Raythune County" and I knew I had to check with Kayleigh.' She paused, and then plunged forward. 'I like to know what's going on in your life, Mom. Everything. Not just the stuff you want me to know about. The hard stuff, too. Like with Nick Fogelsong. You didn't even tell me he wasn't sheriff anymore. Remember? I didn't know for a month. I found out from Kayleigh.' Carla's voice dropped a notch lower. On the way, it became more emphatic. 'I want to know those things, okay? All of them. I want to know. The cases you're working on and the really terrible stuff that happens there and the good stuff – all of it. I want to know about your life. Your *whole* life.'

Now it was Bell's turn to be silent for a moment. Her daughter was right. Bell thought she was trying to shield her, but she was really just keeping her on the outside of her life. And was that for Carla's protection – or her own?

Sometimes she forgot that Carla was not a little girl anymore. She was a young woman. Bright, resourceful. Trustworthy – with a few spectacular lapses now and again, the kind you expected from teenagers, the kind that revealed a fierce desire for independence more than any serious character flaws.

She *did* keep Carla separated from the deepest, truest part of her life – which happened to be her work. Her elected office. And maybe she was wrong to do that. She couldn't tell Carla everything, but she could confide selectively. Bell could draw her closer toward the things that mattered to her, the way you invite someone to share your campfire.

'Listen up, sweetie. Okay? I want to tell you a little bit about Royce Dillard,' Bell said. 'You only lived in Acker's Gap a few years, and that's not long enough to really know. Rusty Blevins knows, and I bet Kayleigh does, too – pretty much anyone who's been born and raised here knows – but they're all caught up in the murder right now. That's all they can see. A murder has a way of doing that. It gets in the way. You can't see around it or over it. But for now, I want you to hear a story.'

'A story.' Carla's voice was fringed with skepticism.

She was nineteen years old, and she didn't need her mother to read to her at bedtime anymore.

'Yeah,' Bell said. 'A story.' She leaned forward, propping her elbows on the table, so that she could hold the cell against her ear more comfortably. 'You've heard about Buffalo Creek, right?'

'Sure. We talked about it in tenth grade. In West Virginia History class. It's sort of like West Virginia's 9/11. It happened, like, a thousand years ago, wasn't it?'

'Nineteen seventy-two.'

'Like I said. A thousand years ago.'

'What did they tell you?'

'There was a flood. The coal companies had dumped this crap – the waste material from when they wash the junk from the coal, this black sludgy stuff – until it made this ginormous pile. And then it rained really hard and the pile collapsed and all the water just went tearing through the valley. And a lot of people died. Old people and little kids – just a ton of people. It was terrible. One of the worst days in West Virginia history.'

'Yes,' Bell somberly confirmed. 'And Royce Dillard was right in the middle of it.'

Bell knew her daughter, and she knew how to interpret her quiet spells on the phone, such as the one that had just descended. Sometimes the silent patches meant that Carla was preoccupied – she was texting a friend, checking the Internet, watching TV on Mute – but sometimes, like now, they meant she was too startled to know what to say. And deeply curious, so curious that she didn't want her own lame questions to get in the way of Bell's explanation.

'So you know the basics,' Bell went on. 'On February twenty-sixth, 1972, a little after eight A.M., a slurry dam burst. Millions of gallons of water were released into the Buffalo Creek Valley. One hundred and twenty-five people died. Over four thousand were left homeless. Royce Dillard was just a baby. Two years old. He lived in Lundale, one of the little towns in the valley. Lived there in a little one-room house with his mother and father – Mike and Ellie Dillard.

'When the water hit, it just smashed that house all to hell. Ellie only had seconds to grab her child and make it out the front door. She was holding him in one hand, and with the other hand, trying to make it out of the way of the water. There was a ridge behind the house. A high spot. That's what she was aiming for – that ridge. To get out of the house and up to that ridge.

'You have to understand how fast the water was coming. Seven feet per second, they say. A wall of water thirty feet high. There was no time to think, no time to plan. You just had to *move*. There were houses and trailers and dead bodies being swept right along, and cars and telephone poles – things that turned into weapons themselves, coming that fast, with that much force.' Bell paused. She closed her eyes and then she opened them again. 'Ellie Dillard was gone. In seconds, she was just – gone. They never found her body. But somehow, Royce survived. Somehow, his father was able to get hold of the little boy and he got him to the edge of that ridge. Mike Dillard had a second or so to decide what to do. And instead of saving himself, he threw Royce to safety. There were people up on the ridge and they called to him, telling him they'd catch his boy, and Mike used the last bits of his strength to throw Royce as high as he could. Then Mike was swept away in that terrible black water. They never found his body, either.'

'Oh my God,' Carla said. It came out as a solemn whisper.

'Royce was raised by his mother's aunt here in Raythune County. When he came of age, he used the money from the settlement the coal company gave to survivors to buy two parcels of land. Put up a cabin on the one out past Sawyer Fork. He's been living there ever since. And the other one—'

'—is the one they want for the resort,' Carla said, finishing the sentence for her. 'Kayleigh told me all about it. That's why Royce Dillard killed that guy, right? Because the guy wouldn't stop pestering him to sell his land? Seems pretty skimpy for a motive, Mom, if you don't mind me saying so. Kayleigh thinks so, too. And so does her granddad.'

Bell rolled her eyes, knowing that Carla couldn't see her do it, but hoping that the eye-roll would somehow be evident in the tone of her voice. 'You know what? Kayleigh and Rusty Blevins are welcome to their opinions. But in a prosecutor's office we have to deal with facts, not opinions.' What she didn't want to tell Carla was that part of her tended to agree with the girl and her grandfather. It *was* a skimpy motive. There had to be more to the story. And more, certainly, to Royce Dillard.

Bell stood up from the dinette chair, needing to stretch her limbs. She looked around. *Uh-oh,* she thought. No Goldie.

Keenly focused on her conversation with Carla, Bell again had lost track of the dog. She wasn't in the kitchen anymore. Had Goldie slipped upstairs to one of the bedrooms? Or was she wreaking havoc in the living room? Same as last time, Bell had visions of canine-engineered chaos: a torn-up couch, claw marks on the maple staircase, puddles of urine lurking in the corners.

'Oh, hell,' Bell said as she scooted back through the hall, her bare feet making a rapid slapping sound on the hardwood floor.

'What's going on?'

'Just hope that damned mutt didn't mess things up out here in the—'

Bell brought her sentence to an abrupt end. She stood in the threshold between the hall and the living room, surveying things.

'Mom?' said Carla, anxious in the wake of the silence. 'Mom? How bad is it?'

Bell watched as Goldie, having wound herself in a tight furry circle so that she could fit between the armrests, quivered and then settled herself more firmly in the easy chair, nudging her nose deep into the soft, giving fabric. Her snores had a faint raspy edge, like an old man's snores. Bell felt a sudden sympathy for this creature who, after all, had been jerked unceremoniously out of her life and deposited here, with no say in the matter, no right of refusal. Despite all that upheaval, the dog still was trusting and good-natured and well behaved.

Maybe, Bell thought, *I ought to be a little more accommodating, while she's here. A little nicer.*

'Mom?'

'Everything's fine. Just realized that I need to do some shopping.'

'For what?'

'A dog dish.'

* * *

Some two hours later, as Bell worked on the unseemly amount of paperwork that she had scattered on the floor around the easy chair, her cell rang. At the sound of the phone, Goldie raised her head; she'd been sleeping on the couch, her snores light and regular now, lacking the raspy edge. Bell had relocated the obliging dog over there and reclaimed her seat.

It was Sheriff Harrison.

'State crime lab just called. All I can say, Bell, is that Carolyn Runyon must have a ton of pull with the big boys in Charleston. We've *never* had forensic results this fast. I kind of wish I didn't know it was possible. Now I'm pissed off about all the times we had to wait for weeks and weeks.'

'Know what you mean. So what did they find?'

'The blood on the shovel is definitely Hackel's. Coroner says the blow came from behind, with the sharp edge of that shovel. At least three very powerful jabs. Took a hell of a lot of strength. Damn near severed the victim's head. He probably bled out in minutes. The lab also analyzed the interior of that wagon of Dillard's – the one he brings to town every now and again – and found fibers from the victim's coat and more of his blood on the bottom and sides. Someone had tried to wipe it down, but they did a piss-poor job of it. Looks like Hackel was assaulted with the shovel, then his body was loaded into the wagon and dumped in Old Man's Creek. They found soil from the creek bank on the wagon wheels.' Harrison took a breath. She was pleased with the deluge of information, and had delivered it rapidly. 'I gave Dillard another shot at coming up with an alibi. Or an explanation for Hackel's blood on his shovel. Didn't say a word.'

'Granted, that's all pretty incriminating,' Bell said. 'But how did Hackel get out to Dillard's property? His car was still at his motel. And Dillard doesn't own a car, so he couldn't have given him a ride.'

'Good question.'

'Fingerprints?'

'Weapon was wiped clean. So was the wagon. But that's typical. Everybody knows about cleaning off fingerprints. Blood and fiber evidence – that's a lot harder to get rid of.'

'The motive still troubles me. Would Royce Dillard kill a man just because he was mad at him? Because the guy made a pest of himself? Surely there's something else going on here.'

'Maybe so. But the evidence against Dillard is strong, Bell. You've gone to trial with a lot less.'

It was a fair point. Bell waited before speaking again. She was perplexed by the unanswered questions, and reluctant to charge Royce Dillard until she'd at least tried to get to the bottom of them. But the clock was ticking. They had to either charge him or let him go. And she had seen, in previous cases, the price of hesitation and delay. She'd seen what happened in Acker's Gap when a murder occurred and the prosecutor's office was slow to charge a suspect. People grew nervous and afraid. A curtain of dread settled over the streets. Wild rumors reared up and were difficult to swat down.

'I know Dillard rejected an attorney initially,' Bell said. 'Has he changed his mind?'

'No, ma'am. Says he doesn't need – and I'm quoting here – any "goddamned bloodsucking lawyer." I've put in a call to Serena Crumpler, though.' Crumpler was a criminal defense attorney in Acker's Gap against whom Bell had fought in several cases. She was young and tough, and often served as a court-appointed attorney for indigent defendants. Bell respected her immensely.

'Good. Maybe she can talk some sense into him.'

'Maybe. But I've seen this kind of thing happen before, and so have you,' the sheriff said. 'A man loses his temper and commits an act of violence. He doesn't want a lawyer because he knows he's to blame. He wants to be punished. Craves it, even.'

'Dillard says he didn't do it.'

'He says that *now*. Just wait till he sees the evidence we've got. And his guilty conscience kicks in.'

Bell let a few seconds tick by. 'So you think Dillard is our man. No question.'

'I do. No question.'

A prosecutor and a sheriff had to work together. Sometimes the prosecutor was more certain about a suspect's guilt, and had to talk the sheriff into supporting the arrest; other times, it was the sheriff who believed they'd definitely tracked down the culprit. Either way, they had to respect each other's instincts. Rarely if ever did they see a case exactly the same way. If she and Pam Harrison were going to be an effective team, she had to start trusting this woman the way she had trusted Nick.

'Okay,' Bell said. 'Let's charge him.'

'Will do. And after that,' Harrison added, 'hopefully Serena will talk some sense into him. He needs somebody on his side.'

'Probably figures he already has that.' Bell's eyes slid over to lock up with Goldie's. The dog, spread out across the couch, had watched Bell during the phone conversation, brown eyes poised and alert, as if somehow she knew whom Bell was talking about.

'You mean a lawyer?' Harrison asked.

'Hell, no. I mean the kind of friend that doesn't give a damn about billable hours.'

13

'They're fine,' Bell said. 'I've talked to the people who are taking care of your dogs, and they're all good.'

Royce Dillard looked relieved. He started to say something back to her – perhaps a word of gratitude – but he didn't. Apparently he recalled that she was one of the reasons he was here in the first place, separated from his animals, separated from his life, such as it was. The questioning light in his eyes shifted back to the flinty black of anger.

'Go away,' he said. He pulled a sleeve roughly across his mouth, as if addressing her even briefly had left a bad taste. He still hadn't met Bell's gaze. Always found a reason to look somewhere else.

This was early Monday morning, and the reality of life in jail had begun to register on Dillard's skin. It had a dry, chalky look.

His new home was a square box with a concrete floor and cinder-block walls painted a tofu-like shade of beige, spiced by the eye-irking scent of industrial-strength cleaning fluid. Dillard was wearing an orange jumpsuit with RAYTHUNE CO SHERIFF'S DEPT stenciled across the back in tall white letters. Jumpsuits came in two sizes – small and XXL – and a medium-sized man like Dillard was out of luck. The XXL suit gave him a clownish look, cuffs crinkling around his ankles, sleeves folded over twice, collar hanging open like an empty sack. Laceless brown shoes completed the outfit; prisoners' shoelaces were always removed, to alleviate the suicide risk, meaning that when he moved, his shoes flapped and shifted. If he got up any speed, he'd run right out of them.

Dillard sat back down on the sagging metal cot with the half-inch-thick line of foam that passed for a mattress. He'd jumped up when Deputy Mathers opened the cell door to let Bell in, unable to hide the eagerness in his face, the hunger for news about his dogs.

'I thought you were worried about them,' she said. His attitude had caught her by surprise.

'I am. That's why I want to get out of here.'

'Well, for the time being, they're being well cared for, okay? All I came to say.' Bell turned. She raised her arm, ready to call for Mathers.

'Hold up.'

She dropped her arm.

'Thing is,' he said, 'I was wondering about Elvis.'

'Elvis.' Bell struggled to match up monikers and dogs in her head. She wished Rhonda was on hand to help.

'Little black one. Looks like a cocker spaniel. Probably ain't, though. Not all the way through, anyways. Gets scared real easy.'

'Right.' She remembered Elvis. Shivering with fright from the drive and the dislocation, the dog had jumped right up into Hickey's arms like he belonged there. 'One of my colleagues is taking care of him. An assistant prosecutor. Hickey Leonard.'

'He got a family?'

'A wife, yes. Kids are grown and gone. Why?'

'Elvis can be nippy with little kids. They annoy him – all the noise they make and the running around and whatnot. Just don't want nobody to get hurt. Wouldn't be the dog's fault.'

'How'd he come to live with you?'

Dillard was hunched over, elbows on knees, legs spread wide. He bounced his legs up and down, causing the cot to shimmy and squeak. He looked at the floor.

'Long story,' he said.

'I've got time.' Not true. She didn't have time. She had a million things to do. But she was intrigued by this man and his mysteries. If he wanted to tell her a story, if he was able to, she would listen.

He waited a second or so, and then something seemed to shift inside him. A knot came undone. 'Most of my dogs, see, they show up on their own,' he said. There was an energy in his voice, an eagerness, that surprised her, because it was so different from his earlier sullenness. As long as he was talking about his dogs, Bell realized, he could communicate just fine. The dogs gave him cover.

'I find 'em in the woods,' he went on. 'Or sniffing in a Dumpster near town. Walking down the road or whatnot. They been abandoned by somebody, just chucked out the side door. Like garbage. The county shelter's always full, seems like – I check there first, every time – and that means that when they get a new dog . . .' He shook his head. The outcome was obvious. 'Some people – I don't know how they live with themselves. You got a creature in your care, a living thing that looks up to you, depends on you. And you throw it away. You leave it to do for itself.' He shook his head again. 'Elvis, though – his story's different. Belonged to a man named Chalmers Remis. Lived over by Blanton Fork. Chalmers used to take that dog with him on these long, long walks in the woods over by my place. I seen 'em from time to time, him and the dog moving so slow you'd swear they'd had some spell put on 'em, so slow that you couldn't believe they'd ever make any progress whatsoever. Me and Chalmers, we'd say hello to each other. Nothing more. Anyway, one day last year I get this letter from a lawyer. Turns out Chalmers died from the cancer. And guess what? He left me his dog. Said Elvis was mine. Now, the funny part is, I was never aware that Chalmers Remis even knew my name. But he recognized me, all right.'

Dillard waited, apparently to see if Bell understood what he was saying. People around here generally knew who he was. He didn't know them – but they knew him. He was the boy who had survived the Buffalo Creek flood, the boy who'd been saved by his father. A grown man now, all buttoned up with his story tucked inside him, like a message in a bottle. 'Lawyer told me that the man's family got a big laugh out of it,' Dillard went on. 'They didn't want that dog, nosiree. And when that lawyer fella was first reading the will to them all and he started the line, "And to my friend Royce Dillard," they all stiffened up, because it turns out that Chalmers had a good bit of money stashed away – and they thought that maybe he'd up and left it all to me. Anyway,' Dillard said, 'he didn't leave me no money. But the joke was on them, because you know what? Elvis – he's a real good dog. I got the prize, after all.'

Bell waited a moment before she spoke. 'Well, you

don't have to worry about Elvis. Hickey says he's thriving. Got a good appetite.'

Dillard nodded, satisfied. 'That's Elvis, all right. Some dogs'll take or leave their food. But others, they'll knock you down if you stand between them and a chicken bone, you know? Don't mean nothing by it. Not bad dogs or nothing. Just their way. They got to survive, howsoever they can. It's in their blood. Instinct. They'd kill you, most likely, if they felt like you was threatening them.'

He licked his lips. His own words were digging at him. 'Know what you think,' he said. 'You think it's the same with me. I had to survive. And so I killed that sonofabitch. Hackel. Well, I didn't.'

She quickly lifted a flat hand, like a traffic cop in a crosswalk. 'Don't want to talk about the case, Mr Dillard. Not without your lawyer present – and like it or not, Serena Crumpler is coming over later today to talk to you about letting her represent you.'

'Don't need her. Don't need nobody.' The belligerence was back.

Like every prosecutor she knew, Bell didn't like defendants to represent themselves, even though it generally ensured a win for her side. Lack of legal knowledge on the part of the accused almost always resulted in a guilty verdict. But it left a bitter residue on her conscience. People shouldn't be punished for pride or ignorance. Or both.

She looked at him. His hair was greasy. The gray stubble on his chin could've doubled as dirt. The jail provided a supervised shaving time each morning, but Dillard, the deputies had reported to Bell, refused it. Hygiene wasn't high on his list.

The real focus of her observation, though, wasn't his appearance. It was his essence, his spirit. From what she had heard over the years, Dillard's withdrawal from a normal life – a life that included other people – had come about gradually, bit by bit, the same way the dense woods had closed over the road to his cabin.

Through his early thirties, he lived just outside Acker's Gap with his great-aunt Bessie Truax. He held down a job – he worked at Lymon's Market – and he built the cabin out on his land as a place for weekends. He was briefly engaged, but for some reason, that fell through. Bessie Truax died. He moved out to the cabin permanently. Began to accumulate dogs. The trips into town occurred less and less frequently. Every now and again, on the anniversary of the Buffalo Creek flood, a reporter might show up in Acker's Gap, asking for directions to the home of Royce Dillard. For a time, he obliged them, and Bell had read the interviews with him in a few newspapers, in a magazine or two. He remembered so little about that day. Just a few hazy details, little shreds and slivers of the maybe–could be kind of memory: His mother's screams. The high black wall of water. Flying through the air, up and up and up, finally landing in hands that reached out and held on, and then a hectic chorus of yells: *I've got him! I've got him!* All he really knew, Dillard would tell the interviewers, was that his father had saved his life. He never knew him, the man who used his last ragged breath to save him. The man who was torn from this world by coal-black water, same as his mother.

And then, about a decade or so ago, Dillard had stopped answering the knocks on his front door. Stopped waving back at people when they drove past him and his wagon on the road into town. He'd told his story for the last time. Maybe, Bell thought, he wanted to seal it off inside him, to make sure it stayed just the way it was, impervious to time and change, the way you might wrap up a keepsake in an old handkerchief – a lock of hair or a charm bracelet or a pocket watch – and then bury it deep.

People said Royce Dillard lived alone, but he didn't, Bell told herself. He lived with his dogs. And he lived with his story.

'Don't need nobody,' he repeated, in case he'd not made himself clear, and the compressed snarl in his tone brought her attention back to the small cell and its blank-faced, leg-jiggling occupant.

'I hear you,' she said. 'But can I ask you something? Your place – the outside's a disaster area, but the inside's fine. Why's that?'

She was sure he'd ignore the question. But he answered.

'Last few years,' he said, 'things have kind of gotten away from me. Stuff just keeps piling up. No excuse. Not proud of it. That's sure not how Bessie taught me to be. I mean, I know better. I do. It's just – I can't – it's hard to—' He stared at the palms of his hands, as if he'd written the words there but they'd somehow gotten rubbed off. 'The inside – well, I've got to keep that picked up. For the smaller dogs. Leave a bunch of crap lying around, they're likely to eat something they shouldn't.' He swallowed hard. 'Got to admit, too, that money's tight. So I don't throw nothing away. Thinking I might need it.' Another swallow. 'My dogs – taking care of them costs a pretty penny, let me tell you. I keep up with their shots. Feed 'em right. It's important. Truth is, here lately I've done some things for money that I never thought I'd do. Things I'd never have dreamed of doing – except for my dogs.'

'If you're short of money, then why don't you just sell your land to Mountain Magic?'

'I need that land more'n I need the money. Perfect spot for my dogs. Not another one like it – that's why I bought it in the first place. Lotsa woods. Big trees and hills and whatnot. One day I'm going to fence it off. Make a place where they can run free – and be safe, too. All kinds of dogs. All together. First I thought it might be okay to sell it – but then I thought, "No, no. Ain't right. I bought that property for one purpose and one purpose only. Got to do what I've been fixing to do for a long time now. No matter what it costs me."'

His eyes bored into a spot on the wall, as if it had given him an argument. 'Folks around here better be careful,' he said, 'else all this land's gonna be taken away. Times get hard – and first thing folks do is start selling land. You gotta hold on to it. You gotta fight for what you love. You gotta hang on even when the thing you love most in the world is being ripped right out of your hands.' He stopped. 'Don't want to talk no more. Talked too long already.'

'You doing okay in here?'

'Yeah.'

'Then I'll leave you be. Just wanted to give you the update on your dogs.'

'Decent of you to look out for 'em.'

'I can't take the credit. It was Sheriff Harrison's idea. Wanted to make sure your animals were in good homes during the trial.'

He nodded. 'How's the other fella doing? The other sheriff, I mean.'

There's only one sheriff, Bell wanted to say. *And that's Pam Harrison*. But she knew what Dillard meant. Nick Fogelsong had been such a big part of law enforcement around here for so many years that he was a little like the mountainous landscape: Any direction you turned, you saw him – or expected to, once the clouds cleared.

'Fine,' she said.

'Don't know him personally, but heard plenty. Most of it good.'

'Imagine so.'

14

Speak of the devil, Bell thought.

She had dropped into JP's for a quick cup of coffee, the visit to Dillard's cell still weighing heavily on her mind. She had interviews for other cases scheduled throughout the day; this was likely her only chance for a break until late this afternoon, when she had yet another errand to run.

And there he was.

Nick Fogelsong, big as life. Suit jacket open, elbows spread, making himself comfortable in a booth that the two of them had occupied numberless times during his days as sheriff, when they'd sit across from each other, blanketing their internal organs with the blackest, harshest, foulest, most detestable – and thereby delectable – coffee that the human digestive system could handle, all the while comparing notes on the most difficult cases they were facing. JP's was less than two years old; it had replaced Ike's, a diner with a long and motley history that had ended abruptly and permanently.

'Hey,' Nick said. He raised his hand. A semi-wave. The cuff link on his dress shirt caught the light.

Bell held back a wince. Nick and cuff links: Nope. Didn't work for her. Didn't work at all.

She paused, and then she moved in that direction, trying to hide the fact that she was rattled. And not on account of the cuff link. She'd just about broken herself of the habit of looking for Nick on workdays, in the courthouse corridors or on the streets of Acker's Gap or here in the diner. For a crazy second, time itself went a little sideways; she half wondered if she was in JP's or back in Ike's, years ago, having just ordered a slice of apple pie from Georgette Akers, causing Georgette to whip out the stubby yellow pencil from behind her right ear so that she could write down the order in her little notebook, even though she didn't need to, of course – Bell always went for apple – and as Georgette reached for the pencil, Bell's eyes followed her fingers and she noticed the sparkly barrettes that propped up Georgette's bright blond hair in a swollen bouffant . . .

No. Couldn't be. Georgette was dead. Dead for more than two years now.

'Belfa? You okay?'

She sat down on the other side of the booth.

'Fine.'

'Look like you've seen a ghost.'

Fogelsong was more of a mind-reader than he'd ever know. Bell didn't tell him how close he'd come to being right.

'Just overwhelmed with work,' she said.

'It's not even nine o'clock yet.'

She shrugged. 'Lots of active cases.'

'Same as it ever was, then.'

Two mugs of coffee appeared before them, steam rising from the tops, a gauzy promise of the bitter heat within. Bell and Fogelsong simultaneously looked up at

Jackie LeFevre, the diner's owner, who had sidled over with the mugs.

'Took a chance on what you'd order,' Jackie said, answering the surprise in their eyes. She wasn't known for spontaneous gestures. 'Never see you anymore, Nick. Guess they keep you pretty busy up at the Highway Haven.'

'They do. But nothing says I can't drop by here more often, Jackie. Count on it.'

'I will.' It wouldn't happen, and they both knew that, but she was too polite to say so. She turned to Bell. 'Anything to go with that? Eggs? Toast, maybe?'

'No, thanks. Just the coffee for now. I'm going to try to make it in for lunch, though.'

Also unlikely, but Jackie nodded, anyway. She was a tall, handsome woman with long straight black hair, an angular face, and dark unreadable eyes. People in Acker's Gap still weren't quite sure about Jackie; her unwillingness to generate and react to banter was a definite handicap. Her late mother, Joyce LeFevre, had owned the diner that previously resided on this spot, and that gave Jackie an automatic boost – family was important around here – but she refused to build on that natural advantage. She was too quiet. A few months ago her ex-husband had come looking for her and caused a bit of trouble one night. People didn't mind the trouble – that could happen to anyone – but they did mind the fact that Jackie never talked about it afterward, never turned it into a story to share.

'Nice as it is to see you,' Bell said to Fogelsong, once Jackie had moved on to another booth, 'I'm curious. What brings you to town?'

Nick took his time with his coffee. He blew on it, sipped it, blew some more.

'Heard about Royce Dillard,' he said. 'You've been questioning him about the Hackel murder.'

Bell didn't reply.

'I knew Hackel,' Nick continued, once he realized that she had no comment. 'Not real well, but we'd talked a good number of times. He'd come by the Haven quite a lot. Wanted to brag about the resort and how wonderful it was all going to be. So I thought that maybe – well—'

'What?' Bell said. 'What did you think?'

'That I could help.' He was stung by her tone, rocked back on his heels a bit, and surprised to find himself there. 'Provide some background. Context. You know.'

'No, I *don't* know. I'll tell you what I do know. I know that you're not sheriff anymore. So I can't discuss an ongoing investigation with you, Nick. Surely you're aware of that.' She took a drink of her coffee. It was savagely hot, but she didn't care. She swallowed the liquid and then moved the white mug to one side, so that she could lean forward and give him a hard look. 'Don't do this, okay? Just don't.'

'Do what?'

'Pretend that we can get back to how things were. Because we can't. It's unethical, for one thing – like I said, I can't discuss a current case with a civilian. And for another, I don't want to.' The diner was busy enough now that her words most likely couldn't be heard outside the booth. The sounds of greetings and laughter and chair-scrapes and coughing fits and the continuous fizzy plash of the deep-fat fryer – it always sounded to Bell like applause – curled around them, ensuring privacy. 'You've moved on, Nick. You made your decision and you moved on. Well, so have I.'

For a minute he didn't say anything. She sensed his yearning, the sharpness of his desire. He wanted to be a part of things again, to feel he was contributing. This was his hometown, whether or not he was sheriff of it. When she'd first heard of his decision not to run again – finding out in a phone call from Sammy Burdette still rankled – she had wondered how long it would be before he realized his mistake. Before he tried to get involved. Tried to insinuate himself in the middle of an investigation.

Well, here it was. The first major case since he'd unpinned the badge from his chest and taken off his hat and walked off into the damned sunset. Here it was.

No way, Bell thought. She wouldn't say the words out loud, but she willed him to read her mind once again. He was so annoyingly good at it. *I've grieved for you, Nick Fogelsong, I miss you like hell every single time I walk into the courthouse – but no. No, you're not a part of my world anymore. You're an outsider now.*

He looked away from her. When he looked back, he was smiling, but she recognized the kind of smile it was: An insincere one. An abstract, let's-keep-things-light-and-friendly smile. The one she'd seen him use any number of times as sheriff, when the situation was dangerous and he wanted to keep the tension from ratcheting up. A professional peacemaker's smile.

'So you got yourself a dog,' he said.

He was so much like her: changing the subject to keep emotions off to one side, out of the picture.

'No secrets around here,' she muttered.

'It's your own fault.' Now his smile seemed real, not contrived. 'You bought dog food yesterday at Lymon's. Opal Lymon asked you about it at the checkout, and you told her. Well, Mary Sue does her grocery shopping on Sundays, too, and so by the time she came in, Opal was ready with the news.'

'Guess I ought to start shopping out of town.'

'Oh, come on. It's not such a bad thing, is it? People knowing your business? Used to bother me all the danged time when I was growing up here, but now I choose to think of it as folks taking an interest. Better than being forgotten, right?'

'Not sure about that.'

'It'll come soon enough. Just take a stroll through any graveyard. You'll get a quick sense of what it's like to be forgotten.'

She dragged the mug back until it sat right in front of her again, feeling the heat of its ceramic side when she cupped her hands around it. *God, how I've missed this man*, she thought. She couldn't let on, but the memory had her in its grip, just as surely as she had the mug in hers: the daily back-and-forth with Nick Fogelsong, the talks about all manner of things, from coffee to law enforcement to philosophy. The give-and-take of news and opinion. The mood-lightening wisecracks.

She felt an anguished, impossible wish – it came over her suddenly, as if someone had dimmed the overhead lights for a second or so – that things had never changed, that the world had stopped its infernal turning and paused right where it was, that the clocks had all gone cold at exactly the same moment, that Nick Fogelsong was still sheriff, that this was still Ike's Diner, that Clay

Meckling was meeting her for dinner tonight, that Carla's room back at the house on Shelton Avenue was still Carla's room and not an empty shell with only the diminishing echoes of the complicated, infuriating, beautiful adolescent life that once had been lived there.

She wanted all of those things. She had none of them. Instead, she had a day packed with obligations.

'Could be,' she said. She plucked a napkin from the dispenser at the end of the table. Folded it over once, twice, and then placed the square under her coffee mug, in case any liquid sloshed over the rim. 'That it? I've got to head out soon.'

'So who's taking care of Royce's dog while you're at work?'

'Ben Fawcett. Vickie Fawcett's boy.'

Fogelsong nodded. The Fawcetts lived two doors down from her.

'Ben just turned nine,' Bell added. 'Good reliable kid. Comes home from school for lunch every day. He'll give her a walk and make sure she's okay.'

Fogelsong lifted and tipped his mug, taking a brief drink. Bell knew he wasn't thinking about the dog – or the coffee, either, come to that.

He finished his swallow.

'Well,' he said, 'if you need my help with anything, you know where to find me.'

She did. And what she wanted to say to him was this: *I'm confused as hell about the case. Even with all the open-and-shut forensic evidence, something's not quite right. I wish I could talk it over with you, hear what you think, then you'd hear what I think, and we'd toss it around for hours, going back and forth with our theories. What made Royce Dillard suddenly lose his temper? What could Hackel possibly have said to him to make him grab that shovel? Jesus, Nick, I wish like hell that things were like they used to be between us.*

But what she said out loud was this: 'Yeah.'

15

The bar next to the Holiday Inn Express up on the interstate was called the Comebacker. The name was both an inducement for return visits and a tribute to the owner's son, Ricky Garrison, who had pitched a few innings in the major leagues a decade ago, and survived a wicked comebacker hit by Derek Jeter in the top of the fifth, leaving the game flat on his back with a skull fracture and a severe concussion, after which he settled down to life in Raythune County with his wife and five children, tending bar for his father. When Ricky was in the hospital, Jeter had sent him a short handwritten note, and Ricky had paid to have it laminated and framed: *Hope you feel better soon. And next time, remember to duck!* Now the note was displayed on the wall behind Harold Garrison's bar, surrounded by pictures of Ricky in his red-and-white uniform during his windup, leg cocked, arms high over his head, body kinked as if his joints were hinged to swing in either direction.

Bell saw Diana Hackel right away. The room was dim, but it was almost empty – standard for late afternoon, before the evening crowd arrived – and a human face stood out, even in the murk. She was sitting by herself at one of the small round tables, leaning forward, elbows bracketing a glass of red wine, fingers of both hands linked to make a small flat hammock on which she rested her chin.

Two days had passed since her husband's mutilated body had been found at the edge of a creek. Bell, approaching the table, sensed that this woman was still stunned, still lost in the daze generated the moment she heard the news.

'Mrs Hackel.'

The face rose slowly, without interest.

'May I sit down?' Bell asked.

Diana waved her hand toward the chair across from her, a half-hearted *Whatever* gesture. The drinks she'd already consumed were apparent in the looseness of her movements. Diana hadn't sounded surprised or apprehensive when Bell had called that morning to request a meeting, but neither was she particularly welcoming.

'My sister's with the kids,' Diana said. She blurted it out, as if Bell had demanded an explanation. 'Back in Falls Church. I was going to have her bring them here, but – but it didn't seem right. They need to be home.'

'How are they doing?'

'How do you think they're doing? Eddie had a lot of faults, Mrs Elkins, but he was a good dad. A really good dad. My boy, Shawn – he's twelve – hasn't said a word since we told him what happened. And Lilly won't eat. Not a bite. So why am I still here, right?' Her eyes sought out the wineglass. 'Why don't I go home to be with my kids, right? They need me. Obviously. So why am I here? Well, I'll tell you. Because I want to make sure that Eddie's killer pays for what he did.' She shook her head. 'We've had to delay the funeral. Until you people finish your work.'

Bell wanted to correct her – in this case it was the state police crime lab, not the Raythune County prosecutor's office, that would decide when the body could be released for burial – but it didn't matter. They were all one thing to Diana Hackel now: The Authorities. The *you people* constituting the target of her discontent.

'I have a few questions, if that's okay,' Bell said.

'Suit yourself.'

'I'd like to get a better sense of your husband. You mentioned the other night that he was good at his job. Lots of energy. Really threw himself into his work.'

'He was a salesman. He liked to sell things. That's how we got together, in fact. He was working for a Toyota dealership. I needed a car. I walked out of there with a Corolla – and a dinner date. A few months later, we got married.'

'Did he enjoy working for Mountain Magic?'

Diana thought about her answer before offering it up. 'I honestly don't know. I mean, he said he did. But no matter where he was working, he always insisted he was having a ball. That was part of the shtick.'

'The shtick.'

'Yeah. You know – the optimism, the pep, the snappy patter.' Diana's tired voice suddenly was infused with the phony zeal of a carnival barker, and she waggled her hands on either side of her face: '"It's all good! It's terrific! It's fan-*tas*-tic! It's un-fucking-believable!"' She relapsed into weariness. 'The pressure was on. That much, I do know. Carolyn Runyon's a total bitch. She'd call the house at all hours, demanding to speak to him. She'd have her panties in a bunch over some big emergency – usually just some routine problem – and she'd be yelling and screaming at Eddie to fix it. Finally he just started staying here through the week, so he could be on site. The motel has a special deal for Mountain Magic employees. He came home on weekends – when he could. That happened less and less, though. Things have been heading to a real crisis point. If they don't break ground soon, they'll never be able to stay on schedule. And if they fall too far behind on the construction timetable – chances are, a lot of the backers will pull out.'

The sole waitress who worked the afternoon shift had finally sauntered over. She stopped chewing gum long enough to ask Bell if she wanted anything to drink.

'I'm good,' Bell said. She looked over at the bar. Ricky Garrison was wiping down a section of it with a striped cloth. His shirtsleeves were rolled up way past his elbows, and even at a distance, even in the dimness, Bell could see the muscles in his right arm as he dug at a spot, muscles that once had hurled a tiny white ball at speeds upwards of ninety-nine miles an hour with uncanny accuracy – his fastball was a thing of beauty – and that now were applied to the mopping up of spilled liquor. She wondered how much he remembered about his playing days; the concussion had left him foggy-brained, with a tremor in his hands.

The waitress, young and henna-haired and skinny, eyed Diana's wineglass.

'Sure, Jolene,' Diana said. 'I'll have another.'

Bell waited for the waitress to leave before resuming her questions.

'Did your husband ever talk about Royce Dillard?'

'Maybe. Could be. Eddie talked about a lot of people. I heard a lot of names. I can't say I specifically remember him talking about anybody named Dillard. But I also can't say that he didn't. It's kind of a blur of names, tell you the truth.' She looked at Bell, fleetingly amused. 'He even mentioned you, once or twice.'

'Me.'

'Yeah. Something about a county commissioners' meeting. You spoke, right? And said you weren't exactly tickled pink about the resort?'

'I expressed some reservations. Mainly about the tax abatements and what the return on those was likely to be.'

'Yeah, well, that was Ed's job. Keeping track of who was opposed to the project and then going to talk to them and bringing them around. If he hadn't come to see you yet, believe me – he was on his way.' She laughed. 'You'd have been putty in his hands. Trust me on that. Eddie Hackel could sell sand to a camel.'

The waitress returned. She tried to pick up the old wineglass and replace it with the new one, but Diana swatted at her hand; she wanted both glasses there before her, every drop available. The waitress shrugged and withdrew. Fine by her.

'When was the last time you spoke to your husband?'

'Thursday morning. I got to my hotel in Charleston on Wednesday night, too late to call him. So I tried him the next day. About nine, I think. I don't know. Check his cell.' She frowned. 'You have his cell, right? It wasn't lost or—'

'We have it.' Hackel's phone and other personal items had been recovered from his hotel room by Deputy Mathers. The missed call from his wife was recorded in the log. That was the only recent activity. 'Apparently he didn't take it with him when he left his room on Thursday afternoon.'

Diana frowned again, deeper this time. 'That's weird. Eddie was one of those guys whose cell might as well be surgically attached to his ear. Never went *anywhere* without it.' She finished her glass of wine and immediately switched it out for the other one. The waitress drifted by again. Diana signaled her for another. 'Look, can we wrap this up? I've got to get going pretty soon. Got to call my kids. Try to explain—' She pulled in a deep breath, and then released it again in the form of a heavy sigh. 'Don't get me wrong. I'm glad you've got the bastard who killed him. I'm pleased as fucking Punch. But I just wish I didn't have to stick around here during the trial, you know? This place is like poison to me now. *Poison.*' She drained her glass. The next one had just arrived.

'Had anyone made any threats against your husband? Did he mention being afraid of anyone?'

Diana gave her a sharp look. 'I thought you already caught the guy.'

'We've charged someone, yes. But part of my job, Mrs Hackel, is to make it clear that we've considered all the possibilities. That we didn't overlook anything.'

'Okay.' Diana flicked a fingernail several times against the side of her new glass, as if to welcome it to the grim party. 'Yeah, he got some threats. I mean, sure, most of the people in your little town here think Mountain Magic's a great idea. Nice big shiny resort and all the business it'll bring. Some of them, though, think the opposite. They think it's just a bunch of rich guys looking for another place to party. And that it'll destroy the land. You know what? They're probably right. But good luck trying to stop it. Money wins. Always has, always will. End of story.'

Abruptly, Diana stood up. She was more than a little unsteady on her feet. She swayed for a few seconds, and then sat back down again. 'Whoa,' she said.

Bell decided to take advantage of this unexpected coda. 'The way I understand it, your husband was trying to persuade Royce Dillard to sell his property to Mountain Magic. Dillard said no, but your husband persisted. Really pushed him. Confronted him every time he had the chance. I take it that wouldn't surprise you.'

'Do you know any salesmen, Mrs Elkins? If you did, you wouldn't ask me that. A "No" to a man like Ed Hackel didn't mean "No." It meant, "Try again. Make me a better offer. Tempt me." Anyway, ever since you arrested Dillard, people around here have been telling me about him. About how he's just plain nuts. Some kind of crazy loner, right? Maybe Eddie just ran into him on a bad day. Said the wrong thing. Maybe Dillard was off his meds. Whatever.'

She uttered a small belch, which didn't seem to embarrass her.

'Look,' Diana went on. 'My husband was no saint. He had a quick temper and he – well, let's just say he liked to have a good time, okay? Partying was a big part of his job. Being sociable. Making sure everybody was nice and loose and happy. But he didn't deserve to die the way he did. Like I said, he was a good father. A really good father. He loved his kids. And you know what's so funny? Want to know what's so all-fired, goddamned funny?'

Bell didn't say anything, so Diana continued.

'This is really none of your business, but here goes. I'm pregnant again. Just found out last month.' She waved toward the wineglass. 'I know. I know I shouldn't.

Won't happen again. Swear. I just couldn't face – couldn't think about raising my kids without – Or the fact that this baby won't ever know—'

Diana stopped. She tried to compose herself. 'That's what Eddie and I were going to talk about over dinner. The new baby. How everything had to change. He was talking about maybe coming home for good, maybe finding another job so he could do that. Was it ever going to happen? I don't know. But he was considering it. And that's the part that just tears me up inside.' Her head wobbled. The alcohol seemed to hit her in a wave. 'He never got the chance to change.' She almost slid out of her seat.

Bell put a hand on her arm to help steady her. 'You're not driving anywhere tonight, right?'

Diana shook her head. That didn't go well, and her face grew even paler from the brief slosh of nausea it brought. 'Going back to my room. Calling the kids from there.'

'Speaking of your kids,' Bell said. She made her voice as casual as possible. 'I hope your family will be okay. Financially, I mean. I assume your husband had a good life insurance policy.'

She'd had to ask. Collecting a life insurance settlement was the most glaringly conspicuous of motives for one spouse when the other one showed up dead – but it still happened. It happened all the time.

'Yeah, well, you know what?' Diana said. Her words were slurred, but filled with resentment. 'When I told Eddie I was pregnant, he said he'd get himself a new policy. A much, much bigger one. 'Cause there'd be three kids now, not just two. That's what he promised me. But guess what? He canceled the old policy, all right. He just never signed the papers for the new one. Too busy, I guess. Too busy getting a bunch of hillbillies to sell their land.' She spat her next word. 'Bastard.' All the warmth she'd expressed for her husband had vanished.

'When did you find out he'd never gotten the new policy?' Bell asked. She felt a rising excitement: This could be it. A plausible reason for someone other than Royce Dillard to have wanted Hackel dead.

'Couple of weeks ago,' Diana answered. 'The insurance guy called me to check on it. That's why I needed to sit down with Eddie. To get him to promise to go sign the damned papers.'

Bell would have it checked out, of course, but if Diana's timeline was accurate, then the widow had known she'd derive no financial benefit from her husband's death. No motive there.

'That's a shame,' Bell said evenly.

'Well, thank God I've got my business.'

'So what kind of business is it?'

'Antiques. Still in the planning stages, but I'm going to open my own store back in Falls Church.' She paused, and then quickly added, 'Dealer in Charleston's been advising me. The ins and outs. How to get started. The basics.' She shrugged. Bitterness seemed to stack up behind her next words, like cars at a roadblock. 'Seems pretty goddamned pointless right now. Everything does, come to think of it.'

With that she lurched away, bumping into furniture as she left the bar, muttering *Fuckit* or *Dammit* each time her hip rammed a chair or an empty table. She kept on going, though, because if she wanted to leave, she had no choice. There was only one way out.

16

Lunch? Bell never had lunch. Lunch meant peanut butter crackers and a Diet Coke at her desk. Lunch meant the last broken-off piano key of a Kit Kat bar that she'd squirreled away in her purse a few days ago; if she brushed off the lint and dug out that funny green dot stuck to it, she'd be good to go. Lunch meant a fifth cup of coffee. Or lunch meant nothing. It was a time of day. That was all.

Lunch most certainly did not mean a date. Which was why, when David Gage called her a few minutes after ten on Tuesday morning and proposed just that – having lunch together – Bell was surprised, temporarily flummoxed by the very notion of a midday social event. *Well,* she'd replied. *I usually don't – well, I suppose that would be – well, okay. Sure. Okay.* Change was good, right?

At eleven forty-five Bell heard the voice of her secretary, Lee Ann Frickie, from Lee Ann's desk in the outer office: 'Got company, Belfa.' Typically Lee Ann, who was sixty-seven years old but admitted it to no one but her doctor and the DMV, would use the phone to communicate, but Bell had left her door open all morning to accommodate a varied, in-and-out stream of appointments, and a slightly raised human voice seemed more effective in this case than any technology.

'Oh, and your sister called,' Lee Ann added. 'Nothing urgent. Said to give her a jingle when you get a chance.'

Bell rose. By the time she'd come around from behind her desk, Gage was already standing in her office, his eyes making the circuit: the shoulder-high row of glass-fronted bookcases and their cargo of leather-bound law books; the leaded windows that looked out on the black-and-white streets of downtown Acker's Gap; and finally Bell's desk itself, an unimpressive block of orangey should-have-been-scrap lumber that some bamboozling furniture wholesaler had unloaded on the county decades ago.

'So this is it,' he said. 'Your lair.'

She smiled at the word and, letting him take her hands in his, leaned toward him. Gage kissed her on the cheek. She did a quick internal check of what she felt at the exact moment of his kiss: Anything? Anything at all? Then she silently took herself to task. *If you've got to check,* Bell thought, *it's not there*.

She remembered – against her will, but the memory came of its own volition – what it felt like when she and Clay first kissed, that melting sensation that had rocketed her back to the emotions of adolescence, that perpetual restlessness, the sort that left you almost airborne, your senses on high alert.

She slipped her hands out of Gage's. Wasn't his fault. Wasn't anyone's, really.

'Where are we going?' she said. 'I usually skip lunch, but today I feel like I could eat a bear.'

'Good. I was thinking about a place over in Swanville.

No sautéed bear on the menu, but they've got a great spinach salad, and they—'

'Swanville,' Bell said, interrupting him. She winced. 'I'm really sorry, David. I should've been clearer when you called. I have to be back here by one P.M. for a meeting. There's just not time to drive all the way over to Swanville and back.'

He nodded. 'So – what's close?'

'Well, there's a diner right down the street.'

'I was hoping to take you out of your daily routine. Bet you're pretty familiar with a place that close by.'

'Other than grabbing a cup of coffee – these days, not so much.' Bell lifted her coat from a peg on the wooden row on the wall. 'Gets so busy around here sometimes, it's like being on an island. I forget there's a world out there.'

All the booths were full, so Jackie LeFevre led them to a table. She left two menus at the table's edge and promised to return with glasses of water.

'JP's,' Gage said slowly, considering it. 'Somebody's nickname?'

'It's short for "Joyce's Place." The woman who seated us is the owner. Joyce was her mother.'

Recognition dawned in his eyes. 'Of course,' he said. 'Ike's Diner. I remember reading about what happened to it. Couple of years ago, right? Pretty big news statewide.'

'Still hard to believe.' Bell didn't add anything. She didn't feel like talking about how close she'd been to Ike's that day, and how the town and so many of its people had been transformed by the tragedy. Gage may have already known. Ginnie Prentice had told him a lot about her; her friend had admitted as much.

'So how's the case?' he asked.

'Which one?'

'The one that meant I didn't get any cheesecake the other night.'

Jackie was back. She planted their water glasses on the table and then waited. Her impatient expression took the place of the phrase, *You two know what you want yet?*

The lunch special was fried catfish sandwich, which enticed neither Bell nor Gage. At his request, Bell ordered for both of them: grilled cheese sandwiches and tomato soup. Joyce gathered their menus and was gone.

'Pretty basic, but really tasty,' Bell said.

She looked around warily. Coming here at lunchtime was a calculated risk. The violent death of Edward Hackel was already common knowledge; news of an unusual event tended to flick instantly over a small town in the high darting arc of a fly fisherman's lure, only in this case, it never retracted. In the morning, customers kept mostly to themselves, half-asleep as they hunched sullenly over their coffee and their plates of biscuits with sausage gravy, but by midday, they spread out, primed for conversation, eager to theorize.

Bell started to stay something to Gage, but here was Sally McArdle, the sole paid employee at the Raythune County Public Library, stumping up to their table. Sally was sixty-one, silver-haired, and hefty. Her right leg had been amputated the year before, on account of her diabetes, and she was still getting used to her prosthesis, relying in equal measure on her quad cane and an abundance of grit. She had stowed a takeout container in the small string bag whose strap she'd slung over a thick shoulder. From the odor, Bell could tell that Sally had opted for the catfish sandwich.

'Afternoon, Bell,' Sally said. Her manner was chilly. She had yet to fully forgive Bell for the death a year and a half ago of one of her best friends, Edna Hankins. Technically Bell was not responsible, but she had set in motion the events that had resulted in Edna's violent passing. Sally had recently told Bell – with an accusatory look in her milky gray eyes – that some nights she still woke up out of a sound sleep, heart beating fast, certain that she'd heard the shy rhythmic squeak of Edna's wheeled walker as she traveled up and down the aisles at the library, adding to her next batch of books.

Clearly, this was not a social stop. Sally had something on her mind.

'Real upset about Royce Dillard,' she said. 'Can't rightly believe it.'

'You know him?' Bell said.

'Nobody knows him. But I was close with his great-aunt Bessie, and she raised him. He's a good person. I'd swear to that. After she died, though, he just sort of – well, drifted, I guess I'd say. Moved away from town. Moved away from everything, really. Lives off whatever's left of the insurance settlement he got for losing his folks when he was so young. Can't be much. Not sure how he keeps body and soul together. Not to mention all those dogs of his. Dogs gotta eat.' She gave Bell a stricken look. 'Do you really think he killed that man?'

'We believe the evidence is substantial. A jury will decide if we're right.' Bell reverted to formal language when asked about active cases.

'Just really hard to swallow, is all.' With a start, Sally seemed to realize that Bell wasn't alone in the booth.

'Well, now. Where are my manners? I'm Sally McArdle.' Out came a small plump hand, which Gage let nestle in his own lean, long-fingered one.

'David Gage. I teach environmental sciences up at WVU.'

'You're pretty far from home.'

'I am. I'm on sabbatical this semester. I have an apartment over in Blythesburg. Doing some research for a book on climate change. In fact, I recognize your name, Mrs McArdle, and I've been meaning to come by and see you at the library. I've heard that your county historical records are very thorough.'

'What kind of history?' Sally was intrigued, but not quite ready to trust Gage. Like a lot of librarians, Sally acted as if the contents of the library were her personal property, and only the worthy – as deemed by her – would be allowed access.

'Coal mines,' Gage said. 'The older ones. I'm testing your air and water quality. Thought I'd consult any old county maps you might have. Make sure I've located them all.'

'Word of advice, Professor.' Sally lowered her voice, even though, by this time, the diner was much too crowded and noisy for her to be overheard, as the lunchtime rush had commenced. 'Next time somebody around here asks what you're studying, just say, "Oh, this and that." Don't say anything about climate change or global warming. Folks're pretty red about that. Can't blame them. Those phrases have usually been the prelude to shutting down one of the few coal mines still up and running. Like we say around here – there's only one thing worse than having a job in a coal mine. And that's *not* having a job in a coal mine.'

Gage nodded slowly. 'I know it's a sensitive topic.'

'Sensitive topic.' Repeating his words back to him, Sally seemed to taste them and find them flavorless. 'Okay. We'll call it that, if that's your preference. Me? I'd call it a life-and-death topic. It's not a matter of tender feelings. These are people's futures we're talking about. And their children's futures.' She looked again at Bell. 'You'll set him straight, I hope.'

As Sally turned to leave, Gage said, 'So I can come by and take a look at your archives?'

She readjusted the strap on her shoulder. 'Hours are posted on the door.' She nodded at Bell and headed back to work, thumping her cane with authority against the painted concrete floor.

'Wow,' Gage said, watching her go. 'You'd think a librarian might be a little more enlightened than that, right?'

Bell eyed him. 'What makes you say she's not "enlightened"?' She made air quotes around the word.

'Well, because – well, her attitude.'

'She didn't say that climate change wasn't happening. She said that around here, it's more than just an interesting subject for people to debate over scones and lattes, after they've finished their *New York Times*. We're not in some drawing room. Or some college classroom, come to that. We're in a place where those abstract arguments stop being abstract. And start being about flesh and blood.'

'Here we go.' He said it the way a kid would, right before the roller coaster started up. Yet his sentence didn't infuriate her nearly as much as did the twinkle in his eye.

'Don't make fun,' she snapped at him. 'Disagree with

me, get mad at me, tell me to go screw myself – but do *not* make fun of me. Or this place. Or these people.'

'Sorry.' The twinkle disappeared. 'Look. I teach at a university, and yes, I've got a PhD. But you know what? I grew up in McDowell County,' Gage declared. 'My father wasn't a coal miner – he sold mining equipment – but my grandfather was, and his father before him. That's how I got interested in environmental science. I saw what life in McDowell County was doing to the people who couldn't get out of there, doing to their lungs and to the developing brains of their kids. I saw what it was doing to the air and the water. Coal's a killer. It's just as bad as any criminal you capture and put on trial. It may make for cheap electricity, but burning it destroys the earth. And mining it destroys the lives of the miners. But I get your point – what's the alternative? Do we just tell an entire generation of West Virginians that they have to starve while we research alternative energy sources? Do we tell them just to shut up and suffer while we theorize and pontificate?'

Gage hadn't noticed, so focused was he on his own words, but the small diner had grown quiet during his address. When he stopped talking, there was a spooky pause – the only sound was the accidental *clink* of a fork dropped on a plate – and then all at once the conversations resumed, as if nothing had happened.

'Guess I'll be lucky,' he murmured, 'to make it out of here alive.'

'You'll be safe as long as you stick close to me.' Bell enjoyed the chance to tease him. 'After that – no promises.'

Truth was, she realized she'd misjudged him, making a superficial analysis based on expectation and prejudice.

She'd assumed she could figure him out, relying on very little evidence. It was a mistake she almost never made in her professional life – so why did she make it so frequently in her personal one?

'Tell you what,' she said. 'I've got this major case on my hands right now, but first chance I get, I'm going to take you out to a mine up off Route 6. Just a couple of men going down there, every now and again, to bring out what's left. It's dirty and ugly and dangerous – and you'll be coughing up a black gob for a week or so after. Guaranteed.'

'Sounds romantic.'

'It is.'

'I was being sarcastic.'

'I got that. But you know what? There's more to a coal mine than just the negatives. There's also something magical down there.'

'Magical.' He couldn't keep the note of amusement out of his voice.

'Yes. Magical.' She peered closely at him. 'You've never been down there, have you?'

'No.' Emphatically. 'And that was the plan. My entire life has been devoted to doing whatever the hell I had to do so that I *never* stepped foot in a coal mine. Seemed pretty impossible at first, coming from McDowell County.'

'But you managed it.'

'I did.'

Bell picked up a little pink packet of sugar substitute from the pile in the plastic bowl at the end of the table. At times she liked to have something in her hands while she talked. She pushed on one corner of the packet, feeling the granules move around under her thumbs.

'When I was in high school,' she said, 'sometimes I'd go down in the mine on Saturdays with Roy Stratton. I lived with him and his wife, Beth Ann, for a little while. They were my foster parents.' She pushed the granules back toward the opposite corner of the packet. 'Roy was a foreman for Milltown Limited. Always had some unfinished business down there, some odds and ends, and sometimes he'd take me with him. He'd find me the smallest hard hat he could scrounge and down we'd go. Down the man-hoist, down into the mine. He wanted me to see it. See the beauty. It's dark, yes, but when you turn around and the light hits the walls, there's the glint of mica. It's like stars. It's almost like you're looking at the night sky. You know you're way, way under the ground, but somehow it's like you're up – not down. You're at the center of the universe. And the smell – it's not a closed-up smell. It's sort of sweet. The sound – well, I can't describe it. Roy used to say that if you know how to listen, the coal sings to you.

'Point is,' she said, hastily winding up her reminiscence, a little embarrassed at having gone off that way, 'it's not all bad. It's mostly bad – but not all.' She dropped the pink packet and dusted off her hands, even though the packet was still closed. There was nothing on her hands.

Gage was quiet for a moment. When he did start to speak, he ended up holding back because Jackie had just arrived at the table, delivering two bowls of soup. Then she backed away, off to check on their sandwiches.

Gage took a tentative sip. The heat from the soup fogged up his glasses. 'Hey, this is really good.'

'Jackie uses a lot of her mother's old recipes. You ought to try the pie.'

She smiled at him, but the answering look on his face told her that he didn't want to talk about soup anymore. Or pie. Or coal mines, either. He put down his spoon.

'Look, Bell,' Gage said. 'I like you. I like you a lot. Everything Ginnie Prentice said about you was right – you're smart. And sexy.' She felt herself blushing. He kept on talking. 'You're a hell of a challenge, and I like that. But I'm getting the distinct impression that you're not really into dating right now. Are you?'

Do we have to do this here? Bell wanted to say, but in a way, she admired his directness, his efficiency: If there was no future, why waste his time, and hers?

'I don't know.' Which was true.

'You went out with me Saturday night,' he said, 'because of Ginnie. I'm aware of that. She'd been talking for months about this friend of hers down in Raythune County, this amazing woman. So I kept after her until she gave me your number and suggested I call you.' He tilted his head, as if he wanted to see her from another angle. 'But today – today was all my idea. I took a chance. And you know what? I'm getting the sense that maybe it's not something you really want.' He looked away. 'Somebody else in the picture?'

'No. Not really.'

'Not really,' he repeated, returning his gaze to her face, a new buoyancy in his voice. 'So I've still got a shot?'

Two platters, each adorned with a grilled cheese sandwich cut on the diagonal and surrounded by a ring of French fries stacked up like greasy kindling, arrived on the table. Jackie, hands on her hips, simmered impatiently until Bell said, 'Nothing else for now. Thanks.' Jackie tucked the check under a water glass.

It was just the two of them again. Gage waited for her to say something. Bell could feel the urgency of his inquiry, not so much the words of it but the deeper meaning – was she available for a relationship, or not? – almost as if it were being communicated to her in a medium other than language. She liked David Gage. She really did. He was – and here she went for the same descriptors he had used about her, because they really did fit – smart and sexy. If she didn't feel, even at this early stage, anything close to the same degree of passion that she'd instantly felt for Clay Meckling – well, so what? Passion came and went. Didn't it? Maybe, after a few years, she wouldn't have responded to Clay that way, either; maybe the heat she felt each time Clay touched her – hell, she felt it each time he walked in a room – eventually would diminish. And finally disappear.

Maybe. She would never know. He was gone, and she'd done nothing to stop him from going. How could she? Raythune County was a place people left, not a place people stayed. She couldn't blame him for going. He'd had a small taste of what lay on the other side of those mountains, and it was the kind of taste that only stoked, rather than satisfied, a hunger.

And besides, Bell herself went through the same private catechism every few months or so: *Why am I here?* Leading to the reply: *Because I'm doing some good. Because I'm not finished. One day I might be, but I'm not. Yet.*

Only seconds had passed. She forced her mind back to David Gage, who was still looking at her across the table, his expression serious but not impatient, because he wasn't pressuring her, not at all, but only indulging in a thoroughly justifiable curiosity: Could she see herself caring about him, or not?

God, there were so many things he didn't know about her. Things that would surely have sent him running out into the streets of Acker's Gap, then hightailing it back to Blythesburg and then Morgantown, without a backward glance. *You don't want any part of this pain,* is the thing she wanted to say to him, the phrase that tolled in her head. She wanted to warn him. Another man, after a brief relationship with her, an affair that left him mildly but constantly frustrated at her elusiveness, had noted that her heart ought to be cordoned off with yellow police tape, the kind with the words CRIME SCENE DO NOT CROSS repeated over and over again. It was only a joke, he said.

Sure it was.

She didn't want to hurt David, and that was the one thing she seemed very good at doing: hurting people. Or misleading them. Or disappointing them. She was glad, all at once, that JP's was crowded, because the presence of others seemed to cushion this crucial moment, to keep it from becoming sharp and painful.

Gage's face relaxed into a smile. Apparently he didn't mind that she had not yet answered him directly. Another point in his favor. As was the fact that he didn't pester her about the murder case. He'd readily picked up on her signals that it wasn't a preferred topic. He'd asked about it – displaying interest in her work – and then let it go.

'So,' Gage said, 'I propose that we spend some time together, now and again. Just hang out. Coal mines, diners – doesn't matter. We'll take it slow. See how it feels. If that sounds okay.'

She nodded, because it did sound okay, and in fact it sounded fine. He was about to say something else when all at once there was a skirmish on the other side of the room that distracted them: a shriek, then laughter and scuffling and a few hoots. A woman, gesturing to make a point, had knocked over a full glass of water, sending the liquid clear across the wide table. The three other occupants of the booth had jumped up as if it were a fire drill. Two old women stood and dabbed with napkins at the laps of their skirts, while a man – his name was Grover Fink and he was seventy-seven years old – frowned at the front of his trousers, knowing what people out on the street would think when they observed the damp spot, knowing how they'd point and giggle behind his back. This town being the way it was, the erroneous news that Grover Fink had soiled himself would, by midafternoon, have spread in all directions, just like the contents of that water glass.

17

Twenty minutes ago she'd been sitting in JP's. Now Bell was sitting behind the desk in her office. At times it astonished her, the speed with which she was required to go from human being to prosecutor, from flawed woman to authority figure whose decisions could cost people their freedom, their future. If she thought about it too often, it got in her head and refused to vacate the premises. It was an impossible job. You did your best, which was all you could do – and you tried not to obsess over the times you'd been too lenient, and not prosecuted someone who then had gone out and committed another crime, or too harsh, and ended up crushing the spirit of someone for whom a lesser punishment might have left a sliver of light under the closed door.

'Appreciate your taking the time for this today, Mrs Elkins,' Serena Crumpler said.

Serena sat in one of the two straight-backed wooden chairs across from Bell's desk. In the other chair was Royce Dillard, looking even paler and pastier than he'd looked when Bell saw him the day before. His right hand was handcuffed to the arm of the chair, and shackles were wound around his ankles in a jangling figure eight. The restraints were a formality, and probably not necessary, but Bell abided by the regulation; holding this conference in her office and not in one of the interrogation rooms was a privilege, and every privilege had its price.

Bell acknowledged Serena's comment with a nod. Her pen was poised above a yellow legal pad upon which she had outlined her plans for the meeting. The outline took up less than half the page. This was business; no matter what assessment she might have made about Royce Dillard's character, this conference was a matter of facts and protocol. Not opinion.

Bell addressed Dillard. 'So you've got yourself a lawyer now.'

'No, I don't,' he muttered, aiming his reply at the front of her desk.

Serena glared at him. 'Yes, you do,' she snapped. Obviously frustrated, she leaned forward and continued to look hard at the side of his face.

'Nope,' he said.

Bell tapped the tip of the pen on the legal pad. 'Make up your mind, Mr Dillard. Either you have legal representation or you don't. If you decide that you want to represent yourself, I can't promise the judge will go along with it. But even if the judge does approve, it's a bad idea.'

'Hold on, Bell. Just hold on,' Serena said. She scooted herself around in her chair, trying to make it harder for him to avoid looking at her. 'Come on, Royce. We talked about this. Hours and hours. Back in your cell, remember? And you agreed.'

'Changed my mind. Didn't do nothing, so I don't need no lawyer.' His eyes explored the floor.

'Yes, you do.' Serena's voice was earnest and determined. She would have made a lousy saleswoman, Bell thought; she was entirely too sincere and transparent. Serena was only in her late twenties, but her extreme thinness made her look even younger. Her straight black hair seemed to polish her knobby shoulders each time she turned her head; watching her nervous movements, you could almost believe that the constant shifting of that hair was the reason her shoulders were so bony – it had worn away the flesh. Sometimes she tied her hair back in a ponytail, but not today. She was wearing an olive green wool suit that made Bell itch just looking at it.

'Serena,' Bell said, 'I think we'd better—'

'Wait. Please.' Serena held up a thin hand, fingers spread, in Bell's direction. To Dillard, she said, 'Do you like to walk in the woods, Royce?'

He snorted. ''Course I do.'

'Okay, then. If you ever want to see the woods again – if you ever want to feel the sun on your face in any way except through a window with bars on it – then by God, you need to stop this foolishness right now and *listen* to me.' She took a deep breath. 'You're facing a charge of first-degree murder for the death of Edward Hackel.' At the mention of Hackel's name, Dillard scrunched up his face as if he'd suddenly smelled sour milk. Serena ignored him and went on. 'Now, Mrs Elkins and I are here today to discuss that charge. I think it's the wrong one. I think Mr Hackel probably showed up at your property last Thursday and he badgered you, just as he'd been badgering you for some time now, because he wanted your land. He was desperate for it. And I think you felt your life was in danger – and that he might harm your dogs – and so you lost control of yourself. When he turned around to go, you struck him repeatedly with a shovel. You saw what you'd done and you panicked. You hauled the body down to the creek in your wagon.

'I think the charge ought to be reduced,' Serena continued. At this point, her speech was as much for Bell's benefit as it was for Dillard's. Bell understood that, and made notes. 'I think the proper charge would reflect the fact that you were frightened and you needed to protect your dogs. You acted in self-defense. Now, if we show the prosecutor that we're willing to cooperate and tell her exactly what happened out at your cabin that day and why, she might decide to reduce the charge against you. We may not even have to go to trial. She and the judge could work out an appropriate punish-ment – maybe twenty years, with a chance of parole at that point – but however long they decide it should be, it won't be for the rest of your life. You'll go to prison, Royce, but not forever. You will walk in the woods again. See the change of the seasons.

'But I can't do any of that unless you authorize me, here and now, to represent you. With no going back on it. None of that nonsense.' She reached out and put a hand on Dillard's forearm. Startled, he shifted it out of her grip. 'People have gone to an awful lot of trouble on your behalf, Royce,' she declared. 'You owe it to those people – the ones who've taken in your dogs – to do what's right for yourself. We've found good, safe homes for Utley and Ned and Goldie and Connie and Elvis and Bruno.' Bell was impressed; Serena had memorized the names of his dogs.

'PeeWee,' Dillard murmured.

'What?' Serena said.

'You forgot PeeWee.' A grin and a nod. 'His feelings'd be hurt if he knew. Has a hard enough time already, that one – got his ear chopped off a few years back. Spoiled his good looks.'

'Fine. Okay. PeeWee, too, then.' Serena's face lost none of its hardness. 'This isn't a joke, Royce. And it's not going to end well for you – unless you give me your consent to be your lawyer.'

He looked at his hands, one of which had a tight metal band encircling the wrist, linking him to the arm of the chair. 'Okay,' he said.

'Okay, what?' Serena said, nailing it down.

'Okay, you're my lawyer. Can't pay you nothing, though.'

Serena's face relaxed. 'A fact that doesn't distinguish you from the majority of my clients.' She turned to Bell. 'We're ready.'

Bell nodded. She made more notes on her legal pad.

'Can we discuss a plea deal now?' Serena asked.

Bell rubbed her index finger along the side of the pen. 'I assume that means Mr Dillard is ready to admit he was responsible for the death of Edward Hackel.'

'I believe,' Serena said, 'that we're heading that way. Royce? What do you think? Maybe it's time to face some facts here. The evidence against you is pretty overwhelming. They found the shovel in your barn – the one that was used to kill Hackel. They found the trail through the woods on your property, where you'd dragged him down to the creek in your wagon. And you had a motive – he was pushing you to sell your land. Land you wanted to hold on to. He threatened you. So you defended yourself. Is that correct?'

Dillard moved his jaw around. Shuffled his feet, even though he couldn't move them more than half an inch or so, forward or back, on account of the shackles.

'This is the only way I'll ever see daylight again, right?' he finally said. 'No other way?'

Serena's expression was solemn. 'We could take a chance and go to trial, but frankly, Royce, I wouldn't be doing my job if I advised you to take that route. I believe the evidence is just too strong. I think we'd lose. And you'd be looking at a life sentence.'

'A life sentence,' he said, repeating the phrase with a kind of wonderment in his voice. 'That's about the size of it, huh?'

Serena nodded.

'Okay,' he said. He was looking out the window now, as if he'd heard a noise or seen a flash of something he needed to check out. Anything to keep from having to look at the two other human beings in this room. 'Okay, I done it. I killed the rat bastard, all right. Happened just the way you guessed it did – I hit him and then I took the body down to Old Man's Creek.'

He'd said his piece in an offhand way that surprised Bell. In her career as prosecutor she had dealt with only one or two truly evil people, people who had committed unthinkably savage acts and then gone home to eat a peanut butter sandwich or finish wrapping a kid's birthday present. People who could admit to horrific crimes with nonchalance, and with no remorse. Sociopaths, the formal term would be.

Royce Dillard was not that kind of person. She'd bet her house on it. And yet he had just casually confessed to a lethal assault on another human being. Moreover, his motivation for so doing still seemed to Bell to be mysteriously inadequate.

Something was wrong here. And while a guilty plea and a sentencing deal might save the county a good deal of money, and the prosecutor's office a good deal of time and trouble, Bell was still unsettled.

She argued with herself, remembering a bit of prosecutorial wisdom that her favorite law school professor, Annabel Jethcoat, had imparted: *You don't have to be certain that an accused person is guilty. You just have to be certain that you can prove he is.* Anything else – determining true innocence or absolute guilt – is way above your pay grade, Professor Jethcoat would add. *We leave that up to God. And He doesn't have to worry about being reversed on appeal.*

Fine. So maybe she should ignore her doubts, her questions – right? But a judge would have to approve any plea deal made by the prosecutor's office. And if Bell herself couldn't fathom why a man like Royce Dillard had suddenly snapped and committed murder – and had no plausible story to explain it – then a judge might very well notice the same thing, and wonder if Dillard's confession meant he was covering for someone else. The judge could reject any deal to which Bell agreed.

'Mr Dillard,' Bell said. 'I need to know why.'

'Why what?'

'You have no history of violence. There's no record of your having an uncontrollable temper. No suggestion of drug or alcohol abuse. You've never been in serious trouble before. So why, out of the blue, did you get so angry at Edward Hackel that you ended up killing him? Even if he insulted you or threatened you – I'm finding it hard to believe that you would have lost your head so completely that you'd attack him that way. What was it, Mr Dillard? What did Hackel say to you?'

'Said he wanted to buy my land. I didn't want to sell.'

'What else?'

'Nothing else.'

'No other threats? Nothing he was going to do if you didn't sell? He had a lot of powerful friends. And a lot of them have important positions. There's big money behind that resort – and you've been holding it hostage. Millions of dollars are at stake. What did he threaten you with, Mr Dillard? A lawsuit? An IRS audit? A bogus lien on the rest of your property?' Even as she listed the possibilities, Bell knew they weren't right. Royce Dillard wouldn't have cared about any of those things. 'Maybe,' she added, 'he threatened your dogs. Was that it?'

Dillard's face congealed into a sneer, a sneer he showed to his own hands. 'You think that me and my dogs were afraid of Ed Hackel? Why, even the little ones made him nervous. They'd give him one bark and he'd be shivering and shaking. Ready to run all the way back to town. Probably peed his pants. The man was a first-class, ring-tailed fraidycat.'

So that wasn't it. But how had Hackel gotten under his skin? What leverage did he have?

'I also need to know,' Bell said, 'how the victim got out to your property. He didn't take his own car. Did someone drive him? Who dropped him off?'

Dillard moved his jaw. He closed his mouth, turning it into a tight slit.

'Mrs Elkins,' Serena said, 'maybe we can move things along by—'

'No.' Bell set down her pen. She folded her hands

together and placed them on top of the legal pad. 'Not until I'm satisfied that Mr Dillard here is telling the truth. And the only way I can be sure of that is if he explains to my satisfaction how Hackel got there – and why he killed him.'

'He confessed to the crime, for God's sake,' Serena said. 'The investigation's over. You've got your killer.'

'Yes, but until I get these questions answered – no deal.'

Dillard shook his right hand, so that the handcuff would rattle and clank. He wanted to get their attention.

'Look,' he said, 'if that's not going to work – if saying I done it won't get me home to my woods no sooner – then I take it back. I didn't kill him.'

Serena rolled her eyes and sagged back in her chair. 'Oh, great. Terrific. That's just peachy keen.' She bolted forward again, her irritation with Dillard giving her gestures a herky-jerky abruptness. 'Listen to me, Royce. This isn't some goddamned game, okay? You're wasting everybody's time.'

He shrugged. 'Told you from the start I didn't do it. You're the one who got me to say I did.'

Bell shared Serena's irritation with Dillard, but didn't have the luxury of being able to let it show. She reached for her phone. 'Lee Ann,' she said into the receiver, 'please tell Deputy Mathers that I'm ready for the prisoner to be returned to his cell.' She hung up and looked across the desk at Serena. 'So he's pleading not guilty. Looks like we're going to trial.'

Royce rattled his handcuff again. 'Got a question for you,' he said to Bell. He tilted up his head. An inch more and he'd actually be looking at her. But he stopped moving it before that could happen.

'Yes?' She wondered if he was finally ready to reveal some curiosity about how the proceedings against him would go.

'Just wondering,' Dillard said, 'how Goldie's getting along. Wouldn't like the other dogs to hear it, but she's my favorite. Nice girl, but she can be right skittish in unfamiliar circumstances.'

The prosecutor's office was quiet now. Didn't happen often, but the rarity of it had taught Bell to savor it, which was always the lesson taught by rare things. Late afternoons sometimes delivered up this gift of a few minutes of privacy and calm, when no one was clamoring for anything, when the day's court sessions stood at recess and the phones forgot how to ring. Soon enough, they would remember.

She reached into a desk drawer. At her request Rhonda Lovejoy had done a LexisNexis search for articles on Royce Dillard and his parents, Mike and Ellie Dillard. On the Buffalo Creek tragedy. The assistant prosecutor had printed out the bounty and put the pages in a file folder. She could have e-mailed it, but she knew that when it came to history, Bell preferred to hold paper in her hand, pages she could touch and sift and sort.

The older articles – the ones published before the Internet made such searches a matter of a few clicks – existed only as hard copies in archives. Rhonda had used a copying machine to transfer the actual newspaper pages onto letter-sized sheets. They all told the same basic story: According to eyewitness accounts, Mike Dillard had given up his own life to save that of his toddler son, Royce. On one of the worst days in West Virginia history, the account of a man's spontaneous act of heroism was a bright spot, a gesture that reminded the stunned, grief-bludgeoned survivors that human beings were capable of more than just greed. About greed, they knew plenty; it was greed on the part of the coal company that had caused the disaster in the first place.

Bell read the article on the top of the stack. It had appeared in the *Bluefield Daily Telegraph* and was dated March 3, 1972:

FATHER DIED TO SAVE SON, 2

(AP) Middle Fork Hollow, W.Va. – Among the dozens of people killed in last month's flooding in the Buffalo Creek Valley were Mike and Ellie Dillard, parents of Royce Dillard, 2. Eyewitness accounts say that Mike Dillard was responsible for his son's survival. The tragedy took more than one hundred lives and left thousands of people bereft and homeless.

'I seen it with my own eyes,' said Vera Tolbert, 22, of Lundale. 'That water was just pounding right along. It wouldn't quit coming. I was up on the ridge. The Dillard house was getting pushed by a lot of other houses that had busted loose, and it started to spin away in the flood. I seen Ellie Dillard and her little boy coming out the window. Just squirting out, it looked like, the both of them, like toothpaste from a tube. Real quick after that, Ellie lost her grip and she went under. She never come up again. Then Mike come along out of the house and he grabbed that boy.

'The people on the ridge – it was me and my cousins and my uncle and some folks I didn't know

– they started yelling at Mike: "Throw him up here! Here! We'll catch him!" It was plain to see that Mike couldn't hang on much longer, not with trying to keep his little boy's head above the water. So he tossed that boy up toward the ridge. Right as he was doing that, a big tree trunk went flying by, and I swear that if he hadn't been heaving that boy up right then, if he'd let go of the boy, Mike could've grabbed that tree trunk and saved himself. But he didn't. Up on the ridge, my uncle was holding out his arms and he caught little Royce. Caught him in his two hands. Caught him like you'd catch a sack of potatoes thrown your way. Once we saw the boy was safe and we looked back down at the water, Mike was gone. It was so quick.'

The child, Royce Enoch Dillard, is now living with a relative in Raythune County. Vera Tolbert and her family said they wish the very best for the boy, and hope that when he is old enough, he will understand his father's sacrifice.

'His daddy gave up his life for his child,' Tolbert said. 'You cannot love somebody more than that – to give up your life for them. I hope that little boy knows about that. I personally would be glad to tell him when the time comes, because I was there and I saw it all.'

Accompanying the story was a grainy, wavy black-and-white photo – all the photos in the early stories were black-and-white, because this was long before smaller newspapers began to use color photography – of Royce Dillard. The photo was taken when he was twenty-two months old, the caption said, a month or so before the flood. It was a family photo, supplied by a relative, and it was amateurish, out of focus: the little boy sits on the floor, wearing only a diaper, chubby legs stretched out in front of him, playing with what looks to be a toy truck, big grin on his round face. At the edge of the frame, two hands are reaching down. Bell assumed those were the hands of Ellie Dillard, eager to pick up her baby boy and take him off to supper, or maybe just to hold him close, kissing his bare belly and making him giggle.

Bell read several more newspaper articles about the Dillard family and that terrible day at Buffalo Creek. She envisioned Royce, once he was old enough, reading the same articles, and then being asked, over and over again, about what had happened. As he grew up, the interview requests had tapered off; people moved on, and there was always another tragedy in the headlines. But that would not matter. Royce still had the memories, whether or not anyone ever asked him about them. This was his story.

She slid the sheets back into the folder. She closed it.

All at once she wished like hell that she could pick up the phone and call Nick Fogelsong, to run some ideas past him. But she couldn't do that. She couldn't talk with Pam Harrison, either, for a different reason: She hadn't worked with her long enough yet to think out loud in front of her.

Bell was on her own.

Fine, she thought. Pride flickered, caught hold, flared. *Fine.*

She had a hunch that was sketchy, half-formed, made from materials scraped off the surface of the known facts, but it wouldn't leave her be. Whatever had happened on the day of Hackel's death, the origins of that violence lay elsewhere – and the destinies of Edward Hackel and Royce Dillard had been linked from long ago, in ways unbeknownst to either.

An hour later, Bell left the courthouse. She had almost reached her Explorer when she heard a loud, annoyed-sounding voice: 'Mrs Elkins!'

Diana Hackel, small face bunched in umbrage, was marching across Main Street. A red beret held her hair in check. A few tendrils had worked their way loose and bounced against her neck. The sun had begun its slow descent behind the mountains and the air was cold; Diana's cheeks looked raw and tender.

'Can I help you?' Bell said.

'Yeah. Yeah, you can. You can promise me right this minute that you're not going to make some sort of plea deal with that scumbag.' She was slightly out of breath from having moved so quickly to confront her. Bell had the distinct impression that Diana had been waiting to intercept her, so that she could have her say.

'Pardon me?'

'Dillard. I heard you're making a deal with him.' She had recovered her breath but her voice still shook with anger. 'It's not fair, okay? My husband's dead. My kids don't have a father – and you're making a deal. With that *killer*.'

A courthouse leaked worse than a slotted spoon. Someone had probably seen Dillard being led from the jail to her office, and told someone else, who told someone else, and word got back to Diana Hackel. Or the gossip might have trickled out through Serena's office.

'Mrs Hackel,' Bell said. She tried to sound more

patient than she felt. 'There's no deal. Royce Dillard is pleading not guilty. As of now, we're going to trial.'

'Oh.' She stepped back, slightly chagrined. 'Oh – well, then. Okay. Good. That's good. Fine. Have a nice evening.'

Bell opened the Explorer door. She had nothing more to say. She didn't want to prolong this encounter. Diana was under stress; she had lost her husband, and Bell would cut her slack on account of it.

But Bell also believed that she'd devoted enough – more than enough – of her day to courts and plea deals and grieving widows. Right now, she wanted to go home. Home to be with Goldie.

Her last sight of Diana came in her rearview mirror. The woman was standing on the sidewalk with a cell pressed to her ear, talking with animated fervor.

18

The house was intact. The hardwood floor bore a few scratch marks, thanks to Goldie's toenails, and the couch cushions sagged with a Goldie-sized imprint, but that was the only significant proof that a dog was now in residence – except for the animal herself, of course, who must've jumped up when she heard Bell's key in the door and now stood alertly in the front hall, tail going furiously, muzzle raised expectantly.

Bell moved past her into the living room, which is when she saw the couch and its mildly pummeled cushions. She'd received a text from Ben Fawcett shortly after the conclusion of her meeting with Serena and Royce Dillard: *she 8 lunch I let her out I cleaned up poop n backyard*

Good to know.

She set down her briefcase. Goldie whined softly. Clearly, the dog wanted something. And the something, Bell suspected with dawning dread, was a walk.

'Can I change my clothes first?' Bell said. Then she realized that she was not only talking to a dog, but also expecting an answer. 'I'll be right back,' she said. 'Stay here.'

She began to climb the stairs. After three steps, she

realized Goldie was following her. 'No,' Bell said, turning to confront the dog. 'No. Go back.'

Goldie's tail swished.

'I mean it,' Bell said. 'Really.' She turned around and resumed her climb. From behind her, she heard the soft padding of a dog's paws.

'Fine,' Bell muttered. 'You can come up while I change. But no cracks about the sweat pants I'm going to put on, okay? I've had them for years and they're kind of droopy and saggy.'

Now they stood once again at the front door. Goldie had been politely silent about the sweat pants, the ones Bell always yanked on after a long day, finishing the ensemble with a battered red T-shirt whose front featured a woodcut of a coal miner crawling along on all fours above the logo *I've Got Friends in Low Places,* plus a gray hoodie with a fleece lining, and tennis shoes. Rhonda Lovejoy had left her a leash. But Bell wasn't certain how the process worked. She wondered if there was a set of magic words she should utter to ensure Goldie's cooperation, such as, 'Let's go!' or 'Come on!' Would the dog walk calmly along beside her, or might Goldie bolt and flee? Presumably Goldie missed her home. Surely she'd make a break for it. *Sure as hell know I would,* Bell thought.

She stuffed a few plastic bags in the pocket of her hoodie, to pick up after Goldie when the necessity arose, and she and the dog headed outside and down the front porch steps. The air was even colder, the sky stained an intense violet; by now the sun had completely disappeared behind the mountains, giving up on this world for another day. Reaching the sidewalk, Bell stopped. Goldie stopped, too, and sat down. She seemed accustomed to a leash, ready to go in any direction Bell led. Which was both good and bad – good because it would make the walk easier, bad because it put all the responsibility on Bell to pick a destination. She flipped an imaginary coin and went left. Goldie followed.

The rest of the houses on Shelton Avenue were a lot like Bell's: venerable, well-worn, three-story stone structures set back from the street, sporting long front porches and a flourish of dormers, turrets, finials, and cupolas, jumbled together in a showy architectural mishmash. Most had been built in the late nineteenth century, when the streets were dirt and the choice of transport either a horse or your own two feet.

'Hey, Bell. Got yourself a pet, didya?'

She was passing Myrtle Bainbridge's house, a large, gray, decaying one with half of its shutters missing, bordered by a falling-down fence and topped off by a disintegrating roof. She hadn't noticed Myrtle up there on her porch, fussing around her flowerpots, getting ready for spring planting. Bell waved. She would've preferred to keep on walking, but living in a neighborhood brought certain obligations.

'Hi, Myrtle. Goldie's just visiting.' At the sound of her name, Goldie's tail engaged in a few energetic loop-de-loops.

'Well, that dog looks pretty happy to me. Might be a longer visit than you imagine.' Myrtle emerged from the shadows of her front porch and stood at the lip of it. Her short white hair rose from her scalp in a delicate little frizz, like the drawings of static electricity in science textbooks. She was vastly, unfathomably obese; her body comprised an almost perfect circle, as wide as it was tall, and her facial features joggled in a rubbery sea of fat. She wore an immense canvas jacket and carried a trowel in one hand and an empty clay pot in the other. 'Can't wait for this weather to turn. Got big plans for my garden this year. I mean big.'

'Myrtle, you class up the neighborhood, no question.' Bell waved again and moved forward. A slight bit of pressure on the leash was all that Goldie required; the dog matched Bell step for step. *Sure wish Carla had been this easy to control*, Bell thought ruefully. *Or my ex-husband.*

She was enjoying herself. That surprised her. She knew what running did for her, even though she rarely got around to it anymore – but walking? Bell had been a runner in high school and college, and relished her time on the track team; she knew the enveloping pleasure of a good long run, the way the endorphins crashed into your system and temporarily chased away fears, anxieties, everything but a sense of the body's brisk motion. Walking, though, brought a subtler satisfaction. She walked every day, of course; her life was spent in motion. But for Bell walking, like driving, typically meant getting from one place to another as fast as she possibly could. Having a destination in mind. A goal. And a timetable, a deadline. This kind of walking – loose, easy, with a dog trotting along beside her – was new, and, to her surprise, nice. It was also conducive to thinking.

What the hell did Edward Hackel do to push Royce Dillard's buttons? With what did he threaten Dillard? How could he possibly have goaded him into a lethal attack? A shadow moved in the back of Bell's mind, like something she had glimpsed a while ago but now could not quite recall, could not put her finger on. A tiny, crucial piece of information floated just an inch or so above her conscious thought.

I'm missing something. It's right there. I can feel it.

Her cell went off. The ringtone told her who it was. She kept on walking as she answered.

'Hey, Shirley.'

'Guess I'm the last to know. What's the deal with the dog?'

'Good Lord. Yes, I have a dog. Not sure why everybody's so damned surprised by that fact.'

'I lived with you, little sister. Remember? I know the hours you keep. Last I heard, dogs need a little more attention than two minutes in the morning while their owner's rushing out the door, late for a court date.' Shirley tried to start another sentence but was thwarted by a cough. She'd put a hand over the mouthpiece but Bell could still hear the massive, gravelly racket. 'Jesus,' Shirley said, voice still strained. 'Sorry 'bout that. Hope I didn't split your eardrum.'

'Don't like the sound of that cough.'

'I'm fine.' Shirley's tone closed down the debate. She was six years older than Bell but in recent years it was Bell, not Shirley, who had functioned as the older sister, the protector, the advice-giver, a circumstance that did not exactly thrill Shirley. After some initial difficulties they had settled into a better place, a place that could usually withstand the sudden gusts from the past that came sweeping by, threatening to tear down the fragile peace they had built.

'Yeah,' Bell said, 'you sound fine, all right.' She knew she shouldn't meddle, but she couldn't help herself. She was not naturally nurturing – except when it came to Shirley.

Her sister's voice was curt. 'So when was the last time *you* went for a checkup?'

'I don't smoke.'

'Yeah. And nobody ever died of anything else, right? Look, before we get too far off topic – I left a message at your office today. For you to call me back. You ignoring me or what?'

Bell winced. Goldie seemed to sense her dismay; without slowing the pace, the dog looked up. Bell rewarded her with a head pat.

'Sorry. Busy time, Shirley. No excuses – I clean forgot. What's up?'

'Just needed to confirm the dog rumor. Couldn't believe it. I mean – this is a real, live dog we're talking about, right? Not a stuffed animal? And not just a *picture* of a dog? We're talking about a living, breathing creature, correct?'

'Oh, for God's sake,' Bell said. 'Yes. A real dog. Her name's Goldie.' Once again, the tail reacted to the familiar syllables.

'And the dog's still alive, right? I mean, you didn't, like, tie her to your back bumper and then forget all about her and just drive off to work this morning?'

'Hilarious. Yes, she's doing fine.'

'That's a relief. Now I don't have to call the authorities. Report animal cruelty.'

'I am the authorities,' Bell shot back. 'My turn to pry. How're you doing?'

She kept her tone light, same as Shirley had, but she needed to know. Right after Shirley's release from prison, she'd had a hard time finding a job, and an even harder time finding the balance between sudden freedom and the self-discipline necessary for a meaningful life. Shirley had run wild. Then she had settled down. They didn't get together often – Shirley and her partner lived in a garage apartment thirty-five miles away – but she and Bell knew things about each other that no one else on earth knew. *Or would ever want to,* Bell always reminded herself, when contemplating their early days, riven as they were with trauma and sorrow.

'Doing great,' Shirley said.

'You always say that.'

''Cause it's always true.'

'How's the job?'

'It's a job. That's about it.'

Shirley was a cashier at an auto parts store in Blythesburg. Not ideal, she'd told Bell, but until she could find something better, this would do. She had tried to make a living as the manager of her boyfriend's band, but it was hard to make ends meet on what he picked up from playing in bars.

'If you need anything,' Bell said, 'like a loan, maybe I could—'

'We're fine, Belfa. Fine.' Shirley cut her off instantly. They'd had this conversation before. Almost word for word.

'I just want to be sure you know that—'

'I know.' Shirley cut her off again, but not harshly this time. 'I do. I really do. Appreciate it, Belfa. But I got this. Okay?'

Bell had reached the end of Oakmont Boulevard. The intensifying darkness persuaded her it was time to head home; she was grateful for the porch lights popping on at random throughout the neighborhood. She executed a wide, sweeping turn, like a battleship with new orders. Goldie turned along with her.

'Okay,' Bell said. She crossed the street, so that Goldie would have fresh ground to sniff.

'So we're good?'

'We're good.'

'Okay.' Shirley hung up. Yes, it was a too-abrupt end to the conversation, but Bell was used to that; Shirley's long years in prison had sliced the manners from her personality, the way you'd trim excess material when hemming a pair of pants. In a place like Lakin Correctional Center, where Shirley had spent more than half her life, manners were a liability. A sign of weakness. Weakness could get you hurt or killed. In a perverse way, then, Bell was grateful for Shirley's lack of please-and-thank-you habits. It had ensured her survival. Brought her back here.

'Love you too, sis,' Bell said into the phone, knowing that her sister was long gone, but saying it anyway.

19

The name was ridiculous. It was stupid and juvenile, like something you'd call a ninety-proof beverage concocted in a backwoods still.

Yet there it was – MOUNTAIN MAGIC – emblazoned in red letters on a white vinyl banner that proudly spanned the stupendous length of the construction trailer, tied off at either end with a big red vinyl bow. Bell could see it from a long way off, and it set her to wondering: How many arrogant, overpaid, squash-playing, Jaguar-driving, latte-slurping advertising geniuses had gathered in a fancy New York City office to come up with *that* embarrassment of a name?

She further wondered what Edward Hackel had thought of it. He must've had to say 'Mountain Magic' a hundred and fifty times a day, give or take. He was the one, after all, charged with hyping the project, with chatting it up, with luring investors and keeping them happy and excited, and then lining up the real estate that would accommodate the hotel and the restaurant and the casino and the golf course and the pools and the riding stables and the helipad. He was the one who had kept the entire project racing along – until it hit a speed bump.

A speed bump known as Royce Dillard.

It was Thursday morning. The sky was the color of polished pearl. Five days had passed since Hackel's body was found in Old Man's Creek; two days after that, Dillard had been formally charged with his murder. And yet Bell still had no real sense of Hackel. No way to gauge how far he would have gone to make the resort a reality, and if his zeal had somehow brought about his death.

Bell parked in front of the trailer. It was surrounded by an alert-looking assembly of shiny SUVs and two-ton pickups in primary colors. Her Explorer was the only vehicle on the lot that could have benefited from the immediate services of a car wash. The others all looked as if they were washed and polished once an hour, with touch-ups at the thirty-minute mark.

She hadn't come alone, but she might as well have, for all the company Deputy Oakes had provided. He was still smarting from having lost the argument over who was going to drive. Bell had prevailed, because the department's Chevy Blazers both happened to be in use this morning. Oakes, the visible embodiment of a bad attitude, had pitched himself into her passenger seat and pulled the door shut behind him with as loud a bang as he could manage to make. Arms crossed, chin turned to the window, he'd barely said a word during the entire trip. He'd edged perilously close to Royce Dillard territory when it came to being uncommunicative.

'Ever been out here?' Bell asked. She reached round and fetched her briefcase from the backseat.

'Couple of times,' was Oakes's sullen reply. 'They've got their own security, but when the alarm's tripped in the middle of the night, they call us for backup.

Every friggin' time, it's a deer or a raccoon that wandered past the motion detector.' He slid out, stood up, and put his hat on his head. He was muscular, and nimble in his movements, with a handsomeness that was more than just an accumulation of pleasing features. He had a hard jaw, black hair, and soft green eyes, but he also had a self-confidence that rode out ahead of his physical appearance and struck its own deal with the world, on terms inordinately favorable to himself. Oakes chewed gum constantly, and he chewed it in that slow, insinuating way that was ultimately more insulting to an adversary than a wad of carefully aimed spittle.

Bell could well understand why his hiring by the sheriff's department had caused such a ruckus among courthouse employees. She also understood Pam Harrison's reason for going outside Raythune County for the pick: They'd had some bad luck with local hires in law enforcement. It was time to acknowledge that people who'd grown up seeing the mountains from a different angle – or had seen no mountains at all – might bring a fresh perspective.

'So you've met the head of security,' Bell said. They were approaching the neat little porch affixed to the trailer's entrance. The porch was accessed by four metal steps and a railing on both sides.

'Paul McGloin. Yeah, sure.'

'You two hit it off?'

'Guess so. Why?'

'Because I'd appreciate it if you and your buddy could maybe go amble around the property and talk about manly things while I speak to Runyon. Divide and conquer.'

Oakes stopped chewing his gum for a moment. He couldn't tell if she was making fun of him or not.

'Okay,' he said, thinking about it as he led the way up the steps. 'So we want to separate boss and employee.' He punch-knocked on the trailer door. 'Gotcha.'

While they waited for a response, Bell treated herself and took in the view. Mountains rose all around this spot like a choir loft in a cathedral. The mountains were three-dimensionally vivid in the crystalline air, still glistening with a whisper of morning frost. The hotel would be located right here, meaning that the windows of every room would look out upon a visual miracle. Beyond the closer mountains were others, and still more after that, crossing in front of each other in receding rows of sweeping rise and steep descent. Bell knew her home state well, but sometimes, when she got away from the parts where the people and all of their sorrows lived, she saw it in a whole new light. It was then that the central tragedy of West Virginia – soaring natural beauty marred by the ugliness of human greed, a greed that doomed too many of its people to live in poverty – was most apparent. The loveliness of this land depressed Bell far more than did its squalor. Squalor was only squalor; the loveliness revealed what could have been.

McGloin answered the deputy's knock. Bell had never met him before, but there were no introductions; the security chief nodded and grunted to Oakes as they entered. Bell had called and made the appointment the day before, yet McGloin still seemed pissed off by the visit, as if she'd interrupted something vital. He wore his dark hair raked back into the pert knob of a ponytail. The stubble on his face was artful; you could easily believe he'd spent hours with a razor, getting it just right. A gold earring dangled from one ear. His clothes were black and tight, just uncomfortable enough to be stylish.

'Mrs Elkins,' said a silky female voice from the far end of the trailer. 'Good morning.'

This was a different Carolyn Runyon from the angry, belligerent woman who had stood in Sheriff Harrison's office on Saturday night. After greeting Bell, she quickly rose behind the large teak drafting table upon which she'd been making notes in a small notebook. Approaching them, the hand she extended was slender and steady; the elegant diamond bracelet encircling her wrist barely stirred as she shook their hands.

'Please,' Runyon said. 'Sit down. And welcome to the headquarters of Mountain Magic – at least until the hotel is finished, after which we can move in there and spread out a bit while we start Phase II of the construction.' She chose a seat on the black leather sofa next to Bell. Oakes remained standing by the door.

'Most of my staff,' Runyon added, 'is out by the lake right now, going over a drainage issue. We need to have it resolved before we break ground.'

'So that's coming up soon?' Bell said. 'Even with the death of Edward Hackel?'

'It's what Ed would have wanted,' Runyon said solemnly. She closed her eyes and dipped her head for a few seconds. Bell took the opportunity to look around.

Arranged throughout the trailer's spacious interior were sleek blond tables with complicated chrome under-pinnings, black chairs and the matching sofa. In one corner, there was a cappuccino maker, mini-fridge, and microwave, all wrapped in shiny reflective black. Multiple surfaces were covered with blueprints, their curled edges held open with delicate stickpins. On one wall, large posters displayed painted scenes that were idealized versions of mountain gorges and summer-bright meadows and frothy rivers, with captions that varied from MOUNTAIN MAGIC – THE DREAM BECOMES REALITY to ALMOST HEAVEN: MOUNTAIN MAGIC! Classical music flowed discreetly in the background.

The construction trailers Bell had seen on other job sites – dirty, cigarette-scented, crammed with tools and crumpled invoices and thermoses and thrown-down jackets and mud-crusted work boots – were nothing like this.

'Look,' Runyon said. Her voice had a just-between-us-girls lilt to it. 'Before we go any further, let me say that I'm really glad to have this chance to clear the air. I was pretty upset last weekend. I know I probably came off as the biggest bitch in the world. But in my own defense, I really do think I was in shock. Ed Hackel wasn't just an employee. He was a friend. A very dear friend.'

'Of course.' Without moving her head, Bell let her eyes rise to meet Oakes's eyes.

He got the hint. 'Hey, McGloin,' he said, hitching up his trousers. 'Mind showing me around outside? Only time I get out here, seems like, it's pitch-black. Never really seen it at its best, you know?'

Once they were alone, Runyon waved a hand toward the cappuccino maker. Bell shook her head.

'No?' Runyon said. 'Well, I think I'll indulge, if you don't mind. I've been here since four this morning. I start getting a little fatigued at about this time of day. Nothing like caffeine to put me right again.'

The machine fussed and sputtered. Carolyn Runyon

kept her back turned to Bell while it did its work, making conversation difficult. Bell wondered if that was the point.

'There,' Runyon said, a few minutes later. She settled back down on the sofa, crossing her long, tautly muscled legs at the knee, holding the white saucer and cup. 'All better now.'

'Four in the morning,' Bell said. 'That's what I call dedication.'

'Don't have a choice. The surveying crew shows up at five, and then the engineers generally get here by six. It's a very tight schedule, Mrs Elkins. One delay can put us months behind. There's a ripple effect. What looks like a small problem in one area can create a much larger problem in another. You'd be surprised how much preparation there has to be. Meticulous planning. By the time those bulldozers start rolling, we have to have every detail nailed down.'

'It's not just the preparation, though, right?'

'Beg your pardon?'

'The holdup. It's not just because you have to prepare so thoroughly, is it? You have to have Royce Dillard's land. And he won't sell it to you.'

Runyon sipped the cappuccino. She took her time replacing the cup on the saucer. 'Ed was working on that. I believe he was close to a breakthrough.'

'Meaning he bullied Royce Dillard.' Bell didn't bother trying to keep her tone casual anymore. 'He badgered Dillard relentlessly. Never let up.'

'I don't think we should speak ill of the dead. Do you?'

'I wasn't. If anything, it was a compliment. As I understand it, that was Hackel's job. Getting the land was his number-one priority.'

'Fair point. And yes, I'd agree. Ed was—' Runyon paused. She made it clear that she was choosing her adjective with great care. *'Effective,'* she said, enunciating all three of its syllables as if she wanted to get them exactly right. There was admiration in her tone. 'He was a salesman. Good salesmen can't be timid. They can't hold back and wait for things to happen. They have to charge ahead. They have to *make* them happen. Believe me, if Ed Hackel wanted something you had, he'd do whatever it took to get it. He was very diligent about research. About figuring out the best way to approach you. Just which buttons to push. Everyone's different. It's all about the research. That's what made Ed such an excellent representative of this company.' She reached over to set down the saucer on a nearby table. 'But I really hope you're not here to suggest that Mr Dillard was somehow justified in his attack on Ed.'

'No. I'm not.'

'Then why *are* you here?'

Bell pulled a yellow legal pad out of her briefcase.

'I'm putting together the trial brief,' she said. 'It's basically a script for what will be happening in the courtroom – as much as we can predict. Witnesses we intend to call, points we'll be making. That way, the judge can be ready to rule on any points of law we reference.'

'And you'll be calling me.'

'Yes. I'll be calling you. I'll ask you to describe what Edward Hackel did for your company. And I can tell you that when Mr Dillard's attorney cross-examines you, she'll want to know why Hackel was repeatedly contacting Royce Dillard about his land, even after Dillard had turned him down.'

Carolyn Runyon tucked her skirt more tightly under

a firm thigh. She was, Bell noted, gym-hardened, one of those women whose slenderness meant that you could easily miss their sinewy strength.

'Well,' Runyon said, 'I've testified before – many times, in fact – but in civil trials, not criminal. There's always a lot of litigation in real estate. My lawyer gets a new BMW every year, and I swear he ought to put my initials on the vanity plates. I'm quite sure my legal fees pay for most of the goddamned thing. Bloodsucking bastard.'

Ah, Bell thought. A flash of the real Carolyn Runyon, the one she'd seen in Pam Harrison's office on Saturday night: cold, bitchy, belittling. Bell wanted to keep that woman front and center. There was more chance of honesty and candor from her than from the mild, smiling, cappuccino-sipping version.

'So what's going to happen now?' Bell said. 'You still need Dillard's land. With Hackel gone and Dillard standing trial, how will you get it?'

'We're not giving up, if that's what you mean. There's simply too much at stake.' A determined smile, brave and hopeful. 'Ed told me repeatedly that Royce Dillard isn't interested in money. He's living out in the middle of nowhere with that pack of wild dogs. Fine. But circumstances can change. You never know.'

'True,' Bell said. She was a believer in the strategic value of suddenly changing the subject. 'Just for the record, where were you last Thursday?'

'You people,' Runyon said testily. 'Jesus.' An irked shake of her head, sending her earrings into a brief tinkling dance. 'You've got a man in custody. You know he's guilty. Yet you insist on—'

'It's standard. We have to account for everyone's whereabouts. Otherwise, the defense might try to float an alternative theory, and suggest we rushed to judgment in charging Dillard. We'll be asking the same question of every one of your employees and all of your subcontractors – the ones who were on site last week. Plus anyone who had any contact with Mr Hackel during the hours immediately preceding his death. Including his wife.'

'Surely she was home in Falls Church. That's where they live.'

'The question is, Ms Runyon – where were *you*?'

'Here, mostly. My staff can vouch for that. And then back at the motel – and believe me, I spend a lot of time in the bar once the workday is over, and people saw me there, too.' She paused. 'I already told all this to the deputy. The fat one. The one who interviewed me Saturday night – and who was very rude, by the way.'

'File a complaint.' Bell leaned forward. 'Tell me about the tension between you and Diana Hackel.'

'Ha. "Tension." Now, *that's* an understatement.' Runyon briefly inspected the nails on her right hand. 'She didn't like the hours I made Eddie work. She thought I was too hard on him. Of course, she certainly didn't mind cashing his paychecks. Thanks to my company, that woman lived very, very well. Big house, nice car, startup money for some silly business. No reason for all those complaints of hers. She was lucky to have Eddie.'

'And did she?'

'Did she what?'

'Have Eddie. Or was there someone else in his life?'

Runyon shrugged. 'I don't pry. If Eddie was indulging in some extracurricular activities around here after working hours – well, that was his business. Not mine.

And it surely wouldn't have been the first time a married man has indulged in a little fun on the road.' Her expression softened. 'Frankly, given what happened to him, I hope he *did* have a little something going on here. You know? Hope he had some pleasure. Heaven knows he got little enough of it when he was home with her.'

'Forgive my bluntness, Ms Runyon – but were you and Ed Hackel having an affair?'

Runyon ran an index finger across the hem of her skirt. Then she looked up. 'What does any of this have to do with his murder?'

'Maybe nothing.'

'Will it have to be made public during the trial?'

'Not necessarily.'

'Do I have to answer?'

'No. You don't. Not now, anyway.'

'I see.' Her finger smoothed the skirt hem once again, this time going in the other direction. 'I don't think I have to explain to you, Mrs Elkins, how difficult it is to be a woman with power. In charge. We're scrutinized in an entirely different way than men are. If we're tough, we're called bitches. If we're not tough, we're too soft for the job. And God forbid we ever try to relax every now and again. Blow off steam. A man can have a hundred affairs and he's considered a stud. Other men *envy* him. A woman has a little fun every once in a while and she's a slut. Other women look down on her. Pity her. I get so tired of the double standard. Don't you? Really, now – don't you?'

Bell knew exactly what she was talking about. She didn't disagree. But she wasn't here for the camaraderie. She remained silent.

Unfazed, Runyon went on. 'Mountain Magic was my

idea. All of it. I grew up in Illinois, and my parents and I drove through here once when I was a kid. Family vacation. We didn't stop – we were on our way to the beach – but I never forgot it. These mountains! They were like something out of a fairy tale. I kept thinking we'd come across flying dragons or princesses on horseback. So when I finally got to the point in my career when I could develop my own project, this was it. I mean, I'd worked for other people's dreams for so long. Now it was my turn. My dream. This resort really *is* going to be magical, Mrs Elkins. You'll see.'

There was a wide window across the back of the trailer, and it drew Runyon's gaze. Bell's, too. They might have been looking at the same landscape, but Bell was fairly certain they were seeing very different things.

The window provided a luscious panorama of an area that, if things worked out the way Runyon and her investors hoped, soon would be filled with the huffing, tanklike machinery of construction, with the giant iron claws that slashed and gouged great holes in the earth. An endless parade of trucks would bring in cement and steel beams and PVC pipes and pallets of bricks and stone. Land that had looked roughly the same as it had looked for centuries – wild and raw, thick with a thousand different kinds of plant and animal life – would be subdued by the heavy hand of progress, tamed and flattened to create a playground for people who could pay for it. It would be nobody's home. It would become mere scenery. Backdrop. The kind of thing that, if it grew too dowdy and frayed-looking, could be touched up with glitter and glue.

'You know, Mrs Elkins, we really do have the best of intentions for this place,' Runyon said.

'That's the problem.'

'What do you mean?'

'It's the people with the good intentions,' Bell said, 'who usually do the most harm.'

The phone rang. It had rung several times throughout their conversation and Runyon ignored it, but this time, she used it as an excuse to stand up and initiate a dismissal. She smiled.

'If you don't mind,' she said, in a voice clearly indicating that she didn't give a damn whether Bell minded or not, 'I really do need to get that. I'll text Paul. He'll let your deputy know that you're ready to leave. You can wait for him outside. Good day.'

20

On the ride back into town, Deputy Oakes told Bell what McGloin had shown him: battalions of shiny new pieces of earth-moving equipment ready to rip out great hunks of unsuspecting ground. Awaiting the signal to attack.

Shortly before they reached the courthouse Bell changed the subject. She wanted to talk to him – casually, as if the thought had just occurred to her – about his habit of winking at women. Bell had no real authority over him, and didn't want to make a major issue of it. She just wanted it to stop. And she certainly didn't want to bring in Sheriff Harrison – who did have authority over him.

She tried to explain to Oakes that, no matter how he meant it, the winking was inappropriate. A lot of men did it, she acknowledged, but few of them were under eighty. It was a throwback to an earlier era, when sexism was pervasive – and overlooked. There was, she further explained, a grossly lascivious subtext when a man winked at a woman that way, as if he'd seen naked pictures of her and was recalling every curve and shadow.

'It's like you're not taking us seriously,' she said. 'It's sort of offensive, frankly.'

Julia Keller

'Nobody's complained about it.' He shifted his posture. 'Nobody but you.'

'Maybe they're too intimidated to bring it up. People respect that uniform, you know.'

'You think I'm dishonoring the uniform?'

'Didn't say that.'

'Then let me get this straight,' Oakes said, in an arch, amiable voice that rose toward a peak of amused incredulity. 'We got a big murder trial coming up and lots more evidence still to collect, plus all of our regular duties – and the thing you're worried about is me winking at a pretty lady now and again? Really?'

'Not "now and again." All the damned time.' She was irritated now. 'And from what I've seen, you wink at all women. Pretty or not.'

'Well, Mrs Elkins, maybe it's my way of making 'em all *feel* pretty. You know?'

She gave up. For the present, anyway. She'd just pulled into her parking spot next to the courthouse.

He waited.

'You're not coming?' he said.

'No. Errands to run.' She needed to drive home and let Goldie out. Ben Fawcett had a field trip at school today and couldn't do it. But that was none of Jake Oakes's business.

He opened the door and eased himself out. Replaced his hat, fussing at the tilt of the brim until he got it the way he wanted it. Crossing in front of the Explorer on his way to the courthouse steps, Oakes paused and looked back at her through the windshield. His hand made its way up to his forehead in a lazy-looking salute. And then he did exactly what Bell expected him to do: He winked.

Jerk, she thought, but there was no heat behind it. Because the truth was, Oakes was right. With a murder trial set to begin, she had a lot more to worry about than an ornery deputy with a flirty streak.

And then he did something she wasn't expecting him to do: He walked over to the driver's side of the Explorer. Twirled his index finger in a little circle, meaning he wanted her to lower her window.

'Listen,' he said, leaning over so that his face was level with hers, the heel of his hand cocked on the sill. 'I know you think I'm just a dumb old deputy, but I did get a little information out of McGloin.'

'Really.'

'Yeah. He took me over by the area where they're going to put in the riding stables. Gorgeous spot. Wanted to show it off. And he got a little talkative. I bet it's because we've already charged somebody for the murder. Doesn't feel like he has to protect the boss anymore.'

'What did he say?'

'First off, he said Hackel was a slick hustler. Wore a nice suit and always had his shoes polished – but nobody trusted him. Total hypocrite. Pretended to be a family man, but spent plenty of company time chasing tail and partying. Matter of fact, first thing Hackel did when he got to town, McGloin said, was start asking certain folks around here where he could score some cocaine. Wanted a reliable source for the duration.'

Bell shrugged. 'Well, we don't get to choose which homicides we work on, Deputy. Got to investigate all of them, no matter what anybody thinks of the victim.'

'Hold on. I'm getting to the interesting part. Turns out McGloin was working late a few weeks ago and he caught 'em.' Oakes grinned. 'Walks into the trailer and finds 'em there. Carolyn Runyon and Ed Hackel. Really going at it.'

Bell nodded a dismissive nod. 'So they were having an affair. Figured as much. And again, we're not the Morality Cops.'

'Hold on.'

'What?'

'You think I mean he caught 'em on the fold-out couch,' Oakes said with a grin. 'Nope. He caught 'em in the middle of a big fight. A real knock-down, drag-out. Plenty of yelling and screaming.'

'Over what?'

'He doesn't know. But whatever it was, he said it sounded like they were ready to rip each other's heads off and then spit in the neck holes.'

Goldie ran headlong around the backyard, smelling everything she encountered. Occasionally she'd stop and bark wildly at the shadow cast by the big silver maple; the shadow spread out across the lawn, darkening the tender fringe of early grass.

Bell watched her from her seat on the back stoop. She wished there were a way of somehow explaining to the dog that it wasn't real, that it was just a shadow. Nothing to be afraid of. But then again, Goldie probably wished the same thing from time to time: Wished she could tell those silly humans that most of the things they worried about were mere illusions, and that even the ones that were real probably couldn't be helped – so why get upset about anything?

Bell pulled out her cell and called David Gage. She realized how much she looked forward to talking to him. The conversation with Carolyn Runyon that morning had left her hungry for straightforwardness and sincerity.

'Hey,' he said. 'I hear that bark. Either you're watching *Turner & Hooch* or Goldie's trying to say hello to me.'

'Wait. I thought *I* was the only person who remembered *Turner & Hooch*.'

'No way. I've been trying to get my girls to watch it ever since they hit middle school. But any movie I recommend is sort of tainted. You know?'

She knew. She'd tried multiple times – with no success – to get Carla to watch some of her favorites such as *The Year of Living Dangerously* and *Streets of Fire*. A parent's selection simply had to be rejected automatically. There was a principle at stake.

'One day,' Bell said, 'your girls will be trying to get their own kids to watch *The Fault in Our Stars* – and then they'll know what it feels like to be sneered at.'

'No doubt.' His voice dropped its jocular tone. 'So how's the case? I know you'll be going to trial soon.'

'Too soon.'

'Can you get an extension?'

'Not unless I want the judge to slash my tires. Or order the bailiff to do it. Judges like to keep things moving along. Can't blame them – the backlog in the courts is bad and getting worse. Too many drug cases, frankly.' By this time, Goldie was back at the stoop, licking the palm that Bell held out to her. 'But we're working hard to be ready. Which is why I called, David.'

'Oh. Okay.'

She heard the slight edge of disappointment in his voice. He'd assumed it was a social call.

'I need to find a child psychologist to fill in some gaps for me,' she went on quickly. 'Thought maybe you know of a good one up at the med school at WVU. Someone who specializes in clinical research about the effects of early trauma. The defendant in this case was a survivor of the Buffalo Creek flood. Lost his parents. But he's never shown any propensity to violence as an adult – before now. So I'd like to get a sense of how the flood might've shaped him, you know?'

'Sure. Know just the person for you. One of my good friends. Well – she *used* to be one of my good friends. I sort of lost her in the divorce. Now she's my ex-wife's good friend. But she's still a hell of a child psychologist. The best. Lectures all over the world. Has published a ton in peer-reviewed journals. Impeccable credentials.'

'Sounds ideal.'

'Her name's Melanie Treadwell. I'll text you her contact info.'

'I'm very grateful.' Bell switched the cell to her other hand, so that Goldie could lick her other palm.

'And – uh, Bell? Know you're up to your ears in work and all, but I thought – well, you still have to eat, right?'

'Theoretically.'

'Then how about dinner tomorrow? I'll be over in Steppe County most of the day, but I'll be driving back through Acker's Gap. Thought maybe—'

'Absolutely, David. Love to.' She didn't know if she'd love to or not, but she knew that she *wanted* to love to. She wanted, that is, to keep trying with him. Goldie had finished with her palms and now lay at her feet, keeping an eye on the giant fuzzy-edged shadow out in the yard and occasionally growling at it, still not quite convinced that it meant them no harm.

21

The list, printed and single-spaced, filled one full page.

It was the record of items recovered from Edward Hackel's motel room. First thing this morning, Bell had opened a manila envelope and tilted it, shaking the contents onto her desktop. Out slid notes, printouts, transcripts, photographs: the tangible record of the investigative phase of the case. On top of the pile was the list. The items themselves were stowed in an evidence locker.

She needed to get a better sense of Hackel, a more specific impression. One that would help her put together the case against his killer. There were different ways to do that. You could talk to the people who had known him – colleagues, loved ones, each with her or his own perspectives, prejudices, histories. She'd done that. Another way was to reflect upon the things with which he'd surrounded himself in his daily life. It was all that was left of him now.

Bell had occasionally seen Hackel around Acker's Gap, and she had watched his presentations to the county commissioners about Mountain Magic. There was a swagger to him, no question about it; he had a big smile and a big laugh. Handshake always at the ready, the big hand stuck out. Square-cut nails, a firm and formidable grip. Never met a stranger. Never looked blue or downcast or even slightly ruffled. No, sir. Blue skies ahead. A *Did-you-hear-the-one-about—?* twinkle in his eye. Big voice. With Ed Hackel in the house, you could not *not* be aware of his presence, which was by design. He was heavy, yes, but like a lot of big men, he carried the extra weight as if it, too, was by design, to give him more of a stake in the world. Ballast. Grounding. Nothing wispy about *him*, by God. He wouldn't go blowing away in the first strong wind. He was here to stay. His handshake sealed the deal. Count on it.

But she knew the other side, too, of all that energy and bluster. The bullying side. She knew that Hackel had pressured Royce Dillard to give up his land after Dillard had changed his mind about selling. He'd cajoled and connived in order to create a shiny new resort for high rollers that would replace a rugged and unique natural landscape.

Was she being unfair to Hackel and his job? Maybe. Maybe she was, at that. Because a resort was surely a better fate for the land – any land – than a coal mine, either the underground kind or the surface-mining kind that whacked off the tops of the mountains with the monotonous efficiency of a bread-slicer. Anyway. In the end, Hackel's morals didn't matter. His personal failings were irrelevant. Bell would work as hard as she could to convict his killer – whom the county believed to be, and would prove accordingly, Royce Dillard. That was her job. And she didn't have to approve of the victim in order to do it.

She ran a finger down the list of items the deputies had found in his room:

A plastic vial of Tic Tacs (Cherry Passion flavor). Axe body spray (Dark Temptation scent). Hair gel. A roll of Tums, half gone. A sleeve of bright green Gas-X pills. A prescription bottle of Zoloft. Tiny white crumbles found on the bathroom vanity; sent to the state crime lab for testing, the substance was determined to be cocaine. Two (2) cuff links, embossed with the interlocking initials *EJH*. Four (4) packages of Trojan condoms. An unopened pack of Marlboros. Nail clippers. A travel-size package of Q-tips. Car keys. Business cards. One Samsung Galaxy cell. One MacBook Air, the Internet search history of which Hickey Leonard – he was the courthouse's resident geek – had dug out and enumerated, finding a dreary series of porn sites. On the desktop were icons that led to files containing artists' renditions of how Mountain Magic would look once it was up and running, from the sprawling, glass-walled hotel to the eighteen-hole golf course, all tucked under the protective gray embrace of a mountain range. His e-mail was mostly business-related. Two e-mails in his Draft file were addressed to his wife, with instructions to share them with his children. They contained links to allegedly funny YouTube videos showing frantic cats scrabbling out of bathtubs, scaling drapes, and being hypnotized by ceiling fans. The e-mails were signed, *Thot you guys would get a kick out of these!! Love, Dad*.

The last item was a small triangle of paper, a corner torn from a larger sheet, found on Hackel's bedside table. Two letters scribbled on it: *VG*. And next to them, a dollar sign and two question marks. Bell had no idea what it meant.

Finished with the list, she moved on to the photos. The first was an enlargement of the Virginia driver's license of Edward Jerome Hackel. His plump face looked happy, satisfied. Big smile. His dark hair was parted on the left; a small curl dipped down on his forehead. It was the face of a man who was trying to radiate certainty and self-importance, a man who knew – who thought he knew – what his destiny was, and strode toward it with a jaunty confidence.

Two more photos were screen grabs from the surveillance cameras at the Cigarettes 4 Less store on the interstate, a store that would have been on Hackel's way home from Acker's Gap. They were time-stamped 4:47 and 4:51 P.M. on the Thursday that had been determined to be the day of Hackel's death. He wore a brown tweed overcoat. One of the photos came from the inside of the store: Hackel was handing the cashier his credit card – the store's records indicated it was a corporate AmEx registered to Mountain Magic – for what appeared to be two hard packs of Marlboros. The other photo came from the parking lot, and showed Hackel opening the door of his BMW. The purchase recorded on the AmEx was the clue that sent Deputy Oakes to Cigarettes 4 Less to check for the surveillance footage. If Hackel had paid cash, they might never have known about this stop. It told them that at 4:51 P.M., Edward Hackel was still alive, and most likely on his way back to his motel room.

The next collection of photos came from the crime scene. Had Bell been unprepared – had this been her first look at what a heavy sharp object, wielded with strength and purpose, could do to the back of a human neck – she might have been sick. But this was not the worst she had seen. She wondered, briefly, what would happen on the day when she reached that point – when she *did* look at something that was the very, very worst she'd ever seen, ever would see. Would she know it? Would she sense it automatically?

The first photos were taken from a few feet away. The object was facedown in Old Man's Creek, snagged amidst the cattails and the scraggly vegetation that grew at the edges of a body of water. If you didn't know what you were looking at, you might be puzzled; Hackel's substantial body looked like a lump of garbage across which someone had tossed an old brown blanket. The next several were taken from a closer vantage point, and included puffy appendages that had to be hands. The most gruesome photo was still to come. It was a close-up of a head unattached to the body.

From the front, the features were lost in a wet wreck of ripped flesh and abject bloating. From the back, the lethal wound gaped in a gruesome series of triangular wedges; the sharp edge had struck him repeatedly at the base of the skull, hacking through skin and bone with an intense driving force. The matted blood adhered in a sticky-looking paste like an old-fashioned poultice. Turkey vultures had snacked on the last trailing tabs of skin that had once connected his head to his body.

Bell pictured the turkey vultures she had grown accustomed to seeing each spring, as they returned to their roosts in those broad-winged spirals of flight, scouting for carrion and then diving earthward. Some people were disgusted by them, because of their diet of rotting flesh. But turkey vultures ate what was already dead. They didn't kill.

With humans, it was a different story.

22

The phone didn't ring anymore. That was an exagger-
ation, but only slightly. Nick Fogelsong's thoughts were
of the dark, bitter, and self-pitying kind on this Sunday
night at the Highway Haven, and exaggerating his
predicament made him feel worse, which perversely
made him feel better. That was the circular paradox of
self-pity: the more you despised yourself for indulging
in it, the better you felt, because you knew you deserved
being despised. Which in turn made you feel worse.
Which in turn made you feel better.

Three and a half weeks had passed since the body
identified as that of Edward Hackel had been found in
Old Man's Creek. Royce Dillard had been arrested and
charged with the murder. The trial was set to begin the
next day.

Fogelsong sat at the desk in his office at the Highway
Haven. It was almost midnight, well past the time when
he should have packed up his briefcase and shrugged
on his overcoat and gone home. Still, he sat there. Chair
scooted back, feet propped on the desk, hands linked
behind his head, he sat.

And stared at the phone, which didn't ring.

He felt like a teenage girl, waiting for someone to call

and invite her to the prom. He felt shunned and vulnerable and needy. He felt, that is, like a damned fool. But at the moment, he couldn't rouse himself to do much more than sit there and stew. The cup of coffee on his desk blotter was cold. So were his thoughts.

He knew what was going on at the courthouse, because he used to be part of the process. Right in the center of it, matter of fact. He knew that Bell and her staff, assisted by Sheriff Harrison and her deputies, had been assembling evidence for the trial. Constructing the narrative whereby they would prove that Dillard had willfully and with premeditation killed Hackel. On the other side, meanwhile, Serena Crumpler – Fogelsong had approved of the news that Serena was representing Dillard – was gathering her own facts and witnesses to prove that the man was innocent. Or at least to raise enough doubt in jurors' minds so that a conviction for first-degree murder was unlikely.

He wanted to help. But Bell didn't want his help. She'd made that abundantly clear.

She hadn't even told him about the arrest when it happened, a fact that stuck painfully in his thoughts like an undigested lump of dinner. He'd had to get the information from – even thinking the man's name made Nick's blood pressure rise so fast that he'd swear he could feel it elevating inch by inch, putting dangerous pressure on those arterial walls – Vince Dobbs.

Fast-talking, empty-headed Vince Dobbs.

So you didn't hear?

Hear what?

They charged him.

You mean Royce Dillard?

Damn straight. First-degree murder. For killing that

Hackel fella. And leaving his body down by Old Man's Creek. You didn't know about that?

Sure I did.

Didn't sound like it. I think I surprised you.

Think whatever you like.

Don't get sore at me, Nick. Ain't done nothing to you.

Not sore.

Sounds like you are.

Jesus, Vince, just move along, okay? Other folks're waiting in line to pay for their gas. This is a place of business.

At that point, Fogelsong had put his hand on the sleeve of Vince's denim jacket and tugged him out of the way. There were six people behind Vince, restless, impatient, starting to shuffle their feet and mutter things under their breath. Vince was just winding up his transaction that afternoon – he'd paid for his gas at the pump, but came inside to buy a Milky Way bar for himself and a package of sunflower seeds for his mother, Esther Dobbs – when he spotted Nick Fogelsong as the latter emerged from the hall that led to the office in the back.

That's when Vince called to him. Nick had waved in a halfhearted way and moved over in Vince's direction, promptly regretting it when the man delivered his information. Information that was not totally startling – Dillard, after all, had been held for questioning from the start, and all the smart money was on his being charged – but it still blindsided Nick, because there was a thing called rumor and there was something else called confirmed fact, and between those two lay an entire world.

I should've known. I should've been a part of it.

He had gone into town that very Monday morning, two days after the body was found, and tried to talk to Belfa. Not in the courthouse, for God's sake. He knew better. He went to JP's, knowing – well, hoping – she would come in. And when she did, he tried to make his position clear: *I'm not sheriff anymore, true. But I've got a contribution to make.*

In response, she might as well have just flung hot coffee in his face. She'd rejected his help, leaving no doubt that that's just what she was doing.

And now that he knew Dillard was going to trial, Nick had waited for the past two and a half weeks for her to call him. Ask him what he thought about the case. What would he have said? Well, frankly, he thought they'd been a little hasty; he understood the pressure to make an arrest, he knew that county residents were richly consoled by what they saw as swift and decisive law enforcement action, and he further knew that the evidence was textbook – motive, means, opportunity, plus the absence of other credible suspects. And yet.

The 'and yet' part was a matter of feeling, not facts. He could not have discussed it with anyone except Bell.

But she didn't call.

Sheriff Harrison, by contrast, had called him that very afternoon; she had needed his opinion on a few things. She never hesitated to reach out. She was grateful to him for giving her a chance as a deputy, eight years ago. Told him so. And he told her – not as a quid pro quo, but because it was the God's honest truth – that she was doing a good job as sheriff. He was damned proud of her. Privately he thought she was a little impulsive sometimes, a little too quick to act – this case proved it – but that was her style. She was entitled to run things as she saw fit.

And then, while he had her on the line, he'd asked her about an idea he had – *Feel free to say no, Pam, it's no problem* – and she had listened and then said, *Maybe. Let me think on it, Nick.*

Bell, though, had not called.

A lot of his days and nights had gone just like this one: He sat at his desk and he waited for the phone to ring. Oh, he was busy enough, all right; a new group of employees had just been hired, and he had to go over the criminal background checks and the credit checks. Other people did the actual labor; he was the boss. He went over their work and made sure it was all done properly. Made sure, for instance, that the company didn't hire a pedophile and put him in charge of the candy aisle. Moreover, Nick had undertaken a top-to-bottom review of security procedures at all the stations, preparatory to a major upgrade. It was important work. Honest work. Work that made a difference. Walter Albright had let things slip badly in his last year on the job, especially at this location. Sometimes Nick wondered if the man had been going senile. Things had deteriorated that much. It took all of his attention just to get the security protocols back up to an acceptable level.

So why was he so miserable?

His cell went off. It was the company cell, not his personal one, so Nick had no expectations when he answered it. He knew it wouldn't be Belfa.

'Hey, Mr Fogelsong.' It was Lee Hume, the Sunday night cashier. 'Got a situation out here.'

Nick grunted and hung up. He yanked his feet off the desk and bolted forward, springing out of the chair as if it were an ejector seat. Sixty seconds later he was out in the store and moving toward the front counter. It was not an easy journey, bearing a certain resemblance to Moses and his Red Sea moment. Sunday nights at the Highway Haven were always monstrously crowded, as truck drivers made their final pushes to get to where they needed to be with their loads by Monday morning, augmenting their petroleum purchases with Mountain Dew, coffee, 5-hour Energy bottles, smokeless tobacco – whatever would keep them awake at the wheel. Other customers threaded through the aisles, too, intent on one last weekend fling before the commencement of the dreary workweek, toting their six-packs, one in each hand.

Hume and a lushly tattooed young man in a T-shirt and skinny jeans were staring at each other across the front counter, fists cocked at their hips, lower lips thrust out.

'What's the trouble, Lee?' Fogelsong said.

'This guy says I gave him a five instead of a ten,' Hume said. 'He's supposed to get ten back in change – and I gave him a ten.' Hume was an overgrown, puffy-looking man, with black glasses and a round hedge of Chia-Pet hair. Broken blood vessels covered his nose like a net. He was fifty-seven years old, which Fogelsong knew because he'd seen his personnel file; other people might have guessed younger. Hume played the age float. It was a matter of dignity. At twenty-five, even thirty, you could shrug off working the front counter at the Highway Haven as a temporary gig until your fortunes improved; at fifty-seven, it was a career.

'You're a fucking liar,' the kid said with a snarl. 'You gave me a five, asshole.'

Hume turned to Fogelsong, his voice high-pitched and petulant. 'Hear how he talked to me? You hear that?'

'Yes. I do.' Fogelsong motioned to Sissy Lewis, who was just coming out of the ladies' bathroom with a mop and a plastic bucket. Somebody had stopped up one of the toilets again. It had happened about a half an hour ago, and when she called Nick to tell him where she was, he'd said, *What'd they stop it up with this time?* and she had replied, *Trust me, Mr Fogelsong – you don't want to know.*

'Hey, Sissy,' he said. 'Take over the cash register, will you? I need to speak with Lee and this gentleman.' She said, 'Sure.' She was a middle-aged mother of four, divorced, obese, and always cheerful, and she worked harder than anyone Nick had ever seen.

He moved to a corner of the store with Hume and the young man. The other customers had been intrigued by the little drama, but now that the line was moving again, ignored it.

'Okay,' Fogelsong said. 'Here's what we're going to do.' He turned to the kid. The kid was so young that his pimples looked first-generation. 'We're going to give you the five bucks. The five bucks you say we owe you. Is that okay?'

The kid's surprised grin was wide. He smirked at Hume. 'Shit, yeah, it's okay,' he said.

Hume started to argue. Fogelsong held up a hand. 'Just a minute, Lee. I'm not finished talking.' He gave the kid a studious stare. 'Here's how it works – just in case you're thinking of trying this again. We've got your picture from our security camera, okay? And from now on, when you come in here and you get change from your purchase, whoever's working the register is going to take the change and lay it out on the counter and you're both going to agree – before you take it – that it's the correct change. Okay?'

The kid's grin slid off his face like something slick from a griddle. Clearly he'd anticipated a repeat performance of his easy-money scheme in the near future.

'Don't matter,' he muttered. 'Never coming back to this shithole.'

'Breaks my heart,' Nick replied. Hume snickered, which made the kid even madder. He slunk away, and the chains that hung from his belt sloshed back and forth, jingling and rattling. When he reached the front door he punched it open.

'Thanks, Mr Fogelsong,' Hume said. 'Best part is, the fucker forget to take what he really did pay for – those two-liter Mountain Dews over yonder. Stupid punk.'

'Get back to work, Lee.'

A couple of hours later, Fogelsong decided to give up and head home. He'd finished a slew of paperwork – which was not why he'd stuck around so late, but he was glad it was done. Late nights in the office were a great time to tackle paperwork. That was one way – maybe the only way – this job was like his sheriff's job. You had no interruptions in the middle of the night. You could focus. Productivity jumped.

He took a last look at his cell before he shoved it into his coat pocket and turned off the office light. The only calls he'd had tonight were from Mary Sue, wondering when he'd be coming home. *Soon*, he told her. *Soon, honey. Go on to bed. Don't wait up.*

Staring at his cell, knowing for certain now that Bell wasn't going to call, he thought about what he would have said to her, if she had. At first he wanted it to be *Screw you – shutting me out like this. How dare you? How fucking dare you?* But that lasted only seconds. The anger drained away. And he realized that what he really wanted to say to her, and what he hoped like hell she somehow sensed from him, no matter where she was right now, awake or asleep, was this:

Good luck, Belfa. I know how much your work means to you and I hope the trial goes your way.

Then he shut off the light, buttoned his coat, and headed out to the front part of the store. Darkness crouched against the windows. The crowd had cleared out now. Highway Haven was down to just a smattering of customers, typical for the scraped-off plain that stretched out between 2 and 6 A.M. A truck driver filled up two jumbo thermoses over at the coffee urns. A woman stood in front of the beer cooler, puzzling over her selection. Hume looked half-asleep behind the counter, an arm propped against the register.

Fogelsong didn't bother to wave. He went out the front door. A blast of cold air met him there, the tricky cold of March, tricky because you half-expected winter to be gone by now and it never was – but you still anticipated that it might be. Hope beat experience every damned time. Fogelsong winced, pulling up the collar of his coat. *Glad I've got a close parking spot,* he thought, a thought immediately superseded by, *Good Lord, I'm getting soft. Next thing you know, I'll be riding one of those little scooters from my car into the building.*

A glint caught his eye. It came from across the lot, near the first row of pumps on the truckers' side.

He looked closer. The lights above the pumps reflected off the chrome. A truck was parked there, a big silver rig, eighteen-wheeler. The driver stood next to it. A short, burly man in a baseball cap with a Peterbilt logo. His green plaid coat was wool, and it looked as if it had last fit him maybe a decade ago. Coat and face were vaguely familiar. Nick knew most of the drivers by sight if not by name, and Green Plaid was a regular. *A regular pain in the ass,* Fogelsong corrected himself. After filling up his truck, Green Plaid made a habit out of hanging around, fussing pointlessly with his vehicle, walking back and forth across the lot or clogging up an aisle in the store. Nick didn't like it, but there wasn't much he could do about it. Not if the man had made a purchase.

Nick decided to go over and say hello. He liked to remind the drivers with his presence that there always might be somebody watching them, day and night. Security cameras, yes – but human beings, too. Not just dumb machines. Never hurt to let them know.

The sound of his steps rang out against the concrete. Green Plaid's head jerked in his direction. He looked surprised, and then he looked afraid.

'Evening,' Fogelsong said. 'Once you've filled up, you might want to come inside. We've got some mighty good coffee. Tell 'em I sent you. It'll be on the house. Just tell 'em you ran into the head of security and he gave the okay.'

At the word 'security,' the man's head jerked again. He was looking past Fogelsong, toward the north side of the store, where the empty propane containers were stacked for refilling. It was dark there. The lights covered most of the lot and the front of the store, but there were a few areas – slivers, really, no more than that – that fell in between, out of the reach of the lights and, more significantly, out of the reach of the video surveillance equipment.

'Okay,' Green Plaid said hurriedly, still looking past Fogelsong. 'Will do.'

'Well, this is interesting,' Fogelsong said, his voice deliberately affable, easygoing. Keeping things on a nice even keel. He had taken a few steps around the truck cab, where he had a better view of the pumps. 'You don't seem to be getting yourself any gas right now, mister. Which makes me wonder why you stopped by here tonight in the first place.'

Fogelsong's heartbeat was accelerating. Cold as it was, he was aware of the moisture on his palms. He had a pretty good idea of what was going on. Green Plaid, more than likely, was here to pick up a drug shipment. He'd been coming regularly to the Highway Haven so that he could figure out the security layout. Tonight, he'd pulled up to the pumps because that's what trucks were supposed to do. If he hadn't, if he'd parked his truck in the shadows, that would have looked suspicious on the security cameras, catching somebody's attention. The person he was here to meet was probably over by the side of the building, waiting for the signal, whereupon that second man would slither out and make the exchange with Green Plaid, keeping to the side of the truck where the cameras didn't reach.

Of course, I might be wrong, Fogelsong cautioned himself. He had to act carefully and decisively, but not do anything provocative. A small voice in the back of his head told him he ought to just call 911 and get a state trooper out here and be done with it. Let them get to the bottom of things. But he knew what he was doing.

Hell, he thought. *I was a sheriff for more than thirty years. I think I can handle this fat-assed bastard and his pal.* And there was also a part of him – he wouldn't have admitted this out loud, but it was true, all the same – that looked forward to Bell's reaction when word got back to her that it was him, Nick Fogelsong, who had busted up a drug transaction. Maybe a big one. Maybe one related to that new gang. He hadn't put himself so far out to pasture that he couldn't do the job anymore.

'Tell you what, mister,' Fogelsong said. 'Why don't you and I take a little stroll? How would that be? Bet you'd like to stretch your legs, after being cooped up in that rig of yours for so danged long. Let's just walk over there to the side of the store – the place you've been looking at so hard, ever since I approached you – and we'll see what's what. Okay?'

Fogelsong turned to face the store, so that he could point to the shadowy space alongside it. To the place where the accomplice surely waited. Now he reached out to procure Green Plaid's puffy arm.

'Come on, now,' Fogelsong said. 'Nobody wants any trouble here tonight.'

At that moment, Fogelsong felt a sharp, hot sunburst of pain in his chest, a pummeling force that knocked him backward, and he heard the crisp zing of a bullet. He slammed hard against the door of the truck cab, arms spread out, mouth open. He slid in a heavy heap to the concrete. The concrete was cold, but he was in no shape to notice.

23

The night before the beginning of a major trial always brought a certain anxiety to Bell Elkins. No matter how meticulous she and her assistants had been in their preparation, she was never sure she was ready. Granted, not much happened on the first day of a trial – but still. It set the tone. If either side was lackluster, tentative, feeling their way, it showed.

The hour was late. Her head was bent over a stack of notebooks on her desk. She was going over the story she would be telling in her opening statement later in the week. Jury selection would take up most of the first few days, along with the back-and-forth motions between her and the defense that were necessary but that still induced exasperated sighs from everyone in the courtroom, including the lawyers who had filed them. A trial without a blizzard of motions just didn't feel right to anybody, Bell had decided long ago; it would be like a hospital without that odd smell. You wouldn't know what to do if it suddenly smelled good. You certainly wouldn't trust it.

At 11:48 P.M., she rubbed her eyes with the heels of her hands and turned off the lamp on her desk.

She wished she had Nick Fogelsong to help her think

this through. The night before a trial, he'd always been an excellent confidante. Good with strategy – and good with wisdom, too, wisdom being a solid arch over mere strategy, like an ancient bridge over the shifting, sliding river. She wondered what he was up to tonight. They hadn't seen each other since the day he'd ambushed her in JP's. A day when she'd been rude to him, cold and withholding. Miffed at his assumption that he could just walk right back into her life as if he were still sheriff.

Late as it was, he'd be home from work by now. Gone to bed, most likely. Reading by the light of the lamp on the bedside table, with Mary Sue beside him.

Lord, she thought. *If only this was a simple, good guy–bad guy trial.* A lot of her major cases these days involved drug trafficking, and with those, it was easy to argue the county's case. The defendants were scumbags. Prosecution was a breeze. But Royce Dillard was different. She had an inkling of what he'd been through in his life: the loss of his parents at a tragically young age, an inability to adjust to the world, the constant rubbing worry brought on by poverty. She knew he was guilty – the evidence was what it was – and she would make sure he was punished for what he'd done. Still, she entertained a fragile hope that he would, at some point in the trial, decide to tell them why he'd killed Hackel. If he told the story, and if he then changed his plea to guilty, she could agree to a sentence that took into account the provocation for his crime. He would serve time, but he would not die in prison. That scenario, however, required him to be forthcoming with them.

An idea occurred to her. *I can't convince him,* Bell

thought. *And Serena can't, either. But maybe he can convince himself.*

She opened her desk drawer.

Chess Rader was on duty tonight. With so few deputies, the county had to rely on civilian employees to take the overnight shifts at the jail. Rader was a young man with whom Bell had dealt three years ago, when his grandfather was murdered in a case of mistaken identity. He was a good kid. A little cocky, but she didn't mind that. She could come across as a little cocky herself.

'You're up late,' Rader said.

'Price of the job,' she said. On to business. 'I'd like a moment with Royce Dillard.'

'Need me to join you?'

'I do.'

Even though her visit had nothing to do with trial testimony, she wanted a witness. It was a matter of protocol.

She followed Chess Rader down the cinder-block tunnel past the row of jail cells, where the only sounds were the grizzled snores of the drunks and the nightmare mutterings of the meth addicts. At night the jail felt even grayer and lonelier than usual; the feeling of human desperation lingered like a greasy sheet hung from a high window to air it out.

Royce was sitting on the bed. She knew he'd be up.

Chess worked the key. Bell entered the cell. All she carried was a notebook. It had a cardboard cover and pages ruled with thin blue lines. The cover had been stamped with a pattern meant to suggest marble, the black and the white patches swirled. She had picked up a dozen of the notebooks last September at the back-to-school sale at Lymon's Market. They'd been stacked up in a display that included white plastic bottles of Elmer's Glue, with the little orange tips; plaid reels of Scotch tape; three-ring binders; cellophane-wrapped packs of unsharpened pencils. Bell always bought school supplies in the fall, even though Carla was long past needing them – she had graduated from high school, for heaven's sake – and stored them in her office, deep in a desk drawer. It was a ritual Bell had hung on to. She wasn't sure why.

'How's Goldie?' Dillard said. Eyes on the wall.

'She's fine. Look here, Royce. Your trial starts tomorrow. When it's over, you could go to prison for the rest of your life. That's a very real possibility.'

'I didn't kill the man. Been saying that over and over again.' He squinted and grimaced, as if he'd been trying to add up the number of cinder blocks in the wall and had lost count. 'So why are you here?'

'Brought you something.'

She handed him the notebook. He stared hard at the cardboard cover and its marbled design before accepting it.

'What's this for?'

'I want you to write down everything you remember about that day.'

Royce put the notebook across his knees. He knew she didn't mean the day of the murder. She meant February 26, 1972. It was the only day that really mattered to him.

'When the trial's recessed each afternoon,' she said, 'you could do it then. Bound to help clear your head. You'll have to get a pen from Chess here or whoever's on jail duty. They'll have to watch you while you write. And then you have to give the pen back.' Prisoners could not keep pens; too many times, they'd been used as weapons, or as syringes by canny addicts.

'What if I don't want to?'

'Can't force you,' Bell said. 'But I think it's a good idea.'

He considered her words.

'Okay,' he finally said. He lifted the notebook and waggled it, the way you shake a wrapped-up gift to hear the rattle so you can guess what's inside. He shrugged. 'I'll give it a try. Write down my damned story. But what're you gonna do with it once I'm done?'

'It's not for me,' Bell said. 'It's for you.'

Death Imprint

1972
Lundale, West Virginia

I remember sitting in a basket in the yard. A straw basket. The sides were scratchy and all I had on was a little bitty diaper, and so I'd end up with these red marks all over my arms and legs, where the pointy ends of the straw would work their way loose from the weaving and nick my skin.

Now, what kind of mother – I can hear you thinking that, as if you'd spoken the words out loud – what kind of mother puts a two-year-old baby in a scratchy basket, when he keeps on getting himself cut in there? Well, the truth is, I wanted to be in that basket. All the time. My great-aunt Bessie Truax told me that. When my mother would go outside on nice days to put the clean wet washing on the line – almost nobody had a clothes dryer back then, not in Logan County – she had to take me with her, so's I wouldn't get into trouble in the house, and I screamed and I yelled and I squirmed like an ornery little devil until she put me in that basket. I didn't care if it was scratchy. I loved that basket. Felt safe in there, I guess.

I didn't have nothing to be scared about – not yet, anyway – but still I felt safe.

Bessie told me the story about the basket so many times that I'm not sure if I really remember it or if I just think I do. You can't tell sometimes. Memory's a hard thing to figure. Your memories are like these little bits of colored glass, all jumbled together in your head, shifting and clacking like a box of peanut brittle. Some of the bits may come from things you think you remember, but a lot of the bits come from other people. And their memories come from bits they've picked up from other people. And those other people – their bits, too, come partially from themselves but partially from other people, too. If you put all the bits together, and you manage to find the shapes that fit with other shapes, I guess you'd make yourself a big glass rainbow. All these pieces of colored glass, rising over the top of your life, with the light shining right through it.

There's a scar on my left hip that I believe came from the morning of the flood. I can't be sure. No one can be sure about anything that's related to that day. Aunt Bessie said I might have gotten the scar when we were fighting our way out of the house, and my mother grabbed me. By that time the water was so deep that our furniture was floating. Can you imagine that, seeing your chairs and your table and all the things on your kitchen counter just go past you, go right on by, like they were toys in the bathtub? And maybe, Bessie said, maybe a sharp edge of something caught me and cut me. When they found me, they said, I had blood all over me, and when they wiped it away it was all coming from the one long cut. The other cuts and scrapes on other parts of me all healed up real nice, but the one on my hip there, it left a scar.

They made me talk to this woman once. I was just a little kid, in school. Maybe third grade. She was old. She wore a real nice dress and had pretty shoes, and she smelled real good. I didn't mind talking to her, even though under normal circumstances I didn't much like talking to anybody. And never about that morning. Anyway, she told me about this thing called 'survivor syndrome.' It's a real medical thing, like the cancer. Or like having a bad heart. There are five parts to it. And the first part is called the 'death imprint.' It means the pictures that stay in your head when something real bad happens. Even if you can't recollect the pictures on your own, even if you don't know that the pictures are there, they're still there, all right.

The lady was talking about the things I saw and heard: my mother holding me one minute and just gone the next, and then the feeling of being thrown up in the air like I was. My father, they tell me, was holding me out in front of him, trying to keep me clear of the rising water. Before I knew what was happening I was going way way WAY up in the air, toward the black sky, and even though nobody believes me – they say I was too young to remember – I swear I looked into that sky and it was like looking into the heart of the devil himself, because it was so black. Terrible black. People were yelling and screaming and crying, and I heard somebody say ELLIE OH ELLIE and somebody else say GOD GOD and then I heard THE LORD IS MY SHEPHERD I SHALL NOT WANT HE MAKETH ME TO and after that, there was a roaring sound and a big whooshing sound, like the world was being torn into tiny bits, and then more dark.

The lady, the one at the school that day, told me my memories were the first part of the survivor syndrome. The death imprint. And while I now understand that she meant the pictures in my mind, the ones that won't go away, even if you don't know you are remembering them, at first I didn't understand her. When she said the words, I thought she meant a real imprint, like a tattoo. Like the scar on my hip. I've seen it, I said to her. I've seen my death imprint. She shook her head and said, No, Royce, honey – that's what she called me, Royce honey, like honey was my middle name, and the funny thing is, I did not mind that, even though my middle name is Enoch – no, the death imprint isn't something you can see, it's something you feel when you remember. It's imprinted on your mind, Royce honey. Not your body. But even now, when I think about the words 'death imprint,' I think about that long cut, the scar that's still there.

She gave me a typed-up list of all five parts of the syndrome. She told me I would want to have the list for later, when I grew up and could understand it better. It might help me, she said. I read that list over so many times that I memorized it:

DEATH IMPRINT
DEATH GUILT
NUMBING
IMPAIRED HUMAN RELATIONSHIPS
SIGNIFICANCE

At the time I didn't know what most of those words meant but she gave me the list anyway and she said, You'll understand them one day, Royce honey. You will.

*   *   *

So they sent me to live with Bessie Truax, my great-aunt. She was my mother's aunt. She lived in a town called Acker's Gap.

I don't remember the first part of my time there. Bessie told me that I slept a lot, and that sometimes I'd wake up and I'd be yelling and kicking, and she would have to come in and settle me down. I had my own room at Bessie's house. Her son, Chuck, had died when he was twelve years old, and that's how she was able to take me. Chuck's room was now my room. His stuff was still in there. When I got a little older and had my own stuff, Bessie took away Chuck's things – he had posters of some Cincinnati Reds players and a bunch of Matchbox cars, and there was an old cigar box filled with stacks of baseball cards and a few marbles rolling around – and she said, 'This is your room now, Royce. You do with it what you will. Go ahead now.' I don't know what happened to Chuck's dad. Bessie never talked about him. Nobody else did either.

Acker's Gap was a good place to grow up. A real good place. It was a lot slower in those days. There was even a bus that could take you into town if you wanted to go. There's no bus anymore. People have cars. And if you don't have a car, you're out of luck. Unless you like to walk, which I do.

Every so often, someone would ask me about Buffalo Creek. There was a lot of interest at first. On the one-year anniversary, a TV station sent a reporter down to interview me – although 'interview' is not the right word to use when you're talking about a three-year-old, I guess. Bessie told me later that the lady reporter stood me up on a chair and told the cameraman to just keep rolling, no matter what. The reporter asked me my name and how old I was and that kind of thing, the things you ask a three-year-old, and I was shy at first but then it was okay, Bessie said. The reporter asked me to sing a song and I said, 'What kind of song?' and she said, 'Any song.' So I started singing, 'Jesus loves me, yes I know, for the Bible tells me so,' and the reporter stopped me and said, 'I bet your mama taught you that song. Does it make you sad to sing it?' I think she was hoping to make me cry. Anyway, I giggled. That's what Bessie said I did. I giggled and I said, 'No, we sing that song at Sunday school!' The reporter said, 'Well, can you sing a song that your mama taught you?' That reporter, Bessie said, would not give up. She really wanted to make me cry. But I just shook my head. I don't remember my mother singing any songs. Maybe she did sing to me, but I have forgotten the songs. Pretty soon the reporter said something to the cameraman and he lifted the camera off his shoulder and they went away. Then Bessie asked me if I wanted a hot dog for lunch. Funny – I can remember that hot dog a lot better than I can remember the reporter. That's a three-year-old for you.

Bessie never asked me to talk about it. Other people did, from time to time. But Bessie did not. If I asked her questions, she would answer them, but that was all. She did not answer a question and then go on to another story, using my question as a way to get to something else. She answered it and then she waited for me to ask another one. Sometimes I did, sometimes I didn't. A lot of times, I had just the one question.

When I got to be maybe seven years old, I started asking Bessie about my mother. I had been wondering for a long time about what she was like, but I was afraid my questions would sound too shallow or trivial. I didn't have those words to describe it, but that is what I meant. I wanted to know: Was she talkative or shy? Did she have a lot of friends? What was her favorite food? Did she laugh a lot? What kinds of things made her laugh? How did she and my father meet? Did she want to have more kids? The questions were like a hunger in me. But I held them back for a while, afraid that they'd sound dumb.

I knew Bessie would have the answers. My mother was her niece, the daughter of Bessie's sister Regina, and before Bessie moved over to Raythune County, she'd lived in Lundale, real close to my parents. Lundale was one of sixteen coal camps in that valley. They were small, these coal camps, and Bessie told me that if you were standing on your front porch and you had an itch, your neighbor could scratch it for you without even stretching very far. That's how close the houses were, and the trailers, too. But it was nice, she said. Real nice. People helped each other out. If somebody was sick and couldn't afford the medicine, the church would take up a special collection. When there were layoffs at the mine, the families of the men who were still working would do what they could for the families in need.

Now, Bessie made it clear that these people weren't saints. 'Saints do not exist on this earth,' was how she'd put it to me. 'Only us sinners, doing the best we can every day to rise above our sinful urges. The saints are all up in heaven. We are trying to get there ourselves by doing good works, but you should never believe that there are any saints here on earth, Royce.' The Buffalo Creek Valley was no paradise, she would say. The people were poor and they worked too hard. The men died early. Coal mining, she called 'a dirty business, top to bottom, start to finish,' but then she would say that coal keeps the country going, and somebody must do it.

Bessie moved away from the Buffalo Creek Valley before I was born. She and my mother wrote letters to each other, she told me, because long-distance phone calls in those days were real expensive. They stayed in real close touch, through letters.

It had been raining for days. Not hard, but steady. My parents did not have a usable phone at the time. Their phone service had been cut off for nonpayment. 'No shame in that,' Bessie said. 'Your mama had to make decisions about how to spend the money and she always said that food on the table is more important than any phone.'

Anyway, my mother walked down to the store and called Bessie that Thursday and she said the sky looked strange to her, and she was afraid. This was not the kind of thing my mother was likely to say, Bessie told me. She was not a person who exaggerated or made up stories. And she was never afraid.

My mother had had a bad dream on Wednesday night, the night before she called. In her dream there was a roaring sound and the whole world was sliding away, just collapsing right out from under her, she told Bessie, like a stepladder folding up, and she was flung into nothingness. Now, I heard later that a lot of people claim they had dreams and visions before it happened. A lot of the survivors said they knew it was coming because it had been foretold to them in a dream. They dreamed that the skies would rip wide open and the water would come pouring down, and the dam would blow apart and the water would come slamming down the valley.

Maybe that's so. Maybe other people did have such a dream. Or maybe they just said they did, after it happened. But the thing is, I *know* my mother had the dream, because she told Bessie about it. And she didn't have it Friday night, the night before the flood, but on Wednesday night. If you want to show off and say that you saw something coming, you say that you had the dream the night before. Not three nights before. So I believe her. I believe that, in some way, my mother knew, and that kind of tears me up inside, because there was nothing she could do about it. Nothing at all. Nobody would have listened to her, even if she'd picked up her skirt and run up and down the valley, hollering, *Look out! Look out! The dam's gonna bust open in two days – you gotta grab everything you cherish in this world and run right now!* She saw it coming, and there was nothing she could do.

I remember the water. I do.

People told me later that I am probably just remembering what I was told, that there is no way a two-year-old child would remember it the way I say I do, but to hell with them. I remember that water: Black as can be. It wasn't regular water. It was thick as dirt, and it stuck to things, like tar does. And it smelled real bad.

It was early in the morning. I was playing on the floor. I don't remember what I was playing with, but Bessie told me later I had a toy truck that I'd gotten for Christmas that year. I loved it so much. I wouldn't play with any of my other toys. So you can be pretty sure that I was playing with that truck. There was a big sound – I don't know whether to call it a bang or a roar, all I remember is that it liked to swallow us up

– and my mother started trembling all over. She had picked me up by this time, and I remember that she was shaking so hard that she had trouble holding on to me. But she did. She held on. I held on to my toy truck, and she held on to me, and we were moving through the house, moving so fast that I was bouncing up and down in her arms. She was yelling. I had never heard my mother yell before. She was not a yelling kind of person. Usually she talked slow and kind of quiet. I don't remember what she said that day, but I remember being scared because she was yelling.

And that is where it stops for me. My memory stops, and so time stops. Time stops right there, when my mother and I are moving through the house, and the house is moving right along with us. It was knocked off its foundation – I learned this later – by the force of that water, millions and millions of gallons of water, coming at us at seven feet per second. Giant walls of water. They just kept coming and coming and coming. The house was spinning around. Out of control. Everything at the mouth of the valley that had been knocked down first – other houses, trailers, school buses, telephone poles, cars, even people – came smashing into our house, just like, a few seconds later, our house was going to smash into the things that were further down the valley from us. That water kept coming for over three hours.

My mother and I made it outside. She got us out through a window. Holding me in her right hand, she used her left hand to fight and reach and claw, wiggling through that open window, while the water beat at her, and churned and spun her around and liked to pound her to pieces. Bessie had talked to the witnesses and so she told me about it. 'Your mama was a fighter,' she said. And of all the things I ever learned about my mother – people have told me she was sweet and a hard worker, and pretty, too, in ways that pictures don't show – that is the word I love best: fighter. Ellie Dillard was a fighter.

I do not know what happened to her. No one knows. I think it was this: I think she was hit in the head with something that came flying at us. A piece of something, like the sharp edge of a car door, or a rock, knocked her out. One minute she was holding me tight, and then she was not. Sometimes I think I can still feel her hands around my waist, holding me, and then I feel her hands letting go, her fingers pried open one by one by the rank terrible force, and then she whirls away from me. There is a shocked look on her face, a look of amazement and horror and sadness, her arms stretching out as far as they can go, her mouth a round O. I cannot stand that thought for very long, though, and so I have to think of something else real quick. The idea that my mama knew she was letting go of me, that she had to watch herself flying away from me and her helpless to stop it, is more than I can deal with sometimes, and I find myself praying that she was indeed knocked out, that something hit her hard in the head and she was unconscious when it happened, that she never knew, and that somewhere, she is resting on a high hill, catching her breath again. She is peaceful and happy, and not being whirled about. And she knows the day is coming when she can put her arms around me once more, and this time, she thinks, this time she will not let go. She will hold on to me forever.

There are people who tell the story about what happened next. My father grabbed me and he threw me up a hill, with the fading bit of strength he had, with the last breath being torn out of his body, and I was caught by some people who were up there on the ridge over Lundale. Then he was swept away, too.

I was cut and I was bleeding, but I was okay. The next afternoon Bessie came for me, quick as she could get there. Later, when I was a grown man and able to bear it, when I asked her about it, she described to me the day that she looked for my parents' bodies. She wanted to give them a proper burial. It was Monday, two days after the flood. She went to the morgue that had been set up in Man High School and she walked up and down those rows of bodies. Up and down, up and down. She bent over to check, again and again, looking for something that would tell her it was Ellie. 'Or Mike,' I said, and she said, 'Yes, of course. Or Mike.' They were black and swollen, those bodies. They were terrible to behold. But she had to look, she told me. She knew she would be sick later, with the smell sticking to her, and she would never, ever get the pictures out of her head: the twisted limbs and the broken necks and the crusty smear of black that slimed over everything, as if all those poor people had been burnt instead of drowned. There were all ages, Bessie said: old people and newborn babies, and every age in between, like a ladder of sadness, and no rungs got skipped. Every single step in life was there, up and down the ladder. Every age.

She never found them. There were seven bodies never found at all, and among the seven were my parents. Ellie and Mike Dillard.

I met her in Lymon's Market, where we both worked for a little while. Her name was Brenda Smith. She had read a story about me in the paper some years ago and so she knew a lot more about me than I knew about her. Well, she thought she knew about me. Let's put it that way.

I worked at Lymon's after I graduated from Acker's Gap High School. I unloaded boxes and kept the place swept up and mopped shiny – that kind of thing. I already had some money from the survivors' settlement fund, the money paid by the coal company, but I wanted to keep it so I could buy land. I still lived with Bessie. I would've liked to get my own place, but Bessie wanted me to stay, and so I stayed.

Brenda came up to me after work one day. I was waiting for my ride home. I used to pay Ray Carpenter a few dollars a week to take me up the road to Bessie's house. I didn't mind the walk in the morning – it was about two and a half miles – but at the end of the day, I was beat.

Anyway, Brenda said, 'Here's that penny.' And I said, 'What?' And she said, 'For those thoughts you're thinking. You look like you're a million miles away.'

I shook my head. 'Well, I got a lot on my mind.'

'Like what?'

'All kinds of stuff.'

'That don't give me a lot to go on,' she said. She was smiling. 'Good stuff or bad stuff?'

She was a cashier, a few years older than me, with blond hair that sort of curled around her face, and breasts that pushed up against her blouse in a way that made you want to keep on looking for a long time. I'd seen her trying to catch my eye when I was unloading boxes in one of the aisles. I would cut the tape on top and pull back the flaps and get out the cans of fruit cocktail or pinto beans or tomato sauce, one by one, and I would stack them on the shelves, row after row, bending down and standing up, down and up, down and up. She was at the front of the store. When there were no customers around, she'd lean out across the little black conveyor belt that ferried people's purchases past the cash register, her elbows holding her up, looking my way with her pretty little smile.

'Bad stuff, mostly,' I said.

That surprised her, I think. We were out in the alley behind the store, because Ray liked to pick me up out there. He didn't like to come to the front. Ray was older. He had sideburns, plus a black mustache that he couldn't keep his fingers off of. Never had a real job, but was always busy, you know? And he had a car. That was all I cared about.

'What kind of bad stuff?' she said.

This had gone too far. I wanted to stop the conversation, even though I knew it was just a joke, just a sort of flirty thing going on, and that she didn't really want me to start listing all the bad things I was thinking about. The older I got, the more the pictures in my head had begun to show up. They had been black and white but now they were in color a lot of the time. Not just the things I remembered, but the things other people remembered and told me about. Including Bessie. She didn't mean to, but sometimes she made things worse. Sometimes when I asked her a question about that day, about my mother or what she was wearing or what our house had been like, I wanted her to say, 'I don't know, Royce. I can't remember.' But she always tried to answer me.

I liked talking to Brenda, as long as she didn't push me.

This day, I just said, 'That's for me to know and you to find out.' She laughed and smacked my arm, as if I was being a bad boy. I looked down and stared at her hand – the one that had touched me – and that made her laugh again. She didn't understand.

Her ride came first and I watched her climb in the backseat of a two-door yellow Mustang. She had loads and loads of friends. There must've been seven or eight other people in that car, all smushed and squished up against each other, laughing and yelling. Brenda disappeared into that car like she'd been folded into something foamy in a mixing bowl and was just absorbed by it, losing the firm edges of herself.

We talked a lot after that. Before and after work. On our breaks. I brought her home to meet Aunt Bessie. I knew Bessie would like her, too. Brenda had dreams – she wanted to get out of here, get away – and she had a way of talking about the world that made it seem like a wide-open place. A good place.

After 'Death Imprint' there are four other things. One by one, those things happened to me, just the way that lady had said they would, all those years ago, even though I was on the lookout for them and would've stopped them if I could. Number Four is 'Impaired Human Relationships.' That is the only way I can explain what happened next. It was like I knew that my friendship with Brenda was going to end, anyway, and so I had to go ahead and end it. Just get it over with.

One Sunday afternoon Brenda and I were sitting on the swing on the front porch, our bellies full of Bessie's fried chicken and mashed potatoes. This was fall. A chill hung in the air, the kind of chill that bothers you, eats at you, like something important you've forgotten to do.

And I just couldn't stand it anymore. I don't know why or how, but I knew I couldn't stand being there on that porch with Brenda for one single second more. My skin started to go cold. I had to be by myself. I truly thought I was going to die, right then and there, unless I got away.

I stood up from that swing and I went inside and I told Bessie I wasn't feeling well. I asked her if she could tell Brenda good-bye for me. And I never called her again. I did not go back to my job at Lymon's Market, either. I never had no job after that. Just couldn't do it. Couldn't stand being around people. Starting that day, I have tried to go easy with the little bit of money I have left but it is running low. Am I worried? I am. Mainly about my dogs. You can eat less yourself, but you can't explain things to a hungry dog.

Brenda called me a few times after that, and left messages, but I think her pride must've kicked in because her messages were not desperate or pleading, just sort of curious. I got the feeling she was relieved. Relieved that I was the one who'd taken the step that needed to be taken. I see her from time to time now. She's not the same girl she was – she's kind of lost her sparkle, is how I'd call it. Well, truth is, she'd have lost it a lot quicker if she'd stayed around me for very much longer.

Everything started to change after that. Bessie got sick and she died, and I buried her, and I moved to my cabin. The dogs came down the road, one by one. They joined up with my life. They sort of made a wall between me and the world. Which is how I survived.

For some reason I'd thought it would be gradual. Thought I'd be less and less able to put up with having people around me. Thought I'd pull away from them, inch by inch, piece by piece. But it wasn't like that at all. It was sudden. It happened right there on the porch, on that chilly Sunday afternoon. I can remember the feel of Brenda's hand, when she put it on my leg. It liked to burn me. Even though I was cold.

I guess you could say it happened the way night comes in the mountains: swift, like the fall of something sharp and heavy. One minute you are still in day. The next minute the world is dark. But your eyes adjust to the darkness. You learn to live there. You make do.

I started reading about Buffalo Creek when I was thirty-one, thirty-two years old or thereabouts. Before that, when I was younger, Bessie did not like to see me reading about it. And so I did not. Bessie was the only family I had, and she was real good to me. So I never crossed her.

But in 1999 she got the emphysema. I used some of the money I got from the survivors' settlement to make sure she was comfortable. I bought two pieces of land with the rest of it. One is the little bit of land that I put my cabin on. The other is bigger. That's the part I'm going to put a fence around for my dogs – no matter how much those bastards offer to pay me for it.

Bessie died at home, like she wanted to, with me right there beside her. And after she died, I started reading. The more I read, the madder I got.

An Act of God. That is what the coal company said had caused the flood, caused that sticky black water to go rushing down the seventeen miles of the Buffalo Creek Valley, tearing out houses and railroad tracks, picking up cars and trucks like they were toys, rubbing out roads and schools and lives.

An Act of God.

Now, if I were God, I'd be upset by that. I think I'd be plenty riled up, getting blamed that way. Because that wasn't any Act of God. It was an Act of Greed.

What happened was this: The coal company needed someplace to put the waste material. After coal comes out of the mine, it is washed at the tipple, and then it drops into the railroad cars and off it goes. But the waste material that comes off in the washing is a real problem. It's solid and liquid both – it's rock and slate and coal waste and black water. Some of it sort of burns and smolders, too, because of the coal. At the Buffalo Creek tipple, which started up in 1947, there was about a thousand tons a day of refuse. They'd truck it over to the mouth of the valley and dump it, day after day, year after year, decade after decade, making a dam of liquids and solids. According to what I read, the dam got to be about two thousand feet high and four hundred feet wide. It must've hung over the people in that valley like a bad dream, the worst bad dream in the world. Just a big, awful, oily pile of junk.

And then it started raining.

Male and female: they died. Fat and skinny: they died. Smart and dumb: they died. Generous and stingy: they died. Good people, bad people: they died. Didn't matter who you were, or how you were. If you lived in that valley, chances were, you died or saw somebody close to you die.

A hundred and twenty-five people died that day. More than four thousand people lost their homes and had nowhere to go. A whole community – sixteen coal camps were there in the valley, stretching from Lundale, where we lived, to places like Saunders and Pardee and Latrobe and Robinette and all the rest – wiped out.

Gone. Just gone.

The thing is, the coal company knew it wasn't doing right by that dam. They knew they ought to keep an eye on it, giving that filthy water a way to drain away instead of just letting it build up with all the other crap in there, too, bigger and bigger, higher and higher, more and more dangerous. But they didn't. They didn't because they didn't care. They could make more money if they just let it be. Fixing it, getting rid of that coal waste a different way, would cost money. So they just kept piling up the junk. Who cared about the people of the Buffalo Creek Valley? We were just coal miners and coal miners' wives and coal miners' children. We were refuse, no different from the refuse piled up at the mouth of the valley. The coal company let the black wall rise. Until the day when all hell broke loose.

'People ought to get to die one by one,' Bessie said to me. This was right before she passed. Lying in her bed, desperate to breathe, every breath a rasp and a gurgle, her eyes all blurred up from the painkillers that didn't really kill the pain but just put it on a high shelf for a while, where she could still see it. 'Matter of dignity. People getting to die one by one. Dying in a big gang like that – it ain't right. Not what the Lord intended.'

It wasn't an Act of God. It was a crime. It was mass murder – but nobody went to jail.

So you can see, can't you, how I got this darkness in me? This angry part of me, that won't leave? You can see why I do things sometimes and don't know why I do them.

These companies, they want to say that they're like

people. I read about this. They want to say they're citizens, too, so they can make all these political contributions. Just like people can. Well, fine. But you show me the person who can pay money and stay out of jail for murder. If a company wants to be like a person, then that company ought to be punished just like a person is punished. The president of that coal company, the head of mining operations, the board of directors – they should have been sent to jail for murder.

They say I killed a man. That is what they say. Well, if I did, then why can't I just pay a fine like the one the coal company paid, and then be on my way? Tell me. You tell me.

The coal company paid some money, but nobody went to jail. That's a crime, too, and maybe a worse one.

Part Two

Part Two

24

She was going to be sick. Bell felt the sour acid leap up into her throat, felt her stomach start to lurch and churn, and only through an intense and focused effort was she able to keep from throwing up, right then and there.

First had come the ringtone. She'd grabbed for the cell with one hand, rubbing her eye with the other. Pulled herself up into a sitting position. Black room. She swung her legs over the edge of her bed. Jesus – why were people always calling her *in the middle of the freakin' night?* Daytime was nice, too. Daytime was a perfectly fine time to conduct business. The bedroom floor felt slick and cold under her bare feet; it was like a sidewalk, but not really. Different from that. Was she still dreaming?

She had listened to the voice on her cell. Heard the words. Absorbed the information, whereupon the bottom fell out of her life.

The fact that she was sitting meant that she could thrust her head between her knees, fighting the heavy pull of nausea, fighting not to faint. Her body was turning inside out, trying to empty itself. The shock was so tremendous – the initial hit and its reverberations, spiraling out like the frantic arms of a pinwheel – that she was dizzy, unstable. Disbelieving. The floor under her feet was still cold but now it was moving, too; it was wavy, it was undulating, it started to shift and buckle.

Nick Fogelsong was in a critical condition. Gunshot wound to the chest. Not expected to survive.

In the aftermath, Bell would have no clear memory of this day. Other people would tell her that she had done fine in court, that the judge was satisfied, that the trial had gotten off to a solid start, but she would have no independent recollection of any of it. She would only know that she had done her job – and then had gotten the hell out of there. Somehow she had propelled her way through the time, plowed headlong through the hours, until court was recessed for the day and she was able to go to the hospital.

Mary Sue Fogelsong had reached her on her cell just after three that morning. She delivered the impossible, unbelievable news: Nick, interrupting a drug deal in the parking lot of the Highway Haven, had been shot in the heart. He'd lost a massive amount of blood. He was still in surgery. 'Bell,' Mary Sue said, 'they don't think – they won't say if— They won't look me in the eye, Bell, and you know what that means. My God, my God, Bell, what're we going to do if—'

Bell was groggy, sleep-webbed, when she answered the call, but suddenly she was as alert as she'd ever been in her life. She was grateful for the cold floor beneath her bare feet, glad for its stark bracing hardness. She fought the nausea. Beat it back, thrashed at it. *Go away. Not now.* She cut off Mary Sue's last sentence. 'Don't say it. Don't you say that.' She fumbled for the switch on the lamp, pushing back against the sickness that tried to tilt her sideways. 'I'll be right there.'

'No,' Mary Sue said. 'That trial starts today, doesn't it? Royce Dillard's trial.'

'Screw the trial. I'm coming.'

'No, Bell – no. He's likely to be in surgery for a long time. That's what they told me. There's no point – you won't even be able to see him. Nobody can.' Mary Sue had recovered her poise. It was as if, by hearing Bell's voice, she had found the ground again. 'You do what you need to do. Come over later. When you can. If anything happens before then, if it turns out that he—' She stopped herself. 'I'll call you. I will. If I can't reach you, I'll tell Lee Ann.'

'Your word on that.'

'Yes. Yes. Of course.'

'Mary Sue,' Bell said, needing to ask one more question. The prosecutor in her was now wide awake, too. 'Did they catch the bastard who shot him? Tell me they got him.'

'No. They didn't. They're still looking. It's Collier County, which is good.' Mary Sue was – had been – a sheriff's wife, and she knew that Collier County had seven deputies to Raythune County's two. It made a difference.

Dammit, Bell thought, wishing the shooter was in custody, wishing she could have a crack at him. Her anger temporarily displaced her anguish. Then the anguish came surging back, overwhelming her. All at once she wasn't sure she could stand up. Or speak. Or take her next breath. Breathing seemed beyond her right now, its simple mechanics lost in the blur of the incomprehensible thought that Nick Fogelsong might die.

My God – he can't—

But he could. Of course he could. On or off the job, it was always there, the possibility that this was how it would end. Just as it was for anybody. Nothing guaranteed that our ends would be commensurate with the way we ran our lives, that good people would go with dignity and peace, bad people with chaos and pain. Nothing. And so, Bell realized with sick dread, there was nothing to prevent Nick Fogelsong from dying in the parking lot of a gas station in the middle of the night, and not in a place reminiscent of those noble battlefields that he so loved reading about – San Juan Hill, Little Round Top, the beach at Normandy. He could perish just as easily on a patch of oil-stained concrete, amidst trash pushed around by the wind. Cigarette butts. Beer cans, crushed double.

'Belfa,' Mary Sue said. Had she sensed Bell's distress? Did she realize that Bell wasn't breathing, that she was sitting on the edge of her bed frozen with fear?

'Belfa,' Mary Sue repeated, and that was the key, somehow, to the unlocking of Bell's limbs. And her breathing, too. Mary Sue, saying her name. Her real name.

'Yes?'

'I've got to go,' Mary Sue said. 'And – listen. Listen to me. You know that he'd want you to do your job. You *know* that. If Nick ever found out that you put a personal tie ahead of your job, why he'd—'

'He'd skin me alive,' Bell said, and they both had a brief restorative bit of laughter, the kind that skims just enough tension off the top to allow life to go on, even in the wake of catastrophe.

After Mary Sue hung up, Bell still sat on the bed,

holding her cell. She heard a noise. Goldie padded into the room and stood there, looking at her. Bell had completely forgotten she had a dog in her house. Goldie moved closer. Closer still. There was a brief, interrogative tail-wag.

Before Bell was really aware of what she was doing, she slid down onto the floor, wrapping her arms around Goldie's torso, burying her face in the thick warm fur of the dog's side. Then Bell did something that was so unusual for her that she knew the exact number of times – three – that she had done it before, and never in front of another living creature.

She wept.

Judge Ronnie Barbour was a tall, rangy man who might have been Daniel Boone in a previous life. The first time Bell had handled a case in his courtroom, she'd thought: Switch out the black robe for a fringed buckskin jacket, plop a coonskin cap on his head, and jam a rifle in his hands, and you'd swear you were in the presence of the frontier legend. Barbour had a lean, hard face separated into strips by vertical wrinkles. His eyes were the color of cast iron, his nose was as straight as a sheared-off side of rock ledge. His gray hair was a little too long, and a little too scraggly. He wore it swept back from his forehead and hooked behind his ears. A small scruff of curls crowded up along his collar.

'Royce Enoch Dillard,' the judge said, 'you are hereby charged with the first-degree murder of Edward Jerome Hackel. How do you plead?'

A flurry of whispers erupted between Serena Crumpler and her client, who was dressed today in a not-new blue suit, white shirt, and pale gray tie. His hair had been parted on the side and wet-combed into temporary submission. Serena hissed something sharp and admonishing in Dillard's ear, advice he seemed to accept only grudgingly. He stood up straighter, looked down at the defense table, and he said, 'I ain't guilty, if that's what you're asking me. But for the record, that Hackel was a lying, no-good sack of—'

'Thank you, Mr Dillard.' Judge Barbour turned his black eyes to Serena. 'Ms Crumpler, that's the last time I will permit a non-responsive addendum by your client. Are we clear?'

'Clear, sir.'

'Good. Mrs Elkins?'

Bell stood impassively in front of the wooden table, hands clasped, face raised toward Judge Barbour's high bench. She was wearing a black suit with a black blouse, dark stockings, black heels. So self-contained was her demeanor, so blank her expression, that few people would have guessed that on the inside, she was in utter disarray and mad panic, screaming silently at the possi-bility that Nick Fogelsong was already dead, that he had died in surgery without regaining consciousness, and that she would never see him again in this life. The things that had kept them separated these last few months – his decision to give up the sheriff's job, her pride and her anger – were nothing, less than nothing. And she would never be able to tell him so.

'The county strenuously opposes bail, Your Honor,' she said in a flat voice. 'Mr Dillard is accused of a violent assault that resulted in the death of a husband and father of two children. Mr Dillard lives alone and has few, if any, ties to the community. Therefore we feel bail should be denied.'

'Ms Crumpler?'

'Mr Dillard is not a flight risk. He owns property in Raythune County and he has no prior record of any kind.'

Judge Barbour's gavel was brought down with a clean stroke between his first and second sentences: 'Bail is denied. I know you have several motions, Ms Crumpler, related to suppression of the evidence collected at Mr Dillard's place of residence. I'll consider those now, and then if there's time today, we'll start jury selection.'

So on it had gone throughout the morning, the motions and counter-motions, the presentations and the objections, as the formal apparatus of a criminal trial creaked and lumbered along like an overloaded wagon, moving in spurts and stops and the occasional surprise turning, covering more distance sideways than forward, or so it seemed. The ancient courtroom with its taupe plaster walls and yellowing pressed-tin ceiling was drafty; cold slipped in through the corners of the old windows. Moisture always gathered on the inside frames of those windows and warped them, leaving long, branching splits in the wood. The frames were painted white every spring but then peeled again the very next winter.

Bell was aware – half-aware, really – of who was there among the spectators, seeing the faces when she turned away from the judge and went back to the prosecutor's table. She saw Diana Hackel – eyes moist, lips pinched, arms wrapped around her torso – and she saw Carolyn Runyon. The two women stayed on opposite sides of the courtroom. She saw three or four strangers, men in dark suits, sitting in the row behind Runyon; she assumed they were associated with Mountain Magic.

She saw the retired people who haunted the halls of the courthouse and shuffled into almost every trial, looking for diversion, entertainment.

The ancient radiators under the windows chuckled and sizzled. And on this first day of the proceedings that would determine Royce Dillard's fate, Bell did what she had to do, said what she needed to say, at the time she needed to say it. Her mind was elsewhere. Rhonda Lovejoy was beside her; she understood that her boss was functioning on professional autopilot and if Bell hesitated, if she forgot what came next, Rhonda would hastily whisper a word or two, reminding her, and Bell would nod and go on.

Earlier that morning, just before they walked into the courtroom, Rhonda had offered to handle the proceedings of this first day by herself. That way, Bell could be at the hospital. The answer was no – just as Rhonda had known it would be. This was the prosecutor's job. And Bell Elkins would not, could not, abdicate her responsibilities, despite the fact that the man who had saved her life so many years ago was now fighting for his.

'Bell,' Serena said, approaching her immediately after Judge Barbour announced a brief lunch recess. 'I just got a text about Nick Fogelsong. Oh, my God – I'm so sorry. I know how much he means to you. To the whole county. Is there any word from—'

'He's in surgery.' Bell cut her off. She couldn't talk about it. Not if she hoped to get through the afternoon session. She knew she was being unreasonable, but she resented Serena for even bringing it up. This was her crisis, her tragedy – hers and Nick's and Mary Sue's – and she didn't want anyone else touching it or even being close to it. Or commenting on it. She was afraid that the more people discussed it with her, even to express concern and support, the more real it would become.

'I'll agree to a recess for the rest of the day if you want to propose one,' Serena said. She was trying. She didn't know what to say, what to do, but she was trying.

'No. Let's move on.'

'Are you—'

'Yes.' Fiercely. 'Totally sure.'

Serena looked at her, sympathy giving way to curiosity. She'd never been able to figure out Bell Elkins. She doubted she ever would. Somehow the courtroom didn't feel quite so chilly anymore; it was downright balmy, compared to what she'd seen in the prosecutor's eyes.

25

At last it was over. Judge Barbour's gavel descended with a level bang that left no echo and the atmosphere in the courtroom instantly shifted. It grew slack and disordered, unraveling into separate enclaves of coat-gathering and scarf-knotting and glove-tugging and murmured conversations. Bell rose and reached for the legal pads strewn across the tabletop, but Rhonda, still seated, put a hand on top of her hand and looked up at her, mouthing a single word: *Go.*

She would have no memory of the trip to the hospital. Later, it would occur to her that perhaps she should not have been driving in that state of mind; violently preoccupied, she was probably a danger to herself and others. She did not remember turning into the parking lot or running inside or pushing the elevator button with the heel of her hand, punching at it repeatedly and with such force that she would find a bruise there several hours later, and she would stare at the purplish yellow mark on her skin and wonder where the hell it had come from.

They were clustered in the hall outside the entrance to the intensive care unit. Bell saw them as soon as she lunged off the elevator. For a strange moment she wondered who these people were – two of them, a man and a woman, in flat-brimmed hats with gold braid and heavy brown uniforms – and then in seconds she realized, the fog lifting, that she knew them all, and had known them for years now: Sheriff Harrison, Deputy Mathers, Mary Sue Fogelsong, Hickey Leonard, and Carlene Radnor, Nick's second cousin, a schoolteacher who lived in Toller County. They stood in a ragged half circle, hands at their sides, looking stricken and lost.

'Bell,' Mary Sue said. She was the only one who spoke. The others just looked at her.

Bell's eyes asked the question.

'No,' Mary Sue replied. 'No news. They're supposed to bring him back up here – to the ICU – after the surgery. It's been hours and hours but – but they say that doesn't mean anything. Not really. The doctor will come and talk to me. That's what I've been told.'

Bell touched Mary Sue's shoulder. They did not hug. Hugs were something that happened in other people's lives, not theirs.

'I'm so sorry,' Bell said. Mary Sue dipped her head to acknowledge the words. She was holding herself in a tight embrace, arms crossed, elbows flush with her body, as if she feared she might lose track of something if she relaxed.

Carlene Radnor uttered a single sharp sob. The high-pitched sound broke oddly against the silence maintained by the other people here. They stared at her. Not in judgment, but in wonder: So that's what emotion sounds like when it is released, their expressions seemed to say. When it isn't locked up inside the body. Held prisoner.

Bell had met Carlene at several gatherings hosted by

Nick and Mary Sue, and she was always struck by how much family members could resemble each other without really sharing any essential features. Carlene was small and dark, while Nick was large and fair, but she had the Fogelsong aura, that admirable sense of not apologizing for the space one takes up in the world. Carlene was thirty-two years old, and had recently gone through a horrendous divorce; her ex-husband, Ollie Radnor, had leveled charges against her of child endangerment that were not even remotely true, but that had caused a splinter of doubt to work its way into the court proceedings. She had been forced to agree to joint custody of their two girls, ages ten and fourteen. Truth was, Ollie was the one who habitually left the girls unsupervised and who called them names – names such as Fat Ass and Beanpole, or Thunder Thighs and Matchstick, as their respective physiques dictated – and Bell remembered the darkness in Nick's face when he described the man's emotional abuse of his children. It was all she could do, Bell recalled, to restrain Nick from driving over to Toller County and slugging Ollie Radnor in the mouth.

'I just can't—' Carlene was trying to speak. 'If something happens to Nick, I swear, I just don't see how I'm going to—'

'We don't know anything yet,' Hickey said. He was a comforting presence here, Bell saw. He was perennially and comfortably disheveled, and the small bit of hair he had left was the color and consistency of broom straw. He had been a lawyer in Acker's Gap for many years before coming to work for her at the prosecutor's office. His age and his deep, steady voice meant that he was listened to. 'But you know as well as I do, Carlene,'

Hickey went on, 'that he's as tough as they come. Right? If anybody can survive this, Nick Fogelsong can.' He put a big hand on Carlene's shoulder.

Hearing Hickey speak, Bell realized how much she'd missed her colleague. She had assigned him to a complicated spate of prescription drug cases, and he was often on the road, meeting with prosecutors in adjacent counties to work out plea deals and jointly executed search warrants. Drug dealers had little respect for county lines.

Bell turned to Harrison. 'What do we know?'

'So far, not much. I've talked to Sheriff Ives a couple of times today. Collier County's running down some leads. Doing their best.' The sheriff took off her hat, thrusting it up under her left armpit.

'He broke up a drug deal, is that still the theory?' Bell said.

'Yeah. Looks pretty straightforward – Nick was working late, he noticed something suspicious, and he intervened. That's when they shot him. A store employee saw it on the surveillance camera and came running out, just in time to spot the truck driver getting the hell out of there. Another guy – the shooter, we figure – got away, too. Shooter'd been back in the shadows. Camera only caught the back of him when he hopped in the truck.'

Harrison went on to describe the footage they'd retrieved from the camera. As she spoke, the scene flared in Bell's mind, a mute midnight drama: A truck waits at the pumps. A man stands beside it. Nick approaches, engages. The shot comes from somewhere else, a spot not covered by the camera. The force of it flings him against the truck door. He drops. Flat on his back now, he bleeds and he bleeds, the blood running across the concrete, filling the little trench along the small concrete island hosting the gas pumps. His eyes are glassy. Breathing shallow, barely detectable. Face a waxy frozen mask of *Not now* and *Not like this* and a plain, plangent *No.* This being Nick, surely it is *Hell, no.*

'The store employee – did he get a plate number from the truck?' Bell said. 'Even a partial?'

Harrison shook her head. 'Nope. And the driver knew just where to park to keep the plate clear of the camera. Squad got there real quick, thank goodness.' She snapped her fingers. 'Oh, yeah. The cashier did say one thing. The truck driver was wearing a plaid coat. The video camera's black and white, so we don't have a color. Just that – a plaid coat.'

'Plaid coat.' Bell practically spat the words. 'That's great. That'll lead us right to the bastard who shot Nick. Terrific clue. Two out of every three adult males in southern West Virginia wears a plaid coat.' In her frustration she wanted to kick an inanimate object – a desk or a chair – but the hall was bare of possibilities, and so she had to settle for salting her words with an extra dose of sarcasm. 'That's a *big* help.'

The elevator chimed and two people got off. Strangers. Here to visit someone else in the ICU. Young boy, older woman. A kid and his grandmother, most likely, because the woman's features – cleft chin, pointy nose, small eyes – were repeated in the boy's face, but in a soft, unhurried version. A face was waiting for this boy when he grew older; it was the grandmother's face, and she would be long gone by then, and so people would peer at him and say, 'You look so much like her!' and he would smile and shrug, not knowing how to answer, because by that time, he would barely remember her.

The two of them pushed through the double doors of the ICU and disappeared, swallowed up by the return swing. The Raythune County Medical Center was a small facility, with only eight beds in the ICU; a lot of emergency cases were Life Flighted to bigger hospitals in Beckley or Charleston. When Bell had heatedly inquired about that – why, for God's sake, hadn't they loaded Nick into a helicopter first thing and taken him to a better-equipped place? – Sheriff Harrison explained: They'd needed to get Nick into surgery right away. No time for a helicopter ride high over the mountains.

Bell looked around at the tan-painted walls, the tan-tiled floor. Everything neat, everything clean and bright. Swabbed nightly with a mop. Waxed to a shine. Nothing could be allowed to accumulate. Not germs, God knows, but not emotions, either, because the emotions would be dangerous, combustible. How many people had waited here just as they were waiting here now, filled with questions and dread? Bell envisioned the grief of all of those people over the years, people like the boy and his grandmother, thousands of them, their grief for a sick loved one widening and intensifying, until the hall finally was so crowded that you couldn't move, you couldn't raise a hand, you couldn't breathe. The emotions had to be cleaned out regularly, too, she thought, so that new grief could have its turn.

This hall, and the ICU unit to which it was attached, were familiar to her. Too familiar. Many times, her cases had brought her here; she needed a dying declaration from a witness or defendant. She had visited Clay here, after he'd lost his leg. And six months ago, she had spent a long night here with a young woman who had been assaulted and who was struggling to unearth the secret of her family's history.

A cell rang. It was Mary Sue's. She answered. They watched her. 'No, I'm afraid not,' she said. 'Yes. Yes, I appreciate that. Yes. Yes, thank you. I certainly will.' Mary Sue hung up, and it was all Bell and the others could do – politeness and decorum barely restraining them – not to fling themselves at her and demand to know the content of the call. Was it news about Nick?

'That was Bud Wright,' Mary Sue said. 'He owns the Highway Haven chain. He's called several times already, wanting updates. He's offered to do whatever he can. Organize blood donations from employees – anything. He's a good man.'

Blood donations. *Damn,* Bell thought. Hadn't even occurred to her. She'd been too preoccupied.

'Was Nick conscious when they got him here?' Carlene asked. She didn't look at anyone in particular. She'd take an answer from any source.

Mary Sue shook her head. 'No,' she said.

The elevator dinged again and the door opened, disgorging more people into the hallway. They were here for Nick. Some, like Bell, had had to wait until their workdays were over before they were free to come to the hospital. Others had just heard. There'd been a lull of several hours, while word spread throughout the town, but now the news was everywhere, an unstoppable force. Bell offered grim nods of greeting to Lee Ann Frickie, Rhonda Lovejoy, Sammy Burdette, and Sammy's sister, Dot Burdette. A few minutes later the elevator arrived once again, bearing another load.

Some of these people, Bell knew and spoke to; others she didn't know, and didn't speak to. They simply exchanged looks of mutual incomprehension: This could not have happened. Not to Nick Fogelsong. He was – that is, he had been for many years – a public man, a man everyone recognized. He was part of the dense everyday weave of life in Acker's Gap. He would always be here. Nothing serious could ever happen to him. And yet somehow it had.

Sheriff Harrison looked at Bell. Her eyes were sheathed, unreadable to most people, but Bell understood. They moved to a place down the hall, away from the others, to speak in private.

'I know how you're feeling right now – how we're all feeling,' Harrison said. 'But I wanted to ask about the trial. Had to leave the courthouse early. Big pileup out on Route 6. Nobody hurt bad, but a real mess.'

'We'll have the jury seated by tomorrow. Next day at the latest. Judge Barbour's an efficient man.'

Harrison nodded. For a moment, neither she nor Bell said anything; rising up behind them were the low-pitched conversations of the others, now gathered in groups of two or three. The concern in their voices, the hum of muffled shock, transcended specific words.

'I had just talked to Nick,' Harrison said. 'Yesterday.' Bell didn't respond, so she went on. 'He said he'd made a mistake. A bad mistake.'

'What did he mean?'

'Quitting as sheriff. It was too soon, he said.'

Bell had no reply. All beside the point now.

The sheriff settled her hat back on her head. She felt uncomfortable when it wasn't in place. Bell sensed that. Already, the outward signifiers of the position – the hat, the boots, the belt – were synchronizing themselves with the inward part, the part that was working its way

Julia Keller

into Pam Harrison's soul. *You'll never have another good night's sleep,* Bell wanted to say to her. *You know that, right? Not with that job of yours. Might as well wear the uniform to bed. Save you the trouble of getting dressed in the dark when you're called out at all hours.* Bell had seen what it had done to Nick Fogelsong. She knew the job could swallow you whole.

But she also knew how much he'd loved it. Could you hate a thing and also love it at the same time? Despise it and crave it, with equal passion and ferocity? Of course you could.

'He told me he wanted to help,' Harrison went on. 'Maybe be a deputy himself again. That's how he started out, you know. As a deputy. Worked under Larry Rucker. Then Rucker had his heart attack and died so sudden-like and—' Harrison wouldn't finish the sentence out loud. It was too close an echo of what seemed to be happening here, right in front of them, in real time: the death of one sheriff, making way for another.

And yet: No. That wasn't the current situation at all, Bell reminded herself. Nick Fogelsong had given up his job voluntarily. *And he's not dead,* she thought, suddenly furious with everything and everyone. *He's not dead. I would know that. I'd feel it. If Nick was dead, I would know it in my bones – and I don't. I don't know any such thing.*

'Be a deputy again?' she said. 'Really?'

The sheriff frowned, as if Bell had strayed off topic, or hadn't understood her in the first place. 'He's been struggling. I think he was just throwing some ideas out there. Brainstorming. Trying to find a way to – well, to get some meaning back in his life, maybe. To anchor it.'

Harrison didn't know where to look, after uttering a

remark that was so wholly out of character for her, and her gaze dropped down to her boots. Bell looked down, too. The boots were black and shiny. Bell had always wondered if Harrison touched them up during the day. Just a quick rub, maybe, with the tip of a rag dipped in black polish, when she was alone in her office. A secret vanity. Everybody had one. How else was she able to keep her boots looking like that, when she spent her days slogging through mud and kicking open trailer doors?

Harrison was talking again. 'I wish you could've heard him. When he told me about being on the outside. He wanted to live a different kind of life – that's why he didn't run for reelection – but I think he found out real quick that being sheriff *was* his life. A good part of it, anyway. More than he'd reckoned.' Once again she looked away from Bell, but this time it was to send her eyes around the hallway, the long, antiseptic-looking space interrupted here and there by knots of nervous people. 'I know you were plenty ticked off when he didn't tell you about his decision,' Harrison said. 'Never even filed the papers. But you know what? He didn't tell his wife, either.'

Another surprise. 'Are you—'

'Yeah, I'm sure. She came to me about it. She was pretty darned mad. He waited until after the deadline and then he told her.' The sheriff shook her head. It struck Bell that she knew nothing about Pam Harrison's personal life. She wasn't married, but had she ever been? Was she in a relationship? Male, female – Bell didn't know. She hadn't asked. Lives in small towns could be like parallel lines: close, but never touching.

'He said he was doing it for her sake,' Harrison said,

her words running over the top of Bell's thoughts. 'So he'd be home more often. And you know what she told him? She said, "If I need you to make sacrifices for me, mister, I'll ask. Otherwise, you can take off that martyr's robe of yours and you can dust the damned furniture with it, for all I care." She's a feisty one, that Mary Sue.'

Bell let the information settle in her mind. 'What did you tell him about coming back?' she finally asked.

'That I'd think about it.' A pause. 'Never had a chance to give him a final answer.'

The same thought seemed to come to both of them at roughly the same time. They had other duties, too, matters they ought to get back to.

'Best guess about the length of the trial?' Harrison said.

'Couple of weeks, tops. Serena can't refute the physical evidence. I don't know if she intends to put Dillard on the stand, but if she does, he won't help himself any.'

'It'll be good to have things wrapped up,' the sheriff said. 'You think he'll appeal?'

Harrison was taking a conviction for granted. 'No telling,' Bell said, wishing she could be as certain about things as Pam Harrison was. *Maybe if I shine my shoes more often. Maybe that'll do it.*

A few minutes later a short, heavyset woman in a white lab coat and dark baggy slacks appeared in the corridor. Her hair was pulled into a tight bun. There was a preoccupied look to her sharp blue eyes, and as she gradually took in the reality of just how many people were standing in the hallway, she seemed a little taken aback by the sheer volume of humanity in residence here. 'Mrs Fogelsong?' she said to the air, hoping that one of these women was the correct one.

'I'm here.' Mary Sue stepped forward.

'I'd like to speak with you, please. I'm Dr Allison. The cardiothoracic surgeon who operated on your husband. Are there any other family members present?'

Someone took hold of Carlene's arm and drew her forward, the crowd parting automatically to enable her to join Mary Sue and the surgeon. All conversation had stopped, and the atmosphere was as tense and strained as a held breath.

'There's a private room around the corner,' Allison said. 'I think it's best if we go there.'

The three of them – Allison, Mary Sue, and Carlene – headed down the hall. Before they rounded the corner, Mary Sue looked back for half a second. She sought and found Bell's eyes.

Her expression echoed the very elements prominent in Bell's mind as well: dread, fear, and a solemn realization that in the next minute or so, depending on what the surgeon said, all of their futures would be changed forevermore. Nick's was not the only life that hung in the balance.

26

He was alive. And he was pissed off, too, which in Nick Fogelsong's case was redundant.

Still woozy from surgery, he tried to sit up. The nurse, a muscular man in sea green scrubs and sturdy black Rockports, restrained him by propping two fingers against his shoulder. That surprised Bell, who was watching from the foot of the bed. It showed how weak he was.

'Lemme up,' Nick said, his words gravelly and slurred as they slowly clambered up through a haze of anesthesia that was dissipating only slowly, like tissue paper in water. 'Gotta go, gotta—'

'You don't have to do anything, Mr Fogelsong, except lie back and get better,' the nurse said. He was clean-shaven but the shadow on his jaw was blue-black, a heavy beard held in abeyance, eager to spring. His words were kind but his tone was not; he'd dealt with patients such as Nick Fogelsong before, Bell surmised, and he understood that politeness got you nowhere. His name tag said his name was Bobby Lee Lustig. The room's bright lights reflected off his shiny shaved head, the way sunlight glints off a chrome fender.

Nick tried to raise his left arm, the one less laden

with bandages, and he gurgled something incomprehensible but most likely profane. Cocooned in thick gauze and IV lines and wires, wires that led to a console of chirping machinery behind him, he looked like a grumpy mummy who'd been awakened and dragged from the tomb about a millennium too soon.

Bell stood next to Mary Sue. They had been here since their conversation with Dr Allison some six hours ago. Nick had stirred and shouted in his sleep, and moaned and tried to kick off his blankets, but it was not until now – almost midnight, Bell noted with a quick glance at her wristwatch – that he really seemed to be waking up. To be coming back to them.

'Nick,' Mary Sue said. 'I'm here. Bell's here, too. Carlene was here for a long time but she had to go pick up her kids.'

At 5 P.M., Bell had texted Ben Fawcett and asked him to take Goldie over to his house for the night, if his mother agreed; she had realized that she might very well need to be here for a very long time. She kept a change of clothes in her office at the courthouse. If she had to, she could go right from here to the courtroom in the morning.

Nick gurgled something else, equally incomprehensible but softer this time. Not combative. Lustig checked several of the monitors behind the bed, adjusted the rate of the IV drip, and then looked down at his patient with an expression that mingled authority with pity. Of the two men in this room, one was upright and in command, and the other prone and helpless, weak and needy; you could call what you saw in Lustig's eyes 'concern,' but it was pity. Nick would hate that, Bell knew, but he was in no position right now to tell Lustig where he could shove his damned pity.

'Okay, Mr Fogelsong,' Lustig said. 'I'm going to let you visit with your family now. But don't cause any trouble, okay? You need to take it easy. You just had major surgery. Promise me you'll rest and I'll let them stay a while. Do we have a deal?'

Nick blinked, which was good enough for Lustig. He nodded to Mary Sue on his way out. 'You all can stay for a little while longer, ma'am,' he said, 'but after that he really needs his sleep. He's still pretty fragile.'

Bell let Mary Sue go to him first. She wanted to be here, but there was an awkwardness about it, too; she wasn't family, no matter what the nurse believed. Right before they went in, Bell had murmured her uncertainty to Mary Sue – *Technically, I'm not a blood relative, and so maybe I'd better not* – but Mary Sue had cut her off: 'You sure as hell are. Now, come on.'

Mary Sue leaned over the rail. 'Nick,' she said. 'Nick.' She was afraid to touch him, and so she stroked him with her words. 'I love you. I love you.'

He moved his lips. They were glued together with dried phlegm. He'd broken the seal once but now it had re-formed.

'Did—' Frustrated, he fought to speak, the effort visible on his face. 'Did—'

'Take your time,' Mary Sue said.

He closed his eyes and frowned. He struggled to make his mouth do what he wanted it to do. 'Did—' Again. 'Did—' His face was turning slightly reddish purple from the push, the fierce desire to communicate, but Bell knew better than to tell him to take it easy. 'Did they—' He clenched his teeth in fury. He was attempting to make a hard 'K' sound, but his tongue kept getting in the way. His tongue, the fuzziness in his brain, his goddamned body – which had turned on him, mocking him. His enemy now.

He tried again. And this time, with tremendous effort, in a rush of mushed-together syllables that perhaps only the people who knew him best would be able to interpret, he finally got it out: 'Did they – c-c-catch the b-b-bastard?'

He had come very, very close to dying. So close that when Dr Allison had tried to describe to them the distance between a dead Nick Fogelsong and a living one, and she lifted her thumb and her forefinger to do so, the visual was less than clarifying; Bell couldn't make out any space between the digits. It looked as if she were pinching her fingers shut.

That close. The line was no line at all.

The .22-caliber bullet had penetrated the upper chamber of Nick's heart, storming into the left atrium. The ER doctor, the surgeon explained, had wedged a finger in the wound in the heart to stymie the bleeding while the trauma team prepped him for the long and complicated surgery that ensued. Yes, it sounded so amateurish, so makeshift, Dr Allison acknowledged, seeing their faces, like a desperate strategy that might have been used on a Civil War battlefield – but it worked. Bell could imagine Nick's reaction to the description of how he'd been saved: *Hell. Why didn't they just patch up my heart with duct tape, while they were at it?*

'Fair to say,' Dr Allison had added, looking at Mary Sue, 'that your husband is a lucky man.'

Luck. The thing you couldn't believe in – until it went your way, Bell thought, and after that it was the most powerful force in the universe.

And then the doctor told them what Nick faced. Her voice was matter-of-fact, not cheerful or reassuring. It wasn't her job to be reassuring. Nick was fifty-five years old. His wound had very nearly been lethal. He faced long months of rehabilitation, hard labor, the likes of which he'd never known before. He would develop an intimate relationship with pain, and exasperation, and the suffocating despair that always comes in the wake of serious injury: Everything was different now. The extent of his recovery would depend upon his appetite for work, and his attitude. And his patience.

'Patience,' Mary Sue had repeated back to the surgeon.

'Yes. He won't be able to do the things that he used to do – and for some people, that's hard to accept.'

'If you knew Nick Fogelsong,' Mary Sue said, 'then you'd know that a better word would be "impossible."'

Nick was in pain. He didn't complain about it, he didn't moan or flinch, but Bell could tell, and she was sure Mary Sue could tell, too. The anesthesia was almost gone now. It was like a sheet whisked off a piece of Victorian furniture, revealing the ornate monstrosity that waited under the white cover. The pain had been there all along, but medication kept it hidden, kept its twisted menace out of sight. A tug on the sheet – and here it was. The nurse came in and out at regular intervals, offering painkillers; Nick, though, would fib about his level of distress and grunt no. The moment Lustig left, Nick tightened his jaw and closed his eyes. Sweat slickened his brow. As the anesthesia inched away, polite and courtly in its retreat, the pain came roaring forward, crazy and despotic. Nick dozed, jerked awake, and then dozed again.

It was almost 3 A.M. No windows in the ICU, which gave the place a sealed-off feel, a sense of being suspended above the fuss and jumble of the world, a snug little island. Here, everything was slow and deliberate and purposeful. Nothing extraneous, nothing but what was needed.

If she looked too long at Nick, Bell felt that she could almost hear the blood hurtling through his veins, valiantly trying to replenish itself after this confusing interruption, and she also felt she could hear the hectic effort of his heart, appalled at this turn of events. Her daughter – thank goodness – had never been seriously ill, but when she was twelve years old she had tumbled out of the big silver maple in their backyard. The surgery to repair her broken arm was complex, which meant a night in the hospital, and Bell had had the same strange feeling back then: Looking at her sleeping child in the middle of the night, she was sure she could see right through the cast and the skin and then on into the interior of the body itself, a body shocked by its wound but now recovering, and she imagined that she could actually watch the delicate infrastructure taking care of itself, sending out fresh new green shoots, branching out, healing the breaches.

Mary Sue dozed in a chair on one side of the bed, her head tucked sideways, her hands loose on her lap. Bell, wide awake, was in a chair on the other side. She watched Mary Sue for a while, struck by the vulnerability of a sleeping person. Mouth slack, consciousness in shards, shields down. How much we have to trust the world, Bell reflected, to get any rest at all. If you thought about it too long, you'd never go to sleep again.

Nick stirred, moaned. Mary Sue's eyes opened.

'What is it?' Mary Sue asked him, leaning forward, touching the rail.

'Just thinking,' he said. His voice was marginally clearer now, but the effort to speak still was arduous. Every word cost him. Yet they knew better than to ask him to stop. 'Thirty years as sheriff and not so much as a hangnail,' he muttered. 'Coupla months at the Highway Haven and I'm shot like a dog.'

There was nothing to say to that, not really, no words of consolation that would mitigate the perverse accuracy of his observation.

Bell held the water glass up for him to see. Did he want any? He blinked, his mouth a tight line. No, he didn't. But he wanted to say something to her, and so he kept his bleary gaze aimed in her direction.

'Belfa,' he said. 'You need to get the hell out of here.'

For a moment she thought he meant Acker's Gap. She thought he was telling her to return to DC, to leave this place with all of its sorrows and its contradictions and its endless bad luck. But then she realized – just in time, just before she upbraided him for meddling in her life, a sin from which not even the fact that he'd almost died could excuse him – that he meant the hospital. He meant she needed to go home. To get ready for Day Two of Royce Dillard's trial, which would begin again in – she'd just checked her watch – less than six hours. After what he'd been through, though, how the hell did he remember the fact that there was a trial going on? It was, Bell supposed, part of the mystery of Nick Fogelsong. And tied up somehow with his affection for this place.

'Town's pretty wrought up,' he mumbled. 'Biggest trial around here in ages. You gotta be sharp. Gotta get to the bottom of things.'

'I'm okay,' she said. 'I'll leave in a minute. Can't believe they haven't thrown me out already.'

She thought he had drifted off to sleep again, but he hadn't; he had just closed his eyes to regather his strength. Now he opened them.

'Pam told you, didn't she?'

'Told me what?'

Nick frowned. She wasn't really confused about his meaning, and they both knew it. Her coyness was a disappointment to him. But she had her reasons. *My God, Nick,* Bell thought, *do you really want to talk about this now?* In a hospital room in the middle of the night, with him groggy and gurgling and wrapped up like something you'd find under the Christmas tree – minus the bow – and her so weary that she could barely keep from oozing out of her chair and landing in a heap on the floor?

Yes, his eyes said. He did.

'Okay,' Bell said. 'Yeah, she told me. About you wanting to come back.' She looked over at Mary Sue, to see if Nick's wife wanted to be part of the conversation.

Mary Sue was silent. *This is between you and Nick right now.* That was how Bell interpreted her expression.

'Hell of it is,' he said, 'doesn't matter anymore. By the time I'm back on my feet from this – they tell me it's going to be a long, long road, and the way I feel right now, I sure believe it – I'll be too damned old. Too broken-down. Can't ever be sheriff again. Not even a goddamned deputy.'

Bell didn't argue. Because he was right.

The silence went on for a while. It was not real silence. The mechanical voices – the beeps and the rhythmic swishes, the ones that sounded like a lonely person sweeping a sidewalk at dusk, going back and forth, back and forth – never ceased. Only the human voices had taken a respite.

Bell was startled when Nick spoke. Once again she thought he had dropped off to sleep, and her plan was to slip out in a minute or two, with a nod to Mary Sue.

'Don't wait too long to do what you want to do, Belfa,' he said. His voice was dark. A sadness seemed to move around inside it, like something caught in a box, and that something was still feeling the walls, getting a sense of the size of the prison. He had to take a break between sentences, recover his breath, but he was able to finish his thought. 'If you want to do something, for God's sake – do it. Don't hold off. Do it now. You never know what dirty tricks are coming down the road. Ready to trip you up.'

Dirty tricks. That was Nick Fogelsong's name for fate. Yes, there were fancier names. More sophisticated ways to refer to destiny. Still, she'd stick with Nick's phrase: dirty tricks. The little twists and kinks and false bottoms. The ironies and double crosses.

She started to answer, but then realized he'd fallen asleep for real this time.

27

When Bell was thirteen years old, she sneaked in the back of a courtroom while a trial was in session. Her foster mother had come to the Raythune County Courthouse on business and Bell accompanied her, even though it was a school day; the woman, whose name was Georgette Slattery, never really cared if Bell went to school or not. She never really cared, frankly, what Bell did or didn't do, at any time. Slattery went off to find the office she needed and Bell roamed the long, echoing hallways. She came across a thick set of double doors and paused to tug casually on one of the big brass knobs, with every expectation that it would be locked up tight as tick, when – Holy crap! – it *actually opened*, and she pulled it back slowly, slowly, so that it wouldn't creak or squeak, and then she slipped in. She felt like a dirty piece of paper sliding into a fancy white envelope.

The courtroom was big and cold and ornate. Around the top of the walls ran a thin strip of wood with intricate repeated carving; it was the loveliest thing Bell had ever seen. Arranged in symmetrical lines across the wooden floor were six rows of wooden benches, divided in half, with a long aisle in the middle, just like in a church. The floor was dark, thick wood, like the wood you'd expect to find on the deck of a ship.

She crept into the very back row on the right-hand side. No one had seen her come in. She was sure of it. There weren't many spectators, anyway, just two old ladies, one old man, and a younger lady. No kids. The windows along the wall were stacked squares of cold sunlight. Below the windows, two radiators hissed and coughed. Up front was a high wooden stand, and behind it was visible the top half a very old, very bald man. The black robe in which his shoulders were swaddled made the shiny white knob of his head look definitely odd, like a pus-filled boil that had erupted from the moist pleated interior of that robe. Two men in dark suits stood in front of the judge. She couldn't hear what they were saying.

Bell had then felt a hard hand clamp her upper arm. A frowning, pink-faced sheriff's deputy stood over her. Brown shirt, brown trousers, black boots. Little pink ball of a chin. His eyebrows dove together, indicating an excessive amount of displeasure in discovering her there. He jerked his head. She correctly interpreted the head-jerk to be his preferred shorthand: *Come with me.* She stood up. Allowed him to haul her roughly back out the big double doors. Once they were in the hall, he said, *Get lost, kid. You got no business here.* She obliged him. Not because she feared authority – in fact, her experiences in foster homes had made her realize that most of the people in the world invested with authority are frauds and liars and hypocrites, including, but not limited to, the people who wanted her to call them 'Mommy' and 'Daddy' – but because it was probably time to meet Georgette Slattery in the lobby. She couldn't be late. Not if she knew what was good for her. Bell turned back only once as she walked away. The deputy was watching her to make sure she didn't sneak into another room. She had to ask him a question. He'd seen that magnificent space, too, with the carved strip around the ceiling and the high windows. *Hey, mister,* she said. *Isn't it beautiful?*

She still remembered the moment, all these years later, especially when she argued a case in the very same courtroom, as she was doing this morning. It was the beginning of the second week of the murder trial of Royce Dillard.

Beautiful?

Well, no. It was well shy of beautiful. But the thing that had impressed her then – how like a church it was, with old wooden pews and a center aisle and a raised pulpit and a kind of gathered reverence for words – impressed her still.

Bell stood behind the table designated for the prosecution. Stacked and handy on that table were the yellow legal pads containing her notes for the day. Rhonda Lovejoy sat in the second chair. She wore a white wool pantsuit and white heels.

'State your full name for the record, sir,' Bell said.

'Rusty Blevins.' The old man added a *So there* head-bobble at the end. He gripped the front of the witness box with his gnarled hands, hands that were now paying the price for a bricklaying career that had lasted more than half a century. He was stooped, and his bony shoulders jutted up so high they could've doubled as earmuffs. Pink tufts of hair sprouted up here and there across his pale crusty scalp. The pink had once been red, hence the nickname he'd borne since toddlerhood.

'Your full name, please,' Bell said.

'What're you getting at?' he rasped back at her, pulling himself even farther forward in the wooden box, suspecting a ruse.

'The name on your birth certificate,' she clarified.

'Oh. Gotcha. Okay, well, it's William Barnard Blevins Junior.' The head-bobble again. 'Always been just "Rusty," though.' He scooted back in his chair, but still gripped the front of the box, twisted fingers hanging over the edge.

'Thank you, Mr Blevins.' In her right hand, Bell held a pencil by its sharpened tip. She softly beat the palm of her left hand with the eraser end. 'Please tell the court what you witnessed at approximately two thirty P.M. on Thursday, February nineteenth, in front of Lymon's Market.'

'Well, ma'am, I was just coming out of the store. Picked me up a little something for lunch, is what I did. Some sliced bologna and saltine crackers. I was leaning on the newspaper box, same as I always do, talking to some folks that were just going in – Fred Larson and Beanie Larson, his boy.' Blevins looked concerned. 'Well, I oughta come clean here, since you made such a point of it. Beanie's not really Beanie – no more than I'm really Rusty. I mean, his given name is Eldred. But folks've been calling him Beanie since he was a little kid. I believe it has something to do with a can of kidney beans and this habit he had of jamming them up his nose. He's grown out of it now. But the name stuck.' Blevins snickered. 'Good thing the beans didn't, am I right?'

Bell nodded. She was so focused on her questioning that she didn't realize he'd made a joke until several spectators chuckled softly. Blevins waggled his head; he was enjoying his moment in the sun.

The trial was now fully under way. Opening statements and jury selection had taken up the first week, and several motions filed by Serena Crumpler had required another three days for the judge to sort out and rule upon. Then Bell had begun her presentation of the county's case. She expected to wrap up her side of things quickly. The forensic evidence was solid and unassailable, and her job was simply to lay out the narrative that would turn the science into a story: the story of how Royce Dillard had lured Edward Hackel out to his property for the express purpose of murdering him, and had done so via a series of blows to the back of the neck with the sharp edge of a shovel, and then transported the body down to the creek bed with the help of a small wagon.

At noon each day or thereabouts, when Judge Barbour sonorously announced the lunch recess, Bell drove out to the Raythune County Medical Center for a quick visit with Nick and Mary Sue. There had been a setback. Two days after his surgery, Nick suffered a slight stroke when a flake of plaque from a vessel near his heart broke off and blocked the blood flow. The numbness in his right arm – likely permanent – meant he would henceforth not be able to handle firearms. Any lingering dreams he might have secretly harbored of returning to a job in law enforcement were now officially over. They should have been over before – he'd said as much to Bell – but she knew Nick Fogelsong, and knew that what he said out loud and what he planned in the privacy of his thoughts were often two very different things. She knew what a blow this was. She also knew he likely wouldn't want to talk about it. She was correct.

In the evenings, when the long day in court was over, Bell would go home to feed and walk Goldie. Then she returned to the hospital. She'd bring Mary Sue a takeout dinner from JP's – fried chicken or beef stew or country-fried steak or a round carton of soup – and the three of them would sit in Nick's room, now located on a regular floor and not in the ICU, which meant there was a window. Even through the darkening scrim of dusk, you could look out that window and see the faint, fading outline of the mountains in the distance. If you had lived here long enough, as the three of them had, you knew what spring was doing to those mountains: persuading them, with a quiet whisper, to shed the gray and the black in favor of green. Bell liked to think of the healing of Nick's body the same way. So much was invisible now, so much was happening under the surface, prodded by a secret clock, like bare branches poised to leap into flower.

And so the three of them sat there, night after night, with little conversation, Nick dozing after a punishing day of physical therapy. Bell would open her briefcase and prepare for the next day's court session, legs crossed, yellow legal pad balanced on her knee, pen busy, and Mary Sue read or slept, and that was how they passed the time.

Rusty Blevins ran his tongue along the inside of his mouth, giving each cheek its due. It was what he did when he was thinking. Bell had asked him how often he'd seen Royce Dillard in town.

'Not too common a sight, grant you that,' he said.

'Once a month?'

'Oh, no. Nothing like that. Maybe every two, three months.' He paused, scrunching up his wrinkled face, double-checking the memory, and then he nodded, having confirmed his recollection. 'Yep. That's about it. You'd see him at the post office, maybe, then over to Lymon's, or vicey-versy. He had a lot of dog food to haul back, so he had this little wagon. Needed some grease on them axles. You'd hear him coming before you saw him. Just squeaking along. But not too often. Like I said – three or four times a year, is all.'

'And you saw him on Thursday, February nineteenth, is that correct?'

'Oh, yes, ma'am.'

'Outside Lymon's Market.'

'Yes, ma'am.'

'Was he going in or coming out?'

'Coming out, ma'am. That little wagon of his was piled yea high with sacks of dog food.' Blevins unhooked a crooked hand from the front of the box and indicated a height close to his shoulder. Then he reasserted his grip, leaning even farther forward. 'I'd seen him earlier that day at the post office, too. Checking his box.'

'Did you speak to him either time – at the post office or at Lymon's?'

'Tried to. He ain't what you'd call overly friendly. Never has been.' Blevins looked over at the defense table, attempting to give Dillard a sickly smile, an intention thwarted by the fact Dillard was staring at one of the radiators. 'Sorry, Royce. I'm under oath,' Blevins said.

Judge Barbour's intervention was swift. 'Mrs Elkins, please instruct your witness to refrain from addressing the defendant.'

'Yes, Your Honor.' Bell set down the pencil on the prosecutor's table, lining it up so that its yellow length was parallel to the edge. 'Mr Blevins, you need to direct your answers to me, not to Mr Dillard.' She allowed herself a quick sideways glimpse at Dillard, to see his reaction to all of this – not just to Blevins's remark, but to the trial itself. She'd had few opportunities to watch him, gauge his mood. It had been her professional duty to argue against bail – with no family, no job, no one to vouch for him, he was a classic flight risk – but she worried that it would be almost unbearable for him, locked up in a jail cell, away from his cabin, his land, and most especially, his dogs. A few years ago she'd prosecuted a man who was a lot like Royce Dillard, a scribble-haired, scraggly bearded recluse who lived off the land up in the mountains, and who could barely form words after so many years of not needing them. He was accused of arson; he'd left a campfire burning and the wildfire had consumed fifteen acres. But before the preliminary testimony was over, Deputy Mathers had found the man hanging in his cell by a bedsheet.

When you're used to seeing the sky over your head every day, Bell thought, it must be difficult to ratchet down your expectations to the sliver of it that could be seen through the window of a jail cell. That's why she was concerned about Royce Dillard.

He looked fairly placid, however, seated next to Serena Crumpler, hands clasped on top of the table, feet flat on the floor, head down. The only slight indication of any nervousness was a faint shimmy of the table, caused by the vibration of his legs. Otherwise, it seemed as if he'd granted himself an excused absence. His body was here, all right, but that was the extent of it. His mind was somewhere else. Probably off with Goldie, Bell guessed; in his imagination the two of them were surely roving across the countryside, thrashing happily through the brown leaves, jumping over fallen logs.

'Mr Blevins,' she said. 'You provided the sheriff's office with a video recording made with your cell phone, is that correct?'

'Sure did.'

'And when and where was this recording made?'

'February nineteenth, ma'am, right there in front of Lymon's Market. Along about half past two. When things started to get interesting I just pulled out my cell phone – my granddaughter's the one who got it for me, because she says everybody needs one these days, it's not optional anymore – and I pushed the button.'

'What do you mean by "interesting," Mr Blevins?'

He grinned. 'Well, old Royce over there was shouting at the man who'd been hanging around town ever since they started up with that resort. Hackel. Ed Hackel. Great big fella. Talked to him a few times myself. No matter what you said to him – Hackel, I mean – he always brought the conversation back to that big ole place they wanna build. Fella had one thing on his mind and one thing only.' The grin had gone away by this time, as Blevins seemed to remember the seriousness of what was being discussed here. 'So Royce was yelling and Hackel gave it right back to him, giving just as good as he got. And then Royce said—'

'Objection, Your Honor,' Serena said. She had jumped up, quick as a jack-in-the-box. 'Hearsay.'

'We'll be introducing the cell phone video shortly,' countered Bell. 'It's already been admitted into evidence.

Julia Keller

The jury will be able to hear the conversation that Mr Blevins is describing. I simply wanted to set the scene.'

One of Barbour's nicknames – each judge had about half a dozen – was Judge Snap Judgment, and he demonstrated why.

'Sustained,' he said without hesitation. 'Let's let the jury see the video, Mrs Elkins, and they can make up their own minds about what's going on in it. Don't think we need the subtitles.'

A TV set on a rolling cart had been brought in that morning and set up next to the witness box. Bell gestured toward it. Then she turned to Judge Barbour's bailiff, who was ready with her MacBook.

'Jessica, please run the video.'

The screen came alive. Two men faced off on a sidewalk. One was Royce Dillard. The other was Edward Hackel. Behind them was the dirty salmon-colored brick of Lymon's Market. The shaky recording was hard to watch; the picture jumped around, tilting first one way and then the other, like a flimsy ship in a bad storm, and the sound consisted of muffled squawks, punctuated by the occasional comprehensible sentence rising above the scramble: *Say that one more time, you dirty sonofabitch, and I'll kill you – swear I will.* The person yelling the threat was Royce Dillard. There was a bout of back-and-forth shoving between the two men, and then Dillard left the frame. He returned a second later, a wicked-looking object in his two-handed grip – a tire iron, maybe. It wasn't clear. He took a wild swing at Hackel's head. Hackel ducked. There was a scream from the crowd, and a scattering of squeals, and then the picture dissolved in a bleary smear of people and general agitation.

Bell waited a few seconds, to let the jury absorb what they had just watched.

'Thank you, Jessica,' she said to the bailiff. She turned back to Blevins, who had watched the screen with avid concentration, right along with everyone else, leaning so far forward in the witness box that he looked as if he might tumble over the front partition.

'Mr Blevins,' Bell said, 'is that the footage you shot on your cell on February nineteenth of this year?'

'Yes, ma'am.'

'And who were the combatants in that altercation?'

'Pardon?'

'Who was fighting?'

'Oh. Okay, well, it was Royce Dillard and that Hackel fella.'

'Will you point to the man who was fighting with Mr Hackel?'

Blevins pointed to Dillard. Dillard had no reaction. His hands remained locked together on the tabletop. His eyes watched his hands.

'Let the record show,' Bell said, 'that the witness identified the defendant, Royce Dillard.' She picked up her pencil again, and once again tapped her left palm with the eraser end. 'Mr Blevins, do you have any idea why Mr Dillard was so angry at Mr Hackel – the man who later turned up dead in a creek on Mr Dillard's property?'

Serena was up in a flash. 'Calls for speculation, Your Honor.'

'And so it does,' Judge Barbour declared. 'Mrs Elkins, your witness is welcome to his views on the possible motivations of the defendant. However, they won't be a part of these proceedings. Move on.'

*   *   *

Serena declined to cross-examine Rusty Blevins, much to his disappointment. He sank back in his seat in the witness box, already feeling the chill as the spotlight swung away from him. Before he climbed down, Serena reserved the right to call him later – her request put a bit of the gleam back in the old man's eye – and then the county's case marched forward.

Bell spent the rest of the day presenting the physical evidence. She called to the stand Wallace Barr, a forensic specialist from the state police crime lab in Charleston. He testified that the blood on the shovel found in Dillard's barn had been Hackel's, and that, after matching the shovel edge to the shape of the victim's wounds, they could say with a high degree of certainty that the shovel was the murder weapon. Barr then explained the hair and fiber evidence found inside Dillard's wagon, following that up with the soil analysis proving that the mud clinging to the wheels had most likely emanated from the bank of Old Man's Creek. Dirt and debris on the bottom of Hackel's shoes, he added, had come from the area in front of Dillard's barn. The preponderance of the evidence indicated that Hackel had been struck and killed in or near the barn early Thursday evening, then placed in the wagon and hauled to the creek for disposal, like an oversized sack of trash.

28

The next morning Bell called Deputy Jake Oakes to the stand. He left his hat on his seat and ambled slowly up to the front of the courtroom. After taking the oath, he sat down and made himself comfortable in the witness box. And then he winked at her.

'Your full name,' Bell asked him, her voice formal and cold, even though he was her witness.

'Jake Oakes.'

'I said *full* name, please. Including middle.'

'That's it. Jake Oakes. Don't have a middle name.'

'Really.'

'Nope. Neither did Harry Truman.' He grinned at her.

'So – is it Jacob Oakes?'

'Just Jake. My folks didn't have very high ambitions for me, I guess. Figured plain old Jake would do me fine.'

She heard Judge Barbour clear his throat, a sure sign that he, too, was now officially perturbed.

'What is your profession?' she asked him.

'I'm a deputy in the Raythune County Sheriff's Department.'

'And how did you come to be involved in the investigation of the death of Edward Hackel?'

Oakes sat up straighter now, the smile gone. 'On Saturday, February twenty-first, at 11:07 A.M.,' he said, 'the 911 operator received a call from a man who identified himself as Andy Stegner. Caller reported finding a body in Old Man's Creek. Said the property belonged to his neighbor, Royce Dillard. Deputy Mathers and I were assigned to go check it out.'

'What did you find?'

'We hiked about a mile or so from the hard road until we reached the creek. After moving along the bank for a while, we came across a dead body. It was covered with a brown tweed overcoat. Later identification proved it to be the body of Edward Hackel.'

'What did you do next?'

'We called the state crime lab from the scene and waited for their arrival, to make sure it was undisturbed. Once they got there, we went up to Dillard's cabin to ask him some questions. He already knew about the body. Mr Stegner had filled him in on what he'd found.'

'Did you and your colleague consider Mr Dillard a suspect at this time?'

'No.'

'But you read him his rights.'

'We did. As a precaution.'

'What was his reaction?'

'Well, he said he didn't know how the body had gotten there or who it might be. At that point we requested his presence at the courthouse, to give us more details, but he was under no obligation to comply. He came voluntarily. Rode in with Deputy Mathers and me.'

'Very well,' she said. 'Later that day you were able to obtain a search warrant for Mr Dillard's property, were you not?'

'Yes, ma'am.'

'Can you tell the court what you found during the execution of that lawful search?'

'I found a shovel. Appeared to be covered with blood.'

'Where did you find it?'

'In the defendant's barn. I set aside several objects that were in plain view and then I saw the shovel, leaning against the back wall of the barn. I bagged it for analysis. Arranged for its transport to the state crime lab. Chain of custody was observed throughout. The shovel was later determined to be the weapon that killed Edward Hackel.'

'Did you see anything else in the barn relevant to this case?'

The puckish side of Jake Oakes returned, if only for a moment. 'Well, ma'am, there were three big dogs. One of them – according to what Andy Stegner told us – was the one that actually found the body. But she refused comment. I can only assume she was following the advice of counsel.'

A stir of chuckles swept across the jury box. They liked Jake Oakes. Bell could see that. This was a grim business, and the deputy was a good leavening agent, his personality a nice way to temporarily balance out the darkness.

'Anything other than the shovel and the dogs?' she said. 'Perhaps later. During a second search.'

'Yes, ma'am,' Oakes said. The levity left him. He was deadly serious now. 'Upon your instruction, I went back to the barn three days ago and searched again. The premises have been sealed off since the victim's body was recovered and the defendant removed to our custody. The only people who've been in there after my initial search are you and assistant Raythune County prosecutor Rhonda Lovejoy.'

'Go on.'

'Like I said, I scoured the place all over again. Top to bottom. And underneath a panel in the rafters I found—'

He hesitated.

'What, Deputy?' Bell pressed him. 'What did you find?'

'I found twenty-four small plastic bags, each containing what appeared to be illegal prescription narcotics. The state lab tested the contents. Found a combination of oxycodone, Dilaudid and fentanyl.'

'Your conclusion, based on your experience as a deputy sheriff?'

'Royce Dillard is either a drug dealer himself or he knowingly aided and abetted drug dealers by allowing his barn to be used as a distribution point.'

29

Royce Dillard. A drug dealer.

From her position alongside the witness box, Bell took a quick look over at Rhonda. She knew the assistant prosecutor would be shocked at the information that had just been unleashed, information that caused a strong gust of whispers to rustle across the courtroom like a hundred pages being turned simultaneously in a hundred different books. Bell wished she could have tipped off Rhonda, preparing her in advance for the revelation. But there hadn't been time. The state lab had not delivered its verdict until minutes before Oakes arrived in court. His wink at Bell had been a signal that, yes, the test results had come back. The pills were narcotics. Until Bell knew for sure, she couldn't bring it up in court, couldn't risk the embarrassment of the contents of those bags turning out to be, say, Flintstones Chewables.

Rhonda's face looked washed of all of its color. She sat behind the prosecution table just as she'd been sitting a few seconds ago, leaning forward, ready to grasp a legal pad from the stack in front of her should Bell request it. But her round chin trembled, and a shudder seemed to run through her big body. For a moment Bell was afraid Rhonda was going to cry – but she under-estimated her. There were no tears. Rhonda quickly got hold of herself, shaking off her astonishment.

On the other side of the aisle, an incensed Serena Crumpler had leaped to her feet so quickly that she startled Jessica Muth, the bailiff, causing Muth to flinch and knock her laptop onto the wooden floor, producing a solid smack. Serena barged up to the bench, demanding that Judge Barbour require Bell to produce the official analysis of the contents of the plastic bags found in Dillard's barn – and demanding, further, to know why Bell had kept the results of Deputy Oakes's second search a secret until Oakes took the stand today.

'Your Honor,' Bell said, having joined Serena in front of the bench. 'I didn't know what – if anything – the search would produce. And the results of the analysis were only made available to me a few minutes before the court convened today. Otherwise I would've shared all of this with Ms Crumpler.'

'Sure you would've,' Serena muttered, acid in her tone. 'Anyway, it's totally prejudicial, Your Honor,' she said, quickly switching her attention back to the judge.

'Mrs Elkins?' he said.

'Judge, it goes directly to motive. We believe that Edward Hackel discovered that the defendant was using his barn as a storage site for illegal drugs. And he employed that information to try to blackmail Mr Dillard into selling his land. The murder, we believe, occurred in response to the blackmail threat.'

Barbour turned to Serena. 'You'll have your chance to explain the drugs found on Mr Dillard's property,' he said. 'Let's proceed.'

Bell watched her opponent march away. Serena's steps were quick, and stiff with umbrage. Bell's gaze also took in Royce Dillard, stone-faced as usual in his seat at the defense table, head tilted down, and then it swept over to Rhonda. The assistant prosecutor's eyes were impossible to read, but Bell could sense her disillusionment. Rhonda had believed in Royce Dillard. Believed in his essential goodness. The new piece of information put that assessment in serious jeopardy.

'Hey – remember me?' Deputy Oakes said. Still in the witness box, he raised his right hand and fluttered his fingers. Two female jurors smiled at that.

Bell dismissed Oakes and called her next witness: Artie Munson. He was nineteen years old, overfed, with gel-spiked brown hair, droopy eyes, and a zipper-like scar that ran from his cheek to his chin. His dark suit looked as if it had just been pulled out of a box in the basement, and would go right back into it again once this ordeal was over.

'Please state your name, address, and occupation,' Bell said, after his swearing in.

'Artie Munson. Trailer park over in Swanville. Ain't got no job.'

'Very well, then, Mr Munson.'

'Artie's fine. Everybody calls me Artie.'

She didn't react to that. 'How do you support yourself?'

'Odd jobs. Helping folks out. Whatever.'

'Are you acquainted with the defendant, Royce Dillard?'

'Sure. I seen him around.'

'And how about the victim? Did you ever meet Edward Hackel?'

'Yeah. Didn't know his name. But when I seen the picture, I knew it was him.'

'How did you come to be acquainted with Mr Hackel?'

Munson waited. He looked apprehensive. He tugged at the bottom of his suit coat.

'Mr Munson,' Bell said. 'You've been granted immunity from prosecution. You won't face charges for anything you tell us today.'

Relief made Munson smile. He knew the terms of the deal he'd made, but wanted to make sure he had it right before continuing. 'Okay. Yeah, well, I got a buddy who works on the cleanup crew out at Mountain Magic, and he told me there was somebody there who was looking to – well, to party. Get high.'

'To obtain illegal narcotics, you mean?'

'Yeah. So I met up with the guy. It was Hackel. Told him where to find what he was looking for.' He pointed at Dillard. 'His place. A barn on his property.'

A stir raced around the courtroom like a tiny car on a circular track. Judge Barbour frowned. The stir ceased.

'How did Mr Hackel react to this information?' Bell asked.

'He just grinned. Grinned real big.'

Bet he did, Bell thought distastefully. She could imagine Hackel's glee at the news that finally, at long last, he had something to hold over Royce Dillard's head. He had leverage. Blackmail bait. He had in his possession a fact that Dillard would be desperate to keep under wraps.

But was it enough? Would it explain to the jurors' satisfaction why quiet, self-effacing Royce Dillard had taken a sharp-edged shovel to the back of a man's neck, after which he'd dumped the corpse in an icy creek?

'Tell them, Royce. Tell them what you told me.'

Serena stood behind Dillard's chair. The prosecuting attorney's office in the late afternoon was dim and chilly. As the sun went down, it snatched back the light and warmth offered up throughout the short day; not even the three lamps were enough to counteract the gloom.

The trial was in recess until tomorrow. Serena had asked for a meeting in the prosecutor's office. Bell sat behind her desk; Rhonda had chosen the couch. Dillard was hunched over in the wooden armchair, his face pale and stricken as he stared at the tops of his knees.

'It was for money,' Dillard said. His voice was slow, as if the words themselves, and not just the shameful truths they signified, were burdensome. 'That's why I did it. But it was a big mistake. I knew right away. See, I needed cash. For my dogs. Two of 'em got to have surgery. Utley's hip is a mess. Pains him something awful. And PeeWee's got a real bad eye infection. So I said they could use my barn. State police wouldn't think to look for nothin' way out there. That's what they told me.'

Bell looked up at Serena, and then back down at Dillard. Clearly he was deeply troubled by what he'd just revealed, filled with embarrassment and regret.

'I never sold no drugs,' Dillard said, the pace of his words quickening. 'Never. I'd already told them to come and get that shit out of my barn. Didn't want it there. No matter what they were gonna pay me. Not enough money in all the world.'

'Did Hackel threaten to expose you? To reveal the fact that you were storing illegal drugs?' Bell asked.

'Yeah.'

'So that's why you killed him.'

Dillard studied the floor. 'I didn't kill him. Told you that already.'

Serena put a hand on Dillard's shoulder. He flinched, but she didn't remove it. 'Bell,' Serena said, 'I'm asking for a little forbearance here. I hope you don't intend to add drug possession with intent to distribute to the charges against my client.'

'No. I think first-degree murder is enough for now. We'll be presenting it as motive for the crime, of course, but no additional charges will be filed.'

Serena was relieved. 'Good. That's good. So we're okay here?'

'As long as Mr Dillard cooperates.' Bell picked up a pen. 'Who did you deal with?' she asked him. 'Who gave you the drugs? I want a name.' She had already tried to get the same information from Artie Munson, in exchange for not charging him, but concluded that he was as ignorant as he looked. Munson was an errand boy. Nothing more.

'Never got a name,' Dillard said. 'Fella just dropped them off. Told me he'd get in touch when he needed to.'

'What did he look like?'

'Big man. Fat. Had a ball cap on, so I never really saw his face. Wore one of them wool coats.'

'Well, what did the coat look like?'

Dillard pondered the question. His eyes traveled along the front edge of Bell's desk and then back again. 'Green,' he said. 'It was green plaid.'

*   *   *

'Do you believe him? About the drugs, I mean – do you believe he'd really changed his mind about storing them in his barn?'

Bell and Rhonda were leaving the office together, walking side by side down the long courthouse corridor, when Rhonda asked her the question.

'I don't know,' Bell answered.

'Royce Dillard is no drug dealer,' Rhonda declared. Heat in her tone. 'He's no murderer, either. I do my job – you know that, Bell – and my job is to help prosecute him, but when I look at Royce, I don't see a killer. I see a victim.'

Serena had taken her leave a while ago; Royce Dillard had been returned to his cell. But Bell and Rhonda had continued to work. They needed to discuss their plans for the next day's court session, when the defense would begin its turn. Before they could settle into that, however, Bell had put in a call to Sheriff Harrison. *Don't know if it's relevant, Pam,* she said, *given the fact that there's a hell of a lot of plaid jackets in these mountains. But thought I'd mention it. Just in case it helps in the search for Nick's assailant.* The sheriff's voice had sounded wrung out with weariness: *Wish we were making more progress. I'm assisting Sheriff Ives as much as I can, but we're short on manpower and long on cases. So's he. I'll pass it along, though. Every clue helps.*

Fatigue had finally worn down Bell and Rhonda, too. They decided to call it a night.

'I appreciate your passion, Rhonda. I do.' Bell paused at the end of the hall. Most of the lights were already switched off. Around the corner was the front lobby of the courthouse. Here, Bell remembered, Diana Hackel had waited for her and Sheriff Harrison on the night

Ed Hackel's body was found. The courthouse was the place where the aftermath of all tragedies seemed to gather, the place where all the sadness in a small town eventually coalesced; here it was sorted out and labeled and ranked, and here is where the propagators of those sorrows finally were made subject to justice. *Sometimes,* she corrected herself. *Sometimes, that's how it happens. If we're lucky.*

Rhonda jumped in before Bell could speak again. 'I know it looks pretty bad for him right now. But I'm telling you – something's going to happen. I can just feel it. Somehow we're going to find out what really happened to Ed Hackel, and we're going to know why, and it's going to take everybody by surprise.'

Bell was too tired to argue. Plus she had a dog to get home to. 'See you in the morning, Rhonda.'

30

Goldie had eaten her supper with unusual relish and now she licked the bowl, dragging her long pink tongue around the circle again and again. Watching from across the kitchen, Bell wondered if she was giving her enough food. She dumped in another half cup of Pedigree. Goldie finished it in seconds and then dropped into a sitting position, an indication that she was satisfied. Her tail swished back and forth – but for her, the rhythm was a bit subdued. It lacked the crazy excitement normally visible in that tail. This was a thoughtful, almost melancholy tail-wag.

'You miss him, don't you?' Bell said. She had abandoned any embarrassment about talking to a dog, and now routinely conversed with Goldie. 'It's okay.' She scratched a small area behind Goldie's right ear. The sweet spot. The tail incrementally increased the vigor of its wag. 'It's okay.'

Bell took her coffee cup into the living room. Goldie followed her. At first Bell had disliked the dog's habit of staying close to her that way, following her as she went from room to room; it felt like having a big hairy stalker with bad breath tracking her in her own home. But in just a few days, Bell had begun to enjoy it. Now she took Goldie's loyal lockstep for granted.

She settled in her chair. Goldie, as usual, repaired to the couch, and promptly stretched out for her post-meal snooze. Bell planned to catch up on some paperwork and then drive over to the hospital to see Nick.

Her cell rang, startling her and awakening Goldie. The dog's big yellow head popped up like a curious periscope.

'Elkins,' Bell said.

'This is Melanie Treadwell. I'm sorry to be calling you at dinnertime, but I just got back from a conference in Stockholm. And your message indicated that this was urgent.'

'Yes. Yes, it is. Thanks for getting back to me.' Bell took off her reading glasses and settled more comfortably into her chair. 'I appreciate this.'

'Not a problem. David Gage has been a friend of mine for years, and he left me a message as well. He speaks quite highly of you. I'm happy to help however I can.'

Bell had Googled her, and David's praise was justified; Treadwell had written and spoken extensively on the psychology of childhood trauma. She traveled a great deal, often visiting war zones and refugee camps, helping young survivors of violence deal with their horrific memories.

'Just to be clear,' Bell said, 'this is a private conversation. I won't be quoting you in court or asking you to testify – nothing like that. I'm just trying to get a feel for a few things about the case I mentioned in my phone message.'

'Understood,' Melanie said. 'Works for me, too. Frankly, Mrs Elkins, I wish I could talk informally like this with every prosecutor in the country. Childhood trauma is astonishingly pervasive. I think it influences adult criminal activity to a degree we haven't even begun to deal with yet – but if you try to bring it up, a lot of prosecutors think you're angling to get murderers off the hook. I've had the phrase "bleeding heart liberal" flung at me so many times that I probably ought to adopt it as a nickname. And "academic" is another word that's somehow become pejorative.' She let out a long, frustrated sigh before continuing.

'I'm not suggesting that a bad experience in childhood ought to excuse anything an adult does. I'm just saying that if we intervene early, and get these kids some help, we could not only stop a fair number of adult crimes before they happen – we could also improve lives. People who grow up with terrible pictures in their head are living a kind of half-life. A shadow life. One part of them is always back there in the middle of the trauma, still hiding, still cringing, still terrified – while the other part is here in the present, trying to function normally. The friction between those two scenarios can cause an immense amount of psychic pressure to build up. And that pressure ultimately has to be released.'

In her impatience to get to the bottom of Royce Dillard's ordeal, Bell hadn't realized how close to the edge of her own history this conversation might stray. And it was not anywhere she wanted to be. Not now. Not ever.

'Okay,' Bell said, eager to move on. 'I get that. But specifically – the defendant in my case was only two years old when he lost his mother and father in the Buffalo Creek flood back in 1972. Would a two-year-old remember enough so that it might haunt him into adult-hood? And if he did – could those memories affect his impulse control? The evidence is conclusive. We're sure he committed the crime. What I'm trying to figure out is the origin of the sudden violence. Was it inevitable – or could the defendant have somehow stopped himself? I'll be making my sentencing recommendation to the judge very soon, and I want to make sure I've taken everything into account.'

'Buffalo Creek.' Treadwell's voice grew ruminative. 'I've read some articles by the psychologists who talked with the survivors. Fascinating cases. Such devastating losses could tear a child to pieces emotionally.

'This area of research,' Treadwell went on, 'was pioneered by Anna Freud. She interviewed children who had survived bombings in World War II. Entire cities throughout Europe ended up as smoking piles of bricks and dead bodies.'

'What happened to those kids?'

'Many of them carried psychological wounds the rest of their lives. And the same has been true of the children of Buffalo Creek. As adults, they've experienced everything from anxiety disorders and phobias to sleep issues and sexual dysfunction. Plus physical symptoms such as chronic headaches and stomach problems. Not to mention alcoholism and other addictions.'

'So even if the defendant was too young to remember—'

'Oh, he remembers, all right,' Treadwell said, finishing the sentence for her. Sadness in her voice. 'They can talk about survivors all they want, but the truth is – when something like Buffalo Creek happens, nobody really escapes. Ever.'

Bell was quiet for a moment.

'Mrs Elkins?'

'Sorry,' Bell said quickly. 'I don't mean to be wasting your time.'

'You're not wasting my time. In my profession, you learn to get comfortable with silence. I just want to be sure I'm telling you what you need to know.'

'Yes. You are. So – what do you think? If someone lived through the Buffalo Creek disaster as a child, could he end up a killer?'

'Whoa.' Treadwell laughed. 'I don't mean to make light of your question, but – well, like I said, "Whoa." That's quite a leap.' She paused. 'Let me answer you this way. There's a phenomenon called survivor syndrome. It has five parts. According to the psychologists who worked with the victims of Buffalo Creek, every survivor – to a greater or lesser degree – had aspects of these five parts in their subsequent behavior. The first is called death imprint. That refers to a memory of what actually happened that day. The picture in your head. And then there's death guilt – you're haunted by the idea that you lived while others died. The third is called psychic numbing. You just shut down, you withdraw from life, so that you can't be hurt anymore. Then there's impairment of relationships. It's why some survivors can't have healthy emotional bonds in their lives – marriage, close friendships. The fifth part of survivor syndrome is called significance. As human beings, we try to find meaning in the bad things that happen to us. We want our lives to matter – not to just be a bunch of random events, random catastrophes. We can put up with a lot – if we can find a frame for it. Some people seek that in religion. In the notion of God's will. But in the case of Buffalo Creek, that was a real challenge. The flood happened not because there was a tornado or hurricane – but because a coal company cared more about its profits than about the people in that valley. Damned hard to find significance there.'

Treadwell had talked longer than she'd intended, and Bell could hear a note of summing-up in her tone. 'Here's what I can tell you, Mrs Elkins. When I'm dealing with young people who have endured great psychic pain, as the children of Buffalo Creek did, I focus on the fifth element I told you about – the thing called significance. If we can see our lives as part of an ongoing story, then even the bad parts are somehow easier to deal with. There's a meaning behind the story. Not just panic and pain.' She took a breath. She seemed to be thinking about how to make her next point.

'The worst thing you can do for someone who's gone through a horrific ordeal,' Treadwell said, 'is to strip away the meaning. To rob the experience of its significance. Because when you do that, all that's left is the anguish. And that can be unbearable.' She paused. 'Did childhood trauma make your man a murderer? I can't say. But human emotions can be wildly volatile. And sometimes extremely dangerous. You have to handle them with great care.'

'Thank you. I really appreciate your expertise.'

'Not at all. And now I'd better go unpack.' She paused. 'Next time you talk to David . . .'

'Yes?'

'Oh, I was just going to have you tell him that I miss him. I really do. Divorces just suck, don't they?' She laughed. 'Jesus – I sound like my son. He's seventeen and every other word is "suck." Or "like." Anyway, what I mean is, things got a little nasty between David and Lesley when they first broke up. I felt caught between them. And I've known her longer. So I owed my loyalty there, you know?'

'I do.' Bell had lost a few friends herself by virtue of the same rough justice.

'But he's a great guy. And an amazing dad. I don't know what you two are – I mean, I don't know if you're—' Another short gust of laughter. 'Oh, hell. If you're dating him, Mrs Elkins, I hope things work out for you.'

The drive from Shelton Avenue to the Raythune County Medical Center took only about fifteen minutes, but Bell didn't want to waste even one of them. She dialed Jake Oakes's cell before backing out of her driveway.

'So how'd I do today?' he said in a light, bantering tone, dancing his way through double entendres. 'Always glad to get a little feedback from a lady, if you know what I mean. Might help me improve my technique.'

'Fine, Deputy.' She was brusque. The night-shrouded neighborhood was whipping past the windows of her Explorer, and she felt precious time slipping away from her as well. 'Need you to do a little more digging for me. Would you have time to make a few calls? I'll clear it with the sheriff.'

'Count on it.' Oakes suddenly became all business, as if her seriousness was contagious. At first she'd been suspicious of his ability to turn on a dime from smart-ass quipster to diligent law enforcement professional, but now it didn't bother her; she had even come to admire it. Maybe that was how he handled the stress of the job. The jokes, the sexy strut – maybe that was how he lived with the things he was forced to look at, day after day, from mauled bodies to the routine sadness

of messed-up lives. Everybody in this line of work had
to find their own way.

'Good,' she said. 'Can you be discreet?'

'Discretion's my middle name.'

'Thought you didn't have one.'

She waited for him to come up with a snappy retort.
To her surprise, he didn't; he was too focused. She told
him what she needed.

31

Rain began to fall shortly after midnight. It tapered off before dawn, and Bell managed to wedge in her early-morning walk with Goldie during that brief blessed interval. Then the rain came back, with clear intentions of settling in for the long haul. It was a wet, gray, mottled world. Waterlogged clouds strung themselves out across the sky.

People arrived in court that morning with a wilted, frazzled look; even those who'd enjoyed the moving roof of an umbrella seemed disgruntled, out of sorts, put upon. There was a feeling in the ancient room of creeping damp, infiltrating corners and moods accordingly.

Bell looked around. In the second row behind her, Diana Hackel was brushing off the sleeves of her raincoat. The belt didn't fit around her middle anymore; secured by the loops across the back, it dangled at her sides like a second pair of arms. In the row behind Diana, Bell saw four courthouse regulars, the people for whom criminal trials were better than daytime TV. Mostly old, they settled into their seats each morning, canes held between their knees, expectancy in their eyes, swaying left or right to see around the heads of the people seated in front of them, each time there was an uptick in the action.

No Carolyn Runyon. And no one else from Mountain

Magic, either. *That was quick,* Bell thought. Once Hackel's value to the company had dropped to zero, owing to the inconvenient reality that he was dead, apparently they'd moved on. Business was business.

Serena Crumpler rose and called her first witness. He was Roland Atwood, vice president of the surveying firm hired to mark off sections of land for various parts of the resort.

'Help us understand something, Mr Atwood,' Serena said, once he'd identified himself and was sworn in. 'Mountain Magic purchased more than twelve hundred acres across Raythune and adjacent counties to build this resort. Why is the single parcel owned by Mr Dillard so crucial? Why not just change things around a bit, so that you don't need his land?'

Atwood was a large, rugged-looking man who clearly spent a good portion of his workday outdoors. The skin on his wide face had the texture of saddlebag leather, and his neck and hands were burnt red from sun exposure. Yet he didn't seem ill at ease in a suit and tie, either; Bell surmised that he also spent time in the firm's home office in Arlington, Virginia. He was obviously accustomed to testifying in a courtroom. He spoke clearly, calmly, if a bit louder and slower than was necessary.

'Yes, ma'am, some people might see that as a work-able solution,' Atwood said. 'Just buy another patch of land on another end of the entire parcel or just make do with what's already procured. But this is about inter-state access, not total acreage. Royce Dillard's land provides the only reasonable and cost-effective way to get to the interstate. If we can't secure his land, we'll have to persuade the state to let us build a new interstate exit – at company expense. That'll add tens of millions of dollars to the cost. And push back the completion date by a couple of years. Maybe longer.'

'I see.' Serena sneaked a sideways look at the jurors, to make sure they understood the implications of this testimony. 'So Edward Hackel, the man in charge of getting Mr Dillard to sell his land, was highly motivated. Highly motivated to harangue Mr Dillard about it, no matter how many times he was rebuffed.'

That elicited a grim smile from Atwood. 'I don't know about the word "harangue," ma'am – your description, not mine – but your point is basically right. Ed had to get that land. If he didn't, the entire project would stop.'

'What was Edward Hackel like when he was opposed? Was he calm, reasonable, patient?'

'No, ma'am. Eddie was a hothead. Screamed a lot, jumped around, made a lot of threats. A real volatile guy when it came to business. With that temper of his, Ed was a magnet for death threats.'

Bell scooted her chair back fast and stood up. 'Your Honor—'

'Got it, Mrs Elkins,' the judge said. 'Ms Crumpler, you know better than that. Unless your witness has knowledge of a credible threat from a specific person, it's hearsay.' He looked sternly at the jury. 'Please disregard the last remark of this witness.' He settled back in his chair again, the black robe folding around him. 'You may continue, Ms Crumpler.'

But the point, Bell knew, had been made. So Royce Dillard had threatened to kill Hackel? Well, a lot of other people had done the same thing. Or wanted to. And at the end of the day, a defense attorney's job wasn't to prove her client's innocence; it was to persuade the jury that the prosecution hadn't proved his guilt.

'Just one more thing, Mr Atwood,' Serena said. 'You've testified that if the victim didn't get that land for Mountain Magic, the project would stop. But why? I mean, couldn't you just wait him out? In a few years, maybe he'd change his mind.'

Atwood shook his head. 'Project this big and complex requires a lot of up-front outlay,' he said. 'So there's millions of dollars just sitting around until we get the green light to break ground. These kinds of investors – they have a ton of other places they can put their money. No reason they should just hang around through all of the arguing and the mountain-moving.'

'Mountain-moving?'

'Yes, ma'am. Without Royce Dillard's land, the only place we can feasibly put that new exit would require us to relocate a mountain. As roadblocks go, that one's a doozy.'

When Bell returned to her office for the lunch recess, Lee Ann Frickie handed her a note upon which she had written, *Dep O wd like u 2 call*. Long before anyone had ever heard of texting, Lee Ann had practiced the art of the tersely compacted message.

Oakes answered his cell before the end of the first ring. 'Hey,' he said. 'Sorry I'm not there in person, but the sheriff sent me out here to Willow Road. Report of shots fired. Probably just some good ole boys aiming at beer cans lined up on a barrel, but you never know. Anyway, I did what you asked.'

'And?'

'Got some mighty interesting things to tell you. Give me a minute to pull over.'

Waiting for Oakes to return to the line, Bell was struck

by how much she'd come to trust him and depend on him in a short period of time. Their rocky beginnings were forgotten. It was Jake Oakes who had tracked down Artie Munson, whose testimony allowed her to prove that Hackel knew about Dillard and the drugs. And it was Oakes who kept a constant eye on things out at Mountain Magic, where, he told Bell, the cranes and the graders and the bulldozers were still poised expectantly in neat, expensive rows.

His voice was steady but excited. 'Okay. To begin with, Diana Hackel's "business" isn't much of a business at all. In fact, it's a big bunch of nothing so far. I checked with the chamber of commerce in Falls Church – there's no record of her trying to establish any kind of business or renting any office space. But just to make sure, I checked with the Virginia secretary of state's office. No request to register a name for a new business, either. Now, when I called the Fairfax County Courthouse, a lady there told me that she does remember a Diana Hackel picking up some forms, with information on zoning and sales tax regulations. But Hackel didn't ask any other questions. Didn't seem real interested in starting a business. Just wanted the forms.'

'A courthouse employee told you all that over the phone?' Bell said.

'Guess my charm doesn't require a personal appearance to be effective. It's a gift.'

She was rather glad he'd returned to his arrogant self; there was a comfortable familiarity to it.

'Okay, go on,' Bell said.

'Checked out McGloin, like you asked. It's in the fine print, but he's not just an employee of Mountain Magic.

He's a major stockholder. Got a big financial stake in the resort.'

'Right. And?'

Oakes uttered a lazy-sounding laugh. 'I felt like a reporter for TMZ, but I got the information you were after. Yeah, Carolyn Runyon has a history of getting involved with her male colleagues. I dug through the public record and sure enough – she was named in a divorce proceeding four years ago in Anne Arundel County in Maryland. Runyon was a VP for the hedge fund where this guy was CFO. Lots of nasty details – racy e-mails, X-rated gifts, that kind of crap. The wife was madder'n hell and wanted it all on the record.'

'Okay. Thanks.'

'No problem. I better go. Those liquored-up hillbillies out there might be turning their attention from beer cans to the family cat.'

Bell expected him to end the call, but he didn't. 'Hey,' he said, as if he'd needed a couple of seconds to work up the nerve. 'Can I ask you something?' Oakes took her silence as an affirmative reply. 'Listen,' he continued, 'I'm happy to help, but I gotta ask – why'd you want me to do all this? Royce Dillard's the one on trial.'

'Grant you that. We've got the right man. But we've got to have a plausible reason, so that my summation to the jury sounds convincing. Would Dillard kill Ed Hackel because Hackel kept pushing him to sell his land? Would Dillard kill him because Hackel threatened to expose his complicity with drug dealers? Or was it something else entirely?'

'Good Lord,' Oakes said. 'How many motives do you *need*, lady?'

'Just one. The right one.'

32

The other car sliced meanly out of the darkness, as swift and ominous as a shark's fin. Bell hadn't seen it behind her, but suddenly there it was – beside her now – as it passed her on Route 6, a two-lane road picketed with frequent and conspicuous NO PASSING signs. It looked less like another vehicle and more like a black slash of restless momentum. If a superhero lived in Acker's Gap, that's what she would drive, Bell told herself, not without admiration. Then she shook her head, realizing that admiration was not the proper response from a prosecutor observing a crime. The car had to be going at least thirty miles over the speed limit, overtaking the Explorer with an effortless karate-kick of speed.

She'd had a long day in court, and then a longer-than-usual time at home with Goldie. The dog wasn't feeling well. Bell had drizzled a little bacon grease on her food; Goldie perked up long enough to lick it off. Then Bell sat on the floor with Goldie's head in her lap, stroking that fluffy, supple yellow fur, murmuring to her. *Good girl. You're a good, good girl.* Goldie's tail finally thumped: A positive sign. She was her old self again. One quick walk, and then it was time for Bell to leave for the hospital.

She had just turned onto Route 6 when the Batmobile boiled up from out of nowhere. For the fraction of a second it was alongside her, prior to its quick shift back into her lane ahead of her, Bell looked over. It was Carolyn Runyon. She was certain of it. All she could see was a dark profile, but there was something in the way the other driver held her chin, the cocky angle of it, that was familiar. Just for the hell of it, as the car's taillights began to open up a wide lead, Bell accelerated, too. She would never have caught up, but they were both stopped by the red light at the intersection with County Road 17.

Waiting for the light to change, Bell kept her eyes on the back of the driver's head. She wasn't surprised that Carolyn Runyon was in such a hurry; she had impressed Bell from the outset as the kind of person who was always in a hurry. Acker's Gap must be a kind of hell for her. She must feel as if the whole town moved in slow motion, like a person walking underwater, every step burdened and deliberate, the pace unbearably turgid.

The dome light in the other car snapped on. Runyon leaned over to her right, exposing her profile. Reaching for something in the glove box, maybe.

Bell realized, to her surprise, that it wasn't Carolyn Runyon. It was Diana Hackel. And then the light changed and the Batmobile leapt away.

When she arrived at the hospital, she found Nick alone in his room. No Mary Sue.

'Hey,' Bell said.

He'd been watching television. The too-loud laughter from a sitcom had been audible from the hallway as she approached, and it surprised her; she'd never known

Nick Fogelsong to be much of a TV watcher. Not of commercial television, anyway. Among his most prized possessions was a DVD series of documentaries about the major battles of World Wars I and II, and she knew he'd watched those enough times to have memorized the voiceover narration – but a sitcom? No.

He aimed the remote-control channel changer at the set bracketed on the wall opposite the bed. One click and both noise and picture vanished.

'Hey yourself,' he said. 'How's that dog?'

'Wearing me out. Three walks a day, and she's always begging for more.'

'It'll keep you young.'

'Or make me old before my time. Could go either way.'

'And the trial?' he asked. 'I haven't been keeping up. Can't focus.'

'Expect we'll be wrapping up soon. Rhonda Lovejoy's doing a great job assisting me.'

'Even though she thinks you might have the wrong man? She's been by here a few times. Mentioned her reservations.'

'Fortunately,' Bell said, 'she keeps that opinion to herself while the jury's present.' She took off her coat and slung it across the second chair in the room, the one usually occupied by his wife. 'I'll move that when Mary Sue gets back. Is she making a coffee run?'

'No.' His head dropped back against the pillows. 'Called and said she won't be coming by tonight.' He reached over to put the remote on the bedside table. His wince when he did it was so deep that Bell could almost feel the pain herself. But he didn't make a sound.

'Oh. Okay,' she said. It wasn't okay – it was damned

strange and totally unprecedented, and they both knew it, yet neither wanted to acknowledge it. 'Needs a night off, I bet. Got a lot on her plate these days, taking care of things at home till you're back on your feet. Speaking of that – how's the physical therapy?'

She didn't look at him while she waited for an answer. She pretended to be fussing with something on the front of her purse, a small discoloration that she rubbed at with two fingers, and then scratched at with her thumbnail. She didn't like to see him flat on his back this way. Hated it, in fact. It was out of the natural order of things. Still. Even though she'd come here every day for weeks now. And would keep coming.

'Going okay,' he said. And then, nothing.

From down the hall came the high-low drift of voices. The squeaky wheel of a cart bristling with medical charts as it went rolling by. A spike of laughter. Somebody else's TV set, tuned to a game show.

Bell finished with the spot on her purse. She folded her hands on top of it, sat back in her chair. It was an unsettling moment. He had always been the strongest person she knew – physically, emotionally – and now he was lying in a hospital bed in a cotton gown that tied at the back of his neck like a child's bib, too weak to raise his right arm more than half an inch or so. She'd seen him try. And fail. And sometimes, not try again for the rest of the day.

Her cell made a noise, indicating a new text. Bell glanced at it:

Dinner soon?

It was from David Gage. Oh, Lord. She slid the cell back in her purse. It was the fourth time he'd texted her today. She'd only answered the first two. She liked him; she really did. But there was no spark. She'd thought she could deal with that. Well, maybe not.

'Sheriff Ives stopped by,' Nick said. 'They're running down some leads. Could take a while, but they might actually find the bastard who put a slug in me.'

'That's great news, Nick. Wish I could do more to help.'

'Not your job.'

'Still doesn't feel right.'

'Doesn't feel right for me, either – lying here like a useless sack of crap while a bunch of drug dealers are running around out there.' He needed to change the subject away from his frustration, and so he did. 'Guess who called me.'

She waited to hear.

'Clay Meckling,' Nick said. 'Wanted to know how I was doing. You know, back when he was going through his rehab, I'd drop in at the hospital, give him a pep talk, cheer him on. Tell him he had to fight. Shoe's on the other foot now.'

'Close as you two are,' she said, 'I bet talking to him will be a big help.' She couldn't risk saying anything else about Clay. She was afraid her voice might give her away. Reveal a depth of feeling she'd rather keep hidden.

'Yeah,' he said. 'Maybe.'

Nick looked at her. After the temporary lift supplied by his mention of Clay, he'd dropped back down again. His eyes had a bleakness to them that alarmed Bell almost as much as would the sight of a deep cut. The wound could be repaired; his pride, she wasn't so sure about.

'Mary Sue's in trouble,' he said, blurting it out, trying to get the words over with as quickly as he could. 'It's too much for her. She's with her psychiatrist tonight. They're looking at changing her medication. Doing something. Anything. The stress – it's wearing away at her, Bell, and it's triggering symptoms. She can't—' He faltered. He tried again, not sure how much he ought to say. He had already violated a substantial portion of his personal code: The things about which he cared the most were the things about which he talked the least. She knew that because it was her code, too.

'She'll be okay, Nick.'

'How the hell do you know that? Nobody knows that.'

'What I meant to say was that she's a fighter. Don't count her out.'

He didn't react. He wasn't looking at her. His eyes were fixed on a spot on the wall across from the bed, somewhere below the TV set. There was nothing there.

'Nick?' Bell finally said.

'Mind your business, Belfa,' he said. His voice was as gray and mournful as fog. 'Just mind your business.'

A nurse came in the room, carrying a fresh IV bag. She was young and moderately pretty, with soft brown hair and perky-looking glasses with maroon frames. A yolk-yellow smiley-face button was pinned to the front of her pale blue smock, next to a name tag that read MICHELE.

'Good evening, Mr Fogelsong.' There was a flirty tease to her demeanor. She smiled at Bell as she switched out the flaccid IV bag for the plump new one. 'Hi, there. Is this rascal here behaving himself?'

She finished fussing with the monitors. She stood alongside Nick's bed, small hands on the rail, and took a long, searching look at her patient. Bell had instantly dismissed this woman when she entered the room because of her youth, her cheerfulness. Now Bell realized her mistake. The nurse was absorbing a great deal of information about Nick Fogelsong just from this seemingly casual perusal; she appeared to be extrapolating, from the sag of his chin and the emptiness in his eyes, the sadness that had him in its grip, a sadness that lived beyond the healing reach of any medicine.

Her window was down, and so Bell could hear Goldie's warning from a long way off. The moment she turned onto Shelton Avenue, the meaty barks and the short, jabbing yaps were instantly recognizable, breaching the walls of her house and riding the cold night air. Bell was returning from the hospital much later than usual tonight. Was that it? Was Goldie just lonely?

As soon as Bell swung into her driveway, she saw the source of the dog's agitation: Someone was standing on the dark front porch. If the Blazer parked at the curb wasn't enough of a tip-off, the wide hat sealed the deal. It was Pam Harrison.

'Happened to be in the neighborhood,' Harrison called out to her. 'Decided to wait for you. Hope it's okay.'

'It's fine.' Bell climbed the front steps quickly and unlocked her front door. Goldie bounced out onto the porch, giving Harrison a thorough going-over with her nose. The sheriff didn't seem to mind; she was as stiff with dogs as she was with people, but she gave it a try, reaching down and ruffling Goldie's fur.

'How's Nick?' Harrison said. 'Haven't had much time lately to stop by.'

'He's okay. Hard road ahead, but he'll get there. Want to come in? I can put on a pot of coffee.'

'No. Won't take long. Can we just stay out here? Then I'll be on my way.'

'Fine.' Bell was mystified, but ready to listen. 'Is this about the trial?'

Harrison stopped petting the dog. She stood upright again. 'A person could get the idea that your heart's not in it.'

'What do you mean?'

'You're doing a good job,' Harrison said quickly. 'It's not that. I just want to make sure you believe in—' She stopped.

'Believe in what? The case?'

'In me.'

Now Bell thought she understood why Harrison didn't want to come inside. Inside meant lights. It meant taking off her hat. It meant exposure of many kinds.

'I know,' the sheriff went on, 'that you and Nick were a team. A great team. I'm doing my best, but I don't know if we're ever going to work together like you and he did. It's a pretty high bar.'

'Takes time.'

'I know. I know that. But it was me who pushed you to charge Dillard. And I just want to be sure that—'

'The evidence is there. The trial's going well.'

'Still not sure why he did it. Could it really have been Hackel's blackmail threat? Dillard wasn't really dealing drugs. He could've explained that, if he'd been caught.'

'Dillard's not the explaining type. You know that.'

Harrison looked out across Bell's dark front yard. 'He's had a hard life.'

'No doubt. But he killed a man.'

'Rhonda Lovejoy doesn't think so.'

'Rhonda Lovejoy's not the prosecutor.' Bell waited.

Harrison still didn't budge, so she added, 'We're doing the right thing. Go home, Pam. Get some rest.'

The sheriff nodded. She readjusted her hat and descended the steps, moving with a sort of nimble glide that Bell was tempted to call grace. She'd never call it that to Harrison's face, however, knowing it would embarrass her.

The Blazer left the curb. Side by side up on the porch, Bell and Goldie watched it go.

33

'Drago Mine Number Four is operated – when it operates at all – by the Brassey-Waltham Company of Pittsburgh, which in turn is owned by Central Energy Consortium – known as CEC – of New York City, which in turn is a subsidiary of Roscoe-Althorp, an international energy company based in Brussels, Belgium.' Bell was reading off a sheet of paper, and she made her voice suitably dry and singsong, like a bored third-grader reciting the Pledge of Allegiance.

'Let me translate for you,' she said to David, folding up the sheet upon which she'd scribbled the mine's provenance, and slipping it into the back pocket of her jeans. 'Every few days a handful of miners goes down and scrapes a few dozen truckloads of bituminous coal out of here – and the rest of the time, it's just a big hole in the ground. Nobody really claims it. Not enough coal production to care about.'

They stood at the gated entrance to Drago No. 4. It was a clear, mild, pink-skied Saturday morning. The fourth week of Royce Dillard's trial would be getting under way on Monday. And Bell needed a break. A break from the trial, a break from her daily visits to the hospital to see Nick, a break from everything. Just a short one – but the scenery had to be completely different.

This would do. She had texted David late the night before with a proposal: If he was still interested, she'd make good on her promise and get them down into Drago No. 4. They could only stay for a few minutes – just long enough for Bell to prove to him that it did indeed possess a singular, rough-hewn kind of beauty – but this was their chance. His return text was filled with exclamation points and YES in all caps.

He had joined her here twenty minutes ago. To the left of the mine entrance was the tipple, and beyond that, a ramshackle building called the bathhouse, where the miners donned their gear at the start of their shifts and, when they came back up, showered off the sweat and the coal dust. The foreman, a man named Dickie Lavender, had rummaged through the bathhouse and come up with the things they would need: one-piece denim coveralls that fit over their clothes, leather utility belts, steel-toed boots, helmets and headlamps. Dickie just happened to be Rhonda Lovejoy's uncle's stepson. When Bell had mentioned to Rhonda that she'd love to take David Gage for a quick dip down into Drago No. 4, a mine that hadn't been updated since the 1950s, Rhonda had snapped her fingers and said, 'Got just the fella for you.'

Lavender was younger than Bell had expected. He couldn't be more than twenty-five or so. He had spiky orange-red hair and freckles of the same shade that stood out like stars against his dead-white skin. Bell wondered what that skin looked like by the end of his shift.

'I'd like to say that I'll be in big trouble if anybody gets wind of me letting you down here,' Lavender opined, 'but the truth is, nobody gives a damn about this place anymore. Nor the people in it. Used to be, the old guys tell me, there was three shifts working here, day and night, every day of the year. Big beautiful seam of coal. Prettiest thing you ever did see. Pocahontas seam. One of the biggest ever. That was forever ago, though. Nobody wants our coal no more. We're like animals that're going extinct, you know? Last of our kind.' He scratched at the side of his head with a dirt-grimed fingernail. He seemed as philosophical as a Buddhist monk. 'Can't be helped, though. It is what it is. You guys ready to go?'

He opened the gate and stepped to one side to let them board. Bell and David walked onto the wooden slats of a small, rickety-looking contraption called a man-hoist. The slats were so far apart that you could easily see between them – and what lay below the platform was a shaft that plummeted some seven hundred feet, a distance impossible to contemplate without a little shiver of dread.

'This here's a real old mine,' Dickie said, closing the gate behind them. There was only room for two. 'Shaft was dug out by hand back in the 1930s. Can you beat that?' Marvel in his voice.

A cool wind wafted up from the bottom of the shaft. Dickie waved and grinned. He pushed a small brass button next to the hoist. Three short bells rang, a signal that the hoist was on its way down. With a jerk and a shimmy, the platform began its creaky descent. David had grabbed Bell's arm at the first twitch of motion, and she patted his hand. 'Think of it like you would a subway ride,' she said. 'For a miner, this is the morning commute.' He nodded. He let go of her arm. His lower lip was tucked under his upper one; he looked like a schoolboy concentrating on a math problem. A schoolboy in a hardhat and goggles, that is. Bell didn't want to contemplate what *she* must look like in this getup; a pair of oversized denim coveralls that gave her the general dimensions of a manatee did not constitute the most flattering of ensembles. No temptation to take any selfies.

The hoist continued its drop. Every few feet it paused, swaying slightly back and forth as if making up its mind if it wanted to keep going, and then, with a reluctant groan, it resumed. The creaks grew louder and more frequent. Craggy gray rock seemed to slide upward past the hoist as they dropped. When Bell looked straight up, she saw that the light at the top was only a frail dot now. The lower they went, the dimmer it grew. Soon, though, a light at the bottom of the shaft began to blossom.

'Still can't believe that a McDowell County boy's never been down in a coal mine,' she said, hoping that a bit of teasing might put David at ease. She pronounced it *Mac*Dowell, the way the natives did.

'Yeah, well, if I had – I think I'd remember,' he answered, in a hoarse, choked-sounding voice. He coughed, as if that was the problem.

The hoist bounced against the rock ledge at the bottom of the shaft, bounced again, and then settled itself with a heavy thud, a brief grinding noise, and another thud. Bright lights burned all around them, lights that seemed to spiral outward from a central core. Miners walked by with purposeful strides, heads bent, intent on their jobs, few of them bothering to check out the new arrivals that the hoist had deposited here. Even the skinny men looked burly, bulky, wrapped as they were in the thick coveralls and boots and helmets – just as Bell and David were, but on these men, it looked different. It wasn't a costume. She and David were tourists, and this was temporary; these men were workers, and this was their livelihood, for as long as it lasted. They looked like men who had emerged not from one of the corridors radiating out in four different directions from this spot, but from the deep and mysterious past, living throwbacks to an era when human muscle and will were the primary sources of energy. Coal, the coal pulled forcibly out of the earth with that muscle and will, was secondary. These men were dirty-faced phantoms from a dying – really, already dead – era.

'Here you go,' Bell said. She stepped off the platform and gestured for him to follow. They were engulfed in a world of shiny black rock. The strong lights gave the sides of the walls a wet look. The air smelled like hosed-down gunpowder. She could sense David's apprehension. The distance from floor to ceiling was about five feet; they had to bend over as they moved. A neck ache tomorrow morning was a sure thing.

'Just step over here a little ways,' she said. 'Got to keep the way clear.'

More miners came along, spines curved to accommodate the ceiling, walking singly or in twos. Some were holding thermoses by the plastic handles, or lunch boxes. They talked in low murmurs, like people in church. Occasionally there was a loud string of laughter that seemed to be passed on down the line, dying out by the time it reached the last man. That group disappeared in a corridor and another three or four men appeared from another. The men had to walk to one side, because rail tracks ran down the center of each corridor.

'A lot of those men are doing what's called dusting,' Bell said. 'They spread rock dust around the face of the seam. Air and coal dust is a highly combustible mix. The rock dust makes it safe. Well – safer.'

Before she could say another word, a violent shaking ensued. The vibration of the rock beneath their feet made it difficult to stay upright. Bell's legs felt liquefied. A massive roar of machinery filled the cavern. This time, David didn't reach out for her arm; he was ready for surprises. The noise went on for several minutes and then suddenly cut off.

'That's a continuous mining machine,' Bell said. 'Just tears the hell out of the rock walls, dragging out the coal. It digs in a sort of square pattern so it makes four walls – a room. In each room, it leaves pillars of coal to hold up the roof. And then it comes back and takes out the pillars.' She pointed down one of the corridors. Visible in the distance was a mammoth rack of spotlights bolted to both sides of a giant black block with enormous mechanical arms.

'Can we go see it?' David asked. Eager as a kid.

'Nope. It's a worksite. We'd be in the way. This's as far as we go.'

'So where's all this beauty you were bragging about? So far, all I've seen is rock. And all I've gotten is a mouthful of coal dust.'

Bell swung her head toward one of the empty corridors. The light from the lamp on her helmet struck the dark wall, and it was as if a secret cache of diamonds had suddenly spilled in their laps: Tiny chips of mica in the rock glittered in a rippling swath. These points of light, caught in the illumination from Bell's headlamp, seemed to leap and dance like living things. During this minute or two when the mine was quiet – no machines, no men – it was as if Bell and David stood in the heart of a dense forest, one that quivered with thousands of fireflies, or were perched in the midst of a night sky that seethed with stars.

She could hear his breathing.

'Okay,' he said. Voice quiet, subdued by awe. 'I see what you mean.'

Finding beauty within the ruins. Finding, in the darkness, something lovely, something that had meaning, if only for the person who beheld it. This was a trick Bell had taught herself early. Given her profession – one that required her to see the very worst that people could do to each other, inflicting all manner of physical and emotional pain – she kept the trick handy, like a magician who never leaves the house without that special deck of cards.

David coughed. It broke the spell; the fragile moment collapsed all around them. His tone turned to one of complaint. 'But how the hell does anybody spend their life working down here? I feel like I want to run my lungs through a car wash.'

'Wouldn't be my first choice either,' Bell said. 'But don't worry. These mines – the few that are left – are doomed. And Lord knows, they should be. They're dirty and dangerous. The coal they produce is doing all the bad things to the atmosphere that you and your friends accuse it of. No defense for it. And far too many men have been killed or injured in mines just like this one.' She turned back around to face him, switching off her headlamp. Now the wall returned to being just an expanse of black rock. Not a trove of diamonds. Not a harvest of stars. 'But before these mines go away entirely – before the only thing that's left of this place is a bunch of sepia-toned photos of men in hard hats with dirty faces – I just wanted you to see it and hear it. To smell it. To feel it.'

She was aware of something in her own throat, but it wasn't coal dust. She swallowed it back down again. 'This way of life – this place – is gone, David. Two-thirds of the coal produced today comes from strip mines, not underground mines. Since 1976, seventy-five percent of these mines have shut down. Coal miners? Down to less than a third of what there were back in the 1970s.'

'And that's a good thing, right? Like you said.'

'Yeah. But what's coming along behind it? What kind of employment is left for people in Raythune County? Salary-wise, these were damned good jobs. Jobs you could raise a family on. Build a life on. Do you really think Mountain Magic's going to offer that for maids and busboys? For waitresses? For caddies and desk clerks?'

He didn't answer. There was no answer.

'Time to go,' she said. She pointed up. 'Back to the future.' And then she paused. One more thing to say. 'Sorry to go all Studs Terkel on you there. I just know how hard coal miners work. And what they've meant to West Virginia.'

He nodded. He let her lead the way back onto the hoist. She leaned over and pushed the brass button, the signal to Dickie Lavender that they were ready to return to the surface.

Slowly, the platform began to rise. It was a smoother ride than the one on the way down, as they climbed steadily past the rough walls of the shaft.

'That is pretty amazing,' David said. He watched the chipped and mysterious rock that looked as if it were sinking down past them as they were hauled up. 'I can't wait to tell my girls about—'

A squeal of machinery, a hiss, and then a popping sound. The lights went out. The platform halted. It jerked once. Again. The hoist hung forlornly in the middle of the shaft, swaying slightly, as if even the contemplation of its current location was making it dizzy. Another jerk. Then it was still.

'Hey,' David said.

'They'll get it going again,' Bell said. 'Just hang on.'

'Don't have much of a choice.' It wasn't a wisecrack. There was an edge to his voice.

'Happens all the time,' she said.

'Really.'

'Yeah. The motor overheats. It's got an automatic shutoff. Once it cools, we'll be good to go.'

'Or good to fall.'

'Relax, David.' She smiled at him. She turned her headlamp on, so that they could see each other. His face was taut with the opening stages of panic.

'Believe me, I'm trying to,' he said.

The platform jerked again; unprepared for it, they almost fell over. Then: nothing.

'Jesus,' David said.

'I'm telling you. We'll be fine.' She didn't know if they would be fine or not, but she'd learned a few things from Nick Fogelsong over the years, and one of them was: When you're scared shitless, act brave. And keep thinking.

'Maybe I'd better turn off my headlamp,' she said. 'In case we're here a while. Might need it later.' Hacked out of the rock on one side were small indentations that ran up the shaft, bottom to top. A last-chance ladder. In an emergency, Bell knew, they could step off the platform and climb. But that step – from solid platform to scooped-out place in the rock that was roughly the size of the front half of your boot, with no railing, and nothing existing between you and the rock ledge hundreds of feet below but your own strength and guts – was harrowing to think about. So she didn't think about it.

They were roughly halfway between the surface and the bottom of the shaft, so the light at both ends was muted, distant, like a faint memory of childhood.

'You okay?' she said.

'No.'

'Dickie knows what he's doing.'

David didn't want to talk about Dickie. 'Look, Bell,' he said. His voice was hurried, but no longer on the precipice of panic. He sounded resolute. 'If this thing ends up crashing down there and I'm crushed to death – but you make it out – promise me something, okay? Promise that you'll tell my girls how much I loved them.'

'Tell them yourself. We're getting out of here.'

'What if that foreman can't make it go again?'

'Dickie will come through.'

'How do you know?'

'Because if he doesn't,' Bell said, 'and we don't make it up, he knows that Rhonda will never forgive him. Trust me – you don't want Rhonda Lovejoy mad at you. She can make life real tough for people she doesn't like.'

'Don't understand,' David said, 'how you can joke right now. I really don't.'

Bell reached out to find his arm. She gave it a squeeze. 'Better than falling apart, don't you think?'

He moved around on the platform, trying to dissipate

his nervousness, perhaps, by staying in motion. But there was nowhere to go.

'Seriously, David – we just need to sit tight. Dickie's working on this.'

'What if he isn't?'

She was just as scared as David was, but saw no point in dwelling on it.

'Okay,' she said. She needed to take his mind off their predicament. Her mind, too.

'Let's play a game. Let's pretend that this really *is* it.'

'Great game.' His voice was glum.

'Come on. You'll see. Okay – so back to what you were saying. These are your last few minutes on earth. What do you want your girls to know about you?'

She heard him sigh. Gradually, though, he was giving in to her question.

'About me,' he said.

'Sure. Things you've never told them. Advice you want them to hear. Or things about your life. Anything.' She and Carla had first played this game one summer night. Her daughter was eleven years old and a terrible storm had taken over the world; the trees looked alive, yanked back and forth by a vicious wind, their tops thrashing, and the thunder cracked so loudly that you could feel the vibration all the way down to the soles of your feet. Rain was flung against the windows with what seemed like deliberate hatefulness. Carla had rushed into Bell's room and snuggled under the comforter. *Mom, I'm scared,* she said. *What if the roof falls in? What if—* Bell, holding her very, very tight, said, *The roof won't fall in, sweetie.* She could sense, though, that the reassurance wasn't hitting home. It was too glib, too pat, too easy. Who wouldn't say that very thing, at such a time? And so Bell said, *Maybe it will.* Carla sat up in bed. *Mom, what do you mean?* Bell replied, *If the roof falls in and that big tree out there smashes us flat, what are the things that were best about your life? What are the things that meant the most to you?* And Carla, instead of focusing on the storm or on her fear, focused on her answer: *The best things, Mom, are you and Dad, and playing basketball. And my Harry Potter books. And chocolate ice cream.* Carla's answer reminded Bell of a scene in her favorite play, *Our Town,* when Emily Gibbs comes up with her own list: *Food and coffee. And new ironed dresses and hot baths.*

'So what would you want your kids to know?' Bell said, prodding him again. 'Doesn't have to be huge, momentous, earth-shattering things. It can be anything you want it to be.'

David's voice came out of the semidarkness at a different pitch. It was stronger now, and thoughtful. 'I guess I'd like them to know that I really tried to make our family work. I didn't want the divorce. I tried like hell to make a go of it with their mom.'

'Good,' she said. 'What else?'

'Well, I suppose I'd like them to know about my work. I changed fields, you know. A lot of my graduate research was in microbiology. Lab work. But I looked around and I realized what was happening to our world. So I shifted to environmental science. I know there won't be any easy answers to the problem of climate change. But whatever those answers are – they'll come from science. Not politics.' She heard, for the first time since they had been shocked by the halt of the hoist halfway up the shaft, a note of hopefulness in his voice. 'Yes. That's what I want them to know. How much I love them and how much I still love their mother. I always will. And how much I love this planet. Corny as that sounds.'

'Doesn't sound corny at all.'

'How about you? What do you want Carla to know?'

Bell started to answer. Then something occurred to her. She would never know if that idea had somehow drifted up from the depths of the Drago No. 4 mine, rising on the back of a rich plume of coal dust, or if it had been in her mind all along, and just needed a jolt to shake it loose.

'David,' she said. 'What if I lied?'

'Pardon?'

'What if I threatened to tell a different story about you? That you were a terrible coward in these last few minutes? That you were disappointed in your girls, and you hated their mother, and you hated your work?'

'I don't know what you—'

'What would you do?'

'Well,' he said, 'I'd be pretty pissed, frankly.'

'How pissed?'

'I'm not following what you're—'

'If I was blackmailing you with that threat, what would your response be? Remember – I'm going to tell a heinous lie about you. A lie the world's likely to believe. So – would you do my bidding?'

'I might,' he said. 'But I'd try to stop you first.'

'Exactly.'

Fourteen minutes later, the man-hoist began to grunt and moan once more. In another five, they crested the surface. They were met there by the sweaty, dirt-seamed face of Dickie Lavender.

'Jesus Christ,' he said, yanking open the gate. 'Shoulda warned you. This thing sticks worse'n a rusty truck door. Gets hung up every few trips. I been outside with the electrician, trying to get 'er going, else I woulda shouted down to you, tell you what was going on.'

'We did okay,' David said.

'Piece of cake,' Bell put in.

David looked over at her. And she realized, based on what she read in his eyes, that he now understood. Sometimes it happened that way: You both tried to make a relationship work, but then you realized, in a moment when you weren't even thinking consciously about it, that it was never to be. No blinding flash of revelation, no grand moment of truth. Just a sober, quiet knowing. It wasn't going to happen between them. And that was okay. Disappointing, perhaps, especially to him – but okay.

On paper, David was perfect for her. In the real world, though, things were different. She knew the man she wanted. And it wasn't David Gage. She might never have another chance with Clay Meckling, and she might be alone for the rest of her life – but she wouldn't compromise. She couldn't. Something in her blood made her that way.

Dickie Lavender, having no idea about what had just passed silently between them, thumped Bell's helmet. Then he thumped David's, too. 'Lotsa people,' he said admiringly, 'scream like stuck pigs when the man-hoist quits like that in the dang middle of the trip. Or they start yelling to Jesus. But you two were as cool and comfortable as a couple of old miners. Oughta be proud of yourselves.'

34

Rhonda Lovejoy stopped the car. She did it too abruptly, with a hard punch of her right foot, and the vehicle's tires shrieked their indignation as the hindquarters fishtailed wildly to the right.

'Holy crap,' her passenger yelped. 'You trying to put me through the windshield, or what?'

'Look over there.' Rhonda ignored his complaint and pointed eagerly. 'On the concrete pad in front of the garage. That black one's an Escalade. The other one's a Lexus. Come on.'

Before Jake Oakes could tell her one more time just how truly bad an idea he considered this to be – how foolish, reckless, and most likely ineffective – Rhonda had already scooted out of her car. She'd parked within sight of Walter Albright's ostentatiously massive brick house in Harbor View, a new housing development located just past Blythesburg. There was no harbor here, hence no view of same; the name had been chosen because the developers thought it sounded snooty and exclusive, as if these were elegant oceanfront estates in Connecticut, not gaudy McMansions set down in a converted farm field in West Virginia.

From here she and Oakes could see a portion of the

lengthy, triple-wide concrete pad that constituted Albright's driveway, and had as well a beguiling peek at his rolling, meticulously landscaped backyard. The house included a two-story, four-car garage, topped by a small replica of a sailboat that served as a weather vane; the copper was well on its way to oxidizing into the classic blue-green shade. Albright apparently liked to indulge in the Harbor View fantasy himself.

Rhonda and Oakes got back in her car. They needed to see the place from another angle. Their suspicions were being richly fed by every frill and accouterment they came across: This was too much house, too much garage, too much everything for a retired state trooper, even one who had worked an additional two decades as security chief for a chain of truck stops. Rhonda had done her due diligence before setting out: She'd checked with her niece, Judy – a real estate agent in Collier County – and discovered that Walter Albright's wife, Gloria, had purchased the $950,000 home just over a year ago. She paid cash. And she filed the title in her maiden name – Gloria Bransted. Judy was able to find out all of this because she was Rhonda's niece. And Lovejoys always knew where to look.

Rhonda was glad that Oakes had agreed to accompany her. 'Agreed' was too generous; 'consented under coercion' might be closer to the mark. Rhonda had stopped by the courthouse early Saturday morning and found the deputy just as he was finishing up the night shift, ready to head home, whereupon she announced to him her plans to drive over to Harbor View and snoop around Albright's property. During one of her visits to Nick's hospital room, Rhonda explained, Nick had talked about Albright. About how inefficient the old man had become at his job, how slipshod and forgetful. Something had clicked in Rhonda's head – and so, she told Oakes, she was going to check it out. Right now.

You can't do that, Oakes said. *Watch me*, she'd snapped back at him. *You're crazy*, he replied. *Could be*, Rhonda said, adding, *But I'll be damned if I'm going to keep sitting around without lifting a finger to find out who shot Nick Fogelsong. He's my friend.* Oakes shook his head and said: *Friend or not, it's Collier County's lookout, not ours, and besides—* At that point, Rhonda started walking away. *Hold on,* Oakes called out. *You can't go by yourself.* And she turned back to him and said, *Well, okay, but you've got to change out of your uniform first. Dressed like that, you can't sneak up on anybody.*

As they drove toward Harbor View he had expressed his surprise that there was a passel of palatial homes in such a benighted area of the state. 'You're making a common mistake,' Rhonda had reprimanded him. 'You think it's all shacks and trailers in these parts. No. There's houses that serve the high end, too – doctors, lawyers, people with real money. Go-to-hell money, we call it. And that's the problem these days. There's high and there's low. But there's no middle.'

Then he'd asked another question: What made her so certain that, if Albright *had* been involved in a drug ring, and profited handsomely from same, there would be sufficient evidence of that at his home? 'Oh, Jake, Jake,' Rhonda said, giving him a piteous glance as she swung her car toward the exit marked BLYTHESBURG. 'What's the point of having more money than other folks if you can't show off to the neighbors? Subtlety is not a virtue much prized by the sort we're talking about. Believe me – if Walter Albright took payoffs to let Highway Haven turn into an open-air drug market, he'd put that money to good use. He'd be conspicuous about it – and he couldn't help himself. In a funny kind of way, all those shiny new toys would help a man like Albright feel better about what he's done. They justify it. Working all those years in law enforcement for peanuts, while the bad guys rake it in – why, it's only right and proper that he finally gets a taste of the high life. You see? Okay, so here's the bet. I say there'll be at least one riding lawnmower, a motor home, a trampoline, a snowblower, and maybe a Bobcat in an outbuilding.'

Oakes laughed and said, 'I'll see your lawnmower, your motor home, your trampoline, your snowblower, and your Bobcat, and I'll raise you a swimming pool and a hot tub.'

While they watched, an overweight man came out of the back door of the house. He headed toward the Escalade. With a jaunty nonchalance, he flipped a set of car keys up in the air and then caught it again. Flip and catch. Flip and catch. It was cold this morning, and he wore a green plaid coat. On his head was a ball cap with a Peterbilt logo.

Oakes pulled Rhonda back behind her car. He unclipped the cell from his belt. Punched in a number.

'I'd like to speak to Sheriff Ives,' he said. 'Tell him it's Deputy Jake Oakes from the Raythune County Sheriff's Department.'

'We got 'em.'

Bell repeated the words triumphantly into her phone – 'We got 'em' – just to make sure that Mary Sue Fogelsong had heard her correctly on the other end. 'Tell Nick that a search warrant for Walter Albright's house and grounds was executed at 2:14 this morning by the Collier County Sheriff's Department. We found evidence that he accepted bribes to compromise security procedures at the Highway Haven.' She paused. 'Sure, put him on the line. I'll tell him myself.'

Waiting for the phone to be passed to Nick in his hospital bed, Bell looked across the table at Rhonda and Jake. Both had taken her up on her offer to buy them a truly epic breakfast here at JP's – eggs, sausage links, grits, hotcakes, waffles, toast, and coffee – on this early Sunday morning, and were currently clawing their way through it at warp speed, like a demolition crew paid by the brick. They'd been up all night and they were ravenous; they had gone along on last night's raid that had dismantled a major drug ring. Even though they had no official role, it was their tip that had initiated the action, and the Collier County Sheriff had taken one look at their eager faces and muttered, 'What the hell. Come on, you two – you can ride with me. But keep your damned heads down, okay?'

Nick's voice on her cell sounded tired. 'Hey, Bell,' he said. She looked forward to the moment when he didn't sound tired all the time. Tired didn't suit Nick Fogelsong.

'Hey.' Bell was excited, and pleased that she had good news for a change. 'We nailed the bastards. It was Albright's son-in-law – Leroy Smathers – who ran the show. He'd been paying Walter for the last year and a half to look the other way while they set up their operation. Walter was more than happy to pocket the cash. Once Walter got fired, though, they had to find another distribution point. That's why they went to Royce Dillard.' She stopped to take a long, satisfied breath. 'Albright's decided to cooperate with us. Turns out that after he lost his job, he wasn't worth a damn to them. So they started treating him pretty bad. Moved into his house, ordered him around. They even trashed the inside of his motor home – and that was enough to turn Albright against his own kinfolk. I mean, drug dealing's one thing, but pouring beer on the Berber carpet? He's jumping at the chance to testify against the lot of them – for whatever amount of time is shaved off his sentence.'

'Good. That's real good news,' Nick said.

She waited for him to ask her for more details. When he didn't, she supplied them, anyway. 'The guy in the green plaid? That's Leroy. Guy who shot you is a scumbag named Tommy Boykins. He's looking at an attempted murder charge. I know some of those Collier County judges. They won't go easy on him.'

There was a pause, and then Mary Sue was back on the line again. 'He's having a rough morning, Bell. Lots of pain. Pushed himself a little too hard in physical therapy yesterday. He didn't want to ask for pain meds this morning – but he finally had to and he's pissed about it. Listen, though – this is wonderful news. You've done a splendid job.'

'Not me,' Bell said. 'It was Rhonda Lovejoy and Jake Oakes.'

At the sound of their names, the two people across from her grinned. Oakes toasted the table with his orange juice glass.

'You tell them,' Mary Sue said, 'that I'm sure Nick'll want to thank them personally. Just as soon as he's able.'

'I will.' Bell ended the call. She placed her cell next

to her napkin. The napkin was still folded; she'd ordered only coffee.

'What did Nick say?' Rhonda asked. She'd had to finish swallowing a jumbo bite of syrup-beribboned pancake before she could speak. 'Got to be a relief, knowing that the man who shot him is gonna be out of action for a good long while.'

'Yes,' Bell said. 'He's looking forward to the day he can shake your hands.' She didn't elaborate. She felt protective of Nick and his despondency; she didn't want to share with too many people the fact of how changed he was, how knocked back by his wound and by his awareness of all that he couldn't do anymore.

'So how'd you spend *your* Saturday?' Rhonda said. She was saucy, sky-high, happier than Bell had seen her in weeks. The Dillard trial was taking a toll on her.

'Let me think,' Bell said. She pictured the scary tick of the minutes trapped on the stalled man-hoist, the rich scent of the coal dust, that dark world. And she thought, *Later.* She'd share the story with Rhonda later. This was their morning, their victory.

The only person in whom Bell had confided thus far was Carla. Her daughter possessed an adventurous soul. Bell knew she wouldn't say, *Oh my GOD. You were WHERE? And you were trapped for HOW LONG?* – the probable reaction of almost anyone else. Indeed, when she'd called Carla last night and described the ordeal, the young woman said, *That is SO incredibly cool, Mom. Sounds like a new ride at Six Flags – the Haunted Man-Hoist.*

'This and that,' Bell replied.

A frowning Oakes was using his fork to chase the last few biscuit crumbs around his plate. 'Can't help but wonder,' he said, 'why a man like Nick Fogelsong didn't suspect Albright right from the get-go.'

'He thought of Albright as a colleague,' Bell said. 'A brother officer.'

'Hell. Colleagues can let you down, quick as other folks can. Fogelsong's got to know that.'

'He does. But it's never going to be his first thought.' Bell saw that Oakes was still frowning, so she came at the explanation another way. 'The minute it's our first thought,' she said, 'that's when we quit. That's when it's all over. We've got to believe there's a bright line between the good guys and the bad. Somebody like Albright is an anomaly, an exception – not the rule. The second we're not surprised by the likes of Walter Albright, the battle's well and truly lost.'

Oakes nodded. He seemed to accept that. 'Well, folks,' he said, his voice turning jocular again, 'I'm mighty glad this all worked out okay, but Sheriff Harrison's going to kill me when she finds out how I spent my time off. Just so you know. All I ask is that you give me a decent burial. Something nice. Not too fancy.'

'Don't worry about it. I'll square things with her,' Bell said.

He winked at her. Then he patted his belly, which never seemed to expand no matter how much food he put away. 'Well, now that I've rejuvenated myself, I've got to get ready for my shift this afternoon. Tell you this much, Rhonda,' he said, offering her an admiring nod, 'if I'm ever in any kind of trouble, I hope they send you to my rescue. 'Cause you just don't quit, girl.'

They watched him leave. Once the red door had closed behind him, Bell looked around the restaurant. It was still too early for the after-church crowd, and so most of the tables were empty. Through the wide window that ran the length of the front wall of JP's, you could see the gray flanks of the mountains in the distance, chipped and scored like the hard-used hides of immense prehistoric animals. She thought about those mountains and what they had witnessed all these centuries: good people and greedy people, happy lives and wretched ones. And endless, endless stories. In this place, history seemed a little closer to the surface of things than it did anywhere else. It was always within reach, like your next cup of coffee. History wasn't a set of ancient fables but a daily reality that you felt and you tasted. It lived in your skin. It lived in the dirt and the sky, just as it lived in the hardships and the sorrows that stretched back into a common past that would never be forgotten. History mattered here. It told people who they were and what their lives really meant.

She remembered what she and David had talked about on the man-hoist. And she remembered the article in the *Bluefield Daily Telegraph*, the one from all those years ago, the one in which Royce Dillard's story had been told for the first time. 'Rhonda,' Bell said. 'I need a favor. I don't know for sure, but it might make a difference for Royce. Look, I know you're exhausted, but—'

'I can sleep when the trial's over,' Rhonda said. 'Tell me what you need.'

35

Rhonda was out of breath. Bell asked her to repeat what she'd said, so that she could understand her; the words had begun to run together in a hasty mush, fed by zeal and fatigue.

'Got back about midnight,' Rhonda said. She plopped down on the couch across from Bell's desk. 'Some hard driving on those roads after dark, I'm telling you.'

It was not yet seven in the morning. Rhonda had left Acker's Gap just after finishing her breakfast at JP's the day before. Her destination was a small coal town in the southern part of the state.

'It's like you figured, Bell,' Rhonda said. 'Ed Hackel had driven over there a few days before he was murdered. He'd been hunting her for weeks. But he didn't have any contacts. And you don't track down somebody in southern West Virginia – somebody who went off the grid in 1972 – unless you know what you're doing.'

Rhonda sat back against the couch. Her hair was flat, even greasy-looking, with none of the usual evidence of its having been fussed over, and the skin around her eyes was smudged and crinkled with tiredness. She had texted Bell at 5 A.M., announcing that she'd gotten back too late last night to call but that she really needed to meet before the day's court session began.

2 excited 2 wait: That was how Rhonda justified her request.

Sunrise had just touched the edges of the tall leaded windows in Bell's office. One of the virtues of an ancient courthouse – something to set against the negatives such as lousy ventilation, appalling plumbing, and warm hospitality toward successive generations of mice and assorted vermin in every crevice and crawl space – was the presence of large and copious windows. More modern public structures, their designers mindful of energy loss through all that glass, featured windows that were little more than slits. Bell loved her windows. She wasn't sure she could function without them. She kept the brown drapes swept back and well secured, so that the world beyond her office was always visible – the world beyond, that is, whatever stories of misery and conflict and loss were being set before her, hour by hour, day after day.

'So,' Bell said. She wanted to give Rhonda more time, but her curiosity wouldn't hear of it. 'Vera Tolbert.'

'To begin with, she's not Vera Tolbert anymore. That's one of the things that made her so hard to find. In 1975 she took up with Orville Gunderson. So now she calls herself Vera Gunderson. It's common-law, though. No marriage records. That's what held up Hackel when he was trying to find her. Can't be done through records. You've got to go there. Chat with folks. Took Hackel a while to figure that out.'

'And she agreed to talk to you?' Bell said.

'Not at first. She was suspicious as all get-out. I walked up to the door and I knocked, and when she opened it, she had a rifle in her hand.'

'You're kidding.'

'I am *not* kidding,' Rhonda declared. 'It turned out to be just a BB gun, but my Lord – if somebody'd been monitoring my heart rate right then, they would've called the squad. Anyway, she opened the door and she held up that BB gun – I could tell by now what it was – and she said, "Wish you people would leave me the hell alone." Her face was all red. She was breathing real hard. My grandfather breathed like that – I'd know that sound anywhere. Too many cigarettes over too many years. Anyway, I just looked her dead-square in the eye and I said, "Ma'am, I don't mean to make things difficult for you, but I'm an assistant prosecutor over in Raythune County, and we're trying to get to the bottom of a murder case." Next thing I knew, she'd lowered that BB gun and invited me inside the house and offered me a cup of coffee.'

'Wonder what changed her mind?'

'The truth. The truth changed her mind. I mean, I asked her that myself, and she said, "You were honest about why you're here. Straight off. The fella who was here before, he lied to me. Lied right to my face. Said he was with the guvmint and was tracking down folks who were owed some money. So naturally I let him in. Turns out that was a damned lie."' Rhonda put her hands to her hair. What she felt there drew a frown. 'Lord, I bet I look like ten miles of bad road. Just couldn't take time for the curling iron. Had to get over here.'

Bell didn't say, *No, you look fine.* Especially not after the issue of truth had been raised so recently. She said, 'You'll have a chance to freshen up before court. Promise.'

'Good thing. Else the judge and jurors are likely to run screaming from the courtroom. Anyway,' Rhonda said, settling back into her story, 'naturally I asked her the identity of her gentleman caller. Yep – it was Ed Hackel. That was the name. I showed her a picture, to make absolutely certain. She sort of snickered when she saw it. "Oh, yeah," she said. "That's him all right. Nice suit. Big brown tweed overcoat. Wore his hair all slicked back. Heavy man. Real heavy. Put it this way – if he stepped on your toe, you'd know it. But still handsome. Kinda like that Perry Mason fella. Raymond Burr." Once she'd let him in her house, she said, he came clean about why he was there. He wanted her to change her story. Her story about what she'd seen on the morning of February twenty-sixth, 1972. Wanted her to say that Mike Dillard hadn't tried to save his little boy. No, sir. He'd left his boy to die.'

Bell nodded. She could imagine Hackel's threat to Royce Dillard: *Sell the land or I'll make sure the world thinks your life story is a lie. A fraud.*

It was the only leverage that would matter to Dillard. It meant more than a threat of exposing the drugs in his barn. It meant more than anything.

Sell the land or I'll have that old lady – the one who saw your father save you – change her story. She'll say whatever I tell her to say. No problem. She'll say your father didn't save anybody. Only cared about himself.

The significance of Dillard's suffering, and his family's suffering: It all came down to what his father had done. The ultimate sacrifice. If that was taken away, then there was nothing. There was only pain. And pain without meaning is unendurable.

Dillard didn't give a damn about the things that most

people did – money, possessions, power, sex, revenge, reputation. The things that could incite people into violence when they thought they were under siege. And so Hackel had to find the one thing Dillard *did* care about.

And he found it.

Hackel, Bell speculated, probably hadn't realized what he was setting into motion when he threatened Royce Dillard's story. Hackel didn't know he was pushing the man toward the abyss. And sealing his own fate as well.

'She said Hackel offered her a nice payday for changing her story, for claiming she'd lied all those years ago,' Rhonda went on. 'A thousand dollars.' A quick lift of her eyebrows. 'A woman like Vera probably hasn't seen a thousand dollars all at the same time ever before in her life.'

'So she agreed.'

'Nope. She didn't.' Rhonda grinned. 'She may be poor and old, but she's not stupid. She took a long look at that fancy overcoat of his, and those shiny shoes, and she smelled that expensive aftershave – and realized that he had a few bucks in his pocket and might go higher. After all, he'd taken the trouble to find her and to come all that way. He must want her to change her story pretty bad. So she said, "Two thousand." Bless her heart.'

'And?'

'Hackel didn't say yes right away. Now, lots of folks in Vera's spot would've backed down at that point. They'd have said, "Oh, come to think of it, a thousand is fine, thanks very much." Not her.'

Rhonda pulled a small notebook out of her purse, in which she had made her notes. 'Here's what she told me she said to Ed Hackel. "I'm sixty-six years old, mister.

I've got arthritis so bad that I can't get out of bed in the morning without groaning so loud that it scares the cat, and things'll be about the same for me, with or without your damned money. So the price is now three thousand. But if you go longer than a few days afore getting back to me, price goes up to five."' Rhonda flipped the notebook closed. 'Gotta admire her moxie. And her understanding of capitalism – the more somebody wants something, the more you can charge for it.'

Bell remembered the list of items on the nightstand of Hackel's motel room. The scrap of paper with *VG $??* scribbled on it. Hackel probably needed Carolyn Runyon's approval to get the cash for the higher payment to Vera Gunderson.

'All she had to do,' Rhonda said, 'was recant her testimony. Just tell a few newspapers and TV and radio stations that the tale she'd spun all those years ago – about what she saw on the day of the flood, the story about Mike Dillard and his little boy, Royce – was a lie.'

'And how was she going to explain changing her story, after all these years?'

Rhonda shrugged. 'Guilty conscience. Wanting to set the record straight before she died.'

'Did she know that Hackel had been murdered in the meantime?'

'Oh, yeah. Just a small item in the paper over there – but she recognized the name right away, of course. And she wasn't embarrassed to tell me that her first thought was, "Dang it. Now I gotta forget about that big-screen TV I was gonna buy."' Rhonda closed her eyes, and used her index fingers to rub at them. 'She asked me about Royce Dillard. Hasn't seen him since he was two years old. But she's sure he isn't capable of murder. Asked me my opinion on the matter.'

'What did you say?'

'I said what you always say, Bell. I said anybody's capable of anything.'

36

Winter was on its way out, and spring was making inroads, but the radiators in the old courtroom were still on duty. They raised their usual ruckus each morning, an amateur symphony of plinks, pops, bangs, hoots, and rattles; a steady high-pitched whistle that made people look around for a hidden teakettle; and a low ominous rumble. By midafternoon they settled down a bit, although they were never completely quiet. Occasionally a small *fwizzzzt* would escape from a radiator's nether regions, causing some of the younger spectators to glare disgustedly at an older person, and the older person to mumble *Sorry* sheerly out of habit.

Bell sat at the prosecution table. She was, for the moment, alone in the courtroom; the day's trial session would begin in ten minutes. She'd come here after releasing Rhonda to go wrangle her hair in the women's bathroom.

Despite all the good news lately – the arrest of Nick's assailant, Rhonda's success in finding the woman who'd witnessed Royce Dillard's rescue all those years ago – Bell was still feeling sad and frustrated, a way it was all too easy to feel in Acker's Gap. If she wasn't careful, if she didn't keep a watch on herself, she could end up feeling this way all the damned time. Frustration was the default emotion around here. A sense that things would never change.

Well, things had changed, all right. Clay was gone. Nick was flat on his back with a wounded heart, in more ways than one. And Royce Dillard was on his way to prison for killing a man who had pushed him to the brink by threatening to tell an unbearable lie.

Once the defense finished with its side of the story, closing arguments would begin. Bell had been contemplating what she'd say to the jury. Yes, Royce Dillard committed murder. But he had his reasons. Dillard must be made to pay for his crime. Yet justice tempered with mercy was still justice. She wouldn't ask for a life sentence. A long one, yes – but not life.

She heard the groan and scrape of the big double doors as they swung open. The flat crash of loafers on old wood. Someone was coming up the center aisle. Bell rose and turned.

'Morning,' Serena said. She clutched notebooks, file folders, and legal pads to her chest. Her black hair was raked back so severely that her face looked even leaner and more pinched than usual. Serena had once told Bell and Rhonda that she lost at least fifteen pounds during every trial. *And I find them,* Rhonda had noted ruefully.

'Morning,' Bell replied.

The two women stood in the narrow chasm between the prosecutor's table and the defense attorney's table. In a few minutes, spectators would begin to fill in the rows behind them, murmuring hellos, shucking off coats, scooting over to accommodate latecomers. A deputy would lead in a shuffling, blank-faced Dillard from his cell. Judge Barbour would enter and seat himself amidst his baggy black robe. With the drop of his gavel, the trial would resume.

For now, though, it was just the two of them. Bell and Serena. Prosecutor and defense attorney. Here in the courtroom they were adversaries, enemies, but in another way, an overarching way, they were sisters. At the start of this case, Bell had seen herself in Carolyn Runyon, and had imagined that by now she might be indistinguishable from the Mountain Magic CEO – if she'd stayed in DC, that is, and had taken the job offer from a posh legal firm. But – no. No, now she saw herself in Serena Crumpler. Serena was younger, taller, thinner; her hair was black instead of brown, and straight while Bell's had a slight wave, just enough to be hard to comb on humid days. Those things didn't really matter. The two women were here. Right here. They had choices, and here was where they'd chosen to live their lives. Here was where they worked, and dreamed of better days. Here – in a place most people left just as soon as they were able. Leaving was easy; staying was hard.

The radiator spat out a wheezy curse. It broke the spell. Serena moved away and sat down at the defense table, anxious to review her witness list for today's session. First up: Opal Lymon.

Opal was seventy-eight years old. For well over a century, her family had run the only supermarket in Acker's Gap. In the 1930s the store almost closed, stomped flat by the Depression, as so many other businesses were, but in the 1940s it sprang to life again, like a newly opened page in a pop-up book. Opal and her brothers and sisters all started working in the store when they were still too small to reach the counter. Their father put a stepstool behind the cash register to accommodate them.

'Miss Lymon,' Serena said. 'How long have you known Royce Dillard?'

Opal was so thin that she looked like a wire sculpture. She had sporadic hair the color and consistency of milkweed. But she still worked twelve hours a day at the store, seven days a week, and she answered in a clear, firm voice.

'Known him since he was a child. His great-aunt Bessie used to bring him in with her when she shopped. Once he graduated high school, he come to work for me.'

'What sort of person is he, Miss Lymon?'

'Royce has his problems. Nobody can say otherwise and be speaking the truth. Went through a lot as a child. Can't forget that. He's what I call crippled-shy – he can't even look you in the eye. Can't speak sometimes. It's held him back, no question. But I'll say this. He's honest and he's true.'

'Did he have any friends while he worked for you?'

'Friends? Royce? No, no. I only ever saw him talk to one other employee. Real pretty gal named Brenda Smith. But only for a little while. Then he quit.'

'Did you ever see him commit a violent act? Or threaten to?'

'Oh, no, no, no. Never. Gentle as they come.' She pointed a bony finger at Serena. 'You know about his dogs and how he coddles them. Everybody does. Well, that tells you all you need to know about a person. He'd never raise a hand to man nor beast.'

Bell's cross-examination was brief.

'When did Royce Dillard last work for you?'

Julia Keller

'Oh, must've been – let's say 2003.'

'And how often have you seen him since that time?'

The wrinkles around Opal's mouth tightened as she frowned. She knew what Bell was getting at. Opal would forgive her – she understood what Bell's job was, and appreciated it when a job was done well – but she didn't have to like it.

'Three, maybe four times a year,' she said. 'Comes in for supplies. Puts 'em in a little wagon. Drags it back home again.'

'Four times a year,' Bell repeated. 'Once every three months – if then. So you really don't have any idea what Royce Dillard is like now, do you? For all you know, he could've changed a great deal.'

Opal shook her head. 'Nobody changes that much.'

'Thank you, Miss Lymon,' Bell said. 'That's all.'

Serena's next witness was Stanley Baker, a lanky young veterinarian. One day last year, Baker recounted, Royce Dillard brought a desperately injured dog into his office. The animal had been hit by a truck out on Route 6 and was in agony from a shattered spine; Dillard had found him by the side of the road, scooped him up and carried him on foot the two and a half miles to the vet's office. Baker, alas, had not been able to save the dog.

'Having observed Mr Dillard in a moment of intense stress,' Serena asked, 'would you think him capable of violence?'

'Absolutely not,' Baker said. 'He's a fine man, from everything I've seen. Decent and peace-loving. A little peculiar – no doubt about it – but violent? No.'

Baker pushed up his glasses on his bony nose and added, 'By the way, he asked for the ashes. Of the dog he'd never even known. He told me that the dog must've loved to run in the woods, and probably just burst out onto the road one night, coming out of the woods too fast for that trucker to stop. So Royce wanted to scatter his ashes in Old Man's Creek. Because, Royce said, when you're lying down for the last time, you have the right to lie down next to what you love.'

The old couple had come to court every day. They sat in the far outside corner of the very last row, bundled up in their thick coats and their muddy boots, muffled by their clothing and by a kind of force field of reticence that seemed to grip them like frost on a pair of fence posts. Early in the prosecution's case, Bell had called Andy Stegner briefly to the stand to give his account of finding the body in Old Man's Creek; after that he would, she'd assumed, go back to his farm and his isolated life. Yet he never missed a day of the trial. Nor did his wife. They paid close attention to the proceedings, but they spoke to no one. Occasionally, as the spectators filed in for another day, someone would nod hello to the couple; the Stegners would nod back, but they seemed locked in their own lives, not unfriendly but simply distant, their minds on other things.

After Baker's testimony, the defense rested, and the trial was adjourned for the day. Royce Dillard would not be taking the stand. Bell understood Serena's decision. Given his odd behavior, his tics and his quirks, Dillard was a risk. His peculiarities might be off-putting to the jury. *A little too Boo Radley* was how Rhonda had described him. She wasn't being unkind. Just accurate.

The trial was nearing its end. In just a few more days it would all be over, Dillard's fate decided, and the people

in attendance today seemed to carry that solemn awareness in their expressions as they departed. The occupants
of each row rose in unison, as if their names had been
called by some invisible authority, and then waited until
the people in the row behind them had made their way
into the aisle, whereupon they followed. All were
funneled toward the big double doors at the back of
the courtroom. The low murmur of talk mingled with
coughs, the occasional explosive sneeze, the audible rub
of slick parkas against wood as big-hipped people nego-
tiated the narrow aisles.

Bell was one of the last to leave. She crossed the
threshold and moved into the hall outside. She heard
her name.

'Belfa Elkins.' It was Opal Lymon. The old woman
stood next to the wall across from the double doors, a
red flannel coat draped across her clasped hands. Next
to her were Andy and Brenda Stegner. The three of them
had stationed themselves out of the flow of the departing
people.

'Hey, there,' Opal called again. She shifted the coat
so that she could lift a bony hand. 'Come on over.' She
used her chin as a pointer. 'Did you know that Brenda
here used to work for me, about a thousand years ago?
She was Brenda Smith back then, but I still remember
what a good hard worker she was. Best I ever had. She
and Royce used to be friends, back in the day. Haven't
seen her in ages.'

'That so.'

Bell needed to get back to her office. She'd sent
Rhonda on ahead, to start the coffee and line up the
legal pads for the first draft of their closing argument,
and she still wanted to speak to Dillard in his cell tonight.

But she obliged Opal's summons. A few minutes of cordiality wouldn't kill her, would it? Regarding the three old people, the names swam forward in her mind.

Brenda Smith.

Now, Brenda Stegner.

Royce Dillard's neighbor had known him from long before. They had worked together, when they were young. She'd been his only friend, according to Opal's testimony.

And so, Bell thought, her brain working so quickly now that she wouldn't have been at all surprised if it had generated a whirring sound and perhaps a burning smell as the gears and sprockets overheated, *maybe she walks over to Royce's place by herself that Thursday afternoon for a visit, but Royce isn't home – he's still in town. Ed Hackel shows up, ready to resume his hectoring. She's surely heard about Hackel's treatment of Royce. Everybody knows how he's hounded Royce, trying to persuade him to sell his land. Now's her chance to stick up for Royce. She tells Hackel to leave him alone. Hackel laughs at her. Tells her to go to hell. Turns around. Enraged, determined to get him to leave Royce alone, she picks up a shovel . . .*

Bell did a quick appraisal of Brenda Stegner's body. She was a heavy woman, solid and strong. A farm woman. Biceps as big as a man's. Would she be able to deliver a death blow with a shovel?

Yes. Yes, she would.

And when her husband came home that Saturday morning and told her what he'd found in Old Man's Creek – what sorts of emotions had run through her? Panic, guilt, fear, shame – what? Had she confessed to Andy Stegner? If not then, maybe later?

353

As she stood there in the hall, gripped by the images generated by her suspicions, Bell realized she was grasping at remote possibilities, at something, at *anything*, that might change Dillard's fate. Maybe she was doing it as much for Rhonda – and her belief in the man – as she was for Royce.

'Hello again,' Andy Stegner said. He shook Bell's hand. His hand was big, hard, thickened by scabs and calluses. A working-man's hand. His face was a simple one, rumpled with age, the eyes steady and stoic. 'I have to tell you, ma'am – we still don't believe it, me and Brenda. We come here every day and we've listened to everything and we ain't changed our minds one whit. Royce is a good man. No way he'd ever—'

'Now, Andy,' Opal said, wagging a finger at him. 'Bell's the prosecutor. She's doing her job.'

'True. True.' He touched his forehead, and spent a few seconds rubbing at a scaly patch of skin. 'Sorry. Just got carried away. Hard to see this happenin' to him. Felt we oughta be here, as often as we could. For support. But the farm's always callin', you know.' He turned to his wife. 'Probably ought to use the facilities, honey, before we head home. Long drive.'

This is it, Bell thought, trying to control the excitement that was rising in her. *This is my chance to speak alone with Brenda Stegner*. If she was lucky – and if Brenda was as remorseful as Bell hoped she'd be – this could be wrapped up quickly.

Bell said good-bye to Opal and the Stegners. Wished them all a pleasant evening. She rounded the corner of the long courthouse corridor. She let several minutes go by. Then she slipped back toward the wooden door marked LADIES. The entrance was in a small recessed area, out of the line of sight of people waiting in the lobby.

Brenda shuffled by. She was a lumpy figure, gray head aimed at the floor, shoulders hunched. Her life seemed to press down on her like a crossbeam she'd been tasked with lifting into place.

Bell put a hand on the woman's well-patched coat. She drew her back into the recessed area. There was no one else in the vicinity.

'Mrs Stegner,' Bell said quietly. 'I'd like a word with you, please.'

Confusion bloomed in Brenda's pale blue eyes. She didn't respond.

'You know Royce Dillard,' Bell went on. 'Like Opal said, you were friends a very long time ago, weren't you? And you didn't like the way Ed Hackel was treating him.' Still no response. 'You're a good woman, Mrs Stegner. You want to protect Royce. He needs somebody to protect him, doesn't he? He can't do it for himself. He doesn't know about the world. He doesn't know what it can do to you if you're not strong.' Bell kept her hand on Brenda's arm. The woman had begun to nod, slowly and tentatively. 'I think you want to tell me what happened, Mrs Stegner. I think you do.'

Now the nodding stopped. Brenda blinked. 'Tell you what happened when?'

'When you killed Ed Hackel.'

Brenda jerked her arm away. 'What are you— No. No, no. You've got it wrong, you hear? I didn't kill anybody. Jesus – *me*? You can't think – you don't really believe—'

'Then where were you on the Thursday afternoon when Hackel was murdered?'

Brenda took in a torturously slow breath. She was a long time letting it back out again.

'I can't tell you that.'

'I need to know, Mrs Stegner.'

'I said I can't tell you.'

'All right, then. I'll have to call the sheriff. We'll go into one of the interrogation rooms and we'll talk about it there. Your husband can either wait for you or pick you up later. Your choice.' She quickly recited the woman's Miranda rights.

The fear in Brenda's eyes had gone through several transformations. Now it reached a crescendo. Her hands began to shake.

'You've got to under— I can't— I won't—' Brenda's sentences kept stopping and starting. The trembling in her hands had expanded into the rest of her body. 'I'm not— I didn't— Please—'

'What happens next is up to you, Mrs Stegner.'

The woman raised her head. The expression on her face was a blend of resignation and heartbreak, with a tincture of something else, too, something small and dark and lost.

'Okay,' she said. 'Okay, fine. You want to know where I was on that Thursday – I'll tell you. My husband doesn't know. If you tell him, you'll destroy just about everything that matters to me – but I can't stop you. You'll do as you see fit.' She swallowed and then winced, as if she'd just had a taste of her own lies. 'I'm a drunk. A lowdown, stinking, shit-faced drunk. Okay? That's how I deal with things. With the fact that there's never enough money. And nothing in my life except work and mud and crap. So two or three days a week – more, if I need it – I drive over to Swinton Falls and I go to meetings run by the Reverend Stony McHale. He'll vouch for me.

'Andy doesn't know. He thinks I go visit my mother. Because he thinks I'm *happy*. He knows I used to drink, but he thinks it was easy for me to quit. See, I'm a lot younger than he is, Mrs Elkins. More'n twenty years younger. You can't tell it now, but I had big dreams. I had plans for my life. You shoulda seen me. Back when I knew Royce, back in those days – I had the boys chasing after me, let me tell you. And then things just – they just happened. That's all. The world just got away from me. I love Andy. I do. I love my husband – but I fucking *hate* my life.'

Brenda didn't kill Hackel. Her alibi was easy to check – so easy that she couldn't be lying. Bell knew Stony McHale and his work. She admired him. He wouldn't lie, either.

I was wrong, Bell thought, regret washing over her. *And I put this poor woman through hell. I made her say out loud what she's spent years trying to push down and forget. But as Opal Lymon said: I'm the prosecutor. I'm doing my job.*

'You go ask him, Mrs Elkins,' Brenda continued, in a voice that was now so low and so hopeless that it sounded like the rasp of a rusty saw drawn across scarred wood. 'You do that. You go ask the Reverend McHale about that Thursday. And all the other Thursdays. And the Tuesdays, too. All the days I have to go talk to somebody so I don't jump clean out of my skin. So I don't grab for that bottle. He'll tell you.'

Brenda lurched away without looking back, head down, thick boots hitting the hardwood floor with the flailing stamp of wild sorrow. She was returning to the husband who waited for her in the lobby, and who loved her without knowing her at all. Her secrets were simple ones, ordinary ones, but they were hers, and they would follow her forever, like the echoes of her heavy steps through the emptied-out courthouse.

37

'Royce,' Bell said. 'It's time. Cards on the table, okay? I know what Hackel threatened you with.'

He wanted to look up at her, but he couldn't, and so he moved his head sideways instead of up. She could feel the stubbornness in his stare, even though she couldn't see his eyes.

Dillard sat on the edge of his cot in the narrow jail cell. His legs vibrated. The motion seemed to be outside of his control, a force that had overtaken him long ago and would keep on running until somebody somewhere – not him – was finally able to pull the plug.

In front of him stood three women: Bell, Serena, and Rhonda. Just outside the cell, slouching against the cinder block wall, was Chess Rader, night supervisor of the jail. It was dinnertime, and the other prisoners were busy with their pudding cups. Chess had delivered the last plastic tray to the last cell in line and then returned here.

'He was going to pay Vera to change her story,' Bell said. 'Isn't that right? That's what Hackel held over your head. We know what he told you – that if you didn't sell the land, he'd give the signal. Set it all into motion.' She made her voice a tick gentler. 'Your whole life would look like a lie. A fraud. Everything people have always believed about your family – twisted, torn up, destroyed. It's no wonder you attacked him. Lots of people would've done the same. He'd hit you with something a lot worse than a shovel.' She held up a manila folder. 'I've got the paperwork ready. You change your plea to guilty. We explain it all to Judge Barbour. It'll work out a lot better for you, Royce, if you just admit what you did, and we can go from there.'

Serena reached down and touched the top of his shoulder. Dillard didn't pull away this time. He seemed unaware that her hand was even there.

'Royce,' Serena said. She spoke quickly. 'It's your decision. If you'd like to think about this, I can ask Judge Barbour for a delay – and then we'll talk about it, just you and me, and—'

'Wait,' Dillard said. He pointed at Bell, without looking at her. 'Yeah. What you're sayin'. That's it. That's what happened.'

Bell felt a flutter in her stomach. Hearing it confirmed, hearing him say it out loud, made this a moment she had both sought and dreaded. She'd thought she was prepared for his confession, but now that he was making it, she realized that she wasn't. Yes, she had wanted to win this case. She wanted it badly. But some small part of her – the human part, not the prosecutor part – had secretly held out a fragment of hope that maybe they were wrong. Sheriff Harrison was wrong. The town was wrong. All of them were wrong – except for Rhonda Lovejoy.

And now, this.

'Okay, then,' Bell said. All business. The jail cell had gone quiet. Bone quiet, Nick used to call this kind of intense stillness, by which he meant the quiet of bones in a coffin, locked into position for eternity. 'Here's how it's going to work. When we go back into court tomorrow,' she said, snapping off the words, 'you'll notify Judge Barbour that you want to change your plea to guilty. Then we'll ask for a recess and meet back here to start working on a plea deal once we've looked at—'

'No. No. Wait. Whoa, there,' Dillard said. His voice was jittery with alarm. 'I never did it. I never killed him.'

Serena spoke before Bell could. 'But you just said—'

'NO.' It sounded more like a punch of thunder than a simple word. Seconds after he had spoken, Dillard's body seemed to recoil from the press of their accumulated stares. 'When I said, "Yeah," I meant you had it right about that asshole,' he added, talking so fast that it verged on a kind of gravelly babble. 'It was blackmail, plain and simple. He was gonna call me a liar. Me and my family. Said he'd gotten hold of Vera. Made a deal with her.' His head whipped around, his eyes landing on and then sweeping past the individual cinder blocks in the wall. 'But I didn't kill him. I didn't do it. No way.'

Bell's sympathy was quickly turning into annoyance. She'd done what she could. She'd explored alternative scenarios, she'd considered other culprits, but everything ended up in the same place: the small dirt clearing in front of Royce Dillard's barn, with a shovel being thrust over and over again at the back of a man's neck.

'Best thing you can do for yourself now,' she declared, 'is to change your plea to guilty. Let your lawyer here work out a deal. Now that we have a motive, we can look at possible mitigating—'

'*I never did it,*' Dillard cried out. Spit bubbled up in the corners of his mouth, and when he wrenched his head from side to side, some of the spit flew out and landed on his shirt. He looked like a man in intense, searing pain, the kind of pain that was far worse than a physical wound. 'I *hated* him – I hated his miserable stinking guts – but I never hit him with no shovel and I never killed him,' Dillard said. His next words came out as a sort of primitive incantation: 'Never, never, never, never, never.'

This was not some swaggering defendant, trying to con them with lies and evasions. This was a man turning himself inside out, exposing his soul. He was vulnerable now, Bell thought. If she could push him just a little more, she could get him to admit his guilt. Then she could agree to a more lenient sentence – lenient only in comparison to spending the rest of his days in prison.

'Royce,' Bell said. 'I'm going to ask you one more time. On the lives of your dogs – on the life of Goldie and the rest, and please don't ask me to name them all, because frankly, I don't think I can – do you swear to me, right here and right now, that you did not kill Edward Hackel? On your mother's memory – do you swear you didn't do it?'

He was breathing hard. The breaths were husky and slow, swimming in phlegm. He shook his head back and forth. His face was somber and filled with pain, but his eyes were bright. Bell had been so certain that he was about to confess – she had named the things most sacred to him, his mother and his dogs – that when he didn't confess, she felt as if someone had yanked out a chair just before she sat down in it.

'On my mother's memory,' he intoned, 'and on the lives of my dogs, I swear I didn't kill that sonofabitch.'

A moment passed. The only sounds came from

prisoners in the other cells up and down the line. One man hummed, then stopped. Another bounced a single time on his cot, making it squeak.

She had tried, and failed. He wouldn't budge.

'Okay, Royce,' Bell said. She was weary, and resigned to what would happen next. She'd given him his chance. 'That's it. I'll leave you be. Big day tomorrow. Get yourself a good night's sleep. Don't imagine you'll be having any more company.'

He lowered his sleeve, with which he'd wiped the spittle from his lip. He was settling himself down. 'Nope. Not unless that lady comes by again.'

'What lady?'

'Owner of that company that's puttin' in the resort.'

'Carolyn Runyon.'

'Yeah,' Royce said. 'She's come by here a coupla times to see me.'

Bell looked at Chess. 'I've never seen her name in the log.'

Chess shrugged. 'Can't say. She hasn't been here when I was on duty. But some of the other guys aren't exactly vigilant about logging in visitors' names. Especially if you wave a ten-dollar bill under their nose.'

Bell's eyes consulted Serena, who shook her head. 'News to me, too.'

She turned back to Dillard. 'So Runyon came to see you.'

'Yeah. Doesn't stay long. Just long enough to say that if things don't go my way in the trial, she knows some real good lawyers for the appeal. Said everybody deserves a fair shot.'

All at once it was clear to Bell. It had not been clear to her earlier because there was too much in the way

– too much history, too much fog, too many mountains.

Bell finally understood what had happened in the last few minutes of Ed Hackel's life as he stood in the gray twilight by Royce Dillard's barn. She knew who had killed him, and she knew why. All she had to do now was figure out how to prove it – and do it before the case went to the jury tomorrow.

38

Sometimes Nick Fogelsong thought about Carlene's two little girls – not so little anymore, but he remembered them that way, and so no matter how old they grew, he would always see in them the three-year-old and seven-year-old they once had been, running around the backyard when they visited him and Mary Sue, hair streaming behind them, moving in and out of the shadow of Smithson's Rock – and he wondered what it would have been like.

Having his own children. His and Mary Sue's.

He'd been thinking about it tonight. He only let himself go there when he was alone. The night sounds of the hospital wound themselves around his thoughts until everything dissolved into one thing: the sounds and his thoughts, neither conscious of the other.

It was a natural thing to wonder about – would they have been boys or girls, dark or fair? But it carried a hurtfulness inside it, too, that kind of speculation, like something shiny and pretty you see on the sidewalk and so you reach down and pick it up, and then discover that it's a piece of glass. Before you know it, you're bleeding.

He lay back in his hospital bed and he remembered.

Early on, they had talked about it. Mary Sue, after all, was still a third-grade teacher then. She loved kids; she was relaxed and happy around them. And him? Well, he could try. He was a serious man. Too serious, a lot of people said. He'd been in law enforcement many years, even before he met and married Mary Sue. But by God, he could try. He'd loosen up. Kids could do that to a man. He'd let himself be soft and vulnerable around his kids. He'd never raise his voice in anger when his children were present. Never be moody or preoccupied.

There had been no children.

Mary Sue had gotten sick. She got sicker. And somewhere along the way, the idea was lost. It fell away like a cliff face into the sea, not in a single shearing-off crash but in a slow crumble. They never discussed it. He wanted to protect her; he was afraid that children would be too much for her. Already, she herself was almost too much for him.

A noise. He looked up.

'Hey, babe,' he said.

Mary Sue stepped into the room. She looked marginally better. Her color was coming back. So much depended on the mix of medication. The right balance.

'Hi,' she said. 'I – I'm so sorry about not being here the past few nights, Nick. I had to—'

'Not a problem,' he said, interrupting her. 'Come on. Sit.'

'Good God. You're the one who got shot in the heart, and I'm the crybaby.' She wiped at her eyes. 'Every time I see you, I think about losing you. And I can't stand it.'

'You didn't lose me.'

'Close enough.' She shook her head. 'Really. I'm okay now.'

'You don't have to be okay. You just have to be here.'

She touched the rail on the hospital bed. He put his hand on top of hers. His good hand. The other one, the right hand, was still weak and unresponsive. Like a dead thing he was forced to haul around. Something had happened to the nerves; that's what they told him. Vague about it. Well, he wanted the vagueness right now. He didn't want definitive information. Vagueness, after all, meant hope. No one could say if he'd ever get the full function back. Odds were, not. But hope still scratched at the door.

'I have to tell you something,' she said.

Black dread drenched his heart. No. It couldn't be. She wouldn't— No. She would not leave him. No. That couldn't be what she was about to say to him. No.

Most people didn't understand. In the wake of her mental illness, in the wake of all the lost dreams, they thought he'd be the one to get weary of taking care of her. If anybody left, it would be him. Right?

Wrong. He needed her. She told him, by her life, who he was.

'I made a call,' Mary Sue went on. 'Night before last. I had to do *something*, Nick. Because you're not getting any better. When they caught the people who did this to you, I thought that might help you snap out of it. But no. You're still wounded.' He started to argue. She stopped him with a frown, a shake of her head. 'I don't mean physically. I mean – in your *soul*. You want to be sheriff – but you're not. And you can't be. Ever again. You're depressed. You've given up. I see it, Nick. I see it in your eyes.' She leaned forward. Put the back of her

367

hand on his cheek. 'So I called the one person who can relate. Who's been right where you are. The one person you might listen to. And guess what? He's coming. He's on his way here right now. He needed a few semesters off, anyway. That's what he told me. He said – and I quote – "You tell Nick Fogelsong that I'm going to kick his butt all the way to Charleston and back unless he stops feeling sorry for himself and gets out of that damned bed."'

'Clay Meckling.' He was pleased. Very pleased. It would be, among other things, a chance to apologize to the man for being such an insufferable know-it-all, a smug jackass, back when it was Clay in the hospital bed and Nick Fogelsong the one standing over him, solid and whole, fat with platitudes. And clueless about what it really feels like to lose everything – your purpose, your ability to do the work you were born to do, your sense of who you are. Your story.

He thought about the last time he'd seen Clay. Loading his father's truck, getting ready to head to Boston. If you didn't know, you'd never have guessed he had a prosthetic leg. After a bad spell, Clay had worked hard on his physical therapy. Damned hard.

'So he needed to take a few semesters off?' Nick said. 'Come on, Mary Sue. Who believes that?'

'I don't have to believe it,' she said. 'I only know that's what he said. He's coming. I didn't argue.'

Nick grinned. Couldn't help himself. Clay was coming home. Dang. Well, if a man like Clay thought he was worth that kind of effort—

Maybe I need to reconsider a few things, Nick told himself. *Maybe I do.* There was a time when he'd envied anyone who left Acker's Gap, when he watched them go and felt a kind of wild yearning, when he wondered why Bell Elkins had ever wanted to come back here – but something was shifting inside him. There was a certain solace to knowing a world this well. You knew its flaws, its shortcomings, just as you knew its beauties. And you learned to love it all. You loved the abundance of it, the sweep and immensity of the land, and you loved the sadness and the lack, too.

To walk each day on ground that had given rise to you: that was a privilege. Not a curse.

'Have you told Belfa?' he asked.

Mary Sue shook her head. 'All happened too fast. And she's been a little busy, to say the least.'

Another thought came to him: Bell hated surprises. Well, maybe it was time she learned to like them.

'Good.' Nick slid his feet around under the sheet; he was restless, and for the first time he found himself looking forward to the next day's physical therapy session. 'Good.'

39

Diana Hackel sat in the gray metal chair, fingers linked in her lap, clearly peeved but trying to be agreeable. On the table in front of her – also gray – she had carefully placed the items she'd brought along: water bottle (Aquafina), package of peanut butter crackers (Lance) and candy bar (Twix, king size). She kept her coat on, as much to drive home the point that she didn't expect to be here long as to keep herself warm.

'I'm hungry pretty much all the time now,' she said to Bell, indicating the snacks with a rueful nod. 'Always happens when I'm pregnant. You ought to see me on court days. The judge calls for the lunch recess and – *wham!* I'm outta there. I go tearing off in search of a sandwich.'

She smiled. She was being friendly. She had nothing to hide. They wanted to talk to her? Fine. No problem. Anything she could do to help.

Deputy Mathers had brought her from the motel to the courthouse. Yes, she'd been surprised by his request. Who wouldn't be? It was well past 10 P.M. She was in her nightgown and robe. She'd had to get dressed again. But – okay. Okay, fine.

Bell sat across from her, face impassive. 'Mrs Hackel,'

she said, 'I have some additional questions for you about the day your husband died. You don't have to answer them. If you like, you can wait until your attorney gets here.'

Diana looked confused, but still affable. 'Why in heaven's name would I refuse to answer your questions? I want Ed's killer to pay for what he did. I'm happy to help.' She picked up the Twix bar, waved it around. 'As long as the snacks hold out.' Another smile.

Bell didn't return it. 'Just to be clear,' she said, 'you have the right to remain silent.' She rattled through the rest of the warning, the one made familiar by innumerable TV shows, books, and movies.

'Okay, I get it,' Diana said. 'But why would I need a lawyer?'

'Because approximately ten minutes ago,' Bell said, 'Carolyn Runyon told us that you killed your husband.'

In the second of the two interrogation rooms in the Raythune County Courthouse, Carolyn Runyon maintained a tense and rigid pose in yet another gray metal chair. She was alone in the room, but the closed-circuit camera kept tabs on her. She was aware of that; she lifted her eyes and looked at the small black box mounted high up in the corner, a steady red light in the center of it. She didn't stick out her tongue – some people did that, usually young men filled with booze and bravado – or give the middle finger to whomever was monitoring the feed, another common reaction. Her arms were wrapped around her chest, her knees pressed tightly together. After looking at the camera for a while, she decided to look straight ahead. The gray wall across from her absorbed her stare as automatically as a sponge does a spill. That was its job.

She had managed to calm herself down. At first she had been enraged, lashing out at Deputy Oakes when he arrived at the construction trailer a short time ago. Roland Atwood had opened the door in response to the sharp knock, and he gave Oakes a wolfish grin that was surely exacerbated by what the deputy could plainly smell: an abundance of alcohol on Atwood's breath. Oakes pushed past him and addressed Carolyn Runyon. She was coiled up like a kitten on the black leather couch, suit jacket off, scarf unwound, black heels flipped across the carpet in a spiky heap, bare feet tucked under her butt.

When the reason for Oakes's visit was explained – he asked Runyon to return with him to the courthouse, at the prosecutor's request, to clarify a few murky areas – the kitten disappeared. It was late, she snarled. This was an *outrageous* imposition. What the hell could possibly necessitate her presence right now, especially when the trial of Royce Dillard was obviously nearing its conclusion?

The deputy clarified: She was not required to cooperate, but he'd been instructed to inform her that Diana Hackel had received the same request. She was already at the courthouse.

Runyon had looked at Atwood. He stood alongside the couch, drink in his hand, tie unraveled, grin spread out across his face, half-amused by the sudden drama. This was not the evening he had envisioned. Runyon wrenched her right shoe roughly onto her right foot. The second shoe received the same treatment. 'Get my coat,' she snapped. She stood up and straightened her skirt. Her jaw was tight. Her eyes sang with anger.

*   *   *

Bell had a brief sliver of time, and barely that. It was a chance that wouldn't come again. A one-shot opportunity.

When she learned about Carolyn Runyon's visits to see Royce Dillard, elements began to line up in her mind, one after another, beads on a string. She remembered that Diana had conveniently been in Charleston and not Falls Church – hence much closer to Acker's Gap – on the day of the murder, even though Diana's business there was bogus. She reflected on the close resemblance between Runyon and Diana Hackel. She remembered how agitated and upset Diana had been at the rumor that Royce Dillard might not go to trial, the rumor that he'd made a plea deal with the prosecution. And she reminded herself that when it came to planning a murder, the conspirators needn't all have the same motive. Just the same goal.

And so she had arranged to have the two women brought here tonight. It was the prosecutorial version of what she now understood that Runyon had done: fling up a Hail Mary pass. A last-chance, what-the-hell, nothing-to-lose move.

Each woman, shortly after her arrival, had waived her right to counsel – but could change her mind at any moment. Bell had expected this initial compliance: Both hoped to maintain the appearance of honest puzzlement, of curious innocence, as long as possible, and to find out what the prosecutor knew. The moment that pose was no longer tenable, they'd be dialing their attorneys so fast that the cell signals would probably get tangled in the air above the courthouse.

Carolyn Runyon had not really said that Diana was responsible for the death of Ed Hackel. In fact, she'd said little more than 'What is this *about,* Mrs Elkins?' before Bell left her alone in the second interrogation room and returned to Diana in the first.

But Diana didn't know that.

'She said *what?*' Diana replied to Bell, in a voice that screeched unbecomingly. The friendliness vanished. 'That *bitch.* It isn't true. Why would she say such a thing?'

'I don't know,' Bell said. 'What do you think?'

'I think she's trying to save her own skin, that's what I think.' Diana was trembling with fury. 'Because *she's* the one who killed Eddie.' Her small fist bounced on the tabletop. The vibration caused the water bottle to flop onto its side. That seemed to enrage her even more and she swept it the rest of the way off the table, along with the crackers and the candy bar. She didn't watch them land.

'Dammit,' Diana went on, so incensed that her outrage seemed to ricochet off the cinder block walls. 'I've got *children* to raise, okay? A family. Responsibilities. A *life.* Doesn't she get that? Oh, yeah.' A bitter laugh. 'Yeah, she gets that, all right. She gets it – but she *doesn't freaking care.* She's never cared. It's all about her. Whatever Carolyn wants – Carolyn gets. I don't know why I ever trusted—'

She broke off her sentence. She looked at Bell. When she resumed talking, her voice was shaky. Anger had given way to a kind of quiet seething.

'The hell of it is – she never really *liked* Eddie,' Diana said. 'But she sure didn't mind having sex with him. Used to call him a loser. Right to his face. In front of other people, too. Nice, huh? Real sweet. He was handy, that was all. He was there. There – and willing. God, yes. Willing and eager. But he'd *promised* me. When I told him I was pregnant again, he promised me. No more, he said. Never again. Changed man.' A hollow laugh.

'So you didn't know he'd resumed his relationship with Carolyn,' Bell said.

'No. Not at first.' She began to cry. Her tears were silent ones, slipping down her small face.

'How did you find out?'

'I called his cell one night. About a month ago. Really late. I figured he'd be back in his motel room – and he was. He just wasn't alone.' Diana used her thumb to capture a tear that threatened to roll off the bottom of her chin. 'He was in the shower. So she answered. And you can always tell, can't you? There's a way people sound after they've just been fucked. It's in their voice. Sort of lazy and sleepy and slurry.' Diana shuddered with revulsion. 'That's just how she sounded. So I knew. I knew right away.' She gave Bell a questioning look. 'Why'd she answer his phone? Why'd she do that? At first I wondered. But now I think she just wanted to rub my nose in it. Just had to prove she could have any man she wanted – hell, she could even have a man she *didn't* want.' Scrap of laughter, then the seriousness descended again. 'You know what? It was terrible. The worst thing ever. Knowing he'd lied to me. Having it confirmed that way – oh, God. It really, really tore me up inside. I knew I'd never forgive him a second time. *Never*. In my mind, we were done. The end. Period.'

'What did she say when she answered the phone?'

'Oh, she tried to lie. Said they were working late. Figured his room was more comfortable than the office. *Sure*. Like I believed *that*.' She rolled her eyes. 'Because I'm just this stupid housewife, right? Just this idiot who's popping out babies and baking cookies? Well, I got her back. I got her good.'

'What do you mean?'

'I started talking about how thrilled we were about the new baby. And you know what? I could tell by how she sounded – oh, she tried to hide it, but I could see right through her – that she didn't know. She *didn't know.* Can you beat that?'

'No,' Bell said. 'No, I can't.'

'She confirmed it later. He'd told her that I cut him off. And she *believed* him! Jesus. She thought she had him all to herself. And *I'm* the fool? *I'm* the trusting little woman? She has a lot of pride. More than anybody I've ever met. And she was *furious.* Absolutely *furious.* She called me a few days later. Made her case. Pointed out that we both had a pretty good reason to make that bastard pay.'

Diana took a deep breath. Closed her eyes. A few seconds passed, and her eyes popped open again. 'So she says *I* killed him,' she said with a sneer. 'That's her story, is it? Right. And just how did I do that? How'd I swing a shovel that hard? And then how'd I get his body into that wagon all by myself? Eddie was six-two. Weighed about two-forty, two-fifty. You tell me that.'

'I don't know,' Bell said. Her voice was calm and even. 'Why would she say it if it wasn't true?'

'Be*cause,*' Diana answered, leaning aggressively over the table and thumping it with her palm, as if Bell was such an astonishing moron that everything had to be spelled out for her in capital letters and then underlined twice, '*she* killed him. Her and that slimy assistant of hers – McGloin. I may have wanted Eddie dead – after what he'd done to me, all the pain he'd caused – but *they* killed him. Not me. Haven't you figured that out yet? Jesus. You're just as stupid as she said you were. What *is* it about this crappy little town? It's like what Eddie used to complain about. You've got one itty-bitty brain cell and you share it between the whole population. Pass it around. Was tonight somebody else's turn with it? Is *that* why you're so slow to catch on?'

'Must be.'

Carolyn Runyon was standing up now. When Bell walked through the door of the second interrogation room, she turned and gave her a look of such excoriating hatred that Bell half wondered if she'd find burn marks on her skin.

'I'm ready to leave,' Runyon said. 'And might I suggest that you find another form of recreation around here to take up your evenings – other than harassing innocent people? Ping-Pong is fun, I hear. Or perhaps a rousing Go Fish tournament – surely that wouldn't tax the limited intellectual resources of you and your friends.'

'It might,' Bell said, 'although I'm partial to checkers myself. Listen, I hate to change the subject, but I need to inform you that Diana Hackel just implicated you in the murder of her husband.' She sat down.

Runyon paused. She'd been cinching the belt around the waist of her coat and she was motionless for a moment, the ends of the crossed belt held tightly in each fist.

Then she laughed. The laugh was loud and fake.

'Oh, Mrs Elkins,' she said. 'This is beneath you. Really. This little game of trying to play one of us off against the other. I suggest you stick to those checkers. Because frankly, I don't know what nonsense you think—'

'Right now,' Bell said, curtly interrupting her, 'Diana Hackel is getting ready to sign her statement. She told us all about it. About how you and she compared notes and decided that you both had ample reason to want Ed Hackel dead. He'd lied to Diana about not having sex with you – and he'd lied to you about not having sex with Diana. You both had the same motive. And it's the oldest motive in the book – sexual jealousy.'

'Bullshit.' Runyon spat the word. She sat back down again. The legs crossed automatically. She thrust her hands in her coat pockets. She was like a switchblade seconds after closing up: still lethal, but sleeker now, the menace tucked away until it was needed.

'I didn't kill anybody,' she said. 'If she thinks she can save herself by trying to frame *me*, she'd better think again.'

She didn't move. She didn't speak. Minutes passed.

Runyon had no intention of saying another word. Everyone in the world knew that they were better off keeping their mouths shut when being questioned. Even people who weren't half as smart as Carolyn Runyon understood that. If it were only a matter of appreciating the strategic benefit of silence, then no one would ever talk to a police officer or a prosecutor. Or a priest, come to that.

But it wasn't about intelligence. It was about pride. And it was about the story.

'You loved him, didn't you?' Bell said. She said it softly, sympathetically, one woman to another. 'You were in love with Ed Hackel and he betrayed you.'

Runyon didn't look at her. 'Shut up,' she said. Not angrily. In fact, she said it casually. 'Shut up,' she repeated.

'He lied to you. I'll bet that hurt. I mean, *look* at you. You're a beautiful woman – elegant, sophisticated. Running your own company. Mingling with the movers and shakers. You have your pick of men. Anybody you want, any day of the week. And yet – who did you fall for? Eddie Hackel. Who was *he* to cheat on *you*? I mean – the nerve of him. The gall.'

'I believe I very clearly requested you to shut up.'

'It must've *enraged* you. The minute you heard his wife was pregnant, it must've been like acid. Eating away at your ego, your confidence. God – Ed Hackel! That useless fool. He couldn't even do the *one thing* you'd asked of him, the thing that would save the whole project. One thing! Nope, he failed. Because he's a loser. And then there's *you* – gorgeous, brilliant, sexy. A winner all the way.' Bell sat back. 'Talk about a power imbalance. On the one hand, we have – Eddie Hackel. Just a guy. A *married* guy, no less. A guy who can't do his job. Can't even close the deal when it's the biggest deal of his life. And then, on the other hand, we have – *Carolyn Runyon.*'

'Shut. Up.'

'And yet – *and yet* – there you were. Hopelessly in love with him. Beauty and the Beast, right? You and Eddie Hackel.'

Silence.

'Finally,' Bell went on, 'to add insult to injury – you find out that *he* was cheating on *you*. Eddie's wife was pregnant again. Here you are, the kind of woman that a man like Hackel can only *dream* about – and *he's* the one who makes a fool out of *you*. It's just not fair. Not fair at all.'

Silence.

'No one blames you, Carolyn. No woman, anyway. We've all been there. That kind of humiliation is just excruciating. There's not a woman alive who hasn't been through—'

'I said *shut the hell up.*' Runyon's head whipped around. Fire in her eyes. 'If you don't shut up *right this fucking minute,* I'm going to—' She bolted up and out of her chair. It was the first graceless move Bell had ever seen her make. 'Let's get this straight, okay? I want to make this absolutely clear, once and for all, to you and the rest of the hicks here in Mayberry. You're wrong. I didn't give a damn about Ed. Okay? All that crap his wife's been spewing – that I couldn't stand the thought of him being with her – is ridiculous. Yes, I told her that. Because I needed her help.

'It was business, okay? It's *always* business with me. We *have* to get that land. Everything depends on it. And Eddie failed. He let that creep – that sicko with all the dogs – push him around. String him along. So we took care of it. I'm a *professional*, do you understand? I do what needs to be done. I don't put up with excuses. I *win*. That's what I do. You got that? *I always win.*'

'Really,' Bell said. 'So how'd you get Hackel out there?'

'Picked him up at his motel that afternoon. He'd just gotten back from Acker's Gap. He'd made another run at Dillard. Tried to blackmail him with what he knew about the drugs. But once again, he'd failed. Once again, Eddie let us all down.' She shook her head, exasperated. 'Well, I'd had enough. We were running out of time. We were totally screwed unless we got that land right away. It was time to pull out all the stops. One last chance. A long shot – but that's what I'm known for. For doing things other people won't do. Because they're too lazy or too stupid. Or too chickenshit.'

She'd said enough. She flung herself back down in her chair.

Bell had to get her talking again. 'Come on, Carolyn. You're kidding yourself, aren't you? You'd fallen hard for Eddie Hackel. You didn't want to, you didn't mean to – but that's what happened. Wasn't it? You were nuts about the guy.'

'God*dammit*. For the last time – *no*. No.' Abruptly, she bolted forward again, determined to make her case. 'I told Eddie we'd both try. We'd work on Dillard together. I'd drive us out to that crummy cabin and wait for the sonofabitch to show up and then we'd threaten him again. Eddie had been working on a new angle – something about a flood and some old lady – and I said, "Sure, whatever. *Just get him to sell us his fucking land*." I'd had it up to here with Ed's little schemes.'

'Hackel didn't take his cell.'

'I told him to leave it behind. His location could've been tracked.'

'Dillard wasn't home yet. So you killed Hackel and framed him for the crime.'

Runyon laughed. 'Nice try, but I already told you that I didn't kill anybody. Paul McGloin did it. He was waiting in the barn. The minute Eddie turned his back, Paul hit him with the shovel. Quick jabs in the back of the neck.' Her expression bordered on a smirk. 'So if you're thinking of charging me – sorry. Paul's your man. He used that silly wagon to get the body down to that filthy little creek. Do the math. Dillard *has* to sell that land now. To pay his legal bills. All those appeals won't come cheap.' Another laugh. This time, a triumphant one. 'Eddie finally came through for the company. Just not quite the way he planned.'

'You were seen in the Comebacker that night.'

'Wasn't me. That was Eddie's little wifey. Pissed as hell at him because of his affair with me. I mean, she really *did* love the guy. But hell hath no fury, you know?' A sneer. 'Eddie had a type, all right. In a dark bar, Diana and I can pass for each other. She just signed my name and room number on the drinks receipt and – presto.' Runyon jabbed a finger in Bell's face. 'That first night you talked to her at the courthouse? When she acted all mad at me? She told me that you fell for it, big time.'

Bell looked at her watch. Right about now, Deputy Oakes would be knocking on the door of Paul McGloin's motel room. McGloin, she was sure, would implicate Carolyn Runyon. Once he was told that Runyon had sold him out, he would be more than happy to return the favor.

They hadn't spoken to McGloin yet. But Runyon didn't know that.

'McGloin,' Bell said, 'tells a different story. He swears you're the one who killed Hackel. And dumped him in the creek. From the look of those nicely toned arms and legs of yours, Ms Runyon, I'd say it's plausible. Which means it'll be a toss-up as to who the jury believes. If it were me, I'd want to be the first one to sign a statement admitting to the plot.' Bell smiled. 'It's just good business.'

Runyon faced forward, staring at the same spot on the wall she had stared at before.

When Bell stepped out of the interrogation room, Rhonda was waiting for her. Like Bell, Rhonda was exhausted, but she was also excited, her eyes bright and keen. She had watched the closed-circuit feed with Harrison in the sheriff's office. The moment it was over, Harrison had headed to the jail to meet Deputy Oakes when he arrived with McGloin.

'Wow,' Rhonda said. 'I had no idea that Carolyn Runyon was in love with Hackel.'

'She wasn't.'

Her eyes widened. 'But you said in there that—'

'She told the truth about one thing. It really *is* all about business for her.' Bell couldn't remember the last time she'd been this tired. She was debating internally with herself about which should come first: a hot soaky bath or a cold Rolling Rock or about a year of sleep. Right now, sleep was the clear favorite.

'She used Ed Hackel for sex,' Bell went on. 'She'd done it before with other men on her staff. It didn't mean anything to her. No more than it means to powerful men who do the same thing with female employees. Hackel was a little below her usual standard, looks-wise. Not exactly Prince Charming. But he was handy.'

'So why were you so insistent that it was all about love? And jealousy?'

'Everybody's got a story. And if somebody tries to tell a different one, the wrong one, we do whatever we can to correct it. Can't help ourselves. It's the deepest instinct we have – preserving our story. There was nothing I could have said to Carolyn Runyon tonight to make her talk – except to get her story wrong. After that, I knew I wouldn't be able to shut her up. I turned her into an object of pity. And she had to set me straight. *Had* to. Because in the end, that's all any of us really have – our story.'

Rhonda looked uncertain. 'Hard to believe she'd kill a man – and frame another – for some land.'

'It's not just land. It's her life. Without Royce Dillard's property, she'll lose everything. There was no other way. Nothing else would work. Dillard was never going to sell – unless he was forced to. Unless he was backed up against a wall – by a murder conviction and a series of expensive appeals. He'd do anything to get back to his dogs.' Bell smiled briefly, thinking about Royce's dogs, and about the ride she and Rhonda had taken that cold day, returning from his property. Cages rattling in the back of the Explorer. One of the cages had held Goldie.

'That,' Bell said, 'is why Diana was so distraught by the idea that he'd cut a deal with us. That's why she accosted me on the street that day, playing the grieving-widow-seeking-justice card. If Dillard made a deal, if he didn't need money for his appeals, there'd be no reason for him to sell his land to Mountain Magic. They'd be right back where they started.'

'Why didn't they just kill Royce? Buy the land from his estate?'

'That estate could've been tied up in probate for years. Meanwhile, all those trucks and backhoes would be sitting there, rusting away, eating up capital. Not to mention the cost of construction materials. Salaries for the crew. No, she needed a better plan. A faster one. And an expendable employee to make it happen.'

'Hackel.'

'Yes. Hackel.'

It could not happen right now – Pam Harrison was too busy with the new prisoners – but at some point, Bell knew, she and the sheriff would talk about this night, process it, and when they did, Bell would look into her colleague's eyes and hope she saw there what she needed to see: an acknowledgement of the fact that sometimes sheriffs got it wrong. Sometimes prosecutors got it wrong. And when they got it wrong, either one or both of them, they needed to do their damnedest to make it right. They had to find the truth, even as the cold mechanics they had set into motion continued the grinding, relentless journey toward a thing called justice – the human version of it, anyway, which, despite their best efforts, bore only the faintest, flimsiest likeness to the divine kind.

As her weariness had increased, Bell began to feel the soft call of her own story, not as a list of events but as something that came back to her in bits and flashes, sounds and colors: Orphan girl. Child of the hills. Violence and loss. Then: Light. Books. Love. The return to this town, these people.

'Carolyn Runyon,' Bell said, 'couldn't stand the idea that I'd gotten her story wrong – which would mean I'd gotten *her* wrong. We'll fight to the death – we'll even give up our lives – to protect our story.'

Bell stood at the top of the great gray sweep of steps that spread from the courthouse door to the dark sidewalk below. It was almost midnight now, arrests made, her colleagues gone home. The town was still. The air was cold, but that didn't matter; the cold revived her, and it made the air feel fresh and filled with promise, like a newly minted coin.

She retrieved the car keys from her purse. She held them in her fist, mind stuck on the memory of Diana's face, a face clotted with hate. Carolyn's face had been different: It was sharpened like an animal's when it is under duress, keen with calculation.

And there he was.

Clay Meckling.

He stood at the bottom of the steps. At first, she wasn't sure it was really him. For one thing, clouds blocked much of the light from the moon, and it was damned hard to see anything at all. For another, a lot of men in Acker's Gap fit his general description: tall and rawboned, blond hair cut so close to the scalp that its actual color was hard to discern even in daylight. Diffident grin. Boots and jeans. Hip-length Carhartt jacket.

But for all that, she knew. Yes. It was him.

'Hey,' she said. Her fatigue vanished and her body suddenly felt light, unbelievably light, her bones like balsa wood, and she was fairly sure she could've risen a few inches off the earth with no problem whatsoever. She chalked it up to lack of sleep.

That had to be it.

'Sorry to ambush you like this,' Clay said. At first he had to look up at her, standing as she was on the top step, but she started down – a steady pace, not hasty, so as not to appear too eager – and then they were standing on the same ground, and close. 'Wanted to call, but you're in the middle of a case. Know better than to bother you. I was coming around to see if your office light was on. Figured I'd watch it for a little while, then be on my way.'

'Just wrapped things up,' she said.

And because he knew her, he didn't question the fact that she was leaving the courthouse at 11:37 P.M.

'Mary Sue called me,' Clay said. 'Says Nick needs

help. I couldn't say no. Not after what the man's done for me – and done for my family. And for this town. So I drove straight through. Maybe while I'm back here – I mean, if it sounds okay to you – I thought we could spend some time together and—'

'I've really missed you, Clay.' The phrase wasn't right – it didn't begin to suggest what she felt for this man, the intensity of it, the passion for him that had never abated – but it would have to do for now. She knew what people had said about her and Clay and would say again now, the crude references to cougars and to *The Graduate*, all the innuendoes. She didn't give a damn.

'Same here.' He looked around the black, bleak, narrow streets, hands stowed in the back pockets of his jeans, all at once a bit embarrassed. 'You're tired,' he said. 'I'm keeping you.'

'Look pretty beat yourself. What is it – a ten-, eleven-hour drive from Boston?'

'Something like that. Okay, so, how about tomorrow? Breakfast at JP's, first thing?'

She started to say yes. Then she shook her head. 'Not first thing. I've got responsibilities at home. But later in the morning – absolutely.'

'Responsibilities?' He was suddenly concerned. Was she involved with someone?

'Name's Goldie,' Bell said. 'Gets her morning walk, no matter what.'

40

There was paperwork; there was always paperwork. It would be many hours before the charges against Royce Dillard were officially dropped. Judge Barbour would listen to the prosecution's explanation and then make a formal ruling from the bench. Immediately afterward, Bell would file charges against Carolyn Runyon, Paul McGloin, and Diana Hackel for a range of felonies including perjury, kidnapping, conspiracy to commit murder, murder, and abuse of a corpse. Bell had a lot of sorting out to do.

In the meantime, the forms required for Dillard's release from the Raythune County Jail would be drawn up, reviewed, signed by all the relevant parties. Paperwork, and more paperwork. As a child, Bell had heard the same story every child hears, the assertion that after a nuclear holocaust, only cockroaches will be left on the earth. As an adult, she disagreed. It would be cockroaches – and paperwork.

She headed for Royce Dillard's cell. She knew he'd be anxious until he was actually released – who wouldn't be? – and she wanted to help him keep calm today. Serena Crumpler was already busy with a new case, another one involving a client who couldn't pay and an outcome that seemed hopeless from the start. Perfect for Serena.

She found Dillard sitting on his bed, palms on his kneecaps, legs jiggling nervously.

'I'm pretty keyed up,' he said.

'Don't blame you. It's a big day.' She stood next to the bars that defined this space. She didn't move any closer to him. By now she knew that if you cared about the man, you kept your distance. He wanted it that way. 'I happen to know that Rhonda Lovejoy took the liberty of restocking your dog chow out at the cabin. You should be set for a good long while. No need to rush off to the store right away.'

He blinked, a bit startled. 'You mean I get my dogs back?'

'Of course you get your dogs back.'

'Huh. Well, I just figured that once folks got a taste of those dogs of mine – they're great dogs, Mrs Elkins, ain't no denying it – they'd do all they could do to keep 'em. Like when you find a ten-dollar bill on the sidewalk. No hurry in giving it back. You take your time. And unless they make you, you don't give it back at all.'

'You run into any trouble about the return of your dogs,' Bell said, 'you tell me about it, okay?'

'Okay.' His legs jiggled a little faster. 'Goldie, too?'

She waited a few seconds before nodding.

'Yes,' she said. 'Goldie, too.' Truth was, as she'd grown closer to Goldie, Bell had conveniently set to one side of her mind the possibility that Dillard might be coming back to claim her. The dog had become a part of her daily routine. She remembered the great consolation of Goldie's presence on the morning she learned that Nick Fogelsong had been shot, a consolation that was not a matter of words but of spirit – and of warm, supple fur. Conversation was superfluous at such a time. And that's why a dog was the perfect companion for a crisis: No words. No clichés. No platitudes. No earnest, supportive speeches that, sincere or not, tended to leave Bell feeling even emptier, even more crushingly alone.

But Goldie belonged to someone else. Bell had known that from the beginning.

For a moment she didn't trust herself to speak. She feared her voice might break, revealing just how devastated she was by the idea that Goldie would be leaving.

'You can come see her whenever you like,' Dillard said. Bell knew how hard it was for him to make the offer. He didn't want human company. Not ever. But he was deeply obliged to her – as much for taking good care of his dog as for finding the truth and saving him from a prison sentence.

'Don't even have to ask,' he said. 'Just show up when you please. But listen – if you bring her a treat, make sure you pack a little something for the other dogs, too, okay? Don't want them to feel slighted.'

'Sure will.'

'Anyway,' he said, 'at least they'll be able to stretch their legs all they want pretty soon. Finally gonna turn that patch of land of mine into a dog park. Got word through Serena that the company's backing off, so they'll leave me alone. Whole danged project's shutting down. Not a surprise – not with that Runyon lady out of the picture.' Wonder in his voice, he added, 'A lot of folks stand to lose a lot of money out there. Millions, I hear tell.'

Bell nodded. She was thinking about money and power and possessions, about the things that, for most people, were the supreme motivating forces in life. Dillard was different. He wanted only to be left alone. There was a brand on him, an indelible imprint; he was marked forever by one cold and horrifying morning in his childhood, and he dealt with it by living the way he did. The way he had to. It wasn't a choice.

She rubbed a thumb along the painted steel of the bar, part of the row of identical bars that had kept Dillard separated from the world – his world, a world of dogs and mountain air – during his trial.

'There's something I still don't understand,' she said. 'Why didn't you fight back? You were innocent. But you barely even tried. From the very first, it's like you were just accepting things as they came. Giving up. It was hard to even get you to let Serena defend you. Why? You were desperate to see your dogs. And you knew you didn't kill him.'

'But I knew I wanted to. Same thing, ain't it?' He shifted his position on the cot. 'And to tell you the truth, if those folks hadn't beaten me to it – I'm pretty damned sure I *would've* done it, too, just as sure as I'm sitting here. I hated him that much.' Dillard made a fist as he spoke, and now he raised it and looked at it, peering intently at the sharp knuckles and the crooked thumb that locked the fingers in place.

'I get that,' Bell said quietly. She knew about anger, anger that hardens into rage. 'Hackel's threat was ugly and vicious. Paying Vera to say your father was a coward – not a hero. Turning your life story upside down. I know how that must have—'

'No.' At the same moment he interrupted her, Dillard opened his fist. Now he stared into the flat exposed palm. 'No, that's not it.'

'Pardon?'

'It wasn't the fact that Hackel was lying about my father. It was the fact that he was telling the truth.'

Bell wished he would look up at her. She was confused, and if she could see his eyes, she thought things might somehow become a little clearer. But Dillard wouldn't do it. He was concentrating fiercely on the lines on his palm.

'Vera lied from the start,' he murmured. His voice was so low that Bell had to strain to hear him. 'She lied when she said my father saved me. Because he didn't. Vera told Bessie the real story a couple of days after the flood. Bessie pressed her on it. And Vera confessed. Nobody lied to Bessie. Not when she was looking at you with them eyes of hers.' He took a breath. 'My father just tried to save his own miserable skin. Didn't do a damned thing for my mother and me. He got himself out of the house first thing – without a single look back at his wife or his child. After that Mama grabbed me and held me and we got out the window, and when she was lost, somehow I got up on that ridge. Maybe a stranger did it and nobody got his name. All I know is that it wasn't my father.'

'But why did Vera lie, all those years ago?'

'Made a dandy story, didn't it? Lots of drama – a daddy saves his little boy instead of saving himself. People ate it right up.' He shrugged. 'Vera got her name in the paper. She was the center of attention and it felt damned good to her. That's what Bessie said. And once Vera lied, once she'd told the tale, the other folks up on that ridge didn't want to go against her. And maybe they weren't sure what they'd really seen, anyway. I mean, it was a terrible day. And such a wonderful story

– the kind of story people needed to hear right then, you know? So that things might seem a little less sad for a while.'

Vera, Bell thought, had been ready to take Hackel's money for lying – when she'd really be telling the truth, at long last.

Her hand still held the bar, tighter than she meant to. She loosened her grip.

'How long have you known?'

'Bessie told me when I was ten years old. When she thought I was old enough to handle it. She'd never liked my father. Hated him, matter of fact. That's why she moved away from Lundale. That's why she wasn't living there when the flood came. Said she couldn't stand to see my mother with him. Said my mother was way too good for that whiskey-soaked SOB – that's what she called him, every time – but she wouldn't go. "He's the father of my baby boy," my mother always said, when Bessie begged her to leave.'

'So you just repeated what everybody wanted to hear,' Bell said. 'You never told the truth.'

'The truth? The truth would've made my mother look like a fool. A fool for marrying that bastard – and a coward for staying with him. Bessie felt the same way. If we'd said what really happened, we'd dishonor my mother's memory.' His voice had turned raspy, roughed-up. He was holding back a giant wave of emotion, emotion that pushed and surged and threatened to break through the walls he had built inside himself.

'Listen, Royce,' Bell said. 'Your parents were so young when they died. Your father never got the chance to be a different kind of man. You don't know how he might've turned out, if he'd had longer to live.'

He thought about this. 'Well, maybe. All I know is that he didn't deserve my mother's love. And he didn't use up his last breath on this earth to save anybody. Not even himself – the only person he ever cared about. He was a selfish bastard *and* a failure.'

'It's not what you do with your last breath that matters, Royce. It's what you do with your life.'

'Yeah. Right.' He snorted his disdain. His words came in an accelerating mess of self-loathing: 'And what've I done with *my* life? Not a damned thing. Just can't ever take hold. Can't stick. Always running away. Times I tried to reach out to people – or them to me – I just couldn't do it. Something took over inside me and told me I had to go. Go, go, *go*. Had to get out of there, fast as I could, so's I could *breathe*. That girl Brenda – I cared about her, all those years ago. I did. And I ruined it. She's married herself now – you met him, it's Andy Stegner, he's a good man – so she's done okay. I don't see her much, but I guess she's happy and that's good. But still. Tears me up something awful – remembering. How I couldn't stand to be touched. Still can't. I just can't deal with – with *people,* you know? Not a one of 'em. Never. Only time I feel halfway normal is when I'm with my dogs, because they don't ask me questions, they just like to run and run and—'

'Royce,' she said. 'Your story's not over yet.'

From her chair in the living room, Bell heard the honk. Goldie bounced down from the couch, her tail making wild scribbles in the air as she barged toward the front door. Even before Bell opened it, Goldie had somehow sensed that Royce was on the other side. Bell had never seen her quite like this: It was as if every molecule of her being was on tiptoe.

Once the dog spotted Royce, her tail went into a kind of hyperdrive. She rushed out onto the porch.

'Hey, girlie,' Royce said. He handed something to Bell. And then he went down on both knees so that Goldie could reach his face with her tongue, and he rubbed her up and down while she licked and sniffed. 'Hey there. How's my girl?'

Bell stood back and watched the reunion. Goldie had forgotten all about her. Had she meant nothing to this dog? Nothing at all? Then she reprimanded herself: Royce was Goldie's world. Others might come and go, and Goldie might care for them, but Royce was her world. That would not, should not, change. That was how it was supposed to be: Royce and Goldie. They were part of each other's story, moving in rugged tandem across the days and the years.

Bell knew now, in a way she could not have fully understood before, that her life story was not her own. She was part of other people's stories, too, the paths tangling and untangling and overlapping, until finally there was only one story, infinitely thickened by all the stories gathered within it since the beginning of stories themselves.

She didn't know what would happen to Acker's Gap, now that the resort and its promise of economic uplift were gone. She only knew that this place was a part of her story, and she of its. She was also part of Carla's story, and the stories of Shirley and Nick and Mary Sue and Rhonda and Pam Harrison and – maybe – Clay Meckling.

Royce stood up again and shook her hand, without

meeting her eyes. They'd said what they needed to say to each other back at the courthouse. He touched the top of Goldie's head. 'Ready to go, girl?' A sharp bark, and another crazy swoop of her tail.

The dog followed him out to the silver pickup truck driven by Chess Rader. Bell waved at Chess, but he didn't see her; he was focused on the map he'd spread out across the steering wheel. They had six more stops to make and he was checking the locations.

Bell looked down at the object Royce had handed her. It was a notebook with a black-and-white cover, the one she had given him at the start of the trial. She opened it to the first page. *Death Imprint,* it said. She would read it tonight, when she sat in her chair and tried to keep her mind away from the ache of losing Goldie.

Her attention was drawn back to the curb. Royce was clapping his hands and calling out, 'Good girl, that's my good girl, now,' as Goldie leapt into the back of the truck without the slightest hesitation. She barked and quivered and turned in circles, out of sheer exhilaration. Royce was with her now, and she was with him. No matter where she was going, she was already home.

Acknowledgments

My one and only trip down into a working coal mine came during a reporting assignment. It was scary, even harrowing, but there was also a singular beauty to that dark place. The best account I've ever read of this loveliness in the midst of peril and toil comes in Homer Hickam's 1998 memoir of his childhood in West Virginia, *Rocket Boys,* which became the 1999 film *October Sky.* Book and movie both are national treasures.

Two other books were crucial to my understanding of the Buffalo Creek flood and the fate of coal: *The Buffalo Creek Disaster* (1976) by Gerald M. Stern and *Coal: A Human History* (2003) by Barbara Freese. For a thorough overview of the geography, politics, and aftermath of Buffalo Creek, check www.wvculture.org/history/buffcreek /bctitle/html.

Once again, it is my great pleasure to thank the friends and loved ones who made the journey possible: Susan Phillips, Lisa Keller, Elaine Phillips, Carolyn Alessio, Holly Bryant, Ron Rhoden, Carolyn Focht, and Joseph Hallinan, along with the wise and indispensable Lisa Gallagher.

At Minotaur, I am grateful as always for the efforts and talents of Kelley Ragland, Elizabeth Lacks, and

Julia Keller

Hector DeJean, and at Headline, Vicki Mellor and Darcy Nicholson. And I'm pleased to add a special word of thanks to copyeditor Christina MacDonald, who did her job with skill and grace.

Keep reading for an extract from the latest Bell Elkins short story

headline

It was a good place to go at the end of a long and complicated workday. Not because it was a happy place – God knows it could never be that – but because it instantly sucked all the self-pity out of you, and the petty complaints and minor frustrations, too.

Step through the door and they disappeared. Just like that.

This place was – this place had to be – about other people. It forcibly eliminated the self-indulgence of introspection. And for Belfa Elkins, who looked too long and too often into her own soul yet had always felt unable to stop, this place was a bracing tonic and a stern corrective. She would never have described it that way out loud, but that was what it was. It provided a rugged sort of solace, and it restored perspective. It cleaned the slate. It cleared her head.

It was called Evening Street.

This was the place where they treated the babies who were born addicted to narcotics. Their mothers were addicts, and a nasty little corollary to addiction was that when you had a baby growing inside you, the baby came along for the ride. The baby had no choice. She was addicted, too. Before that new human being had even crossed the threshold of her mother's body and emerged into the world, she was saddled with a grievous burden.

The year before, the Raythune County Medical Center had run out of space in the neonatal intensive care unit because of all the babies born addicted to opioid pain-killers. More and more and more. Each year, the number rose. Addicts' babies were crowding out the babies born with other needs, other maladies.

The solution had come from Henry Smathers, a retired tobacco broker who'd made his fortune from another kind of addiction. Compared to pain pills, cigarettes seemed courtly, benign. They were hardly benign. But they did their damage stealthily, over the long haul. It was easy to ignore it. For a while.

Smathers donated a yellow-brick warehouse that his company no longer used. The warehouse was located at the far end of one of the scruffy side streets of Acker's Gap, West Virginia, a long stretch of empty storefronts and heaved-up sidewalks and burnt-out streetlights known as Evening Street. Smathers also paid to have it remodeled into a specialized medical facility, a clinic that would treat the newborn babies who suffered from the effects of their mothers' addiction. This is where Bell went at the end of her workday, whenever she could.

'Hey, there,' said Lily Cupp. She said it softly. She was the head nurse here, and in her arms she was holding an impossibly tiny infant swaddled in a light yellow blanket. The baby's eyes were closed. He opened his mouth over and over again, like a frantic goldfish missing the water, but he wasn't crying.

'Hey,' Bell replied.

It was 7:20 P.M. Bell had just arrived in the large square room dotted with basinets. Each small bed was connected to stacked rows of talkative monitors and serious-looking equipment. The overhead lights in the drop ceiling were dim, so that the infants wouldn't have to squint up into the harsh glare, but the space was still well illuminated by the lights on the machines.

Bell had walked over here from the Raythune County Courthouse. At the checkpoint just inside the front door, the guard, a burly man named Delbert Ryerson, had given Bell the once-over, paying particular – and particularly disgusting – attention to her breasts, and then waved her on through. He'd pushed a button under the desk to release the lock. Ryerson's head was as thick and fibrous-looking as a root vegetable, and his tiny gold spectacles were almost lost amid the folds and pinched-fat creases of his face. He was, Bell recalled, related to somebody. Somebody with influence. That's how he'd gotten this job. Such was the usual hiring routine in these parts, she knew; the very few new jobs that ever popped up were almost always spoken for, earmarked for somebody's brother-in-law. She even called it that: the Brother-in-Law Factor. Ryerson might have been qualified for security work, but if he was, you could chalk that up to sheer coincidence. The Brother-in-Law Factor was the salient reality that had netted him this job. Not competence.

On her way in, Bell turned her cell to vibrate. Lily strictly enforced that rule. The infants needed calm and quiet. They also needed – more than medicine, perhaps, more than machines – skin-to-skin contact.

'This is Abraham,' Lily said, holding up the tiny bundle. 'Two days old. Abe, say hi to Belfa Elkins. She's our prosecuting attorney. Don't get into any mischief if she's around – that's my advice, mister.'

Bell leaned in to look. The infant resembled a famished old man. His wrinkled skin was an odd gray color. It was the shade of a newspaper left out in a rainstorm.

Abraham began to shake violently. At first, Lily tried to hold him steady, but it wasn't working; the child's shaking intensified. And then, even more suddenly, the shaking stopped. His tiny head reared backwards, and his limbs froze in place.

'Can I do something?' Bell said.

Lily ignored her. She walked quickly across the floor and settled Abraham in his basinet. She prepared an IV.

Someone else spoke. 'He's having a seizure.'

Bell turned. She hadn't seen the second nurse approaching, and the sentence took her by surprise.

'It's pretty common,' the nurse added. 'With these babies, it happens all the time.'

Bell nodded. 'I know. Unfortunately, I've seen it before. I come by as often as I can.' She put out a hand. 'You're new. I don't think we've met. I'm Bell Elkins.'

'Oh, right. Lily told me about you. The prosecutor, right? I'm Angie Clark.'

'How long have you worked here?'

The woman looked down at her wristwatch. 'About four and a half hours.'

'Wow – you really *are* new.'

'Yeah, first day on the job. There's a lot of turnover. Some people just can't take it – watching newborns suffer like this, from all the drugs they've been exposed to in the womb. You feel so helpless. So useless. But I guess you know that. You've seen it yourself, visiting regular like you do.'

The nurse was about thirty, Bell guessed. She had sallow skin, short straight dark hair, red glasses, and a

solid, thick-thighed physique. Her blue scrubs were
about one size too small for her.

'I have,' Bell said.

'Want to sit?' Angie gestured toward the row of black
folding chairs along one wall of the large room. 'Lily
might be a while. Abe's got serious problems. Diarrhea.
Irritability. Dehydration. He can't sleep, either. I know
it's a terrible thing to say, but sometimes I think he'd
be better off if —' She bunched up her mouth into a
tidy frown, letting silence finish the thought for her.
Then she sighed a grave and heavy sigh. All of it struck
Bell as theatrical. There was something about this new
nurse that she didn't much like.

Bell walked over and sat down in one of the chairs.
Angie went with her. There were several rocking chairs
on the opposite side of the room, and that was where
Bell usually spent her time when she was here; Lily
would pick out an infant and bring her or him over,
settling the child in Bell's arms. Bell would rock back
and forth, humming, talking softly to the wizened
lozenge of flesh, flesh that might be black or white or
brown. Mostly she murmured vague words of encour-
agement such as 'There's a good girl' or 'You're going
to grow up to be big and strong and smart, aren't you,'
but sometimes Bell ran out of words. If the day had
been long and demanding, if she'd had to spend a lot
of it talking, she couldn't find any more words. She felt
as if she'd used them all up. She needed to say something, though, because it was important for the babies
to hear loving human voices, and so Bell would revert
to sentences she knew as well as she knew her own
name, adding softeners at the end of a curt phrase: 'You
have the right to remain silent, you precious thing, you.

If you give up that right, anything you say can and will be used against you, punkin. In a court of law, sweetie.'

At the moment, though, Lily was too busy with Abraham to set her up in a rocking chair with another infant. Bell would have to wait.

'Hope I'm not keeping you from your work,' Bell said to the new nurse. *Because I'd rather you just went away*, she added to herself, wishing she had the guts – and the bad manners – to say it out loud.

'Oh, no problem. I'm on a break,' Angie replied breezily. She thumped down in the adjacent seat. 'And I needed it, you know what I mean? We've been swamped today. We got two more this morning. A little girl named Marie Christine and a boy named Tyler. Funny – these mothers always have the names all picked out. They practically inhale those drugs and they guzzle alcohol all through their pregnancies, and it's pretty obvious they don't give a shit about anything but the next party – but by golly, they know what they're going to name that baby, don't they? First and middle.'

If you can't wait to read more from

Julia
Keller

Go to www.headline.co.uk to discover the rest
of the Bell Elkins series

THRILLINGLY GOOD BOOKS
FROM CRIMINALLY
GOOD WRITERS

CRIME FILES BRINGS YOU THE LATEST RELEASES FROM
TOP CRIME AND THRILLER AUTHORS.

SIGN UP ONLINE FOR OUR MONTHLY NEWSLETTER AND BE THE FIRST
TO KNOW ABOUT OUR COMPETITIONS, NEW BOOKS AND MORE.

VISIT OUR WEBSITE: WWW.CRIMEFILES.CO.UK
LIKE US ON FACEBOOK: FACEBOOK.COM/CRIMEFILES
FOLLOW US ON TWITTER: @CRIMEFILESBOOKS